Vespertine Blue

Vespertine Blue

Torion Oey

For the haha.

Prologue

There were twelve subjects who showed up at the tower's front door. Nine male, three female. Heights ranged from 5 feet 6 inches to 5 feet 10 inches, the variance being 4 inches. All roughly with the same build, the females naturally being a slight more diminutive. An oddly homogenous group. She didn't care. All she wanted was for the test to work.

Tearing her eyes from the window, her excitement sapping her patience from gazing any longer at the group below, she bustled along the metal stairway spiraling down at the back of the tower. She folded up the sleeves of her blood red cloak to rest above her elbows as she went. The other magicians already were lined up alongside their respective workstations. Twelve oak tables fully stocked with multiple vials of seawater and the substance. *Her* substance. Enough for multiple trials should the need present itself. The remaining two tables that occupied the tower's perimeter were empty. She paced across the stonework and placed a hand on the door, stopping and taking a moment to glance to either side at the stationed magicians. Their cloaks' sleeves were already folded out of the way of their hands. She nodded and pulled the door open.

"Thank you for coming! Your work here will be most beneficial! Now, come." Her tone shifted from marginally-amiable to one-hundred percent business, the half-step down in pitch causing several of the subjects to shift uneasily. She didn't notice as she had already turned around and swept back across the stone floor to one of the empty tables at the back of the tower, closest to the stairs. Turning, she pushed herself up into a sitting position atop the table and instructed, "Pick a work station. Any will do."

1

The remaining subjects who meekly stood outside hurriedly filed in, the last closing the door. With slight haste, not quite quick enough for her approval, the subjects dispersed among the tables. Almost in sync, the magicians pulled tall wooden stools out from beneath the tables for the subjects to sit on. They all sat.

Releasing a breath she had not known she was holding in, she clasped her hands together. "We will start with the lowest dosage. A friendly reminder—even an undiluted intake will not harm you."

The magicians' cloaks shimmered in the flickering light provided by the overhead bulbs as they manipulated the vials. Each used a dropper to pull bright blue liquid from one vial and dispensed one drop into a vial of seawater.

Blinking furiously, she then stared at the nearest diluted vial. The magician shook the vial lightly several times before resting it on the table. "Wait thirty seconds before drinking," she said. Her voice had become hushed, as if she were reverently speaking to King James.

Just then the door of the tower opened and in walked the king himself, followed by his advisor.

Filento, she thought. Wiping the grimace from her face, she stood up and held her arms straight at her sides. "King James, what are you doing here?"

One of the subjects got up from his stool and knelt on the floor, bowing his head. The others stayed sitting, though bowed their heads as well.

Sighing, she glared at Filento. "Your presence is disrupting our research."

"Yes, I know," James said sardonically. "I wanted to see if this thing you've been concocting works."

"All right," she said, resigned to the inconvenience. "Step over here. They are about to begin the first test."

James and Filento moved to stand on her right, right in the way of the work station she had been observing. Annoyed, she stepped around them and glared once more at Filento. Somehow, for some reason, he had wriggled his way into any and every important event occurring in the kingdom. His bushy moustache bent upward as did his mouth in an aggravating smile. *Let him mock my curiosity* she thought, turning back to the work station. "It is time. You may drink when ready."

The man kneeling on the floor stood up fast and returned to his stool. Gingerly, each of the subjects picked up their vials and brought them to their lips. Tipping the vials just a fraction, she watched as the dilution drained into their throats.

Silence ensued. The subjects replaced the empty vials onto the tables and looked around, uncertain. The magicians did not move, watching their respective subjects intently.

She walked to the closest work station and looked down at the subject. "What did you taste?" she asked.

The subject's lips parted as he thought. "It tastes… like water," he said lamely.

Her breathing hitched as if his answer was anything but lame. "And? Was it salty?"

The man shook his head. "No. It was like river water."

"Did it taste fruity?"

Confused, the man paused. "Uh. Yeah, a bit."

3

Stepping hurriedly to the next station, she asked the subject if there was salt in the liquid. The answer was no. "Did it taste chalky?" she asked.

"It... did," the female subject said.

She went to the next station. "Was it salty?"

"No."

"Did it leave your mouth dry?"

Slight pause. "Yes."

Next subject. "Was it salty?"

"No."

"Did it taste bitter?"

"Yeah."

She continued like this around the tower, checking each subject for how the liquid tasted. Finally, she returned to her spot beside James and Filento. "The salt is gone," she said softly.

"Purifying seawater has been a common practice in Oala," Filento mused.

"That's *not* it," she growled.

James asked, "Why did each liquid taste different?"

"That's the thing," she whispered, nudging Filento aside and getting closer to James. "They don't taste different."

"What do you mean?" Filento asked, folding his bulky arms across his chest.

"Each liquid contained the same substance," she said. "Each subject affirmed what I asked it tasted like, the exception being salty. They would have only said it tasted like water if I asked the broad question 'What did it taste like?' "

"Can you know that after only one test?" Filento countered.

Once again, she glared at him. "Trial two!" she called, her voice echoing loudly around the tower. All of the stationed magicians flourished a new vial, silently concealed it beneath their robes for a moment, then handed it to the subjects.

"Go ahead and drink," she instructed.

The subjects obeyed.

"Now," she said, looking at Filento and flashing a thin smile. "Ask them how it tastes. Be as eclectic in your questioning as you'd like."

Filento gave her a hard look before grunting and walking to the first station. "How did it taste?"

"Plain water," came the response.

"Was there a faint taste of... cumin?"

"...Yeah."

He moved to the next station. "What did you taste? Lemons?"

"Hmm... Yeah."

And the next. "Did you taste saffron?"

"It did taste something like that."

Instead of continuing on to the next station Filento doubled back and returned to the first station. "It actually tasted like strawberries, didn't it?"

"Huh. That's weird, it kind of did."

Having had enough, Filento went to take up position on the other side of James. "Your subjects could be very unreliable," he suggested quietly.

She tilted her head, though nodded. "They could, but it is unlikely. That trial's purpose was to see if there were any delayed or diminished effects. All they drank was purified water, no substance included."

"So you've more or less created a substance that... what? Increases people's suggestibility?" James drawled, though his eyes were alight with intrigue.

Raising her arms, she clapped her hands twice and announced, "There will be no need for further trials. I want each of you back here tomorrow, at the same time. You may go."

Without waiting, the subjects all stood up from their stools and exited the tower discreetly. The magicians waved their hands at their tables, and each of the used vials vanished and reappeared in a bin set beside the stairway.

Giving James her attention now, she beckoned for him to follow. She made a point of not looking at Filento, though he, too, followed her up the stairs. Coming to the same window she had used to mark the subjects' arrival, she stopped and turned. "To answer your question, generally speaking, yes. However, it seems to be incredibly potent given its success shown tonight."

"What do you mean?" Filento asked. "How much of the substance did you use?"

"Before you walked in," she continued, "I had my magicians put in one drop."

"*One drop!?*" James breathed. She looked at James whose face had frozen. It slowly morphed into a smile. "One drop," he said again.

6

"If I were to administer the substance alone, the effects could be along the same lines as Mind Control." Filento's eyes darted to her before looking around the otherwise barren second floor of the tower. She didn't notice, and went on. "Mind Control without one's continued, vigilant will to make it work. One of its major complications and, simultaneously, achievements is that the one under the substance's effects can be manipulated by anyone. A non-magician can influence the intoxicant."

"We're getting ahead of ourselves," James said. "This substance supposedly works on *everyone*."

Filento nodded, adding, "It could easily be used against us."

"Yes, though I'm developing an inoculation," she replied. "It's rather simple and uses some of the substance's base components, making it easy for someone like me to control."

"Someone like you," Filento mused. "How did you create the substance in the first place?"

"Alchemy." Silence. The woman watched as James and Filento stared at her. It was Filento who spoke first.

"You're saying—"

"Yes. I've created a new branch of magic, the kind which Dunlon himself could not master. At the present, though," she said, pausing to hold out her hand. Nothing seemed to happen. Eventually, the three began to smell the faint odor of salt in the air. "It is limited," she continued. "I can change chemical components of fluid entities. I cannot, shall we say, make gold."

James and Filento went on looking at her. Again, it was Filento who spoke. "What you've done is a marvel."

Blinking, she glanced at him. "Hm. Thanks."

"One question, however," Filento said, "Why was salt the exception to what the subjects could taste?"

She considered the question shortly since it was a fair one. "The subjects were only told the experiment would involve a new water purification method. That the aim of the experiment was to remove all salt from the water. And so, in some way, maybe due to their will to please the experimenter—me—or due to some expectation to not taste salt, they had a preconception that was enough to resist the basic suggestibility the question 'Was it salty?' contained. Your presence may have contributed to it as well," she noted, flicking a hand briefly at James. "It wouldn't look as good if the experiment failed and they tasted salt. With further experimentation to test responsiveness to different dosages and types of questioning, and even outright statements, I'm sure the subjects will succumb to the substance, no matter how strong the mental barrier."

"This also means the substance... What are you going to call it?" James questioned.

"Vesper," she said.

James smiled and nodded. "After you. Fitting. This means you can create an endless supply of this vesper?"

"Yes," she said, now turning to look out the window. "It will, of course, require a lot of water."

"We can have some Teleporters fetch some," James suggested.

"I already have a plan for that," she said, pointing a finger out the window at the horizon.

The two mens' eyes followed the invisible line from her finger to the shimmering blue expanse beyond the land's edge. "The sea?" James asked.

"The Stirling," she affirmed. "I can turn it into the largest otherwise freshwater body of water in the world."

"That would have global consequences," James said. "What about the fish?"

"I don't like fish. If they die, they die."

Filento stood up straighter. "The fish won't matter. What we have… or rather, what you've created is a means for world rule."

"Indeed," she said.

"How long will it take?" he asked.

"If subsequent experiments of the vesper are successful, along with the inoculation, I'd give it around 12 months."

Filento nodded, folding his arms once more, a slight smile playing under his moustache. "The prospect of world rule in a year." He turned his head to look at James. "I'd like to see it happen."

James's eyes mystified while looking at her. "I'd like to see it happen," he echoed. "Vespertine."

Torion Oey

10 Months Later (Present Day)

Torion Oey

Chapter 1: Not

"Attention, citizens of Telnas! Lanmar!"

The dozens of thoroughfares converging at the palace's front gates spread out through the city, their side-streets interweaving and connecting to each other in a weblike pattern. Important-looking arched buildings both tall and short which all belonged to royalty loomed over the streets, their doors and windows thrown wide open. Each street and every building are filled with people.

"Today marks the end of an era!" I pause and look down at the crooked writing scribbled atop the yellow parchment I hold in my right hand. "Really? The end of an era?" I mutter, tilting my head toward Darren. He glares at me, his eyes a piercing pale blue.

Rolling my eyes, I continue with my proclamation. "King James is dead."

"What are you playing at?" a man's voice shouts up at me, followed by some jeers.

That doesn't seem right. I glance down at the parchment and see *pause* written between the line I just read and the next. Yes, there's supposed to be a pause here to allow for gasps and thinking. There isn't supposed to be shouting.

"You're James!" another man shouts. Several more begin to shout, the majority of their words incomprehensible in the rising charivari of noise. I catch someone complaining about my speech being an elaborate ruse to instate some further laws on exportations.

I drop my right hand and raise my left, palm out. Surprisingly, the crowd quiets down. Raising my right hand again, I continue reading. "I am Not James," I declare loudly. "Though I look like James, I am not him. There have been rumors lately about a man who looks identical to James. That man, who is Not James, is me."

Another pause. I take a moment to glance around the crowd below, then eye the servants and guards lining the wall on either side of me. The majority of them are shifting their legs, their glinting plate helmets turning toward me.

"You all may doubt me, however, it is the truth. Look—" I gesture to Idrid, who steps out from behind me to take up position on my right. She easily raises the body of my twin brother in her large arms up high, the wound I inflicted on him semi-dressed to prevent too gruesome a sight. The blood along his chest has long since coagulated.

Now the crowd gasps and begins talking amongst themselves in diminished voices. I scan the rest of the paper in my hand and sigh. There's still a page and a half to read.

I crumple the paper in my hand and toss it on the floor, earning myself a growl of annoyance from Darren. The paper disappears from the ground and I hear the paper crinkle behind me as Darren unfolds it.

"I know what you all might be thinking," I press on. " 'The king is dead. What now? Who will ascend the throne?' Well, being the king's brother and all, it is my responsibility. However, I will not. I refuse, and I decline."

The talking has ceased and all the people stare blankly up at me. "You're losing them," Darren says, his voice dangerously low. I feel him urgently brushing the parchment with the speech against my back, trying to get me to take it without drawing attention to himself.

The clattering of metal greaves and boots against the stone floor alert me to a crowd of what look to be royals heading toward us atop the wall. I catch a strange whiff of chloramine in the still air that follows the crowd of royals. I glimpse their multichromatic tan and green dresswear and realize they are magicians from one of the Occult Towers.

Darren moves from behind me and meets them before they can reach me. "Where have you been?" he asks them.

A woman, most likely prominent given the way the others form a semicircle around her, responds. "Given the circumstances, we were put on high alert to protect the tower at all costs." She walks around Darren and takes up a position beside me on my left. After a momentary glance, she addresses the crowd. "And so, there will be a shift in governance. In the coming days the Magic Guild will appoint members to a new ruling body. This body will be known as the Concilium."

Darren whirls around, his face pale. I watch him, curious about his reaction.

"We will, of course, be taking applications starting tomorrow at dawn," the woman continues, unperturbed by the lot of the guards turning toward her, their hands slowly reaching for their weapons. "These may be picked up from the majority of the royals' houses along this district, or in your respective district's royal houses within Telnas. We welcome any person looking to guide Lanmar toward a brighter future to apply."

I look around, confused by Darren and the guards' behavior. Idrid kneels down and lays James's body against a parapet before rising, a similar frown of confusion on her face.

The woman magician extends both arms outward as if giving the crowd a large hug. "For Lanmar!" she shouts.

A majority of the crowd fails to echo her, though several return the cry.

"For Lanmar!" she shouts again. Only a half-dozen more pathetically call back "For Lanmar!"

The stench of rotten eggs mixed with chloramine overwhelms me as Darren teleports beside Idrid. I watch silently as his hand grips her forearm and together they disappear. The combination of unnatural smells indicating the use of magic as well as his sudden flight tell me one thing: *danger is here.*

Magicians of the Occult Tower walk slowly toward me, though a flick of the woman magician's hand causes them to freeze. She shouts one last time, "For Lanmar!" before turning to me and asking, "Where did your friend go?"

Her brunette bangs are cut in a straight line along her eyebrows while the rest of her hair curtains her neck and shoulders. Beneath the eyebrows her eyes are a soft brown like that of the bottom of a still pond.

"I'm not sure," I say truthfully, gazing back down at the crowd as if to search for her, knowing fully well I wouldn't find her. "Perhaps she went to get an application form and be ahead of the game."

"It would be good to have a Giant in the Concilium. Despite the Royal Court's actions in the past, we hope to unify all of Lanmar's peoples." Her tone is completely serious and genuine, even while euphemizing the attempted genocide by the Royal Court as simply "actions".

"Half-Giant," I correct. Noting the surrounding guards have become still, I try to find the source of the strange smell of chloramine now that Darren's rotten-egg-smelling magic is gone. My nose directs me to the woman's hands—it is as if the woman had been rinsing her hands with the substance, though they are completely dry. Is it residue or is she currently performing some sort of magic?

"All the same," she says. "We must forgive our past selves," she continues, pointedly looking from me to the body of James and then back to me. "And look to the future. You are welcome to join us, however—" she pauses, smiling at my head shake, "—you've already mentioned your unwillingness to rule."

Wary of the guards around us, all of whose attention is fixed on us, I prepare myself for a fight. The woman turns around and waves. "Do as you like," she calls back. "You're welcome here."

The rest of the magicians reform the semicircle around her and proceed along the wall before descending down a stairway.

A light sound of something falling to the floor catches my attention. At my feet is the crumpled parchment I had used for my speech. Bending over, I scoop it up and uncrumple it. Turning it over to the back, I see new words written below the final line in fresh ink: *Red-light District*.

Torion Oey

Chapter 2: Maia

*W*here are they? Maia thinks, glancing about the first floor of the tower. *What are they doing?* Darren's unexpected interruption had postponed the Conjuring students' quiz to the following day. Maia recounts the prior evening's events in her head: first, she had snuck out and scaled the tower exterior; second, she had overheard Darren talking with Master Aveve about important (although somewhat boring) political stuff involving the king and his brother and some bad-sounding group called the Concilium; then, Aveve had pretended to be a member of the Concilium and Maia had attacked her, destroying part of the tower in the process; and finally, Darren had teleported away, warning her and Aveve of something big that might be about to happen.

Shaking her head, she glances once more around at the other students' faces, searching for her friends Mark, Lin, and Tricia. Maia wonders if she should ask Aveve about them. Although, they *had* followed her outside to observe her spying on the clandestine meeting, something Aveve did not know, so they may be lying low. No matter, the quiz is currently happening and they should be here by now!

Another student who wears the tower's standard uniform that Maia has yet to be afforded—a grey shirt and slacks—takes the center of the floor and conjures two pale blue handkerchiefs in the same hand. The student walks away from the center and is replaced by another. This student conjures two pieces of string.

"Okay, Maia," Aveve coos. "We didn't get to you last time since Darren interrupted. If you please—" She gestures for her to step forward.

Already Maia had learned to conjure several items at once. Despite this, she is thankful for the time to practice the technique. Maia paces to the center of the tower, working the staff she had retrieved like a cane. Stopping at the center, she levels the staff to aim at a point in midair. A moment passes. *Pop.* Two rubber balls appeared and fell to the floor, bouncing several times. The other students move to try and catch them. While they do, Maia moves back to the outer ring of students, purposefully standing back in a spot closer to the door. If they aren't going to be at the tower today, she will visit the town nearby where they lived.

The last students take their turns conjuring their items. Aveve claps her hands excitedly once the final student completes the quiz. "Congratulations, everyone! You all pass!"

"Like not passing would mean anything," Maia hears another student mutter.

"I've been thinking," Aveve goes on, "that pop quizzes may not be all they're cracked up to be."

If anything, they produce a good amount of anxiety Maia thinks.

"I've decided that I won't be doing that for the rest of the year, so you can all rest easy!"

Maia lets out a breath. She was tested by her student guide, Greg, at her previous tower every day and was never nervous. She supposes this is because he never referred to them in terms that implied consequences. She remembers hearing horror stories from non-magic students who had returned to her hometown Fairbreeze after attending places of higher education. They mentioned exams that were pass or fail and the exams could only be taken twice. Students who failed both times were removed from the institutes without receiving any credential related to the field. It scares her that

20

even with extensive education or training that one test could prevent your progress. But that is the regular system for non-magic people. Given her own experience with Greg at the Elementalist tower, magicians likely have a better system of education.

"Instead of springing a quiz on you in another week's time, your next quiz begins now! The task is this: conjure an object that doesn't exist. You all have one week to complete it, which should be plenty of time. You also have as many attempts as you can manage in that time! Oh, and since I forgot to mention it before the last quiz, any of the quizzes that you fail will mean you can no longer attend here! Good luck!"

Maia stiffens, her heart picking up speed. *Is this real? Had Aveve been reading her thoughts?* She flinches when Aveve spins and looks directly at her, the other students returning to their respective friend groups and eagerly discussing the quiz.

"Maiaaa!" Aveve calls, strutting over to where she stands by the door. Aveve's long boots sharply clack on the stone floor. "I haven't seen a certain three students since yesterday's quiz," she says in a marginally quieter voice. "I distinctly recall them being with you. If you could, go to Chalman's residential district and tell them about the new topic for this week. They may also finish the previous quiz when they come back."

For her part, Maia nods, though consciously takes in another breath of air. Her chest feels like it's barely containing her heart.

Aveve flashes her a smile and winks at her. "I know you're new, so I wouldn't simply send you home if you failed the last quiz," she says soothingly. "But after seeing your natural talent and acuity when it comes to magic, it sparked something in me. And that feeling I want the other students

21

here to have. That is why, from now on you're going to have to give it your all."

"Uh..." Maia stalls, uncertain. "A feeling? Aveve, what are you talking about?"

"There's only so much you can do on raw ability alone," Aveve continues. "But after that, what then will you do? I'm looking forward to refining you." She gives Maia a final smile before spinning around and making her way toward and up the spiraling stairs of the tower.

Maia is even more confused, though remembers Aveve saying to go tell Mark and the others. All she is certain of now is that Aveve will only continue teaching her Conjuring if she can meet her requirements. She does not know where to begin or even how to interpret the current quiz. *At least, on my own.* She can maybe find help from her friends.

She pushes open the tower door, its hinges swinging fast and the resounding *bang* of the wood knocking against the outside of the tower hard, and begins walking along the packed earth toward Chalman. *There's only so much you can do on raw ability alone.* The words echo in her head. Maia does not believe all she had done up to this point was only because of talent. She had spent at least two years training in Elementalism alongside Greg. Could she immediately cause the air to go still or suddenly rush? Could she immediately crystallize water? Could she immediately soften stone?

No she thinks, though recalls what she had done with the mysterious tree on the lower level of the Tower of Bel. She herself did not know what she had done or how she did it, but the tower's master, Kellen, had described it as either Conjuring or Mind Control. Wait, no, he had said it was a *mix* between the two. Could such a thing exist? And over the past few days the first thing she conjured was a mixed meal for herself of mashed potatoes, apple slices, and chicken breast, along with the plate itself. That had to be several steps more complicated than the task of the quiz she had just taken, and she did it on her first day.

Maia relents, gazing up from her feet to look at the path winding ahead around rolling hills. She will not say it out loud, but Aveve has a point. But that does not mean she is totally right. Smiling to herself, she begins to jog. If Aveve thinks she has not put any work in, she will prove her wrong. She will push herself in her own way. A way that could not be gotten through raw ability.

Her arms move faster back and forth as she picks up speed. Rather than clenching her fists, she holds her hands open with her palms flat and perpendicular to her torso. Each time one arm reaches the bottom of its arc she concentrates on pushing the molecules in the air.

The way she looks must be silly, kind of like a seal using its flippers to move across the ground. She does not follow that thought. *When I want something, there's no need to worry about appearances.* She continues until she's flat-out running, visualizing the air behind her palms being shot backward as if by propellers. Only, that is not enough. She realizes that the mental image is imperfect since a propeller is fixed rather than swinging like her arms. But it is close.

She adds a component to her mind: a tunnel of wind extending out from her palms. Concentrating, she feels added pressure on her hands. It's as if she's pushing against a pliable surface.

Pushing herself harder, her legs moving even more rapidly, she races along the path. She is beginning to get tired. For a brief moment she lets go of the mental image and breathes in rapidly while still moving. She has to steady her breathing first so she does not overexert herself or wind up getting distracted. Anything uneven could potentially interfere.

Finding her rhythm, she concentrates once more, though only on one hand. She visualizes a tunnel of pure air, spinning wildly away from her palm. Then, she swings her right arm back. At the end of its arc, her hand slaps the air hard.

She feels a slight force extend out from her hand, pushing her hand backward to a slightly higher point in its arc. She slams her legs into the ground to stop herself and look back. There is a good distance between her and the tower while the outskirts of Chalman are now in view. Glancing down at her hand, she smiles. It wasn't enough to push her whole body forward and it had lasted less than a second, but she had felt it. She had made one step toward gliding.

This, she thinks, *will take work*. Maia continues to walk onward to speak with her friends, eager to begin training her Conjuring alongside her Elementalism.

Through the pane on the uppermost floor of the tower Aveve watches Maia race along the path toward Chalman, a smile playing on her lips. She wonders if Maia will be up to her challenge. Behind her she listens to the other students either gossiping or discussing the quiz. It is not like they haven't had similar tests laid before them, though she also wonders if they will be ready.

"Master Aveve?"

She turns to look thoughtfully at the female student. "Yes, what is it?"

"I was wondering what you meant by 'conjure something that doesn't exist.' Is it a riddle?"

Aveve blinks twice and folds an arm across her stomach to rest her other arm's elbow atop, tapping her chin with a finger. "No, it's quite literal."

"Oh. I see," the student says. "It's just that... everything we conjure technically doesn't exist until we conjure it."

"You're right," Aveve says, her voice playfully lilting upward in pitch. "But you're conjuring something that already exists. If I remember, you conjured two flowers. They were lovely chrysanths. I've only seen their kind in the south."

Understanding dawned on the student's face, her eyebrows rising. "You want us to conjure an object that doesn't *exist*. That's going to be difficult."

"In many ways, it will be," Aveve agrees, resting her head on her hand now.

"The only thing I can think of that doesn't exist are mythical creatures... like a salamander."

Aveve shakes her head. "I'm sorry to say, those are actually real. But, even if they weren't, if you managed to conjure one you wouldn't pass my quiz."

The student's eyebrows rise higher. "They're real?" Aveve nods. "Hmm. I wouldn't think to conjure something like that, anyway. For one thing, it could kill me by eating or burning me alive."

"And everyone else in the tower," Aveve adds.

Swallowing, the student continues, "And for another, it would be a living thing, so I couldn't conjure it anyway. But what do you mean it wouldn't count even if they weren't real?"

"They're regarded as mythical creatures, though people have a general idea of what they look like. Every

25

conjuror needs an image of what they're conjuring, and if the image exists then you'd be considered cheating."

Thinking for a moment, the student nods. "I guess so. Still, it seems like a negligible technicality since conjuring the thing would be an awesome achievement."

"Half the task is creating the thing in your head," Aveve says. "I expect everyone's creativity to shine here."

Thanking the tower master, the student gives a slight bow and walks away. Aveve looks back through the window pane once more though no longer sees Maia's form on the path. *She's fast* Aveve thinks, smiling again.

A mushing sound catches her ear and she glances to the wall beside the window. A hole the size of a fist has opened, and beyond that is the empty horizon and sky. Stepping closer, Aveve puts her face up to the hole. *What caused this?*

Gentle wind flows through and brushes against her face, drying her eyes. Blinking several times, she draws back and begins to conjure the tower's wall back. Before she can, a rush of wind blasts her and envelops her entirety. The students all around her gasp and shift back.

She feels the wind violently rushing across her body and causing her clothes to flap uncontrollably. The female student she had been talking with rushes back and reaches out a hand. "Don't—!" Aveve tries to call to her, though her words dissipate almost instantly in the vortex. The student's hand is wrenched away, wrenching her body along with it a couple feet.

Once again before Aveve can conjure a piece in the wall to cut off the source of the wind the wind subsides slightly. It no longer envelops her, though is focusing to a single point. Aveve's eyes widen and her heart begins to race. *Could it really be?*

Free of the currents, Aveve tilts her head so that the rushing air blasts against the side of her head and sends strands of her hair dancing. Finally the air continuously rushes only to the small space of her left ear. Its sound is like the ocean crashing.

"Aveve," a man's voice, barely audible, wafts calmly in the noise.

Aveve smiles wide. *Kellen!*

"Aveve," Kellen says again. "Aveve. Now that I've said it three times, you should know it's me."

I don't need a stupid mantra or code to know it's you she thinks, though remains silent so that she can hear what he says next.

"The king is dead. The Concilium has taken his place."

Dead? Then Darren was right, the Concilium did do something big. But what does it mean?

"There is no telling what the people will do. Be on your guard. And mind the border." The wind abruptly ceases, and the hole in the wall reseals itself.

Aveve looks around at the students who are all still and wide-eyed. Clenching her fists, she grits her teeth. *He only gave me an update? That man...*

"All right, everyone!" she calls loudly enough so that her voice rang down to the bottom floor of the tower. The students on her floor flinch, sensing she is upset. "I'm closing the tower for three days! In that time, continue working on the quiz I've assigned!"

"Master Aveve!" a male student says, interrupting her. "What if we complete the quiz before then?"

"Then you can show me after I re-open the tower!" Aveve's voice booms, traces of vehemence sinking into her words. "And no matter what happens, I expect you all to complete this quiz! If you don't, I will do more than expel you from this tower!"

At that, the sound of the students rushing for the one door on the first floor echo throughout the tower. The students on her floor stream rapidly down the stairs, leaving her alone. Aveve moves to another window at the back of the tower and gazes out at the sea of trees. Kellen's comment about the border is troubling. If it's true the Concilium has ties in other nations… She has to prepare.

Chapter 3: Not

"**O**f all the places, you choose the Red-light District," I state in a soft voice while glancing back and forth at the scantily and suggestively clad denizens walking the streets. Turning to Idrid, I give her a thumbs up. "I didn't know you were into this kind of thing, but I approve."

"Shut up," Idrid growls, folding her bulky arms over her chest.

"I chose the place," Darren says.

"Oh! Nice one, Darren!" I turn and give him the thumbs up.

"Because no royals live in this district and we're less likely to run into Concilium members," Darren adds exasperatedly.

"Mmmm, sure," I say, looking across the street at one of the more glamorous brothels called Ferry Fancy. Leaning back against the cold stone archway we are huddled beside, I blow strands of my bangs away from my eyes. I notice the people, despite their flamboyant dresswear, are keeping some distance from us. "Who was that woman who upstaged me, by the way?"

"Her name is Vespertine," Darren says. "She's one of them, though wasn't wearing the Magic Guild's cloak. Nor were the others. I've suspected her of being a part of the Concilium, though she was always holed up in her tower doing experiments and rarely visited the palace. I don't know much about her other than the type of magic she uses."

"Man," I say, sighing, "I didn't even get halfway through your speech before she came and interrupted, Darren. That sucks."

"You weren't even following my speech," Darren says, irritation seeping into his voice. "And are you listening?"

I stand up straighter, nodding. "You mentioned her being holed up in 'her tower.' You mean she's Vale Tower's master?"

"You know about the tower masters?" Darren asks.

"I only know the Occult Towers' names, their respective branches of magic, and that they are led by a master. I don't know the masters personally."

"Who taught you?" It is Idrid who asks, her dark eyes staring into mine. "I know you weren't raised like normal royalty and your family was less than kind to you. Did someone else tell you?"

"Indeed," I say. "Instructor—That is, my instructor in the south desert did, after I ran away from my family."

"It's not like this information isn't common knowledge," Darren says.

"I didn't exactly grow up in Lanmar," I respond. "At least, after the age of 5."

"You ran away when you were 5?" Darren asks. I nod. He looks at me hard for several seconds then shakes his head in wonder. "The more I learn about this kingdom the more I learn it's rotten to the core."

"Indeed," I say. "I mean, look at you. You were a part of it and you didn't even know."

Darren glares at me. "I only became 'a part' of it a year ago. And I was not actively 'a part' of it."

I shrug. "I don't mean to say you're rotten, too. I just mean that even so, the people have long despised the way they're ruled."

"There's not much I could have done about that," Darren says in a low voice.

"Indeed," I say, remembering the fact James himself was mind-controlled for who knows how long. Not much you can do in that situation. "Back to Vespertine. She's a Teleporter like you, then?"

"She is, supposedly. I've never seen her do magic. That's why I believe she can use Mind Control, and why I suspected she was a member of the Concilium."

"She's not a Teleporter, then," I say, thinking. "Yet she is the tower's master. Rotten, indeed."

"Stop saying 'indeed,' " Idrid says, annoyed. "You sound like textbooks describing the history of Lanmar."

"You're right," I agree. "Wouldn't want to sound like one of those dull books. You might start to enjoy me."

Before Idrid can respond Darren waves a hand, his own Magic Guild scarlet cloak glistening in the sun and lights shining from Ferry Fancy's billboard letters. "Enough. We're going to need to think of a plan."

"For what?" I ask.

"Stabilizing the kingdom, of course."

"Oh. Right. Well, it's no longer a kingdom, is it? And we already did what you asked us to do by coming back to the palace and delivering that speech."

Darren sighs. "You didn't get to finish the speech I had written."

"Right. Vespertine seems to be a step ahead. After you two teleported away she seemed to know about me and you," I say, pointing a finger at Idrid.

"Knowing about me isn't so surprising," Idrid states. "How does she know you?"

"Ah, acknowledging that I'm an enigma! A woman after my heart."

Idrid raises a fist twice the size of mine threateningly.

"From what she said, she seemed to only know me so far as I had killed James. You, on the other hand, she seemed to imply knowing more. As if she knew about your past." I glance between Idrid and Darren, noting Darren's curiosity. Opting to keep that secret seeing as I had already annoyed Idrid enough, I say, "She also wanted you to be a part of the new governing body."

"Vespertine was interested in Idrid?" Darren asks.

I nod, releasing a sharp breath to blow my hair out of my eyes again. "She said she wanted to unify the people. Seems like she has the same goal as you, Darren."

"Right," Idrid says sarcastically. "I bet her idea of stability is exactly the same."

"Well, for now there doesn't seem to be any use doing anything," I say, and begin pacing away.

"Wait, where are you going?" Darren asks.

"You said we needed a plan. Vespertine's goal is too vague to try and make a plan to counter, so the best option is to wait for more information."

"Doing nothing may lead to something worse," Darren warns.

I pause and turn back, feeling the red gemstone I had stolen from the palace pressing against my foot within my sock. "Waiting and doing nothing aren't the same thing," I say, stooping low to retrieve the gem. I stand and look down at it in my hand. It shines a brilliant crimson, as if it's alive. "Idrid, I'd like to ask you for a favor."

"What?" she says rather than asks. The annoyance is gone. She is ready to do whatever I tell her.

Smiling, I say, "Do you think you could take Vespertine up on her offer and join the Concilium?"

Idrid thinks for a moment before nodding. It goes unspoken, though we communicate; Idrid has faced off against Filento, a Mind-Controller, and resisted the magic; though she isn't immune, Idrid can gain information about the Concilium; additionally, she can learn more about her own past if Vespertine knows about it.

I draw my arm back and toss the gem to her. It glints almost blindingly in its trajectory. Idrid catches it in her right hand.

Wincing, she tosses the stone between her hands rapidly. "Ow! What did you do to this stone, Not?" She pulls at a part of her shirt to form a pouch and drops the stone inside it. "It feels like it is on fire. Did you leave residual fire from that magician you fought earlier in it?"

"No," I say, curious. My mouth quirks upward, and I wave. "Perhaps Darren can help you figure out more about that stone. Assuming you can't find the answer in a book."

"Wait!" Darren says again. "What will you do?"

"I'll do what I was going to do before," I say. "Go south. I have a longing to see the desert again."

"Hold on." This time it's Idrid. I look at her and notice her frown. She's worried, though not about herself.

"Before we went into the palace I met someone. A swordsman. Remember? I mentioned him to you, he said he lived on the southern border of Lanmar."

"A swordsman," I repeat, racking my brain. "What about him?"

"He said he wanted to kill you," she says.

Ah. Him. "Thanks for the reminder," I say, waving again. Turning, I begin walking toward the closest way out of Telnas.

"He seems dangerous," I hear Idrid say at my back.

"I have a sword!" I call over my shoulder, and break into a run.

Chapter 4: Maia

It takes Maia less than an hour to reach Chalman. Yet, by the time she steps foot in town she is out of breath and has all but exhausted her will. All she managed to do the rest of the way is recreate a small blast of air behind either of her hands while running. *I'm tired and I didn't even do it simultaneously with both hands!*

Breathing rapidly, she glances between the stone buildings minimally coated with plaster to give the structures a smooth and flat surface. Each building's slanting shingles look as if they could have gone for a replacement months ago. Taking several seconds to catch her breath, she paces to the closest door.

It takes a knock and brief period of waiting before the door is answered by an older-looking woman (not old enough to be considered an elder) who is wearing an apron the color and texture of salmon scales. "Hi," Maia says quickly, appraising the apron and reminiscing of her home town by the sea. "I'm looking for some students who practice at the Tower of Vern. Would you know where they live?"

"That depends," the woman says, her calm expression unwavering. "A lot of kids here go to the tower."

"Their names are Mark, Tricia, and Lin," Maia says.

"Mark lives two houses down. Right there." The woman steps outside her doorway and points past the house to Maia's right to the next one over. "I don't know the other two, so I can't tell you where they live."

"Thanks!" Maia says and walks over while the woman returns inside and shuts the door. Maia pauses at Mark's door, noting that just about every house lacks windows. It is

35

very different than the houses in her hometown of Fairbreeze. *Then again, there isn't much to look at outside,* she thinks while knocking, looking around at the dirty and crudely constructed pavement weaving between the buildings. Just about everything is an eyesore save for the ornamental streetlamps placed at intervals every several feet. They curve outward halfway up where a sconce may be lit.

The door opens and it's another older-looking woman who is behind it. Unlike the last woman, this one's straight and black hair falls around her pale face, creating a ghostly effect. "Hello?" comes a wavering voice.

"Hi! Is Mark here?"

The woman blinks at Maia while looking her up and down. Maia shifts self-consciously under her gaze, becoming more aware of the places her clothes cling to her body from sweat. "Who are you?" the woman asks finally, changing from uncomfortably inspecting Maia to uncomfortably staring into her eyes without blinking.

"I'm a—a student at the tower," Maia starts. There are several more seconds where the woman does nothing but stare at her. Holding herself higher, Maia says, "Master Aveve wanted me to notify students who weren't there of an exam."

The woman doesn't react. No, wait, her face is changing. Very slowly, the woman's eyes widen and her mouth opens, revealing clenched teeth. Maia, bracing herself for something, shifts a step back. Parting her teeth, the woman screams. "MAAAAAARK!?! YOU WERE SUPPOSED TO BE AT THE TOWERRRR!?!"

Somehow the woman's screaming comes out as stated questions, something Maia thought to be impossible due to being contradictory. Maia places a hand over her mouth in surprise.

36

Banging resounds overhead and the sound of footsteps rattle as someone races across the second floor. There is a crash of something falling, someone stumbling then cursing, and finally the footsteps reach their level.

The woman, whose eyes that are stretched wide and bore into Maia's, steps further in and away from the door, allowing Mark to plummet through. He just barely pulls himself back to avoid running into Maia, though his momentum carries him past her and he has to skid to a halt. "Maia? What are you doing here?" His short, dark brown hair is disheveled and sticking out in clumps at weird places. The sign of bedhead. He wears a plain grey shirt and brown shorts. The getup makes him look even younger than his actual age.

Realizing the time she is spending looking at him is drawing out uncomfortably long, Maia says, "Oh—I was instructed to find you."

Running a hand through his hair (though doing nothing to keep it smooth), his eyebrows furrow in thought. "Instructed. You mean Master Aveve told you to get me? I suppose it makes sense since I missed the quiz."

A long, ragged breath draws inward behind Maia, and she freezes when she remembers the woman is still there. "You missed... a quiz...!?" Now the woman is speaking remarkably quiet but at the same time with great power, something else Maia thought to be impossible. She sounds furious. Wait, is this... Mark's mother?

Maia takes several steps away from the door to stand beside Mark. "Uh... Aveve said he can make it up, so it's okay," Maia says in a tenuously pleasant voice, trying to calm the woman.

"You will take this quiz... then return here..." The woman's eyes as hard and still as glass stare at both of them

37

while one of her long, pale arms reaches and shuts the door slowly. The door stops at a crack, leaving enough space to see a dark iris surrounded in a pale white halo. It glares at Mark and Maia for a long moment, and then is gone behind the door.

Glancing at Mark, Maia releases a breath. "Who was she?"

Mark puts his hands in the pockets of his shorts and trudges away quickly. "Come on, we shouldn't stay here," he says. "That's my mom."

Maia jogs a bit to catch up before setting her pace alongside Mark's. "Is she always so tense?" she asks.

"Only around new people," Mark replies.

Nodding, the two lapse into silence. By the time they reach the edge of the town she remembers she isn't there only for Mark. "I forgot!" she cries out, startling him. "I need to tell Tricia and Lin about the quiz as well!"

Mark follows Maia as she heads back into town. "They weren't at the tower either? Actually, I'm surprised most of the other students still went."

"Huh?" Maia asks, confused. "What do you mean?"

"Oh yeah, you don't know yet since you're pretty much living in the tower. King James was murdered a few days ago."

She is too stunned to say anything to that.

"Several criers brought the news this morning. It sort of distracted me from the quiz…"

"Oh yeah, about that," Maia says, "Where did all of you go? You never came back after we snuck out."

"Sorry," Mark says, embarrassed. "After we saw you disappear into the tower's top floor we thought something bad had happened to you. But before long the person wearing the fancy red cloak appeared behind us and asked us what we were doing."

"Darren," Maia supplies.

"After we told him we were your friends he relaxed a bit. He said you were fine and then teleported away."

"He didn't say anything else?" Maia questions.

"No. By the way, what happened?"

Maia hesitates, wondering why Darren would not bother telling them if he knew that she would likely tell them herself.

Mark watches her, then looks away. "Seems important if you're reluctant to say. Well, whatever it is, I assume it has to do with the king's death. It can't be a coincidence one of the Magic Guild stopped by the tower. Anyway, we also got news that a new governing body was taking the place of the king and that citizens of Lanmar could sign up to become a member. That was another reason I didn't return to the tower, since my parents work under the treasurer of Chalman who works for the treasurers in Telnas. They are unconvinced the Concilium will benefit Lanmar's economy."

Maia's eyes widen as she looks at Mark. "Did you just say the Concilium?"

"Yeah. That's what they're calling the new ruling body."

Thinking hard, Maia decides it does not matter if she reveals what Darren told her now. "Darren and Aveve met to discuss an underground group of what are essentially evil magicians who go by the same name. Darren had also said they were planning to do something big. Does that mean they killed the king?"

Mark shrugs. "Probably. Rationally, no one else other than magicians could enter the palace and do it since other experienced magicians guard the king."

That's not entirely true Maia thinks. "There was one person Darren mentioned," Maia says. She remembers the man's pale grey eyes under silver-grey hair, slim and tall standing on one of the hills south of Chalman. He wasn't alone; there was a woman who was very large and a bit taller than him, though Maia remembers the man more since he was wearing the same cloak Darren wears. "A possible brother of King James. Darren said he was going after the king."

"A brother to the king?" Mark asks. "That seems unlikely. There hasn't been any news of the royal family having more than two kids. The second died in early childhood around two decades ago."

"Well, whoever he is, he isn't just some guy," Maia continues. "Apparently he resisted Darren's magic. Or, I guess Darren said he was immune to it."

"Immune to magic?" Maia smiles at the fact Mark is repeating what she's saying. If her bad habit was telling people to wait, his was repeating statements as questions. "How is that possible?"

"How is magic possible?" Maia asks, giving a shrug of her own. "I don't really know." She stops walking at one of the main thoroughfares where crowds are gathered around market stalls. "Could you guide me to where Tricia and Lin live? I really don't have any idea where I'm going."

Without responding Mark turns and walks down the thoroughfare, ignoring the various wares. Maia, much the opposite, looks back and forth, admiring each stall.

"Care to buy anything?" a stout man sitting behind a peculiar stall calls. His stall has nothing but gadgets, though Maia is unsure what any of them do. After shaking her head the man turns away and waves at others passing by to get their attention.

"Oh, there's also something else Aveve wanted me to tell you," Maia says. "She just assigned a new quiz due by next week. It's to conjure something that doesn't exist, but I have no idea what that means."

"Something that doesn't exist, huh?" Mark takes his hands out of his pockets and begins drumming his fingers against the sides of his legs. Maia watches him as he thinks, his eyes cast toward the ground in concentration. "It can't mean just conjuring anything," Mark comments. Maia doesn't say anything, figuring he is thinking aloud. "Though it doesn't seem to be too complex to be taken as anything not literal. It must mean we have to conjure something that doesn't exist *yet.*"

"What do you mean?"

"Ah! But I also still have to do that other quiz, too!" Mark, suddenly flustered, runs both his hands through his hair, causing it to become even more wild.

"But you're a second year," Maia points out. "You can easily conjure two things at once."

"You're right," he says with a nod. "Though I don't like having to make up work. Tricia and Lin will probably have the most trouble..." He continues staring at the ground before his eyes slide over and meet hers. "Oh, right. What I meant before is that we have to conjure something new. Like... well, you've conjured apples, right? Apples are things that exist already, and you already have a clear image of what they look like. I'm thinking the quiz is to test our ability to conceptualize objects."

41

Maia thinks about it. "Huh. You're smart," she says after a while. Giggling, she looks away.

"What is it?"

"Uh. Nothing. I guess I was thinking of something stupid."

"What?"

Embarrassed, she says, "Well, I was thinking, if the quiz is what you're saying, I could try conjuring an object that is a combination of two existing objects. Like... uh, an orange and an apple. An orapple."

"An orapple?" Mark laughs. "What would that be like? Would it have the skin of an orange but the inside of an apple?"

"Maybe," Maia says, laughing along with Mark. "Well, I'll actually decide on something once we talk with Tricia and Lin."

"Sure," Mark agrees.

A figure in full-body cloth trails a block behind the two kids. The person moves smoothly among the townspeople, pausing every now and again to weave into a side street before returning to the thoroughfare. The figure's face is shrouded by a tan hood, though strands of long dark hair spill out into the light.

Stall keepers wave at the figure, calling out their wares, though the figure continues silently to move between the streets. The kids ahead turn and step onto the front patio of a house. Swiftly, the robed figure steps over to a stall and stoops, pretending to gaze at a piece of jewelry.

"Like what you see?" the woman behind the stall asks.

A hand unravels itself from the figure's robes, followed by a slender arm. It picks up a ruby ring and turns it over to catch the light. On the figure's hand is a similar ruby ring, though it shines brilliantly as if emanating its own light. "No, I think I like mine better," comes a deep woman's voice from within the hood. Placing the ring back, the figure turns to see the two kids are walking back her way and are now accompanied by two others. Three girls and a boy, all students of the Occult Tower outside of town.

Without moving, the figure watches as the group of kids pass by. None of them notice the figure watching them. Once they are a block's distance apart, the figure moves to follow. One of them is important, the one she's looking for. But she does not know which one yet.

Torion Oey

Chapter 5: Idrid

"**A**re you sure about this?" Darren asks her for the third time once they enter the royal's house. A single-file line the length of a block trails behind their spot and twelve people stand between them and the royal who supposedly lives there—whoever he is, he must be on the lower rungs of royalty. The entryway had been noticeably altered despite them not having been there before. A rack for shoes haphazardly lay in a doorway on their left leading to a living room, apparently now being used as a barrier to prevent guests from wandering. An elegant gold welcome mat with curving letters stitched into the fluffy felt lay underneath the rack. Welcomes only go so far. "If you feel so much as a pinprick in your mind, it may be too late."

"I can handle it," Idrid replies for the third time.

"Are you both immune to magic?"

"No," Idrid says. "But I've felt more than a pinprick, and I'm fine." Darren's head tilts, his eyes focusing ahead. Another applicant in line exits the room in the back. Idrid notices his clear nervousness. "I'm more worried about you. Have you never experienced the effects of Mind Control?"

The man immediately in front of them turns his head and glares at the two, letting out a soft grunt. "That stuff ain't real," he mutters before facing forward.

"Perhaps now isn't the best time to discuss *this*." Darren hisses out the last word, his body shivering involuntarily when the line shifts forward at another's exit. It takes a moment's pause before Darren speaks again. "No, I haven't."

Idrid looks at him for several seconds. *He's more nervous than I am about Mind Control.* The line moves forward. "I have a tip, then," she says.

Darren lets out a sudden laugh that surprises them both. "Sorry," he whispers, his eyes shifting nervously back and forth. "I thought it funny, being a member of the Magic Guild, getting advice from a commoner about magic."

Her expression changes to confused interest. "A commoner?"

"What else should I call you?" he asks, taking another step forward as the line shifts again.

Only Not, among a scarce few, thought of her as just another person. "That's fine," she says. "If you really don't want to, you won't—or rather, can't be forced."

The line moves forward. Darren's eyes focus on Idrid, his nervousness temporarily absent and replaced by calculated thinking. "So at least the innate instincts of survival, such as not wanting to harm yourself, will be a barrier to Mind Control?" Once Idrid nods he follows up with the question, "To what degree can you counter it if it's not a basic value? If you're being forced to do something other than, say, harming yourself or someone else you care about?"

"Depends on how much you care," Idrid says. "I think. I'm not absolutely sure." She notices his barely audible sigh and stops herself from rolling her eyes. *Maybe I should be more scared.* "You'll know."

Darren gives a questioning look.

"If it's happening, if you're being… controlled, you'll know. You'll feel pressure on your brain. Whether you're able to resist it, I don't know, but you'll feel it for sure. But if you're being manipulated to do something simple or inconsequential, then there's probably nothing you can do to stop yourself."

Darren becomes nervous again, and the line moves forward.

Idrid thinks back to the day her clan, including her family, was murdered by Elementalists. She remembers the man behind the attack standing absolutely still with a smirk on his face. She didn't know him then, but it was Filento. The fact he orchestrated the attack still leaves her stomach cold, though a new sensation—a jitteriness, but something else she fears to reason—steadily creeps through her body that she had noticed when Darren first mentioned others like Filento exist. Not only that, they belong to the same group Filento did. "The Concilium," she murmurs to herself. It had crossed her mind that he wasn't alone in killing her people, and it is more than likely all in the Concilium played a role. She feels the cold in her stomach rise, reaching her heart. If she joins them, she can find out who they are. And then...

The line moves forward, only a couple applicants ahead of them left. Idrid murmurs, "Having a firm idea of something you want helps too, with... you know. Why do you want to join the Concilium?"

Darren thinks for a second. "To prevent Lanmar from falling into further ruin."

"Huh. Well, aren't you just? You don't want anything more selfish?"

"Not really. Do you?"

"Yes," she says immediately.

The last person ahead of them in line leaves through the door in the back, and the royal, sitting in a chair, beckons them forward.

She had expected the royal to be sitting behind a desk. Instead, the line ends just before where he sits in an ornate chair. He pushes closed a middle drawer of a filing cabinet behind him that he had been placing the former applicants' forms in. "Papers, please," the man drawls, holding out a hand. Although he's a royal, he is not dressing the part; the unbuttoned cuff of his simple white long-sleeved shirt flaps about his wrist as he waves his hand impatiently; and he taps a sandaled foot below plain traveler pants. The pants, for their part, look unworn. He swiftly takes Idrid's offered application form and scans it. "Step into the back."

Idrid stiffens and stays motionless, thinking. All the others in line had taken at the least a minute before being sent into the back. Looking at the man sitting before her, she catches him glancing at her while putting her paper in the bottom drawer of the cabinet where none of the other applicants' forms had been placed. Something isn't right.

It's Darren pushing her lightly on her back that gets her moving toward the door. Nothing to do about it. Without looking back, she turns the glass knob and steps through the door. On the other side she finds two chairs facing each other in a rectangular room with a single light on either end. The chair at the far end is occupied.

"Idrid." The woman she had briefly seen atop the palace wall before Darren teleported her away casually sits facing her. She wears a deep red cloak that loosely fits her body, and her brunette hair spills over the hood in the back. Her brown eyes beneath her straight-cut bangs watch her. "Have a seat," Vespertine says, gesturing to the only other seat.

Idrid feels the cold in her heart travel down her arms and numb them slightly, though follows the woman's directions. The chair, much more ornate than the one the royal in the previous room sat in, looks sturdier and manages

48

to hold her when she sits. The contrast between the two women is significant; Idrid is practically twice Vespertine's size and sits back in her chair, uneasy; Vespertine is slim and sits forward, upright. She could be broken with just one of Idrid's hands though she is totally unconcerned. The opposite of intimidated, her eyes are fixated on Idrid's. She looks *excited*.

"I didn't give you my name," Idrid states in a monotone voice. There is no way she could have known it, unless… There is more to Mind Control than she knows. Does that confirm that Vespertine had used Mind Control on her already? Idrid stiffens, pressing her hands against her lap to prevent them from fidgeting. If so, she had not felt a thing. This is bad.

"Gallain gave me your name when you handed him your forms," Vespertine says.

Idrid blinks. So she had not used magic on her, at least yet. But the man taking forms in the front had not moved from his spot nor said anything. Then how had they communicated? Come to think of it, how did they know to send the next applicant into this room?

Gazing behind Vespertine, Idrid sees another door below the single light bulb that illuminates the back of her head. It is the only other way out, but there is no conceivable way Idrid can think of for them to communicate without magic. Is there some other signal or code they're using? Idrid glances up at the light behind Vespertine's head. Perhaps they are using the lights somehow…

"Gallain is a Mind Control magician," Vespertine says, shifting in her seat even further forward. "He can place thoughts in my mind."

It takes her by surprise, but Idrid manages to control her reaction. There is no reason for Vespertine to be this honest with her, making her believe she isn't actually being honest. But on the other hand there is even less reason to make such a thing up. It also makes sense what she said about Mind Control. If they can manipulate others, it's not out of reach to place thoughts in others' minds. This makes them even more dangerous if they can place false memories. Tilting her head and opening her mouth slightly, she says, "I didn't know Mind Control was a type of magic." *I can't let her know what I know* Idrid thinks.

"Really?" Vespertine asks. "Darren didn't tell you anything?"

"I don't know Darren well," Idrid responds. *That's right, all she knows is that we've met as per the circumstances of the murder of James.* Even if she lies, there is no way for Vespertine to prove it. *Unless, she can use Mind Control and make me talk.*

Vespertine continues to stare at her intently. "You're a Giant," she states. "You are aware the kingdom—*former* kingdom—is the cause of the routing of the Giants to the north?"

What is this? "Yes," Idrid says.

"And you were among those clans?"

Idrid can't tell if Vespertine is asking her or telling her. For now, she has to trust that she does not know. And yet, there is no reason to lie. "Yes," Idrid says, figuring the less lies she tells the better.

"I see," Vespertine says, nodding sadly. "I apologize on behalf of the former kingdom."

Idrid's hands tighten against her lap, the pressure she's using to force herself to not move causing pain in her legs. If she asks the question she wants to ask, it may become apparent what her motives are. But if she does not ask, it would seem suspicious.

"Why did you apply?"

Slowly, Idrid lets out a breath. The question may have given her an opening to thread the needle. "I want to hold Lanmar accountable," she says.

"An admirable goal," Vespertine replies. "This last question I'm going to ask is unrelated to whether we accept you, but I want you to be honest with me." Unblinking, she waits for Idrid to nod before continuing. "What do you know about Filento?"

So they knew each other. It was very likely in Idrid's mind that they did, but now that Vespertine mentioned his name it fills her with resolve. "Only that he was directly responsible."

"How do you know, if you don't mind me asking?"

If Idrid truly wants to get more information she figures it is going to have to be gotten through give and take. "I saw him that day, among the other magicians who stormed the hills."

Vespertine remains silent for a full minute. Not once has she broken eye contact since Idrid entered. Her lips form a chilling smile, crinkling the corners of her face. "That's quite a memory, to remember his face. The kingdom's attack on Giants was more than a decade ago. You must've been only a young child when it occurred. Memory... it's an interesting thing. It's thought to be the basis of what makes us who we are. The more importance we place on events we experience tends to be of great importance in ourselves as a consequence. It's almost like we are reflections of our past. Almost." She pauses, sitting up straighter. "It's also thought that the memories we value, wonderful and terrible, are more vivid and better retained. I can only imagine what reflection you saw when you faced Filento again. An unfathomable monster? I wonder if he similarly saw your past when he faced you in his final moments."

Idrid is too preoccupied with what Vespertine is saying to notice her body has gone deathly still. She gazes back at the other woman's dark brown eyes, both of them unblinking.

"I don't think memories are who we are," Vespertine goes on with the same tacit smile. "Not entirely. They're fairly messy, even the ones we hold close. Details, even emotions related to the memory, are subject to change. I don't see people as being as messy. If I were to describe each metaphorically, I'd say people are paintings while their memories are only the colors on the palette. Does that make sense?"

Idrid reacts to the question seconds later, the silence causing her to become self-aware again. "Vaguely," Idrid says, a slight tremor in her voice.

"I'm rambling," Vespertine says apologetically. "What I'm saying is what's done is done. We don't have to be slaves to our memories. But, we must do our best to make sure they have meaning. To that end, it will be easier if we had you," she says finally. Before Idrid can ask what she means she adds, "You're accepted." Standing, Vespertine bows slightly at the hips, and her eyes lower to the floor.

Idrid stands as well, feeling as if a weight lifts when the other woman's gaze leaves her. Her mind is reeling a bit from all that was said, though she knows the process is far too simple. Yet Idrid doesn't have time to question it. Or, rather, she has a feeling her time is limited. She wants to get away from this woman. Fast. "What do I do now?"

"You may exit back through the door you came in. Tell Darren he's accepted too and that he doesn't have to come in," Vespertine adds, then turns and walks to the other door. "Those accepted will meet at Vale Tower tomorrow evening at seven o'clock." She leaves without turning back.

Seconds pass as Idrid watches the far door curiously. It opens and a different woman wearing the same red cloak enters. "Please make your way out," the woman says. "More applicants will be coming."

Idrid leaves the room, and the first thing she does is search for Darren. He is still waiting at the head of the line. Idrid walks briskly past, giving him a tug on his own cloak and saying, "Come with me."

"What? Why?" Darren follows her despite his confusion, and together they leave the royal's house and walk in the direction of Earl's place. They had made arrangements with the elderly man, Idrid's former guardian, to stay with him temporarily. "What happened?"

"She was there," Idrid says vaguely. "She said we're both in."

Darren's eyes widen. "She? You mean Vespertine? What do you mean we're both in?"

"We're now members of the Concilium," Idrid says. "Our first meeting is tomorrow evening in Vale Tower."

"That's far too easy," Darren objects. "This has to be a trap. She didn't even interview me!"

"She left after interviewing me," Idrid goes on. "Another interviewer came in after her. I think she was specifically there for me."

"How did she know where we would be submitting our applications? There are dozens of royals' houses in Telnas."

That does give Idrid something to consider for a while as they walk. "She also mentioned how Gallain—the guy taking our applications in the line—used Mind Control to communicate my name."

"She told you that?" Darren lets out a huff. "This screams bad news. Are we really going through with this?"

"If they can use Mind Control as one-way communication without looking at the person they're communicating with, she could have been notified as soon as a royal saw my application form. And then... I suppose someone teleported her there if she wasn't close by already."

Darren thinks about it. "It makes sense," he says after a few moments. "Though it seems excessive to go through the trouble just for you. No offense."

"I doubt it's just for me," Idrid replies. "You were with me, too, and you got accepted. It's more likely they want both of us."

"I suppose." Darren shakes his head. "I've been thinking about the gem Not gave you," he says suddenly. "There was an Elementalist I met who had a similar gem in a ring on her hand. It could contain fire. The woman used it to set part of the palace ablaze, and almost got me with it."

Idrid's eyes drift sideways to look at Darren. "A rogue Elementalist? Who was it?"

"She was looking for Not, actually. Her name's Jasmine. Do you know her?"

Idrid sighs, looking away. "Only that Not stole her cloak."

"That's what she said. Anyway, I think both gems are enchanted with the ability to contain fire."

Idrid wrinkles her nose. "What an odd ability. Who'd want a rock that contains fire?"

"Someone who needs to start a fire?" Darren suggests.

Shrugging, Idrid walks on. "Magicians are weird."

Torion Oey

Chapter 6: Maia

"What do you mean the tower's closed?" Maia asks desperately. "I just left and everyone was working on the next quiz!" She starts pacing back and forth just outside the tower's single door, glaring at it. Several students milling around the tower watch her.

"Master Aveve said she wouldn't reopen it until three days had passed. We don't know why." The second-year student whose name Maia found out is Pina shrugs resignedly and walks off down the path, the other students who had remained choosing to trail after her.

"What the *heck*!" Maia kicks a foot out, knocking the base of the door. It lets out a hollow sound but refuses to open suddenly with the usual bang. "Now where am I supposed to stay?"

"You could stay at my place," Mark suggests. Tricia and Lin stare at him. "Just a suggestion," he says.

"Our houses are small," Tricia says.

"I doubt my parents will allow you to sleep on the floor," Lin says.

"We have a guestroom," Mark says.

"You and your *governmental benefits*," Tricia says, tilting her head away in a semi-disgusted manner.

"I wish our houses had a second story," Lin says.

Maia considers the idea of staying in Mark's house. The thought of being in the same house as a boy, much less one she only recently met, makes her nervous. Granted she hasn't had a chance to know anyone well enough given she had only recently arrived at the tower, and she had warmed up to him along with Tricia and Lin, it still feels like she would be doing something forbidden. And then there is the problem of his creepy mother.

"My parents wouldn't mind," Mark says as if responding to her thoughts. "At least, they won't once I tell them your situation. My father is out of town, but my mom can be… persuaded."

"What does that mean?" Lin asks.

"Nothing," Mark says. "You wouldn't understand unless you met her."

"I guess there's nothing else I can do," Maia says with a sigh. "But I also guess my problems aren't as big as yours. You all still have to take two quizzes."

"How is having to do a couple quizzes worse than needing a place to stay?" Mark asks.

"Quizzes are scary. Plus, these ones will determine whether we can continue practicing Conjuring." Maia shudders.

"Oh, Master Aveve's done this before when Master Kellen came to visit," Mark says. "She must be fired up about something. Maybe it has to do with why she closed the tower as well."

"You think she's preparing for Master Kellen to stop by?" Lin asks with a giggle.

Mark looks upward at the top of the tower where the roof converges to a single, sharp point. "Who knows?"

Maia turns away from the tower and notices a figure wearing drab robes standing about twenty meters down the path. Whoever it is seems to be watching them. "Who is that?"

Mark, Tricia, and Lin all turn as one and see the figure. "How should we know?" Lin says. "I can't see their face."

The figure starts to move toward them, the robes barely shifting in the motionless afternoon air. It takes a few seconds before the figure is an uncomfortably close distance away and whoever it is has still not said a word.

"Do you need something?" Mark asks the figure in a challenging tone when the figure suddenly stops walking and crosses his or her arms.

"Which of you is Maia?" the figure asks, her voice deep yet feminine.

Maia, having thought whoever it is was a man, crosses her own arms. "Who are you?"

"Jasmine," the figure says, pulling the hood of the robes back and revealing an attractive face. It's angular and sharp in just the right places to not resemble a school teacher's sternness, but pleasingly regal. Her dark eyes gaze out softly under and between darker hair that could be mistaken for black.

"Oh," is all Maia says, taken aback by actually getting an answer and seeing the woman's features. She can't help but be slightly jealous of the woman standing before them, and notices the other three are appraising her in subtle awe as well.

"Is anyone else here?" Jasmine asks, looking the tower up and down before gazing again at Maia.

"Master Aveve locked herself inside," Mark says quickly, no longer wary of the woman.

"Strange," is all of Jasmine's response. "No one else you've seen?"

"Who are you looking for?" Maia asks.

"You, Maia," Jasmine says simply. "That is, if you are Maia. Maybe one of you other two are her. Or perhaps I'm a bit early. I guess there's nothing to do about it."

Early for what? Maia wants to ask, but she realizes that's not very important. "How do you know my name? What do you want with me?"

Jasmine lets out a light sigh, her rosy lips parting slightly. "I'm going to be bored for a while, so I guess you can entertain me. Show me what you can do with your magic."

Confused, Maia shifts her weight between her feet. "Why?"

"I just said I'm bored," Jasmine says exasperatedly. "Can you conjure anything?"

"Fine." Maia holds out one of her hands and one moment later an apple appears. "Are you no longer bored?"

"Ugh, I think I'm even more bored," Jasmine says, yawning. "Is all you can conjure simple objects?"

"No," Maia says, annoyed. She tosses the apple onto a patch of grass beside the tower and conjures two small cloth napkins.

"Ooh, you can conjure two things at the same time," Jasmine says mockingly.

"Can *you* conjure anything?" Maia challenges the woman. She doesn't know why this became a contest, but she's annoyed to the point she wants to prove Jasmine wrong in some way.

"No, I'm not a Conjuror," Jasmine speaks as if it's obvious.

"Well, I'm not either," Maia retorts. She tosses the napkins in the air. Mark, Tricia, and Lin gape at her. Watching the napkins fluttering and beginning their descent, she raises her left hand and makes a pushing motion. From her palm she sends a gentle breeze that passes over Mark, Tricia, and Lin that barely reaches Jasmine and causes strands of her hair to shiver. The napkins are pulled along with the breeze.

"Ooh," Jasmine says again, though this time with genuine interest. She snatches the two napkins out of the air and conceals them somewhere beneath her robe. "You can perform two magics?"

"Yes," Maia says with a hint of pride.

"Easy, Maia," Mark warns. "We don't exactly know this woman."

"How about a contest?" Jasmine says, a wicked smile appearing on her face. Somehow it does not dim her charm but morphs it into a different kind. A feral beauty. "You can consider it a game. A game of tag. If I tag you," she points at Maia, "I win. If you tag me, you win."

"Maia," Mark says again in warning.

"Your friends can play, too," Jasmine offers, surprising the other three. "If any one of you manage to tag me, you can consider it a win."

That gives each of them pause. Maia won't back down from the challenge, but she senses that the woman is tricking them in some way. "Is there a prize for the winner?" Maia asks.

"Why, yes," Jasmine says, her smile growing a centimeter wider. "If you tag me, well, you'll get something good. If I tag you, I get to follow you for as long as I like."

"What?" Maia clutches the sides of her arms with either hand in shock. "Why? What are you, some kind of stalker?"

"I prefer the term 'hunter,' though you're not my prey," Jasmine says in a quiet yet edged tone. "What do you say?"

Mark and the other two huddle close to Maia, forming a circle. "This is too strange," he whispers.

"Is she just playing with us, or is she doing this for some other reason?" Lin asks.

"It's probably both," Mark replies.

"Do you really want her following you?" Tricia questions Maia.

"No," Maia says, "but that's only if we lose. Besides, there are a lot more worse things I could think of."

"You can also decline this 'contest,' " Mark says. "There's no reason you actually have to do it." They each glance over at Jasmine who is standing motionless watching them with the same smile only slightly diminished and appearing more thoughtful than feral.

"I have the feeling she won't let us go so easily," Maia says. "She's probably a magician, though, even if she isn't she's hiding something." Breaking from the group, Maia paces directly up to Jasmine, stopping seven feet in front of her. "I'll play," Maia says.

Jasmine's face sets into a somber calmness. It isn't the reaction Maia expected. "Then begin."

Everyone is still for three full seconds. In those seconds Mark, Tricia, and Lin all grapple with frustration and unease. Each do not want to have to do any of this and are annoyed with Maia's recklessness. If anything, practicing for Master Aveve's quizzes should be their priority.

Meanwhile, Maia predicts Jasmine to immediately move and try to tag her. She will wait until Jasmine makes the first move, having deliberately walked close enough to tempt the woman. As the seconds pass she gets more and more annoyed herself. *Why isn't she moving?*

On the third second Mark moves. He dashes over to Maia and lifts a hand up and toward Jasmine. Jasmine remains still, though her eyes narrow at Mark. *Pop!* A pitch black blanket appears and unravels from his hand, blocking Jasmine from their sight.

Maia understands what he's doing quickly, and causes another breeze to blow over the blanket. It sways in the air, wrapping toward Jasmine. If they can cover her up, she will be easy to tag.

The blanket gently wraps around the woman's form and settles, totally enveloping her.

Yes! Maia thinks. *We've got her.*

A ripping sound cuts the air. At the top of the blanket where Jasmine's head should be a thin piece of silver appears. It moves upward, the sound of the blanket ripping unsettling Maia and the others.

The line in the blanket the piece of silver leaves opens slightly, revealing Jasmine's calm face. She stares out at them unblinking.

Maia hears Mark gasp beside her, and glances at him confused.

"Kn-knife!" Mark whispers. He yanks her away from Jasmine, and Maia looks in time to see the length of silver cut rapidly through the blanket at an impossible speed. "She has a knife!"

Mark and Maia race back to where Lin and Tricia are standing. They turn and stare as the blanket that had enveloped Jasmine bursts apart as if from an explosion and falls around the woman in tatters. In either of Jasmine's hands is a foot-long knife that curves wickedly toward each's point. The sight makes Maia shiver.

Jasmine deftly spins the knives in a circle then catches them in a backhanded grip. She remains in her spot though takes up a fighting stance. "If that's the best you can do, I suppose I won't even have to use magic," she says.

"When you said you could think of worse things, was getting ripped apart by her dual-wielding knives something that crossed your mind?" Tricia asks frantically.

"Obviously not!" Maia retorts. "Regardless, we have to figure out a way to tag her!"

"What!?"

"I'm with Maia," Mark says, surprising the two girls. "This woman is clearly dangerous and wouldn't have let us go if we hadn't accepted her game. At least this way she can continue toying with us."

"Gee, that's a lot better," Tricia says. "I still don't see the reason we should get anywhere close enough to touch her."

"Maybe… maybe getting something good means we don't die," Lin says.

Tricia exhales sharply, an empty laugh, though doesn't respond.

"If you're done talking, can we continue?" Jasmine calls.

Mark takes a step forward. "If our opponent's using weapons…" The air pops and suddenly Mark is holding a crossbow.

"What the heck, Mark!" Lin cries with a shudder. "Where'd you learn to conjure that?"

"Like I told you before," he says, raising the bow and pointing it at Jasmine. "I'm a second year."

"THAT DOESN'T EXPLAIN ANYTHING!" Lin shouts.

Mark fires the crossbow and the bolt flies wickedly fast at Jasmine's stomach. Jasmine spins her knives again once, holding the blades in an overhand grip. She moves her arms and crosses them over her stomach in an X. The bolt violently clangs against the knives before falling harmlessly to the floor.

"She's not only good with knives but is strong," Mark comments, another *pop* resounding within the crossbow indicating he has reloaded it. Rather than firing again, Mark conjures a second crossbow and offers it to Tricia. "She may have trouble if we both fire at her."

"I don't even know how to use one of these," Tricia comments, though takes it. She mimics the way Mark holds his and directs it vaguely at Jasmine.

"There's a trigger under your right index finger," Mark instructs her. "Pull it on three. One. Two. *Three.*" They both fire, and the bolts rush toward Jasmine. Tricia's flies lower than Mark's, her aim off, though the bolt will hit Jasmine's left leg while Mark's will hit Jasmine's left shoulder. There's no way she can block both.

Jasmine shifts her weight to her right side and the bolts fly by her, grazing her grey robes.

"Okay," Mark says, "This is getting annoying."

"Conjure another for Lin," Maia says. "When you all fire, I'll prevent her from moving." Not waiting for agreement, Maia begins walking away. She follows an invisible line to a point in a spot of grass that is the same distance from where Mark, Tricia, and Lin stand apart from Jasmine. Upon reaching it, she looks back and sees the three are ready each with a crossbow of their own. Mark looks visibly tired, likely after conjuring so many things. The crossbows themselves are incredibly intricate and would require perfection to work properly, Maia realizes. This next attack will likely be their last.

She feels her will stirring, preparing to do her best to trap Jasmine where she stands. Gazing at a point between Jasmine and the three others so she'll have the reaction time to act, Maia waits for them to fire.

A second passes and then she hears the *twang* and sees the bolts rush through the air. In that second Maia unleashes her will into the ground. Its current travels across the loose dirt's surface towards Jasmine far faster than the bolts. The ground rises up next to Jasmine's feet in chunks and clamps down, securing her in place.

What happens next confuses Maia. Jasmine, in an instant, conceals the knives beneath her robe and lets her arms hang loosely at her sides, waiting and watching as the bolts fly at her. *Is she going to let them impale her?* Maia thinks, suddenly scared. *Have I accidentally killed this woman?*

Only, the bolts don't. Instead of continuing on their path, they freeze in midair. Then they fall to the ground, having lost their momentum.

It's then that Maia realizes what's happened. The woman had caught the bolts in pockets of air. They never had a chance of hitting her. Jasmine is an Elementalist.

The realization is too late, and Jasmine turns toward Maia, the earth around her feet breaking apart. "I'll give you credit, you actually did manage to make me use magic." Crouching low, Jasmine's body rushes forward, carried on an impossibly strong gust of air.

Maia can't react, and only has time to blink. Jasmine flies by Maia, and in that moment Maia feels the back of Jasmine's hand brush the side of Maia's arm.

Whirling around, Maia faces Jasmine who plants her feet in the ground and skids to a halt.

"Looks like I win," Jasmine says.

Instead of anger, Maia feels relief that the woman did not kill her. So it was just a game after all. Then she remembers what the woman said about following her around, and she lets out a groan.

"Maia!" Mark, Tricia, and Lin all come to her side, pointing their crossbows at Jasmine. Mark is shaking and panting, clearly exhausted. "Are you okay?" he asks while glaring at Jasmine.

"I'm fine," Maia says. "Though we lost."

"Oh." Slowly, he lowers the crossbow, then drops it and lets himself fall to the floor where he lies on his back.

"That was impressive," Jasmine says, walking closer to them. "I never would have thought a kid could do so much. Keep it up, and you'll not have to exhaust yourself."

Mark tilts his head on the ground to look at the woman, regaining his breath slowly. "Whatever," he says.

"I'm more disappointed in you," Jasmine says, looking at Maia. "The magic you used only shows that you're a beginner in both Conjuring and Elementalism."

"Well, I am," Maia says, annoyed that the woman thinks that it isn't good enough.

"That won't do," Jasmine says with a sigh, placing a hand over her face disapprovingly. "Looks like I'm going to have to teach you. I can't let such potential go to waste."

"You're going to teach me?" Maia is surprised, though is suddenly thrilled. She just saw Jasmine use the technique she wanted so desperately to learn to let her fly through the air. "I accept!" Maia says loudly.

"Aren't you eager?" Jasmine comments. "You might want to be more wary of strangers in the future."

"Then should I trust you?" Maia asks.

"It'd make things easier," Jasmine says.

"What about Master Aveve's quizzes?" Lin asks.

"I can work on the one I still have to do with Mark," Maia says. "I'm taking you up on that offer of sleeping at your place." Maia pauses, realizing what she said sounded weird.

"Great," Mark gets out between his panting. "I'll tell… my mom…" He finally sits up and looks sideways at Jasmine. "If anything bad happens… I'll blame you."

Jasmine's lips part, her face a mix of surprise and glee, and exhales a single, light laugh. "No need to worry. Besides, your tower's master has been watching over you." She raises her hand, pointing a finger up at the top of the tower.

They all gaze up and see the window facing them glinting harshly back, obscuring everything within. "How can you see that far?" Maia wonders aloud. "And how does it not hurt your eyes?"

"You'll learn once I teach you," Jasmine says. "Now, come with me. Let's go where we won't be disturbed." She paces away across the field to the west, away from the tower and boundless forest behind it.

Maia starts to move, but Mark stops her with a raised hand. "Be careful," is all he says.

Maia nods, then rushes to catch up with Jasmine, leaving the other three in confused wonder.

Torion Oey

Chapter 7: Idrid

Telnas's streets in the royal sectors are largely barren as Idrid and Darren walk toward the Occult Tower. Not many want to wander there for fear of being punished by chance by indignant royals, or perhaps messed with by magicians. Idrid had heard such rumors and fears mentioned in the taverns she visited before she met Not, and had heard similar rumors in other taverns while traveling with Not though told more scarcely. She doesn't put it past the royals and their guards, nor the magicians who frequented the place, though she's more wary of what will happen once she and Darren enter the tower.

"What's your reasoning for all this?" Darren asks. It is the first question after seemingly running out of them the previous day after Idrid's short interview.

"You're only asking me this now?" Idrid comments while looking at the neatly packed cobble path ahead.

"Why are you taking all these risks to be a part of the Concilium?" he pushes. "I know you managed to best Filento and his magic, but this is still very dangerous. It's probably twice as dangerous."

"Because I want to." The jittery cold sensation returns, tingling her bones. *Relief. I'm relieved Filento wasn't the only one responsible.* She hates it; it's disrespectful to her family, to everyone else who died; it's revolting. *But what else can I do with the anger I've had for over a decade?* They turn at one of the main thoroughfares that should lead them directly to the tower's front eventually. "I'm not one to talk about personal things," Idrid adds. "I hope you'll forgive me."

"I don't need to forgive you," Darren says. "But... maybe there's someone you need to forgive."

Idrid looks at him, the light from streetlamps catching her eyes. "What?"

He raises his hands in defense. "I'm just worried you're not thinking things all the way through."

"I've thought this through," Idrid says, anger tinging her words. "All I'm doing is getting the knowledge I need."

"What more do you need to know?" Darren asks.

"Everything left to be learned. All that was left out of history books, all that isn't common knowledge or taught or spoken. Starting with why."

It's gone unspoken since they came up with the plan to join the Concilium, though Darren has implicitly known that Idrid is being driven by her past. Idrid's head turns back ahead, stonily looking at the tower's face looming in the distance. Sensing she is going to lapse into silence again, Darren asks, "What will you do once you know?"

"Does that require an answer?"

Darren sighs. "Well, no."

"Good."

"I have to tell you, though," Darren says, his own voice getting serious. "While I share your goal, I do not share your purpose."

Idrid glances over at him and shows surprise, the first expression other than a blank, slightly solemn face. "What do you mean?"

"The Concilium aren't known for who they truly are, but for those who do know of them they're a notorious group that manipulate people to do things against their will. By their very nature they are evil. But there is still the fact members of the Concilium and members of the Magic Guild overlap."

"What are you getting at?" Idrid asks, still watching him.

"There are members that are my friends." He pauses though doesn't look Idrid in the eye. "If your purpose leads you to more... let's just say, violent ends, I will stop you." He finally looks at her and they're each met with the same level of resolve.

"I'm not after just anyone," Idrid assures him. "But if I find out anyone, whether they're your friends, whether they're *you*, who had anything to do with my home..."

The implied threat lingers the rest of the way as they remain silent, walking ever closer to the tower. They glance at each other upon finally reaching the tower and nod in unison. "Ready?"

Before they can knock the wooden door opens and reveals the circular room within packed with thirty or so people bunched in various groups. About a third of them wear the same deep red cloak Darren wears, and among them is Vespertine who slides the door open further and beckons them inside. She scrupulously descries Idrid the same way she had during the interview, barely giving Darren a once-over look, while closing the door behind them. Idrid and Darren shuffle to the outer edge of the room where one of several barren work tables sits, save for a pitcher half-filled with water and several serving cups. Vespertine breezes through the crowd to the back of the room to what looks like the remains of a metal stairway. The stairs lead toward the second story but rise only halfway up several dozens of feet before abruptly ending. Idrid gazes at the top of the stairs where the metal seems to have melted from incredible heat. Idrid wonders what could have possibly caused the stairs to melt but not damage anything else in the tower. Vespertine spins around and appraises everyone from her vantage point at the height of the stairs. Idrid takes the moment to do the same.

Of those that aren't wearing the red Magic Guild cloaks which Idrid doesn't distinguish from the Concilium there are mostly those wearing upper-class finery from men in unbuttoned overcoats and smooth cloth shirts and pants to women in shiny dresses and sashes that accentuated their waists. Only three others wear what Darren would call "commoner's" clothes similar to Idrid's that are made of simpler fabrics like linen and wool. One of them, a man with bushy greying facial hair that covers the lower half of his face, has a large winter coat wrapped around himself with the hood up.

"It seems we have everyone," Vespertine announces, drawing Idrid and everyone else's attention. "Applications are still being handled in Lanmar's outer cities and towns, but they're yet to be accepted won't be meeting with us. At least, not yet." She gazes out, taking her time to look at each person in the room individually. "I'm sure each of you are eager to begin talking politics, though I'm afraid that can't happen until we—that is, those of us who are founding members of the Concilium—finalize the placements of our new members."

"What are you talking about?" one of the fancier dressed individuals, a man in a black overcoat reaching down to his knees, questions. "Aren't we all new members?"

"Not quite," Vespertine says. "Some of us worked within the government alongside James as part of a group called the Magic Guild. See those wearing red cloaks."

Everyone aside from the Guild members look around at those wearing red cloaks. Idrid continues to watch Vespertine whose gaze has finally locked with hers.

A woman in a flower-patterned blue frock standing in a group with two other men near the half-staircase speaks. "You said we're not going to do anything until new members are finalized? How long will that take?"

"About two months," Vespertine says.

There's an outcry from several people. "What are we doing here, then?"

"Why so long?"

"Can the country manage without any ruling body?"

"Is all this just cocktail talk while the rest of Lanmar suffers?" This last gruff complaint comes from the bearded man in the winter coat.

"We have an interim body, those of us already within the Magic Guild, that will handle matters for the time being," Vespertine explains, her gaze slowly shifting from Idrid to Darren and onward to the left side of the room. "Our meeting here is to describe how we'll continue the process of assigning new members. As you all have been notified during your interviews, you've been accepted. What your interviewer happened to leave out is that you haven't been accepted into the Concilium yet."

Another outcry resounds around the room. Idrid takes the moment to pour herself some water in one of the serving cups on the nearby table while the first man in the black overcoat asks again, "What are you talking about?"

Vespertine quickly silences the room by raising her hand slightly. For a moment Idrid thinks she's used Mind Control on everyone, her serving cup half-raised to her mouth, though considers it unlikely since it would be practically impossible to manipulate so many people at the same time. She takes a drink and Vespertine says, "What you've been accepted to is the next phase in our search for members. You each will participate in a total of three trials in the coming days. The first trial will begin in… about twenty seconds."

Before there's yet another outcry the Guild magicians all gather at the front on Vespertine's left beside the stairway. Darren is the only one who remains where he is next to Idrid. The sounds of their clothes rustling and feet clonking on the floor stirs up unease among the others. Two of the Magic Guild magicians lift up a rectangular bin and begin taking out its contents and handing it to the other Guild magicians. From where Idrid is she can't see what they're holding.

"What's the trial?" the first man, apparently the most impatient one in the room, asks.

Once the words come out the air in the room seems to change and all at once the Guild magicians throw out their hands. Circular metal pieces half the size of an average person's palm whose widths are barely more than a centimeter begin appearing on the front of people's clothes. It takes several moments before one appears and attaches itself onto Idrid's shirt while another one appears on the left lapel of Darren's cloak.

"They're all Teleporters?" Idrid says loud enough only for Darren to hear.

"Not all of them," he says warningly, staring at the back of the tower while fingering the strange metal object on his cloak.

"What we've given you is a marker," Vespertine announces. "It will be vital for the trials ahead. As most of you know, if you're going to be working for Lanmar you will need to know your way around the palace. It, by far, takes up the single largest-most area in Telnas and consists of many parts. Your task will be to find your way around and see each part of the palace. Your markers will keep track of what areas you've been to and which areas you have not. You will know once your task is complete and your marker makes three long beeps. You will have the rest of the week to complete this trial.

"Those who no longer wish to participate may simply leave now. The markers are detachable and can be thrown away. If you wish to continue, I highly recommend never taking your marker off. Once you've completed the trial you are free to spend the rest of your time within the palace enjoying its amenities as if you live there. You may also choose to leave the trial at any point once you begin, though you may find it difficult. Of course, you may complete the trial and then choose to leave, which is also acceptable. Any questions?"

"Yes," the first man says. "What if, for whatever reason, one of us fails to explore the palace before the week is up?"

"You will not be able to progress in the process and will thus be dropped from our sample of viable candidates," Vespertine says.

"What's the true purpose of this?" the man in the winter coat growls more than speaks.

Vespertine looks at him for a good two seconds before answering. "You're asking what, other than testing whether you're each qualified, is the point?"

The man shifts his stance and rephrases, saying, "How will making us run around the palace looking at different rooms accomplish that?"

Giving a thin-lipped smile, Vespertine says, "You'll see once you begin." The crowd remains silent as she steps down from the half-stairway and moves to the center of the room. "If you're all ready," she says, suddenly breathless, "drop down this trapdoor. It will lead you to an area beneath the main palace where you may begin." She stoops down and lifts a door up from the ground Idrid hadn't seen for all the people gathered in her way.

Putting down the cup on the wooden table, she watches as the closest people to the trapdoor begin filing inside the room beneath one by one. Vespertine remains beside the trapdoor, holding it open while watching each drop down.

"Shall we go?" Idrid asks Darren as the crowd thins out, most of the tower's first floor empty save for them, Vespertine, and the rest of the Magic Guild magicians.

Darren nods, and paces alongside Idrid as they approach the trapdoor.

Idrid stops and looks at Vespertine for a moment. "Will none of those magicians participate?" she asks, casting a glance to the ten cloaked Guild members.

"They will, though they will be taking another way," Vespertine says, the corners around her soft brown eyes wrinkling with another thin smile. "Technically any of you taking the trial may enter the palace at any point within the next seven days and from any direction, though this is the fastest way there," she adds, pointing down at the room below which appears to be a passage that the last few candidates walk down.

"You're saying we don't have to begin now, nor here?" Idrid states, folding her arms. "That seems like it could've been useful information for the others."

"The trial has begun, Idrid. The rules I explained to the others should be sufficient for them to have reasoned that they would not be disqualified until the time runs up. Since no one seems to have chosen to wait and get some rest before starting, they seem to have chosen to get it over with as soon as possible which is a fine strategy in itself."

"Or they were heavily swayed to believe they had no other choice than to start now," Idrid says.

Vespertine's mouth opens, her smile showing teeth. "Like I said, the trial has begun. Whether they could have reasoned their other choices with the information I gave or not, they could have asked me more questions. You, on the other hand, took the initiative and got more information out of me."

Idrid murmurs a doubtful agreement. She hadn't known the Guild magicians had strategized some other way to go about the trial, rather she had thought they were simply going to spectate. She also hadn't specifically asked the reason why the other Guild magicians would not be going to the palace yet. It is more like Vespertine had chosen to feed her some information, as if she favored her for whatever reason.

"Do you still want to go?" Darren asks her while eyeing several of the Guild magicians and waving at ones who Idrid assumes are his friends.

"Take care, country bumpkin!" one, a woman, says with a laugh. Darren blushes.

"Yeah," Idrid says quickly. "I'll be bored doing nothing else." Darren drops down the trapdoor before her, his cloak swishing against the stone floor below.

"Before you go, Idrid," Vespertine says, "I wanted to ask you if the water on the table over there tasted all right. The other candidates had mentioned it having a strange taste. Was it slightly acidic?"

Idrid blinks. She had forgotten the taste, though faint bits of lemon seem to linger on her tongue. "It was."

Vespertine's soft eyes sparkle as she nods. "Good luck," she says, and Idrid turns and drops down into the dim passage.

Chapter 8: Not

*M*y trip to Lynnor is making good progress I think as I gallop across the countryside. I had bought a lovely brown-spotted horse with some personality on the southwest outskirts of Telnas and rode along the Old Town Road. It divided the Abador Fields that sprawled yet further southwest towards the coast where scarce houses are cropped along the countryside. From the road's endpoint I cut directly south when I saw that the land near the coast was mostly overrun with water and too uneven to travel safely on. I was disappointed to be kept from the coast, but it was just as well. The way I need to be going, should I still want to have a nice and deadly interaction with Tang, is due south. Still between us are two-to-three towns on the way. The closest one to the border is Brelen, and once I pass by there it'll be a couple leagues before I run into him.

A faint musty scent peppers my nostrils amidst the crisp and cold air. *It might be time for a bath.* It has been over two days of riding and the sun has already set on the third. My horse, Egol, follows where I position my reins, reacting swiftly to the smallest of my movements. He whinnies and shakes his head, something he's done every so often ever since I found him in the stable. He had been doing it nonstop before I paid for him and I figured he had grown bored being cooped up for an extended period of time. Now he seems to be doing it out of enjoyment. Leaning forward for a moment, I pat his strong neck once.

The land before us is dim, semi-lit by the darkening blue sky in the west and bright light reflected from the moon. Egol's hooves push through the foot-tall grass we ride across. I allow myself to get lost in the hoofbeats and serene environment. It has been too long since I enjoyed the feeling of being alone in such a large, empty space.

A passerine's bright call echoes somewhere in the east. I must be getting close to another town. Egol rushes forward at tremendous speed as if sensing it too. Dark forms appear on a faraway hill ahead and to my left. Dots of light flicker in and around the buildings as we draw closer. I consider the idea of taking a break, though hear Egol whinny again. If I do stop to rest some Egol may get restless again.

I angle the reins slightly and we turn again to the south so that we won't ride right through town but still pass nearby. I shift my gaze ahead and notice another single dark building resting far away from the rest of the town. It's fairly large, tall, and both sides of its angled roof are the same length, reaching down from an edge running lengthwise along the center at the top. That might be a decent place to rest without meeting anyone.

In no time at all we cover the remaining field and I pull back on the reins slightly, slowing Egol. Shaking his head as if to say no, Egol nonetheless slows and comes to a stop outside a metal wire chicken coop.

I hoist myself down from Egol and use a post on the coop's corner to tie him to. Soft clucks emanate from the strutting forms within the coop. "I'll be back shortly," I tell Egol, then walk around the coop to the front of the building. The lights inside pour through a window over the coop, indicating someone's home.

Finding the door, I knock. There is no response. I wait a good thirty seconds before knocking again. Still nothing. Taking the door's long handle, I try pulling. It's locked in place. I also try pushing, since I've made the mistake of not checking before breaking into other places, then squat down and pull out a pair of wires I use for picking locks and begin my work.

I get the amount of clicks I'm looking for before I can open the door. Carefully, I ease it open and quiet my footsteps by stepping with my toe down before rolling to the back of my foot. I gently close the door and look around. The front of the house consists of a rectangle room whose length runs from left to right, and a single hall goes further in with a long scruffy rug leading the way. There are no other furnishings in the room, though there are various pieces of metal littering the floor.

Using the rug to aid my softened footsteps, I creep down the hall, stopping to check every doorway for any signs of life. There's a kitchen which is the room with the window looking out at the chicken coop, another empty room with nothing but metal scraps on the floor, and a bedroom where only a single-person bed occupies the room. I reach the end of the hall and prepare myself before entering what is likely the final room. It's the only room whose door is closed.

Taking the handle, I push and step inside.

"HEY, WAIT!" I vaguely register the woman's shout, the rest of my mind focused on what I see before me. It's another room like the entrance, though a work desk is laid at its center where the woman has her arms frozen in midair. On the table is a contraption of smooth metal plates and crossing wires. Her hands hover around it, holding tools that poke into the contraption's body. The contraption, I realize a fraction of a moment later, is in the shape of a chicken. Its plastic eyes, transparent though tinged with red, are flashing at me.

My instincts take over, and in an instant I've unsheathed my sword from my back. I swing, aiming for the creature's jugular which is actually just where the largest bunch of wires coil up in the neck area. My sword cuts cleanly through, though I swing several more times, eviscerating the metal creature's body.

Only two seconds had passed. The next second, the contraption falls apart as if it had been smashed by a boulder.

"I HAD JUST FINISHED PUTTING THAT BACK TOGETHER!"

I finally take the moment to appraise the woman who had recoiled out of the way when I drew my sword. Her face switches from anger to recognition then back to anger. "Lauren?"

"No, we're not doing the thing where we greet each other like long lost buddies," she says, slamming her tools down on the table and causing the remaining bits of the chicken contraption to fly everywhere. "You just destroyed my exploding chicken."

"Good, that means I saved you."

"It was going to explode *you,* stupid! You wouldn't have needed to 'save' me if you didn't show up."

"I was going to wander in here one way or another, so consider yourself saved."

Lauren huffs out a breath and stands up, pushing the stool she was using back. "What are you doing here, Not?"

"I've been traveling south and wanted to see if I could take—ask for some food."

"The town's just over yonder," Lauren says, swiping her long strawberry blonde hair out of her face and shoving past me.

"You should really think about decorating your place more," I say, following her into the kitchen. "It could use more than parts lying around."

"I don't want to buy any more furniture than I need," she replies, pushing a lever and rinsing her hands in the sink's basin.

"Grime suits you," I comment. "Especially when it's on your face. You know, you could build some furniture yourself rather than making these toys."

"They're as much toys as your sword is."

"That's harsh. I'm sorry I angered you with my presence—"

"That's not what angers me, Not!" she cries, spinning around so fast the droplets of water on her hands splatter me. She blinks furiously trying to hold back tears. "It's the fact you left without saying anything."

"Instructor told me not to—"

Lauren laughs sarcastically while grabbing a towel to dry her hands and wipe her face. "You still call him that? Even now that he's—"

"Dead, yes," I say. "Are you mad at me for that too?"

"No," Lauren says. "But the others are, or were. Especially Tang."

"When's the last time you saw them?" I ask.

"I thought I told you I didn't want to do the whole long lost buddies thing. Besides, I don't care to remember. They left sometime after you left, and they're gone now. Go talk to them about whatever."

"Well, I'm glad I found you."

That gives her pause, her eyebrows rising. "Why?"

"Well… I'll just start from a couple weeks ago." And so I tell her an abridged version about meeting the Woodlanders in Talwood, traveling to the palace, murdering James, and discovering an evil group of magicians.

"Hold on. You murdered the king?"

"Yeah, but it turns out he wasn't totally evil and was being manipulated by an advisor named Filento. And that advisor was apparently part of the evil group called the Concilium, who all use Mind Control."

Lauren's fists are clenched and she's looking at me even more furiously. "Did you happen to kill anyone else on your little adventure?"

"Not me, no. The days after James's death were weird. Some magician I had met on my way to the palace bumped into me again and convinced me to make a speech or whatever to notify the people, and that got mixed reactions—anyway, I did some of Darren's dumb speech and that's when—"

"Darren?" Lauren's hands relax and she hangs the towel on the rim of the basin. "So he's safe?"

"Relatively, yes. I'm guessing you know him?" Seeing her nod, I continue, saying, "All of us—that is, Darren, Idrid, and I—found out the Concilium was coming out of hiding and taking over as the new ruling body in Lanmar."

"I already knew this stuff about The Conclium," Lauren says. "Except for the Mind Control bit. So they're not just looking to expand their numbers, they have an alternative agenda?"

Thinking for a moment, I say, "That sums it up nicely, yeah. Darren and Idrid stayed in Telnas to apply to the Concilium while I traveled south. Which brings me to why I'm glad I found you." Turning, I leave the kitchen without telling her to follow me. I exit the building and walk around the corner to the chicken coop where Egol is still tethered and beginning to neigh restlessly. I push my hand inside a satchel I have adorned on Egol's side and feel within for what I'm looking for. Finding it, I pull out the red cloak I had stolen from Jasmine and wave it lightly at Lauren who hasn't moved from her spot within the kitchen. "There's no telling what the Concilium is planning to do, so I figured it'll cause more trouble if we prepared some resistance."

She pulls the window open and asks, "What did you just say?"

"Just take the cloak," I tell her.

"Why? What is it for?"

"It's one of the cloaks worn only by the highest level magicians. I figure you can use it to help fight against the Concilium, whatever they're planning to do."

"I've seen Darren wearing one of these," she comments, reaching a hand through the window and pulling it in. "But why should I join this fight against the Concilium?"

"I assume you don't want to be mind-controlled or something," I reply, then remember the way Lauren began acting after I had mentioned Darren's name. "And you wouldn't want me, Darren, and Idrid doing all sorts of dangerous stuff alone, would you?"

"I don't care about you," Lauren says, running a hand along the cloak thoughtfully.

"Think of it as me asking you this time to come along rather than leaving without saying anything."

She looks out at me, thinking. "I'll help, but I'm not coming with you."

"I didn't mean literally come with me. I only have one horse."

Lauren puts the cloak somewhere out of sight and then throws a brown parcel at me. I catch it and give her a look. "It's food," she says. "Three days worth."

"Thanks," I say, putting it away in the satchel and untying Egol's tether from the chicken coop.

"Why are you going south?" she asks, pretending to show disinterest.

"Just my instincts." I jump lightly and get atop Egol. "A feeling like I'll find something in the desert. And, what better place is there to train?"

"Don't tell me you're seriously going *there* to train again? Didn't you almost lose all of your limbs?"

"That was when I was eight," I say, affronted. "And it only would have been one limb, if the lizard was lucky."

"Be care—No, I'm not gonna say that. Don't be dumb," she says, closing the window.

"You too," I say, knowing she can't hear me. I lightly nuzzle Egol with my legs and he immediately begins galloping away from the house.

Chapter 9: Maia

"All right, Maia, take a break." Jasmine's hands relax and the solidified air surrounding Maia disperses, allowing her to move freely again.

"I can continue," Maia pants, her shoulders heaving.

Jasmine, no longer wearing her old robes but a low-cut black dress that Maia considers indecent for practicing, puts her hands on her hips. "Sure, but you'll exhaust yourself and be unable to practice the rest of the day. Take a seat and let me teach you a bit about magic since your supposed tower master doesn't seem to have done so already."

Maia lets herself fall back onto a patch of grass at the base of one of the low hills between Chalman and the tower they've been using as practicing grounds. "Kellen and Aveve taught me enough to learn by doing. What else is there to know beyond the basics?"

"The actual basics," Jasmine says. "What have you been doing to strengthen your magic?"

"Endurance exercises," Maia replies, finally no longer needing to pant. "Manipulating elements for prolonged periods of time. I only just started Conjuring so I don't know many exercises for it."

"You do seem marginally better at Elementalism," Jasmine comments. "But there's more than simply doing magic to be better at it. You should at least know the basis for all magic, right?"

"Will," Maia answers.

"That's the colloquial term for it, but even so, only partly correct," Jasmine says, bending down at the hips to stare aggressively into Maia's face. "Will only vaguely refers to the process of doing magic and isn't just some catch-all term. In more learned circles it particularly refers to the last step which involves, as you put it, the *doing* of magic. If you're about to do magic, what comes first?"

"Uh… you first want to do it?"

Jasmine leans in closer, intruding Maia's personal space to the point of almost touching faces. "Again, partly correct but not entirely. Wanting to do magic is the third step. First, you must think!" She stands up straight and paces several steps away, giving Maia more space. "Thinking always comes first. Think: what is it I'm trying to do? Once you've got the focus in mind, you move on to the second step. But first, think. Do it!" Jasmine suddenly commands while whirling around, her hair flying around her face.

"Okay!" Maia quickly thinks of something.

"Let me guess," Jasmine says, "You're thinking about the action of performing magic, aren't you?"

"I don't know what else to think about," Maia says gloomily.

"Think about yourself!" Jasmine commands. "Think about your body. Think about its shape, its capabilities, its potential, and its limits."

Maia had also been thinking that thinking was boring, though the thought just occurred to her that thinking is a lot more complex than she thought.

"You don't have to think fast, since this is only practice and you don't seem to have practiced thinking much. Think each thing in turn. First, your body. It's small. It's a child's body. You're young and are growing. There're some things you can do while there's more you can't do yet. Are you getting the picture?"

"Yes, I'm inept," Maia says self-deprecatingly.

"Somewhat," Jasmine agrees, "But given you know that, you do have a knack for learning quickly which is something. Now, you've thought about yourself alongside the action of performing magic. Thinking of the action is also necessary since it is part of your ultimate goal, so don't stop thinking about it. You should also focus on what purpose the magic will serve. Next, the second step is defining your thoughts. That means you put it into words, either in your mind or out loud."

"But aren't I already defining my thoughts by thinking?"

"Not all thoughts are in words," Jasmine says. Removing her hands from her hips, she gets into a loose, normal stance with her arms limp at her sides. "First, I think." She remains quiet for several long seconds.

Maia wonders what is taking her so long to think, but suddenly feels something in the air change. It's not everywhere, just in the air immediately around Jasmine. Maia can't describe how she senses it since it's beyond mere feeling, though it's similar to the sensation she had when feeding the tree in the Tower of Bel. What's new about it is that she both feels it—Jasmine's will, without touching it—and sees it. It's like trapped smoke surrounding the woman's body.

"Second, I define." Breathing in slightly, Jasmine says, "I am going to tag you." The smoke surrounding Jasmine sharpens and becomes clearer when she finishes saying this.

Maia slowly gets up, wary of what Jasmine is about to do.

"And the third step involves wanting to enact your goal. You intensify your will." Again, the smoke that covers Jasmine sharpens, now no longer shifting like normal smoke and instead becoming a translucent layer around her. "And finally, you will it so by doing."

Jasmine's will flares up and Maia catches only glimpses of it causing the air behind the woman to push her forward. Jasmine flies towards Maia and taps her on the shoulder before throttling by.

Maia turns to see Jasmine land around twenty meters away, halfway up the incline. Maia watches in awe as Jasmine uses the same technique to carry her back, gliding through the air smoothly to land where she started.

"Does it all make sense to you?" Jasmine asks, putting her hands back on her hips.

"More or less," Maia says quietly.

"That's good enough. I want you to practice only the first step for the rest of the day while retaining the knowledge of the other steps."

"But—!" Maia tries to object though Jasmine cuts her off with a scowl. "Ugh, fine. So all I'm supposed to do is think until I see you again tomorrow?"

"Thinking isn't boring when you think well."

Maia nods and starts walking off toward Chalman. A question comes to mind, and she turns back. "Why don't the tower masters teach this?" she asks.

Jasmine shrugs, flicking a lock of hair behind her ear. "Magic is still pretty unknown in terms of what it can do. I'd guess people are more interested in the fact they can do normally impossible stuff without needing to know all of why they can. I bet the tower masters know, they just don't feel the need to teach it unless someone is looking to learn it."

"And how did you learn this?"

"I'll tell you tomorrow," Jasmine says. She turns and walks off towards the forest. Maia also wants to ask her where she learned but the woman walks too fast and is already out of talking distance.

Not wanting to shout, Maia continues toward Chalman, repeating the steps she had just learned in her head. *Think, define, intensify, do.* Sighing, she looks ahead. Mark's going to think she's acting weird when she gets back to his place and finds her sitting on the guest bed seemingly doing nothing.

"Has Jasmine stopped following you around?" Mark asks the next day. He sits in the guestroom beside her bed in a wooden chair while she puts on her shoes.

"I think she's confident I won't try to escape her," Maia says. She finds it strange how not strange it is that Mark has come into her room to wake her. She figures it's customary for guests since she's never lived anywhere out of her home before.

"What exactly are you two doing?" he asks. "Last night you were pretty quiet."

"She's teaching me the basics of magic," Maia says. "That's right, I should have told you but I got caught up in my thoughts. I don't suppose you know the basics of magic, do you?" It comes off harsher than she intended, though Mark's response isn't offended.

"Not really, beyond what I know of will, which isn't much. I guess I never thought to ask Master Aveve."

"Well, Jasmine said there are four steps. First, you think. Second, you put your thoughts into words. Third, you strengthen your will. Fourth, you put your will into action."

"Huh." Mark considers it while Maia gets off the bed and stretches. "Seems like sound advice. The way I perform magic I guess I just go through the motions without really knowing what exactly I'm doing."

"I think it's partly the reason why Jasmine and the tower masters are stronger in terms of doing magic than other magicians," Maia says. "Partly," she repeats. "I think it's going to take me much more learning to get better. I can't get what Jasmine said about my magic out of my head. The thing about being able to do two magics but being bad at both."

"She said you were a beginner in both," Mark corrects her, though his eyes soften. "Sounds like you're underselling yourself."

Before Maia can respond there's a creaking noise at the door to the guest room and they both turn. Mark's mother, Prytia, is leaning her head just into view with her curtain of black hair falling in strands over her face.

"Breakfast is ready," she says slowly, before slipping out of view.

"Tell me again why she's acting creepy?" Maia whispers for fear of Prytia staying still just behind the door frame.

"She's not acting," Mark replies, standing up and exiting the room. Maia follows him while smoothing out her shirt and pants. Together they follow the stairwell down into a lounge and enter a kitchen where a four-person table sits beside a countertop. The counter has a bowl of scrambled eggs and a separate bowl of fruit. Behind the counter is Prytia, somehow managing to stand upright and still with a blank face while appearing to leer at them behind her curtain of hair.

"How are your quizzes going?" Prytia asks in a breathy voice.

Mark, scooping some eggs onto his plate, says, "They're going well. I think I've decided what I'm going to conjure that doesn't exist."

"I haven't even thought of that yet," Maia states while grabbing an apple. "I was too busy… well, thinking about other things."

"That will not do," Prytia breathes out. "Mark, you have to help your friend. You only have four days left."

"Maia's working on her own thing," Mark says.

"YOU MUST HELP HER," Prytia says intensely. "She's gone off alone two days now, and you call yourself friends? You will go with her today and make sure she gets an idea."

"Fine," Mark says. "You don't mind if I come with you, do you?"

"No. Why would I mind?"

Prytia stares silently at the two for a second then sweeps out of the kitchen, leaving them alone.

Mark says, "Let's eat fast, then go."

The two finish their breakfast and quickly make their way outside without being confronted by Prytia again, then follow the path out of Chalman towards the Tower of Vern. "So… your mother seems caring… in a weird way," Maia comments slowly.

"To be honest, she only gets like this when she sees another girl my age," Mark says nonchalantly.

"I thought you said she was always like this with others?" Maia feels her face getting warm and focuses ahead. "So… another girl. There've been other girls, then?"

"Not really," Mark says, cupping the back of his head with both hands and gazing skyward. "The only people she's seen me with are people from the tower I walk home with. I wouldn't consider them my friends, though my mom always tries to set up some meeting with just me and them. It's like she's trying to get me to go out with them."

Maia nods, swallowing. "I guess she's finally succeeded, then." *Where did that come from?* Maia thinks, trying to steady her breath and think of something else to say.

Mark turns to look at her in surprise. His face breaks out into a grin and he laughs while turning away bashfully. He freezes and does a doubletake.

"What?" Maia asks, slightly annoyed by his delayed reaction. "It's technically true. We're going out." *What am I saying!?*

Stiffly, Mark turns forward again. "Uh. Yeah, I guess we are."

A period of awkward silence ensues as they walk. It is miraculously cut short when Jasmine flies down one of the low hills and lands gracefully in front of them. She still wears the low-cut black dress from yesterday, Maia's annoyance growing further now that Mark's there.

"You brought your friend," Jasmine comments. "That'll be good for today's topic. Let's move off the road."

The two follow Jasmine back up the grassy hill she came from and then down the other side. "Where are you staying?" Mark asks, looking in all directions and only seeing Chalman and the top part of the tower with the forest spanning behind it. "Do you sleep outside?"

"Forget where I sleep," Jasmine says, "Have you been thinking, Maia?"

"Yes. I've thought without doing anything else."

"Good. Before we run through the basics again I want to make sure your friend—what's your name?"

"Mark," Mark says.

"Mark, you know the basics?" Jasmine asks.

"Maia briefly told me this morning. They were thinking, putting your thoughts into words, strengthening your will, and acting...?"

"Perfect," Jasmine says. "I want you both to follow the steps all the way through now. Don't try anything beyond your ability, since it won't work."

"Mark gets to do it without thinking all day first?" Maia asks, a bit jealous.

"From what I've seen of his magic I'm sure he's thought a bit more than you," Jasmine says. "Now, no more blathering. Go through the steps and describe them as you're doing them."

Mark makes a small, nervous smile, though immediately drops it before Maia can see. "So... first I'll think about what I'll do. Right?"

"First I think," Maia says. "Then, I put it into words..." She breathes in, then out. "I'm going to protect myself."

Mark, watching Maia while she talks, repeats once she's done, "I put it into words. I'm going to create something new."

Jasmine looks as though she is going to comment, though intrigue keeps her quiet.

"Now, I strengthen my will," Maia says, Mark repeating her. She feels herself, rather her will, hardening around her. The same sensation is echoed by Mark's will just beside her, though his is different. "And finally, I make it happen." Maia brings her hands up with her palms facing out toward Jasmine. The air between Maia and Jasmine becomes still.

"Good job," Jasmine says, moving her own hand to press up flat against the air. "You've created a wall out of the air." She walks parallel to Maia, her hand running along the invisible surface, then her hand slips about five feet away where it reaches the end of the wall. "A fairly sizable wall, too." Her gaze shifts to Mark who is standing still.

Maia takes the moment to look at him as well. She sees the same smokiness that shrouded Jasmine yesterday around him, though it seems a different color despite not being totally visible. Jasmine's will appeared white, whereas Mark's almost blends in with the grass he stands on. It is a warm green.

"I make it happen," Mark says finally, then holds out his hand, palm up. *Pop.* A black slab appears in his grasp. He smiles and looks up.

"What is that?" Maia asks.

"Something that didn't exist," Mark replies cheerfully. "Jasmine, catch." He tosses the slab to her. Jasmine reaches out a hand to catch the flat stone, then somehow misses. The slab bounces away from her hand and falls to the ground. "It works!" Mark says proudly.

"What is it?" Jasmine asks, genuinely intrigued. "I didn't even touch it. It seemed to avoid me."

"I still don't know what to call it," Mark says. "It was an idea I had from the quiz Master Aveve gave several days ago. She gave that lecture about money and how magicians have machines that can check if money is real or fake. Not only do the machines check if money is fake from normal means, it checks if it had been created or tampered with magically. Since my father and mother are economists I'd been thinking about it a lot. Then I thought of creating something that wasn't just made for detecting fake currency, but rather another person's will in general."

"You created something like that?" Maia asks in wonder. "That's... kind of incredible."

"While it can be useful, it is just a slab of rock," Mark says. "The hard part was figuring out how to make it so that it reacted to another person's will."

"So it doesn't react to your own will?" Jasmine asks.

"It didn't slip out of my fingers, so I think only my will is compatible with it," Mark answers. "Maia, try conjuring something and letting it touch the slab."

Maia releases her will that had been keeping the wall of air up and conjures an apple. Warily, she places it on the slab where it lies on the ground. Just before the apple touches the slab it's met with some resistance that prevents it from staying still. Maia tries pressing against it, though the slab pushes the apple back. Finally letting go, the apple rolls off the slab and into the grass. "Anything that is made of will or has will can be detected by it," Maia states. "Doesn't everyone have will, though?"

"Not everyone's will is tapped into," Jasmine speaks. "That's what differentiates magicians from non-magicians. So the slab of rock is essentially a magic identifier. Let me test it with something." She waves a hand and the slab levitates into the air. The slab gyrates as if being tugged in multiple directions. "I'm holding the slab in a pocket of air," Jasmine explains. "I wanted to see if it could detect an Elementalist's magic the same way. It seems to..." Her fingers curl and Maia senses the pocket of air getting smaller. The gyrating slab begins to still, though still barely seems to be shifting. "Oh, wow," Jasmine breathes out. Her hands unclasp and the slab drops back to the ground. "I was giving it my all there, though it didn't break. Not only does it detect magic, it seems to be immune to it."

"I'm not sure that's quite accurate," Mark says, picking it up. "If it came into contact with enough different people's will, it might be destroyed. Of course, it can also be destroyed the old fashioned way." He grips the ends of the slab and breaks it in half. "It can also be destroyed by me, since I made it." With a *pop* the broken slab disappears from his hands.

"Bravo, both of you," Jasmine says, clapping her hands. "You both followed the steps. You may not have noticed, but your wills became sharper because of it. With practice, you can do it as easily as breathing, and your own magic will be stronger for it. Speaking of, Maia, don't do what you just did with conjuring the apple. Every time from now on until I say so you'll be performing magic carefully with all four steps."

"I don't think I'm going to be able to come up with something as great as that," Maia says with a sigh.

"Cheer up," Jasmine says. "You're still able to practice two magics, which isn't something most magicians can do."

"Huh?" Maia blinks, confused. "But wait, Kellen—I mean, the Elementalist tower master told me magicians could if they discovered they were magicians before they matured."

"Like most other things you've been taught, that's only partly true," Jasmine says. "He was likely referring to the process of attunement."

"Attunement?" Maia and Mark ask in unison.

"When magicians mature, they attune to the type of magic they have a proclivity for," Jasmine explains, putting her hands on her hips, the sign she's shifting into teaching mode. "Most magicians only have a proclivity toward one and cannot access magic from other fields. A magician attunes to their magic as they grow, and because they specialize in it it becomes stronger for them. Since the process of attunement at maturity heightens the type of magic the magician is most practiced in, the ability to practice other types of magic goes unnoticed even if they could use multiple magics, and since many magicians don't discover they're magicians until they're adults they've already attuned to the magic most compatible with their body.

"Magicians who have the gift of being able to perform multiple types of magic are called splinter magicians. Their bodies have greater capacities for magic which allows them to perform more than one type of magic. You, for instance, Maia, are a splinter magician and have large capacities in both Elementalism and Conjuring. Have you tried other types of magic?"

Maia shakes her head. "I haven't met anyone other than a Teleporter, though I don't really want to practice Spatial magic."

Jasmine's face sours. "You wouldn't happen to be talking about a Magic Guild Teleporter, would you?"

"He didn't say what kind of magic guild he was a part of. He wanted to keep it secret."

"There's only one," Jasmine says.

"Oh. Well, then yes. His name is—"

"Hush!" Mark says suddenly. "Do you really want to just tell her this? She may be teaching us, but we don't know if she's part of... you know, *that* group."

"I already know you're talking about Darren," Jasmine drawls, bringing a hand up to her face to look at her long nails while absently rubbing the back of her head with the other. "We had a pleasant little meeting just around here, in fact. That was before he knocked me out and took me to the palace."

"You met him around here?" Maia asks. The most recent times he had been there was when he teleported her from the Tower of Bel to the Tower of Vern, and then a few evenings ago just before King James was murdered. The first time she remembers him having trouble with the guy called Not, and after that he mentioned having other business. "How long have you been spying on me?"

"Only a few days ago. I haven't seen Darren in a while." Her hands clench and her face scrunches, suddenly mad. "I'm going to find that piece of crap and kill him!"

Maia and Mark take a step back. "You're going to kill Darren!?"

"No, Maia, not Darren. Despite hitting me, he unwittingly gave me the opportunity to get a few things from the palace. He even allowed me to go free after James and one of the Concilium caught me sneaking around."

"Wait, so you're not part of the Concilium?" Maia asks.

"No... ah, so that's who you suspected me to be. How do you kids know about the Concilium?"

"Uh..." Maia looks at Mark who seems to no longer have any qualms about telling her. "Darren mentioned them before King James was murdered. Did you have anything to do with that?" she asks, suspicious.

"No," Jasmine says, rubbing her face. "I haven't heard any news about the king's death, only that the Concilium are adding new members under the guise of forming a new government for the sake of Lanmar."

"Who are you going to kill, then?" Mark asks.

Jasmine sighs, her anger subsiding. "I'm not going to actually kill him. At least, I don't think."

"Who?" Maia repeats the question.

"Not," Jasmine says.

"Not? The guy who supposedly looks like the king?"

"It seems we know a lot of the same people," Jasmine comments.

"We don't know him," Mark says. "Maia heard about him through Darren."

"I actually briefly met him while traveling here with Darren," Maia says. "He was wearing one of those Magic Guild cloaks."

"Damn him!" Jasmine spits, stomping her foot into the ground. "That's the cloak he took from me."

"You're part of the Magic Guild?" Maia asks.

"No, I stole it from someone who is part of the Magic Guild, and also probably the Concilium since she tried to rob me first."

"What are you all, a bunch of thieves?" Maia asks, feeling a twang of hypocrisy since she herself has stolen things in the past.

"You answered your own question," Jasmine says, her face smirking. "Only I'm not evil. I'm just occasionally bad."

"Why are you teaching us anything?" Mark asks. The question comes out of nowhere, though Maia has been wondering about it in the back of her mind.

"I received a fortune in Picaroon Port," Jasmine says with a sigh. "It was vaguely about a special girl to the east who would lead me to what I want."

"And I'm the special girl?" Maia asks.

"I should hope so. With everything I've explained about splinter magicians you're the only special one. The fortune also hinted at the girl knowing two magics, and I haven't found anyone else who does, and who's named Maia."

"How did you know I could use two magics before you confronted us?"

"Your individual orenda," Jasmine says. "And before you ask, orenda just refers to nature's energy. It's the proper term for what you call will. If you really followed my instructions to think yesterday, I'm sure you've begun to become more aware of other people's orenda. Most know it by its abbreviated form, ora or aura."

Maia sees the thin white smoke shaping itself around Jasmine's body and the similar green smoke wrapping around Mark's. "Does it look like smoke?" Maia asks.

"Yes," Jasmine says, nodding her approval. "Have you looked at your own?"

Maia looks down at herself, her eyes tracking the length of both arms then legs. Nothing resembling smoke or wisps encircles her. "I don't see anything."

"Yours is barely visible, but it's there," Jasmine says. "I almost mistook you for a non-magician whose orenda is locked within their body. It's a sign you have yet to completely tap into your own will, which is why I'm having you go through the basics. Also, I'm a generous person."

"A generous thief?" Maia asks dubiously. "That's like a benevolent king, either rare or nonexistent."

"It beats skulking around in the shadows while following you," Jasmine says. "Your orenda is special because of its color. I'm sure you've noticed mine is pale and white while Mark's is green. Yours is a deeper shade of purple."

"What do the colors mean?" Maia asks.

"They're general indicators of the magic one can use, though they're not perfect indicators since they can change depending on the magician's emotions. Purple is unique and indicative of a splinter magician."

"Is there another way to check to see if someone's a splinter magician?" Maia asks, looking at Mark. "Something like Mark's slab thing that reacts to another's will?"

"There is. A handy test that also indicates the magic one *can* perform. But you can't take it yet," Jasmine says quickly, raising a hand to stop Maia from asking. "Your orenda isn't pronounced enough. Once you can reliably draw it out of yourself you can take the test. Though, if you want to take the test, Mark, you'll be able to."

"Hmm." Mark stares off at the forest's edge, thinking. He shakes his head finally. "Nah. I'll wait to take it with Maia."

"I see," Jasmine says. "Well then, let's start drilling the second step into you."

Torion Oey

Chapter 10: Not

It's getting to be close to noon and I've made significant progress. Already I've passed Brelen, the final town near the southern edge of Lanmar, and I'm nearing the border itself. It's been a while since I've been to Lynnor, though according to Idrid there is still an obstacle in my way. I could easily turn off the path and cut across the wastes nearer the highlands, though that would be too easy. There will be a time I meet Tang again, and if I can put him in check, the sooner the better. *And of all of Instructor's students, he's likely the most capable. Including myself.*

The path Egol carries me along is bordered by contrasting landscapes. On the left are the wastes, a barren land with nothing more than dead or dying grass and dry earth. On the right, a vivid expanse of wildlife with mesmerizing colors from too many species of flower to count. The meadow is equally as flat as the wastes, though isn't an eyesore. A building crops up to the right, sticking upright out of the greenery like a mole, what I assume to be the toll house.

I slow Egol to move at a trot as I get closer. Its sanded oak walls are brushed lightly by the tall grass shifting in the light breeze. Slowing further, Egol's hooves the only sound other than the sound of the blades of grass touching each other, I peer at a window facing the road and finally bring Egol to a halt. Squinting against the reflecting light, I try to make out anything within. Something shifts, a shadow moving, and the ovular face of Tang, long, unkempt bangs and all, peers back out. His face is a deep frown.

Shifting in my saddle, I wave. Tang's face disappears. Two seconds later the door of the building opens and Tang steps out.

"So you've finally come back south." His voice is deep, deeper than I remember. It retains the same level of irritation and spite it had before, though. Tang smirks. "Not much has changed."

"I heard you want to kill me," I say. "I want to give you the benefit of the doubt that you have good reason, but, I must ask, what's that about?"

"You're still your all-too-friendly self. Not much has changed at all."

"Is there a way I can convince you not to kill me that doesn't involve fighting?"

"I doubt it," Tang says. "Your presence makes me angry."

"I could go," I offer.

"Your irresponsibility makes me angrier," he continues. "You pissed off the others when you left without a word. I'm just the only one who still cares."

"I saw Lauren on my way here," I say. "She was also angry. She told me you were the most upset."

"Why wouldn't I be? Instructor died and you left!" His face blanches for a moment before he calms himself. After all these years it's funny in a way how both of us still refer to him as "Instructor."

"Do you blame me for his death?" I ask. I remember the rules Instructor had laid out for us while he taught us to fight. His last rule was that if he never returned after a week, assume he was dead. It had occurred to me none of the others knew how he had died. I knew the consequences of not returning to tell them what happened, though I couldn't face them.

"Should I?" Tang asks.

"I couldn't stop him from going after it," I say.

"Did you even try to stop him?"

"He was going to go with me or without me. If it makes you feel better, he died how he wanted."

Tang lets out a long sigh. "No, I don't blame you for his death. I blame you for the seven days not knowing he was dead. Most of all, I blame you for not including us."

The words hang in the air. The way he says it hits me hard. "I was afraid you—all of you, would blame me."

"There was something Instructor said," Tang says. "About a primal need to see the end in both enemies and friends. That there is a sense of release in affirming the death of someone you love and someone you hate."

I feel a pang. Lightly, I get down from Egol and guide him to the stoop where Tang stands. I tether Egol to a supportive beam with a rope.

"You should have brought us along," Tang hisses. "If not to prevent his death, to witness it."

"I'm sorry," is all I say. Slowly, we both reach for our swords. My right hand rises to grasp the hilt sticking up behind my back, his left hand reaching across his waist to grasp the hilt hanging by his side.

In unison we draw our swords, the metal hissing following each out of their scabbards. His sword is the traditional Lynnorian scimitar, a slightly curved blade that he lightly holds in his hand, pressing the end of the hilt against his stomach.

I smile sadly at the familiar sight. As kids we would spar much the same way. I wriggle my fingers on my own hilt, feeling the warm metal fit snugly in my hand. I wait for him to make the first move. He blinks, eyeing my sword.

"When'd you get a new blade?"

"It's not exactly new," I answer truthfully.

His eyes narrow. "Wait. That's…"

"Instructor's sword," I confirm.

All at once his face becomes stony. "Unbelievable." His left hand flicks his scimitar imperceptibly fast into an overhanded position, and in the same motion he brings his arm out in a lunge. It's characteristic of his fighting style; swift and aggressive. It fits his nature.

Rather than deflecting his blade I leap back and away from the stoop and Egol, noting Tang is putting all his weight into his lunge. He is unconcerned with defending himself. He seems to be welcoming any attack. His goal is only to inflict pain.

Tang rushes forward, continuing his lunge. I sidestep to force him to shift into a swing. He does, and recklessly so. Our swords finally meet, the metal ringing thin in the air. I step back, my foot pressing into the dry grass on the other side of the road marking the wastes, and keep my sword up and pushing back against his.

He lunges again, this time getting close to switch his fingering back to his backhand, then twirls around to bring his sword swinging toward my other side. I bat at it with my own to force its progression to momentarily stop and take several more steps back. Tang follows, his swings gaining speed.

It's not until we're a fair deal away from the road and kicking up dirt that I choose to counter. I feign a swipe at Tang's unguarded side then swing upward diagonally toward his abdomen under his scimitar. He doesn't move to block. Taking me off guard, I quickly alter the course of my swing.

I barely manage to prevent my sword from cutting deep into his stomach and instead only make about a centimeter-deep nick that runs an inch long.

Tang puts a finger against the cut. "Didn't Instructor teach you to end a fight as soon as you could?"

"He also taught us not to leave ourselves obnoxiously open," I say.

Tang flicks his hand, spinning his scimitar along the curved handle in a circle. He does this fast enough so that he creates afterimages that blur together. Slowly, he extends his arm toward me with the scimitar still swinging with dangerous speed like a propeller blade. Even without the edge, the sheer force of being hit would be deadly.

I give up trying to follow the blade itself with my eye and track its trajectory while backing away. There's only a brief moment, likely a millisecond, every full cycle where Tang's hand wraps back on itself to catch the hilt and continue spinning the blade in which it slows, though not enough to be a particularly useful opening.

There's always the easy option, which is to thrust my sword forward and stop the scimitar from spinning, but that is too easy. For that matter, a lot about this fight has been too easy. If I didn't know any better, I'd think Tang is trying to lose.

Ignoring his spinning blade, I make a quick swing at Tang's right side. Tang's sword-arm moves to follow, but too slow. I make another similar cut above his hipbone.

"You're going to have to do better," Tang says, returning his spinning blade to his left side. He moves closer, forcing me back.

I look at his right side. It's apparent where he's trying to make me swing.

"Come on," Tang says. "If you really try, there's no way I could stop you."

Swallowing, I swing at his unprotected side. His face is set as his eyes follow the arc of my blade to his right arm. I make a horizontal slice along his upper arm, cautiously avoiding any arteries. At the last moment Tang twists his arm.

"No!" It's too late. My sword glistens with his blood, its arc going clean through his inner arm and sending a splatter of even more blood flying through the air, and I see yet more blood begin to pour quickly from the inside of his arm. I had cut his brachial artery.

Tang, wincing slightly, manages a smile. "Well, Not," he says, letting his right arm hang loosely at his side with blood seeping down while twirling his scimitar with his left. In an instant, his scimitar stops spinning and is held in an overhanded position toward me. "I'd say I have an hour at most. Think you can last that long?"

I get into a defensive position, biting my tongue. I'd be lucky to last more than ten minutes.

With impossible speed, Tang lunges again. It's unlike any of the previous lunges. His body ripples forward as if carried by a wave.

I barely follow the movement with my eyes. I parry just enough while twisting my body out of the way.

Tang's left foot slams down into the ground, sending up a clot of dirt that hovers in the air. In another flash, he's slashing at me. It's all I can do to block while maneuvering away.

Suddenly he's shifted forms and is attacking my other side, his sword in his backhand. It's the same move as before but over in an instant. The only way I manage to counter is due to my knowledge of his pattern of attack. And yet, still, his movements grow faster while the blood drains from his right arm in large swaths.

We return to trading swings at lightning speeds. The metal sings through the air, the blades' crashes violently ringing out across the wastes. I hear Egol's loud, nervous neighs from the road.

I can no longer track Tang's movement with my eyes. I switch to tracking his aura like Instructor taught while using my eyes to gauge the intention of his swings.

The change allows Tang to make a cut on my right arm. It, like my first two attacks, isn't deep, though it indicates he is reaching the limits of my speed and is about to surpass them.

In another flash, I switch my sword to my left hand.

"Finally getting serious?" Tang asks.

I don't respond, knowing that it would only give him another opportunity. I bend my left leg, crouching down while extending my right leg out for balance. The change causes Tang to begin swinging downward at me. Aided by the force of gravity, Tang's swings become more forceful while retaining their speed. I am putting myself at a disadvantage, though I'm hoping with enough force I can deal enough damage to his sword for it to no longer be useable.

His swings rain down on me while I barely manage to block them all. Drops of his blood fleck my shirt. Though he is panting with his furious attacks, he is only getting faster.

By this point I catch the intention of his next attack before he makes it. Swiftly, I use the force of my legs to push myself up toward his swing, my blade perpendicular to his. I press my right hand against the bottom edge of my blade right where I know our swords will clash.

The swords meet and there is a resounding *clang*! My sword digs into the palm of my right hand and I feel blood begin spreading. But the force is enough. The upper half of Tang's scimitar shatters, breaking off at the point where I blocked. I move out of the way of where it falls, carried by the momentum of Tang's swing in an arc that misses my head.

Tang's face blanches, his eyes alight in fury. "What is your sword made of?" he says in a low voice. "It's not even scratched! For that matter, it should've broken ages ago!"

I stand up and stick my sword into the ground, hilt up. It slides in smoothly despite the hard earth and sticks there when I let go. Clenching the cut on my right arm I breathe in fast and heavy. It had to have been less than five minutes and I hadn't noticed how out of breath I was. "You need to stop the bleeding," I tell Tang.

"I can still kill you!" he growls, throwing his broken sword at me. Despite having counted on it, it's too fast for me to dodge.

Minimizing the damage, I turn my body so that the broken blade, still sharp enough, plunges into my left side somewhere below my stomach. Gasping from the sensation, I yank the scimitar out by its handle. Dropping it, I take a weary step toward Tang.

"What are you doing!?" Tang shouts.

Sighing, I stop. "You've already won," I say. "You won't be able to survive without help. Let me at least stop the bleeding before you kill me."

"Don't come near me!" he says sharply, taking a step back. I realize it's the first time he's retreated in the fight, even though it's over. "Why didn't you try to kill me?"

"Because I didn't want to," I say, moving my left hand to grip the steadily bleeding hole in my lower torso. "And because you wanted me to."

Tang freezes. "I didn't—"

"Like I said," I say, the pain of my wounds becoming more and more of an annoyance. "There was no reason for you to leave yourself that open."

"That was so you could wound me enough so that I could beat you!" Tang snarls. We both know it's a lie. Tang stands there silently, his head tilting down so that his long bangs obscure his face. "You're a bastard," he says softly. Then, he falls to the ground, unconscious.

Shaking my head, I walk awkwardly to his body to minimize the pain in my stomach. Looking down, I make sure he isn't faking it by tapping him with my foot. He doesn't move.

"Well," I say, looking over at Egol standing beside the toll house who is still neighing fervently. "That went well."

Torion Oey

Chapter 11: Idrid

"How long have we been down here do you think?" Darren asks.

Idrid checks around a corner of one of the innumerable corridors making up the palace underground. "A day maybe." It has been a while since they've run into one of the other magicians undergoing the same trial. They had stopped at a storeroom of various foodstuffs (primarily dried fruit) to rest and even then no one had come in to bother them. She still has a phantom feeling of the sack of potatoes she had used as a pillow pressing uncomfortably on her head. Turning the corridor once she is satisfied no one or thing is lurking around, she beckons Darren to follow. "What more do we have yet to explore down here?"

"We haven't found the jail room," Darren responds. "If we find that, I'll know my way out and we can quickly find all the remaining rooms in the palace proper. I'm sorry I'm not of more use right now since I've practically lived here, I just never explored this labyrinthine underground."

"Seems like a great place to conduct evil plans," Idrid comments. They approach another branch in the corridor and Idrid peers around its corner. She spots a figure walking away in lightweight servant's attire of pristine linen bearing the crest of Lanmar. "There's a palace servant."

The two quickly round the corner and hustle to catch up with the servant. Hearing their approach, the servant turns around, bringing up his hands to defend himself in fear. His eyes quickly register the marker on both their clothes and lowers his arms. "More applicants? I was sure they had all gone upstairs already."

"Can you show us the way out of here?" Idrid asks. The servant appraises her large form, causing Idrid to narrow her eyes. "What're you looking at?"

Shrinking in place, the servant murmurs, "I can take you up, but you have to answer several questions of mine."

"Riddles?" Darren asks. "Isn't that played out?"

"No, they are just questions," the servant says indignantly. "If you can't answer at least three correctly, you'll lose half your remaining hours from your trial time."

"Geez," Idrid breathes. Still, she would rather the consequences of losing time than continuing to wander around lost. "Well, go ahead and ask, I guess."

"What is the Concilium?"

Idrid is taken aback by the question. She hesitates to answer, unsure of whether the answer is what is publicly known or the actual truth. She glances at Darren and tilts her head to prompt him to answer.

Darren says, "The Concilium is an organization of high-level magicians whose purpose is to help Lanmar, as well as the world's other nations."

"Correct," the servant drawls, suddenly bored. Idrid wonders how many times he's had to ask these questions. "Next question: Where is the Concilium based?"

Idrid blinks, thinking the obvious answer of Telnas being too easy and therefore incorrect. She skims her memory of what she's read about Lanmar's history. Up to around half a century ago Lanmar was a suzerain nation though broke the relationship with its natal nation. Even though it's been so long, there's a possibility the Concilium originated from Thalidan, the nation to the north that is dominant in both power and land over every other nation in the world. Struggling, she tries to remember its capital.

"Do you know?" Darren asks, looking at her. "I can answer, though I feel like this is a trick question."

"Hmmm," Idrid says while the servant taps his foot impatiently. "I think I have an answer. You don't mind if I answer, even if I'm wrong which is likely?"

"Go ahead," Darren says.

"Endovir," Idrid answers.

"Correct," the servant says with a tonal shift from bored to impressed. "None of the others knew the answer to that one. Next question; if you get this right, I'll guide you: who killed James?"

"Not," Darren and Idrid say in unison.

"What?" The servant looks at them both, confused.

"That's his name," Idrid says. "You didn't know? Did you want, instead, his relation to James? They're brothers."

"Oh," the servant says. "Uh. Correct. I'll guide you now..." he trails off, giving them a skeptical look. Without another word, he turns and walks onward to the end of the corridor.

Darren and Idrid share a look before following. Several turns later they reach a wide, carpeted stairwell leading up. "We were that close?" Idrid mutters.

"You were," the servant says. "I was stationed to patrol nearby corridors since the closer you get, the easier it is to get turned around. Don't forget to step into the jail room before you go up," he says, waving a hand further down the corridor where firelight flickers along the smooth stone walls through a doorway. "That is, if you want to continue with the trial. Goodbye." Turning, he paces back the way they came and disappears around the corner.

"Some progress, finally," Darren says as they make their way through the doorway. A table with a bulky registry of what has to be names of prisoners sits to their right, and on the left is another doorway leading to a dim hallway completely made of stone.

"We should have asked the servant what time it is," Idrid says. They step into the jail room and pace down the hallway, their feet clicking on the floor. "It'd be nice if these marker things beeped when we entered a room we're required to enter."

"I'm sure there's more to this trial that will both help and hinder us," Darren states. "Perhaps some more quizzes from servants. That last one seemed to be priming people with some necessary knowledge for a position in The Concilium. Anyway, I now know where we are and I know the layout of the rest of the palace. If necessary, we can enter every room until we find all the required ones."

"What if we've missed one down here?" Idrid asks.

"Then we'll have to come back," Darren says. "But we shouldn't worry about that now. Let's hurry and see for ourselves what time it is."

The two make their way back to the stairwell and ascend the steps. "I don't know how much you've explored of the palace while you were here with Not, though it's relatively straightforward as far as palaces go," Darren says when they reach the top and find a hallway going in both directions to their left and right. "Think of it as a square with adjacent halls and rooms set at various intervals. As long as you remember these halls encircling the heart of the palace, you'll never get lost."

"Great," Idrid says hurriedly. "Let's get this over with."

Darren, a bit put off by Idrid rushing him, whisks himself to the left. Several seconds of walking along the carpeted floor past several decorative suits of armor and lit sconces along the walls later they reach a branching hall running perpendicular to the right. "Where there's a branching hall, that is the direction of the palace's heart," Darren says. "So if you see a door to your left, that leads to outer rooms."

Idrid nods. Darren skips the hall and takes them further along the hallway. "Are we getting the perimeter rooms over with first?" Idrid asks.

"Yes." Darren halts suddenly, holding out a hand to stop Idrid. "Did you feel that?"

Idrid waits and listens. Subtly, the ground quivers beneath her feet. Ahead, the floor ripples from some unseen force. Like a wave, albeit blockier, segments of the floor rise and fall. It comes toward them, slowly. Without moving, they both wait for the floor to reach them.

Darren crouches just when the floor ahead is about to rise, then leaps over the upturned floor. Idrid simply stands, letting the floor pick her up for a moment then drop back into place. The wave abruptly stops at the same place Idrid stands.

"Why didn't you jump over it?" Darren asks.

"Was I supposed to?" Again, a rumbling resounds from ahead, although this time it is louder. At the very end of the hall where it juts to the right, a mob of people appear and are shouting while running toward them.

"It was some kind of Elementalist magic! I think you touching the wave set off an alarm!"

"Should we run?" The mob rushes forward and Idrid sees the people shouting are other applicants due to the markers on their clothes. Several are magicians wearing red cloaks. One is the burly man wearing the winter coat, his hood bobbing rapidly as he runs. She isn't sure what the applicants are running from since all that's behind them are more people who appear to be servants. The servants are holding pieces of silver that Idrid recognizes as silverware. "Are the servants attacking with forks and knives again?"

"What do you mean again?" Darren asks.

"Filento manipulated servants to attack us and they were throwing knives—never mind, I'm not up for fighting anyone right now." Turning, Idrid picks up into a jog that carries her swiftly down the other way with Darren rushing to keep up.

"Which one of you touched it!?" comes a shout from behind.

"Which one of you didn't jump!?" comes another.

"All the servants in the palace are going to attack us now!" someone else shouts.

"Oops," Idrid says. A door on her right pops into view and she quickly maneuvers it open. Darren rushes in behind her and she closes it. "There's no lock," she comments, gazing around the room for something to block the door.

"Are we going to leave the others to fight?"

"They're magicians, aren't they? They can handle it." Her eyes find a low bookcase reaching up to her knees sitting under a window at the far wall. In two strides she makes it to the bookcase then stoops down, reaching her arms to pick it up from both sides, tilting it back so as not to fling all the books out from its shelves, then she places it in the way of the door.

"You're very strong," Darren notes.

"Thanks." Loud bangs erupt from the other side of the door momentarily before they cease and the shouts of the applicants fade away, likely being chased further by the silverware-wielding servants. The creak of a door opening catches their attention. Across the room from where they stand, beyond a smooth, lengthy table covered in thin glass and surrounded by twelve ornate chairs with tall backs, servants begin filing in. The servants encircle the table somberly, separating themselves out with every other servant moving to the same side of the table. A total of ten servants step up to a chair at the table, the last servant who enters shutting the door.

"Welcome," the last servant says, taking his seat at the head of the table. "You've arrived at the Matching Room."

"Matching Room?" Darren questions. "This is just one of seven meeting rooms. There's nothing special about it."

"Each room has been given a specific purpose for your trial," the same servant says. "The theme of this room is matching. You see before you a number of seemingly identical servants. Your task is to match each servant to discover their role in the palace."

"What if we leave?" Idrid says, not particularly fond of these random tasks.

"You will fail the trial," the servant replies.

"What?"

"Tasks are given to all applicants. Refusing to participate in any renders the trial at large pointless." The servant bends his head forward while meeting their eyes menacingly. "If you do not sit, we will assume you're refusing and you both will be disqualified."

Silently, Idrid and Darren take the remaining two seats, Idrid taking the chair at the other head of the table with Darren taking the chair to the side on her left.

"We may begin," the servant says. As soon as he finishes the sentence he procures a stack of playing cards. With scary speed he flicks them between his hands back and forth. One by one, he tosses a card forward and it slides facedown along the table to a servant who slams his or her hand down to prevent any possibility of showing the other side. Once each servant has their hand over a card, they pick them up and show them to Darren and Idrid. The servant at the other end puts the stack away and holds up his own card.

Idrid barely has time to glimpse a king of diamonds card being held by the male servant sitting directly beside her before the servants throw their cards through the air at each other. They trade cards four times this way before catching them. Their hands hold the cards still for Darren and Idrid to clearly register which cards are held by whom.

"There are ten of us, and we come in pairs. Our pairs are indicated by the card that was passed at least 2 out of 4 times to us. Where the card began is of no consequence. Now tell us if you spotted a pair."

"How does this relate to matching roles?" Idrid mutters to Darren.

"I'm not sure," he replies. "Did you catch any of the same cards flying to two of the servants?"

Idrid looks at the servant next to her to see the king of diamonds back in his hand. She doesn't know if it had been passed to him earlier since him starting with it doesn't count. Even if he was passed the king of diamonds 2 out of 4 times, she is not entirely certain who his partner is that was also passed the card 2 out of 4 times. Already her memory of the midair shuffle is getting confused. She vaguely remembers him passing it to the servant sitting two seats away from Darren who now holds an ace of spades. If there is no choice but to guess, she'll go with that option. *It is a better chance than blindly guessing since the total 4 times has only one pattern of passing; the pattern is that the card goes to the first servant who passes it to the second servant who passes it back to the first who passes it back to the second. However, there would be a significant problem if two of the same cards were at play...*

She glances around the table to make sure none are holding the same card. There may be some sleight of hand as well, meaning a card not being currently shown was put in while all the servants were passing their cards around and then concealed at the end. Thinking about it, those who first were passed their "pair" card must have held a different card at the start before the passing. Additionally, they had to have ended with a different card unrelated to their "pair." Since there are 10 people, meaning only 5 cards mattered that indicated pairs, there were 5 cards at play that did not matter—meaning five patterns of cards being passed for each of the four times the cards were tossed did not matter. And since there was only one restricted pattern of passing yet there are 5 irrelevant cards, there had to be some sort of sleight of hand... Maybe. Unless the "pair" card *had* been held by the person a servant was paired with, in which case they would've been tossed the same card back immediately. Head hurting, Idrid asks, "There is only one card of its type being used, correct?"

"Yes," the servant at the other head of the table says.

Nodding, she points to the servant to her right and says, "You." She moves her hand to point at the servant two seats away from Darren. "And you."

"Correct," the two servants say. "We are—were, the king's personal servants." They rise from their chairs and exit back through the door they came in.

"Eight servants remain, meaning four pairs," the servant at the other head of the table announces. Slapping his hand on the table, the servants begin passing the cards between themselves with deft flicks of their hands.

Idrid and Darren stare intently, trying to follow a single card's path. After eight passes the servants catch the cards and hold them up facing the two.

"There were 8 passes," the same servant says. "The pairs are whichever servants received the same card 2 out of 8 times. Tell us if you spotted a pair."

This is more difficult for Idrid. The passes were faster this time, and now that there were more total passes there were more possible patterns. Although, there is still a way to narrow it down since the card could only be passed to non-paired servants once. Idrid had unfortunately lost track of the card she was following somewhere in the middle of the passing.

Darren comes to her aid. "You," he says, pointing at the servant directly next to him, "and you." The second servant is the one opposite them at the head of the table.

"Correct," the servant at the other head of the table says. "We are the palace's footmen." They both stand and the servant beside Darren exits while the other servant moves to the middle area of the room on the left side facing the windows to overlook the table. "Six servants remain, meaning three pairs." He claps his hands and the remaining servants commence their passing.

Idrid again barely has time to pick out a card to follow before all the cards begin whizzing around the room. They're even faster now, the servants' hands beginning to blur. Despite the speed, the removal of four servants is significantly easier. As she thinks this, she notices the card she's following passes to the same person four times in a row before being passed to a new servant. That can't be right. If the minimum is 2 passes they'd already far exceeded it. Finally the hands freeze and the cards are held still facing her.

"There were 16 passes," the servant standing to the side of the table says. "The pairs are whichever servants received the same card 8 out of 16 times. Tell us if you spotted a pair."

"You and you," Idrid says, pointing at the servant who had traded the jack of spades card at least more than four times with another servant.

"Incorrect," the leading servant says. "You may no longer participate. You may still try," he says to Darren.

"Did I fail the trial?" Idrid questions, slightly shocked.

"If your friend succeeds in picking the correct pair in this round and the next you both proceed. Otherwise, you will get a time reduction."

"How much time will we lose?" she asks.

"For each servant left, that will be the number of days you will lose."

Idrid stares at the remaining servants. With six left, if they fail now they'll have already run out of time and will fail the trial due to having spent the previous day underground. She looks at Darren who is deep in thought, gazing at the remaining six servants.

"You," he says finally, pointing at the first one Idrid had pointed at. "And you," he moves his hand toward the servant furthest from him on his side of the table.

"Correct," the two servants say. "We are the palace bakers." The two stand up and exit the room.

"Four servants remain, meaning two pairs," the lead servant says beside the table. He claps his hands twice and the remaining four all stand. And then they begin throwing cards at each other rapidly. Before they had been using only one hand to catch and send cards around. Now, they swing both their arms aggressively, catching and sending cards incredibly fast. Idrid's eyes whirl in their sockets trying to keep up with it. Every now and then a servant would catch two cards at the same time before sending them off in different directions. Then, a card flew over the last servant on Darren's side of the table and is caught by the lead servant. He chucks it back in and another card whizzes into his hand. For whatever reason, he is being included in the passing now.

After too many passes for Idrid to count, the servants finally freeze and turn to look at Darren, their cards held still for him to observe. Idrid wants to object to the inclusion of the lead servant who had already been caught as a pair, though she stays silent since Darren is concentrating hard.

Slowly, Darren smiles. "You and you." He points out the lead servant and the last servant standing on his side of the table.

Idrid blinks several times, unsure of his answer. She has no idea why Darren picked the servant with his back to the lead servant. The only times she descried a card going to the lead servant was when it was thrown by one of the other three servants.

All of the servants turn their bodies to face the two. The lead servant lifts a hand to his stomach, the other servants following suit, and bows. "Correct," he says. "You've found the last pair. I, too, have another job at the palace. I am a porter."

"We three are cooks," says one of the female servants. The four servants turn and leave the room while the lead servant remains.

"Congratulations," the lead servant says, stepping over to where they stand. He pulls out a strange device that looks like a pen, except at its end is a tiny brush. He reaches out and slides it across the markers on Idrid and Darren's clothes. "Because you've completed this task you have now been rewarded by finding all the required rooms on the palace's first floor."

"But we haven't been to all the rooms here yet," Idrid says.

"That's why it's a reward," the servant says simply. "You're significantly ahead of the other applicants now. Good luck." He turns and exits through the door at the other end of the room.

"How did you guess the correct pair?" Idrid asks Darren.

"I'm a Teleporter," Darren says. "I need to have good eyesight. Come on, let's get started with the second floor."

Torion Oey

Chapter 12: Not

Sounds of loud banging resonate from inside the toll house. I stand up slowly from the chair I had brought out to the stoop to sit, holding a hand over my stomach where I'd cleaned the wound Tang had given me. The thick bandage forms a protrusive lump beneath my shirt. It seems Tang's awake now. I look over at Egol who shakes his head, sending his brown mane of hair spiraling around his neck and face.

I turn away from the fading evening light and move inside, gingerly so as not to open my wounds again. Tang rests in a corner of the single-room home. His narrow bed is sandwiched between the wall and a counter that marks the beginning of the kitchen area. I watch him kick out his feet under the uncharacteristically bright pink cotton sheets, hitting the counter. His right arm rests haphazardly on a bundle of other sheets I found in the house in order to keep it elevated. Tang's eyes glint through the dim room at me.

"You're a piece of crap," he says, kicking his feet against the counter again.

"Would you stop that?" I say, pacing over to his bedside. "You're still badly hurt and I can feel your aura spiking. You might end up breaking the counter." Despite his persisting anger he keeps his head and arms resting on the bed. His long bangs fall around his face and shoulders.

"You have the nerve to break *my* sword," he snarls while kicking the counter again, "and then tell me *I* won?"

"You would've overpowered me if you stopped talking," I tell him. "And you got me good in the stomach, see?" I lift my pale white shirt and show the red-soaked bandage covering my stomach.

"Should've thrown it at your head," Tang mutters.

"Nah, I'd prefer to be alive." I step away and place a pot in the sink that I begin to fill with water.

"What're you doing?" Tang asks.

"Making pasta. You have pasta, right?" I searched the place while Tang was out and already know he does. I flip open a drawer and take out a cotton bag of long, raw noodles.

"How did you manage to break my sword?"

I glance over at Tang who is frowning deeply. It goes well with the pink sheets. "I'm surprised you don't already know." I catch myself about to play a question game with him that would make him give his own answers, thinking better of it. Sitting the half-filled pot on the stove, I say, "My sword cannot break. It was specially made."

"Where?"

I take a moment to light the stove before answering. "Remember the last few days we were practicing up on the Lynnor Highlands?" I say, gesturing beyond the front of the house and past the wastes to where the mountains in the distance rested. "Instructor told me one day that he had found it. He was referring to the forge he always talked about."

"He never talked about anything outside practice," Tang murmurs. "Except for the forge. So it is actually a place that exists. And it was in the highlands the whole time?"

"More or less," I say.

"Don't be vague with me," Tang spits, kicking the side of the counter again. "*Where?*"

I acquiesce. "On one of the peaks."

Tang lets out a soft chuckle. "That sounds ridiculous."

"It's true. It's called the Forge of Light for a reason."

He shifts in his bed, moving his left arm to cup the back of his head so he can glare at me more easily. "So this legendary forge," Tang says skeptically, "uses light from the sun and stars?"

"From the stars," I repeat while staring down thoughtfully into the warming water in the pot. "Yeah, I suppose it does. Light from the stars and moon at night, the sun at day, and everything else."

"What else?" Tang asks.

"Light is just another word for energy," I say. "You know as well as I do about energy. We learned it from Instructor. Everything has its own energy. The forge essentially takes energy from everything around it. I bet it takes light reflecting off the ocean far to the west in addition to its immediate surroundings. Like the forest and mountains themselves."

"That also sounds ridiculous," Tang says. "How exactly… did Instructor die?"

I pour the noodles in when the water in the pot begins to boil and look at him for a moment. "Instructor taught us about our own energy, calling it our aura and will as well as some other word I forget."

"Orenda," Tang puts in.

Nodding, I say, "He taught us how to use it, and we both developed our own abilities with our aura. Your aura goes crazy whenever you're hurt or tired and you become stronger. I guess it's connected to your stubbornness to not lose, since it always pissed you off when you did."

"It's helped me survive," Tang says.

"When you're backed into a corner, I suppose it would help you. Though when you try to use it offensively like today it looks more like you're trying to kill yourself."

"Only because I hate you," Tang murmurs. He lets out a slow breath, relaxing marginally. "You're saying all this to tell me that something happened to Instructor's orenda?"

"The forge took it," I say finally. "Or rather, Instructor gave it away."

"Instructor gave up his life?" Tang asks incredulously, lifting his head slightly.

"He had found his purpose in life," I reply. "It was to find the forge."

Tang groans and shifts again, letting his head fall back onto his pillow to look up at the ceiling. "What was he thinking…"

"Before he did, he told me that life can be experienced many ways. The forge was a testament to that. He said however it is, whether it's a withering leaf that's fallen from a tree or a newborn bird in that same tree, life can be equally gratifying as how humans experience it. He wanted to experience it another way."

"Why did he bring you?" Tang asks.

"He wanted someone to make sure he experienced his new life fully." I walk away from the kitchen area to the door where my sword is resting in its sheath along the floor. Picking it up, I stroll back to Tang and lean it against the side of his bed. "That's how the sword was made." I return to the stove and use a long spoon to stir the cooking noodles. It's several moments before Tang thrusts his legs out and kicks the counter again.

"YOU'RE TELLING ME HE DIED AND BECAME A SWORD?"

"When you put it like that, it sounds stupid," I say, disapprovingly waving my spoon at him. "Instructor's aura was like ours. It was special. It still is, if you take a moment to observe it the way he taught us to." Tang goes silent. I move back to his bedside and pick the sheathed sword up and lay it atop Tang. "It's unbreakable because he made it unbreakable. His will is to experience fights like he has never done before. That is, from what he told me."

Tang's left arm runs along the sheath. "Why did he bring *you*?" Tang asks with a hint of jealousy.

"We were all pretty equal in swordplay back then," I say thoughtfully. "Though I think I've come out ahead slightly."

"Pfft."

"It's probably because of my own ability's compatibility. You remember what that is?"

"You're resistant to others' orenda," Tang says.

"I'm immune, actually," I correct.

"You weren't before," he spits before relaxing. "But you could control it so that instead of resisting others' orendas you absorbed them."

"That's right," I say. "I can store others' energy. This is only useful when facing magicians since they specialize in extending their aura outside themselves. Instructor taught us the opposite, to hold in our aura and augment our bodies to be stronger and faster than normal. Thinking about it now, the skills he taught us were purely defensive rather than offensive.

"But I digress, Instructor could do something very similar to absorbing others' energy. Rather than what I can do, which is absorb energy before compounding it and sending it back, he absorbed it to make himself stronger. And, in that way, he became the perfect sword. My sword is unbreakable, and when it absorbs others' energy it becomes stronger. With my power, I can also release that energy."

"How can you call it *your* sword if it's really Instructor?" Tang asks.

"That's what he called himself at the forge," I say. "He told me he would be my sword and that I would use him to fight. He trusted me, since I only fight seriously when it's worth it."

Tang groans again.

"If you wanted him to take you instead of me to the forge you shouldn't have been so oppositional and quick to fight anybody," I tell him. Glancing over, I see him continuing to stare at the ceiling while holding my sword in his left hand. The water in the pot emits the warm sounds of gentle bubbling and faint smell of cooked pasta that wafts through the otherwise dingy air of the house. It is spacious enough for a family to live in, though the only furniture is an ovular mat in the center of the room with fraying edges and a framed map of Lanmar hanging on the wall opposite the front door.

"What was it like? The forge."

Turning my attention back to him, I say, "You should find a girlfriend."

"What!? Where did that come from?" Tang snaps, his feet slamming the side of the counter.

"I was thinking it's a little cold in here," I say. "The forge at first seemed similar when we reached it. The peak was cold, though it was also bright. Like an empty house."

"How is an empty house bright?" Tang asks.

"Well, if the light's left on it could be, but that's not what I mean. An empty house holds a lot of memories that you may not know or understand, but you can imagine them. At the forge, everything's energy was the same way. It was cold, mostly because of the altitude, but it was bright, because you could see and feel the energy of the place. It was like you could see and feel everything."

"What was the forge itself like?" Tang asks insistently.

"It was barren. There were no anvils or furnaces. Just an outcrop on the peak. There was a single flower, though," I say, my hand automatically touching a pouch hanging along my waist. "The flower allegedly absorbed the energy that gathered at the peak. Instructor ate it, and I don't really know exactly what happened next, but he was gone and a sword was lying on the peak with me. My theory is, with all the stored energy coming from everything everywhere, the flower gave him what he wanted like a wish."

"A flower that grants wishes," Tang murmurs, shaking his head atop his pillow.

"There are stranger things. Speaking of, you've met my Giant friend, haven't you?"

"You mean Idrid?" Tang's fingers draw closer to the hilt of my sword.

"Yeah. Hey, you remember her name! Oops!" I drop the spoon I'm using to stir the pasta into the pot and quickly rip my sword away from Tang. "Don't want you getting any ideas, now."

Tang kicks the counter. "I'm going to kill you," he growls.

"If you kick the counter any more and ruin our food, you very well might through starvation. What'd you think of her?"

"Think of who?" Tang asks as I rest my sword at the front of the house beside the door. When I come back I see Tang's eyes flare up and glare at me. "You're still talking about a girlfriend?"

"I don't really know Idrid's type, though you have similar personalities," I muse to myself, fishing the spoon carefully out of the boiling pot. "One-track minds, stubborn, hate about 90% of the things I say… You could do with an appearance change, though. You've got a rough-and-tumble look that's too similar to mine, though I'm more charmingly rugged whereas you're more like a wild man. A haircut would do you some good."

"I like my hair," Tang mutters stubbornly.

"If you're not going to cut it, then how about some curlers? It'd look majestic if your hair rolled down your shoulders in light waves."

"Stop talking about my hair," Tang growls.

"Will you come with me?" I ask suddenly.

"Stop trying to set me up with your friend," Tang growls.

"No, no, I'm not doing that, my eager friend. That can come later. I'm talking about the coliseums where I'm going."

Tang gives me a confused look. "Why do you want to go back there?"

"It's been a while, right?" I say excitedly, nodding my head in thought. "A place where the best of the best fighters gather to battle one another. It's just the place Instructor would love."

"Weren't you just talking about him wanting you to be picky with your fights?" Tang comments.

Ignoring him, I continue, saying, "Challengers coming looking to be the best, the best coming looking to find the better... An endless challenge for both! I wonder who's the top ranked right now. From what I remember the top rank changed almost twice a week."

"It's just a glorified battlefield," Tang mutters.

"I forget what my highest ranking was. But the food and the winnings were amazing, weren't they? So many people all in one place, I could spend my life there happily."

"Your only purpose in going into Lynnor is to fight for a living?" Tang asks.

"No," I say, finally acknowledging him again. "I'm betting some of the others are still living around there. It's where most of Instructor's students came from including you, right?"

"That's where all of Instructor's students came from, stupid," Tang says. "You were the exception for being a runaway."

"When I find the other students, ideally after I have at least one good fight, I can convince them to come back to Lanmar with me," I say.

"They're no longer students, and what would be the point of that?"

"To save the world!"

Tang silently looks at me for a long time. "You really are stupid."

"Not at all!" I say, waving my spoon at him, sending several hot droplets flying onto the counter. "Dark forces are afoot. I can sense it. Well, there's also the fact one such force going by the name of the Concilium is taking over Lanmar, though I prefer to think I'm going by instinct alone rather than solid evidence."

Tang's feet collide with the counter. "Shut up. Did you just say the Concilium?"

"You've heard of them? That means you know I'm right, right?"

With a sigh, Tang says, "I'll go with you to find the others."

Biting my tongue to prevent my immediate response, I smile to myself. "The pasta's about ready. You have any cheese?"

Chapter 13: Maia

"We've been at this for days!" Maia laments, falling onto her back on the crisp grass. "Aveve reopened the tower already and I haven't even come up with a thing to conjure for her quiz!"

"You have until the end of today," Mark says. "I'm sure you have something in mind."

"What!?" Maia looks up between Jasmine and Mark frantically who both stand over her. They'd moved from practicing in the fields to the edge of the Talwood since the sun is particularly strong today. Streams of sunlight drip through the canopy of leaves overhead, blanketing them from the heat. "I didn't know it was the end of the week already! Now I'm doomed to fail!"

"You've got the basics of magic down, though," Jasmine says encouragingly. "You're ready to take the test to see what kinds of magic you're able to perform."

"Oh!" Maia throws herself up into a sitting position, her mood changing instantly to excitement. "I want to know!"

"Tomorrow," Jasmine says. "I'll need to prepare the tests."

"Awwwww!" Maia moans, falling back onto her back. "That means I'll have failed the quiz by then!"

"You're not going to fail," Mark says, stifling a laugh.

"What're you laughing at?" Maia huffs. "I'm not some weird smarty-pants who can come up with something brilliant."

"How about this," Jasmine says. "If you can pass this quiz your master gave you, I will allow you to find out what magic you can do."

"AWWW!" Maia moans louder, sitting back up. "Not only will I fail, I won't know what magic I can do! Ever!"

"You're seriously thinking you're going to fail the quiz?" Mark asks.

"If I haven't come up with anything yet, how will I ever?" Maia asks.

"Well, I don't have much else to do here except wait, so I'll be leaving. See you tomorrow." Jasmine waves and then runs off deeper into the Talwood.

"Dang it! Frickedy frick!" Maia punches the ground with a fist.

"What do you know a lot about?" Mark asks, sitting next to her.

Maia, suddenly hyper-aware that they're sitting alone, dials back her emotions. "I—uh, I don't know. What do you mean?"

"You grew up in a harbor, right?" Mark's gaze is focused on her. "Do you know much about boats? Or trading?"

"Not really," Maia sighs, forcing herself not to look at him for fear she'll get even more awkward. "I didn't pay much attention to that stuff."

"But you must have seen a lot of stuff being traded," Mark says.

"Well, sure. I was interested in some of the stuff being bought and sold and transported since they were mostly foreign."

"What was the weirdest thing you saw?" Mark asks.

"The weirdest thing…" Maia thinks for a while. "I guess it was a pot. It was large, around this size," she says, outlining in the air how big it was with a finger. "Like the size of four chickens. It had a weird design like a cross between a human's face and a cat's. It was also made out of some strange material that looked like copper."

"A pot, huh?" Mark thinks. "Do you know what it was used for?"

"Whatever pots are used for," Maia replies. "Containing things. Probably food or flour. Why am I thinking about this, though? I want to think of something cool and useful like you did!"

"The quiz doesn't require the thing to be useful," Mark says calmly. "But if you want it to be useful… instead of thinking of the thing, try thinking about what you want it to do."

Mark's comment causes Maia to remember something she read about not too long ago. It was in a book about different types of magic Kellen had given her to read before she had left to learn Conjuring. One of the fields of magic she had been interested in was Enchanting. It would be awesome to conjure an item that had unusual uses. *But that's an entirely different field of magic!* Maia thinks, scolding herself internally. *Never mind that. What's something I would like this object I haven't thought of yet to do?*

Maia glances at Mark who is still watching her. Blushing, she quickly looks away. Mark had come up with the slab that detected magic, or will. It would be nice if whatever object she could come up with interacted with magic in some way…

"That's it!" Maia says suddenly, her eyes lighting up. She looks at Mark excitedly. "Your slab thing didn't just detect magic, it repelled it, right?"

"Yeah," Mark says, smiling. "You've thought of something?"

"What if I conjured a pot that could contain magic?"

Mark's smile grows. "An item that neither absorbs nor repels magic but contains it, huh? Pretty genius."

Maia's face flushes again and she forces herself to turn her back to him and concentrate. The material isn't important. At least, she doesn't think it's important. As long as it can contain another person's will it would be something that doesn't exist. Hopefully. "Pots that contain magic don't exist already, right?" she questions Mark over her shoulder as she focuses her will into her hands.

"From what I've read in the tower, it's theoretically the same as Enchanting," Mark says, dashing her hopes on the floor. "But Enchanting contains the Enchanter's will in objects to have unique effects. Even if an enchanted object was made to contain others' will, your conjured object that does the same thing would be fundamentally different."

"How?" Maia asks slowly.

"Well… an Enchanter's will is added to the object after it's been created. A Conjurer's will is an inherent part of the object when it's created. And… yeah, the Enchanter's will slowly drains from the object from use and can only be recharged by the Enchanter. That wouldn't happen to a conjured object."

"Hmmm…" Maia isn't liking the idea of conjuring an item that has virtually the same use as what an Enchanter could do. Even if it's technically something that doesn't exist, she isn't sure Aveve would be satisfied. She wants to make it physically different from anything that exists as well. Automatically, she begins running through the four steps Jasmine had repeatedly drilled into her. She thinks about what she wants. Then, she says, "I'm going to create something new."

Holding her hand in front of her out of sight of Mark, she focuses her will. With her practice she's gotten more aware of her own energy and she can see it flowing over her skin down to her hand and forming a small globule in the air above her hand. It is purple-colored, like Jasmine described. Finally, with the pot's image in her mind, she conjures it. *Pop!*

In her hand appears an octagonally-shaped metal ball with smooth grooves running around each side. All but one of the sides are openable, a hinge allowing a metal covering to slide diagonally aside to reveal the hollow space within.

Grinning, Maia turns around swiftly, startling Mark. She holds out the octagonal pot and lifts aside one of the coverings to show him.

"Whoa," he breathes. "It's... rather elaborate. Are you sure this is a pot?"

"If you can't tell what kind of container it is, that means I've created something new!" Maia says gleefully. "Stick your finger out here," she instructs him, placing the metal pot down and pointing at the opening. "I want you to try putting some of your will into the pot."

Nodding, Mark sticks his pointer finger into the pot. Maia both sees and feels Mark's will concentrating into his finger; it's a warm green energy. Maia counts down from three, and on zero she lets go of the covering which slides back into place and Mark withdraws his finger.

There's a satisfying metal *dink* as the covering clamps over the opening. "I think some is inside," Maia says. She slowly opens the pot back up and sure enough a single dot of

Mark's will remains within the pot. "It works!" Maia cries in triumph and awe. "Although… now that I think about it, it doesn't seem very useful. It can only capture will if another magician is close enough, and I don't know if there are any ways to efficiently use will for anything other than the magic I've learned."

"That doesn't matter," Mark says. "It's an idea, and it's new. You can pass the quiz now."

"All right!" Maia stands up, leaving the pot on the ground. "Do you think you can make it disappear?"

"Sure," Mark says. Maia concentrates to see the movement of his will when he points his hand at the pot, though fails to distinguish anything out of the ordinary. The pot makes a *pop* out of existence.

"Strange," Maia says. "With magic conducted at a distance I don't see the magician's will moving outward. It always remains around the magician."

"We should ask Jasmine about that," Mark says, standing up beside her. "But first, I still need to finish the two quizzes. Come on, Tricia and Lin are going to get suspicious that we're spending so much time alone together."

Maia laughs at that, though her laugh becomes awkward when she thinks about what she said earlier. They begin walking out from under the trees and back toward the tower. "Uh. Mark," she begins to say.

"What?" he asks.

"You don't… have… a girlfriend… do you?"

"Have what?" Mark asks. "You got quiet all of a sudden and I didn't hear."

Maia bites the inside of her mouth. "A girlfriend!" She says it loud, startling herself. "Uh… I mean—Oh frick."

She starts to think of a way to change the subject when she's suddenly aware of a sound coming toward them. She looks up and sees a form bundled in what look to be horrendous brown-and-black drapes rolling down one of the low hills.

"Pertect yer valyables!" the man shrieks in a rackety voice, tumbling head over heels onto himself again and again in somersaults. The way he tumbles with his head guarded by his hands he doesn't even seem to be trying to stop himself.

Maia jumps a bit back when the man slides to a halt in front of them, Mark for his part staying still while staring at him.

"Hoo boy!" The man unfurls himself and stands up to his full height, roughly a foot taller than the two. "That's wut I calls a canter-wafflin'! Didja see?" The man, who has a full-on bushy black beard covering half his face looks wildly and expectantly at them.

"I—we saw," Mark says. "Not exactly sure what, though."

"A canter-wafflin'! I jus' tolds ya!" The man lifts his scruffy (and too hairy for Maia's liking) hands up and ruffles the duck on his head.

Wait. Maia does a double-take, staring at the orange-beak sticking out of the man's short yet wild hair. Two beady eyes under a small, smooth dome of feathers peer back at her. "Uh. Sir, why do you have a duck on your head?"

"Why don't *you* have a duck on *yer* head?" the man barks harshly. "Gilly wiggadorp, they says blood is thick'r than wat'r, but I says dirt is thick'r than both which is what you two're worth!" The man struts away back up the hill, his arms swinging dramatically. Maia hears the man mutter something about not getting his beard shaven when he had the chance.

Mark turns to look at Maia, a strange look on his face. "You asked if I had a girlfriend?"

"I—ahhh!" Maia screams. The strange man had been the perfect opportunity to change topics, but Mark hadn't shifted focus in the least! "You're still thinking about that!?" Maia starts to scold him. "What about what just happened? You didn't think *that* was weird?"

"It was," Mark agrees, "though I don't care as much about that."

Maia begins walking again fast, chewing her lip nervously while tucking her hair behind her ear. "Well! Yes, that's what I asked!" she says emphatically. "Do you?"

"No," he says. He laughs suddenly, the skin around his eyes crinkling. "You're very direct. Not many people are like that."

"Whatever!" Maia glances up the hill where the strange man disappears over its peak. "Would you... like one?"

Mark's eyes dart to her for a brief moment before looking away. "I haven't really thought about it. Except for the times my mom tried setting me up with girls. But no, not really."

The breath Maia had been holding remains inside her. Somehow a feeling worse than the thought of failing the quiz starts to flow through her chest.

"Unless.. you know, you'd be willing."

Maia's thoughts about finding a cemetery to bury herself in almost drown out what Mark says. She blinks, her gaze lifting to the tower ahead. "Wait," Maia says slowly. "What?"

Mark sighs, clenching his fists. "I'd be interested if you were," he repeats.

Maia holds her hands together out in front of her, clasping and unclasping them nervously. "Then we already are!" she cries, looking at him. He's looking back, a confused look on his face. "I said before, we're going out! So... that means we... are, like... you know!"

"Boyfriend and girlfriend?" Mark says with a smile.

Maia's beating heart almost explodes and it's everything she can do to force herself to not look away. Clenching her teeth, she gives a single, fervent nod.

"I'm glad that's cleared up," Mark says. The moment is interrupted by some more noise coming from the tower. Twenty meters ahead of them there appears to be a small mob banging on the tower's door. "Now what's happening?" Mark asks, his smile gone. He breaks into a jog, Maia following unsteadily behind.

"We've had it with magicians!" a man in the mob calls out, thrashing a leg out and kicking the door. The door slams outward fast before shutting just as quickly. The front row of the mob cringe backward for fear of being hit. "Are you people using magic on the door to attack us? You're barbaric!"

"Aren't you the ones trying to break down the door?" someone within the tower calls.

Mark pulls up beside the door and stares the mob down, Maia arriving a few seconds later.

"Who're you?" another man within the mob calls out.

"I'm a student here," Mark answers calmly. "Who are you?"

Simultaneously the faces of the people in the mob grimace. "Another student, huh? Where's your tower master or whatever?"

"In there," Mark says, hooking his thumb over his shoulder.

"Why don't you bring him out for us so we don't have to keep arguing with you yapping kids?"

"Sure. I'll bring her out." Mark turns and lightly pulls the door open which slams once more against the outside of the tower. The crowd reflexively flinches back again while Maia slips inside behind Mark, pulling the door closed behind her. Shouts from the mob outside begin to erupt again, though they ignore it.

"What's going on?" Maia asks a second mob within, only this one is made up of students.

The students look between Mark and Maia, then one boy responds. "Hey Mark, haven't seen you in a while. They came by a few minutes ago shouting about how it's unfair magicians are going to take over Lanmar."

"That has nothing to do with us," Mark says. "And wasn't everyone allowed to join the Concilium if they applied?"

"Apparently only magicians were accepted," the girl Pina says. "A lot of them are parents of the students going here."

Mark shakes his head as if to clear it. "Okay. Where's Master Aveve?"

"Upstairs as always," the first boy says. Two girls Maia recognizes detach from the mob and greet Maia and Mark.

"Where've you two been? It's been hectic around here." Lin scratches her face and Maia notices her nails are starting to get creepily long again.

"We've been out practicing this whole time," Maia replies.

"You two were alone?" Tricia asks.

Maia, blushing, waves her hand. "Not the entire time, but that's unimportant right now. We should get Aveve down here."

"Oh, yeah, we should," Tricia says, Mark taking the moment to leave them and climb the stairs up. "But later you're going to tell us a bit more."

"Yeah," Lin mutters conspiratorially, sneaking to Maia's other side and nudging her with an elbow.

"What?" Maia says, her voice raising an octave in feigned innocence.

The two girls, hunched over slightly, emit low laughs while clasping her arms on either side. "Something happened," Tricia says.

"She was staying at his house so something was bound to happen," Lin agrees.

"I don't—Did you guys finish the quiz?"

Tricia and Lin both let go of her arms at the same time. Lin gives her a thumbs up. "We did both of them, so now we're both caught up!"

Tricia also gives Maia a thumbs up. "Lin conjured this weird doohickey. What was it again?"

"A gyrotrocheton! It stores medications that you swallow like cough medicine!"

"Yeah whatever," Tricia says, breezing over Lin, "I conjured a rock!"

"A rock?" Maia questions.

"But! Not just a rock!" Tricia waves her hands around in circles mysteriously, then holds her hand out. *Pop.* "It's a *spiky* rock!"

Maia observes the grey rock that has four distinct points sticking out of its body. "Oh. Interesting."

"Master Aveve said the same thing!" Tricia says, beaming at Maia.

"So you both passed?" Maia asks.

"Yep!" the two girls say in unison.

"Maia!" Aveve calls, descending the stairs in her usual rush. Her hair flies in streams behind her. Maia gazes further up to see Mark descending the stairs at his own pace. She blushes when she catches herself forgetting to respond to Aveve who has already reached her.

"Hi, Aveve!" Maia says. "Mark and I are ready to do our quizzes! But there's a mob outside yelling about stuff," she adds, turning her head around toward the door.

"I wanted to ignore them but I suppose leaving them there may be more trouble," Aveve says. She paces over to the door and puts her hand on it. The door bursts forward and remains open while Aveve steps out. "Hey everyone!" Her all too cheerful and emphatic cry carries over the mob outside and quiets them. "I just wanted to let you all know that we're sorry for whatever inconvenience that brought you here! Students are currently learning, so, if you'd all be so kind, come back tomorrow if you have any further grievances!"

"We don't give a damn about your students!" a member of the mob shouts. "It's you people who're oppressing us!"

"Yeah!" another person shouts. "We've lived long enough with James and his lenient use of magicians! We're not going to stand by while magicians take over!"

"You don't give a damn?" Maia recognizes the low, whispery voice that speaks up and she moves to peak around Aveve. A curtain of dark hair bobs through the crowd, making its way forward. Finally the mob at the front parts and Mark's mother, in all her creepiness, turns on the mob. Her hair hangs in straight strands down the side of her face. Her pale complexion is made eerier with the angry grimace she makes. The people at the front shrink back, recognition dawning on their faces.

"Crap! Is that Prytia? She's a magician who's been working with the government for years!"

"You all should go back to town," Prytia's subdued yet dangerously sharp voice pierces the air. "Before I don't give a damn about you."

Now the entirety of the mob flinches back. Maia is impressed, since she's only seen such coordinated movement from ship-hands whose movement was like clockwork.

"W-We'll be back tomorrow!" a member of the mob shouts, and they all run away down the path toward Chalman.

Aveve puts her hands on her hips and nods delightedly. "Well, I'm glad that's taken care of!"

Maia stares between Prytia and Aveve in wonder. Aveve, persistently chipper and seemingly carefree, stands up straight and watches the mob leave with an unreserved warmth. Prytia, considerably less affectual, stands at an equal height and watches the mob leave with unreserved malice.

The contrast of the two keeps Maia captivated for a few seconds.

"I'm going back to the third floor," Aveve announces, twirling in place and walking back inside. "Oh!" she adds, almost bumping into Maia, "You still have to take the quiz! If you're ready, follow me up there." She careens around the doorway and rushes back up the stairs before Maia can say a word.

Mark, who had just reached the first floor, leaps out of the way. "Are they gone already?" he asks.

"Yeah," Maia says while watching Prytia give her a cold look before the woman paces away down the path as well. "Your mother was in the crowd and scared them away."

"Huh." Mark looks over Maia's shoulder to see Prytia walking away. "She always scared away people who wanted to bother our family when they came to our door. I suppose it's why we haven't been robbed yet." His eyes flick almost imperceptibly to Maia's and he smiles. "We should be good for a while."

"Oh. Yeah." Maia wonders if what happened before was real or not. Either way, she has been experiencing an elated feeling that sends tingles down her arms and legs since Mark said they are boyfriend and girlfriend. But does Mark know what that means? For that matter, does she herself know what that means?

Mark beckons her wordlessly up the steps. She follows, not noticing that Tricia and Lin are smiling at her. At the top floor Aveve is standing expectantly by the window where Maia had previously attacked her. Her long boots tap out a vague rhythm as she shifts from side to side.

"Don't you just love summer?" Aveve asks as the two approach.

"Yeah," Mark says. "Though isn't it autumn?"

"That isn't stopping the sun from its glory," Aveve states happily. "Are you both ready to finish your quizzes?"

"Can I do both mine at the same time?" Mark asks.

"Of course!" Aveve says, beaming at him.

Mark holds out both of his hands and conjures two of the same black stone slab he had done before.

"Ooh!" Aveve coos, stepping closer to get a good look. "What do we have here?"

Mark kneels down and places the slabs on the wooden floorboards. They begin to shudder and shift and rattle against the floor. "They react to other people's magic," Mark explains while watching the slabs slide along the floor like butter in a hot pan.

"Very nice, Mark! You pass both quizzes!" Aveve notices the slabs moving toward the center of the tower where the floor drops away and quickly waves her hand, causing the slabs to disappear. "Are you ready Maia?"

"Sure," Maia says. Holding out her hand, she internally follows Jasmine's four steps once more. The image of the octagonal metal pot forms in her head and a few seconds later appears in her hand.

"Another interesting invention I see," Aveve says. "What is it?"

"It's a pot," Maia says. "It can hold other people's magic." She moves one of the metal openings to the side before clamping it closed again.

"These are something special," Aveve says excitedly. "Most of the other students conjured objects that are new only in appearance. You both made something that does something new as well! You both pass!"

Maia lets out a breath of relief, her fear of being expelled from the tower lifting. "Can you make this pot disappear too?"

Aveve obliges, and the pot pops out of existence. "I can see the progress you've both made. Especially you, Maia. You've found a good teacher."

Maia and Mark look at each other awkwardly. Does she think Mark taught Maia everything?

"The Elementalist woman knows her stuff," Aveve goes on, ridding Maia and Mark of their worries of needing to explain.

"Jasmine mentioned that you saw us several days ago," Mark says. "What were you doing in the tower all this time?"

"Prepping," Aveve answers vaguely. "Speaking of, you two should relax while you can. In a few days we're going to get real busy."

"Busy with what?" Maia asks.

"There's going to be a tournament after the end the month," Aveve says. "All of the Occult Towers have been notified, as well as the major cities. Couriers have been sent outside Lanmar to the other nations as well. It's going to be a big event."

"A tournament for what?" Maia asks.

"Magic," Aveve says. "I suspect magicians from all over are going to compete. Since every tower was notified first it's likely the towers will be the ones primarily competing, so we're going to have to practice nonstop to show the other towers' students who's the best."

"Where is it going to take place?" Mark asks.

"In the center of Lanmar, at the Holt of Dunlon."

"The Holt of Dunlon? Isn't that place haunted?" Maia crosses her arms to prevent herself from involuntarily shivering.

"It's abandoned, not haunted," Aveve amends.

"I heard it was abandoned because it was haunted," Maia says.

"What were you told about the place being haunted?" Aveve asks.

"Sailors in my hometown said an experiment by Dunlon himself caused a catastrophe and dozens were killed. They said their bodies came back to life and wander the hill and surrounding forest to this day."

"Do you believe that story?" Mark asks, his eyebrows arching in bemusement.

"Well, my dad said that hearsay is more reliable than what you read about in the news," Maia says seriously. "But that wasn't all. The sailors said that the dead endlessly search for people that are still alive to repeat the failed experiment over and over, adding to their numbers." Maia feels a chill run down her spine. Mark and Aveve exchange looks, causing Maia to get annoyed. "What are you so happy about, Mark?"

"Nothing," Mark says softly, covering his mouth with his hand. His shoulders shake with suppressed laughter.

"What?"

"Haunted or not," Aveve interrupts, "Any magician worth their salt can handle it. Run along, now. You're wasting your time off."

Maia grumpily walks away, starting down the stairs.

"I wonder if Aveve secretly knows Jasmine," Mark says behind her when they pass the second floor.

"Everything seems so busy all of a sudden," Maia says, forgetting her annoyance. "Darren showing up, Aveve giving out quizzes and closing the tower, Jasmine showing up, a random mob of townspeople showing up, and now we have to get ready for this tournament. I've never heard of a tournament being held while I was at the Tower of Bel."

"Seems to be a new thing," Mark says. "Either that, or it happens rarely." They reach the first floor and see the remaining students scattered around the outer edges of the tower while Tricia and Lin remain waiting at the foot of the stairs. "You're also forgetting you showing up," Mark comments. "Transfer students are rare. Maybe you attract this sort of stuff."

"I don't attract duck men!" Maia objects.

"Oh yeah. I'd forgotten about that guy."

"Duck men?" Tricia questions.

"Attract?" Lin adds interestedly.

"Do you both know about the tournament?" Maia asks, changing the subject.

"Yeah, Master Aveve told us," Tricia says. "It's exciting. I wonder who's running it?"

Maia and Mark look at each other, sharing the same thought. "I wonder."

Chapter 14: Darren

"Congratulations on passing the trial," Vespertine says, greeting both Idrid and Darren at the palace gates which are currently closed. "You both finished with a time of 94 hours. Three others finished before you, though not by much. You're all one step closer to being members of the Concilium. Congratulations."

"What's the next trial?" Idrid asks, wanting this meeting to be over quickly.

"The second trial is to travel," Vespertine says with a cool smile. "There will be an event held at the Holt of Dunlon in which all Concilium applicants will be participating."

"An event?" Darren probes.

"The Magic Tournament," Vespertine continues. "It'll be a public event not only for Concilium applicants. Other nations will be participating as well, so you should get prepared."

"I'm not a magician," Idrid says.

"Indeed, you're the only non-magician applicant we've accepted," Vespertine says. "Though the Magic Tournament will only be a moniker. Anyone can participate. Something else I should add, participants in the tournament who do exceptionally well can replace Concilium applicant positions."

"What?" Idrid asks.

Darren says, "You're saying that anyone, even people who didn't apply, can be made a member of the Concilium. Then what was the point of the first trial?"

"Think of it as preparation for the final trial that'll give you an edge."

"The Magic Tournament is the final trial?" Idrid asks.

Vespertine nods. "The second trial is traveling to the site of the third trial."

"That should be easy," Darren says.

"Getting there will be more difficult than you think," Vespertine says. "The tournament will start in about a month. More than enough time to get there, so feel free to take your time." She takes several steps away heading back toward the palace before turning for a moment. "Do your best, Idrid," she says, then walks away.

"That woman's planning something," Darren comments. "It's not coincidence you're the only non-magician who's still an applicant. Given this, it's more than likely the tournament, despite being made public and available for even non-magicians to participate, is rigged for magicians."

"She wants me to do my best," Idrid says slowly. "If she truly wants me to be a part of the Concilium, I might as well see it through. Even if it's furthering whatever plans she has, she's given more information than we have."

"She's too transparent," Darren says. "Politicians who are straightforward and honest are acting that way because they're in control. Or, at least, they think they're in control."

"She hasn't been totally honest about the Concilium, though," Idrid says. "The way she's described it and the way the trials are set up is to instill the idea that the Concilium is benign when we know that isn't true. She has to know we know this. If she's being honest about everything else, why is she being dishonest about that?"

"It's probably the one thing she needs to hide," Darren replies. He looks at the ground then up at the sky. The sun's light fades in a clouded mesh of carmine and cyan in the west over the palace walls. A tangle of wisps pushes across the sky directly overhead, dimming the palace grounds which consist of meticulously-cut grass patches and interweaving pebble pathways. "I just don't get it."

"We should get going," Idrid says, moving to a side of the gate and searching around for a way to open it. "Vespertine mentioned it being another sort of challenge to get there and she gave us a month's advance to get going. If there are more servants stationed on the way ready to dock us time or fail us I'd prefer to do it sooner."

"I still don't see how it'll be a problem," Darren says. "I can travel across Lanmar over twenty times in a day."

Idrid stands up straight, having squatted down to see what looked like a lever set in the wall but is only an unlit torch. "I forgot you can teleport. Let's go to the top of the wall then." They move into one of the gatehouses and climb a brick staircase up. Reaching the top of the wall, they gaze over the city of Telnas. "Okay, let's go."

"I think we should rest since it's getting to be night," Darren says. "There's no rush."

"I want to get a head start," Idrid says, taking Darren's hand in her own which is twice as large. "You can stay in Telnas, but I'm going. Teleport me to the southern part of town and I'll go from there."

Darren shakes his head and obliges. The two disappear from the top of the wall and reappear in a mostly empty street below. Several people walking along gape at their appearance, though it's only a moment that Idrid sees them since she and Darren have teleported again further ahead. Only two more teleports and they're standing at the edge of town where the fields stretch outward. "Are you thinking of possibly finding Not?" Darren asks.

"He's far beyond the Holt of Dunlon," Idrid says. "There's no way I'd catch up with him, much less find him."

"It's a bother he ran off without telling us anything. Does he have some sort of plan?"

Idrid shrugs. "All I know is he has a sword. He left the gem he stole with me, so he must have an intention of coming back at some point." She starts walking, then picks up her pace and begins to run at breakneck speed across the field, leaving Darren flabbergasted.

"She seems eager," Darren mumbles to himself. A gentle breeze flutters over him, sending ripples along his cloak. He freezes, recognizing the sensation immediately. The next moment the air around him stiffens and then roils madly, strong gusts battering him from all sides.

"Darren," comes Kellen's breezy voice through the air. Darren shifts his gaze from Idrid's racing form slightly to the west where he senses the strong wind coming from. "Come to the Tower of Bel. Quickly." The wind's rushing cuts off as if met by a wall and disperses just as fast as it began.

Frowning, Darren teleports over the Abador Fields, heading southwest. Whenever Kellen talked to him through his unusual yet effective methods he was more invitational. Whatever it is, it has to be urgent. Which means he couldn't pay Lauren a visit no matter how fast he teleported.

He reaches the outer edges of the wetlands, a sturdy bank overlooking the damp grass and waterways running all the way to the coast. He teleports along the banks and reaches the shoreline. His feet get wet after he teleports to a spot just next to the sweeping waves. From here he sees the uppermost part of the sun shimmering across the ocean, its light casting the water in a brilliant blue. Darren admires it only for a second before teleporting along the wet sand further south. Soon enough a shimmer of tan interrupts the horizon, marking the Elementalist tower: the Tower of Bel. Darren teleports four more times before he comes to a stop at a spot on the beach closest to the sandy tower rising out of the ocean just off the coast.

Darren squints while looking at it; it's just as plain yet dazzling as every other time he sees it. While it's made of sand, it catches the sun's rays while shining back, creating a warm image of innumerable tiny beacons. His eyes follow the tower's progression up until he notices that, close to the very top, a portion of the tower has morphed and created a sort of lone balcony. Kellen's figure stands atop it and Darren feels his eyes on him.

The next moment Darren's standing beside Kellen atop the tower. It's significantly more windy up there causing his clothes to thwap around him. "Can you do something about this wind?" he asks.

Kellen makes an almost imperceptible nod and the wind eases down around them, leaving them in a relative quietness save the sounds of water lapping at the base of the tower below and waves crashing along the shore.

"Thanks," Darren says, smoothing his cloak and shirt with his hands. "What's going on?" He looks Kellen up and down, appraising the tower master. As always, he wears high silver ankle boots where the cuffs of his black pants hang along with his blue jacket over a white button shirt. His face is deep in thought as he gazes down at the ocean absently.

"I've been thinking," Kellen says, his voice a touch less airy than it sounded when talking through the wind but still very much airy. "The ocean is looking awfully blue lately."

Darren follows Kellen's gaze at the shifting waters. He can't tell, though the water does retain a warm color. "I suppose?" Darren states uncertainly. "There's still some daylight left," he adds, turning to the retreating sun on the horizon. "The ocean always looks different depending on the time of day. Even then, each season brings its own color."

"True," Kellen says. "Whenever I look at it, it's like I'm seeing something for the first time. But the thing is, for a while now I've been looking at it. And lately I've been thinking it's like I've seen it before."

"What do you mean?" Darren asks.

"I'm not sure," Kellen says. He continues to watch the waves rise and fall, the pleasant sounds of lapping water continuing to rise up to them. "It just feels like it's not as different as it was before. Like it's becoming dormant."

Darren nods slowly. He lifts his head and looks sideways at Kellen. "Did you call me here to talk about the ocean?"

"Hm," is all Kellen says. He lifts a hand and strokes his chin absently. Moments go by in which Darren thinks Kellen isn't going to respond. "No," he says finally, still gazing at the water. "I called you here because of that." Kellen moves his hand from his chin and extends his arm downward at the ocean.

Darren looks once more to where Kellen directs him and feels his heart turn cold. A shadow half as large as the tower they stand on pushes toward the surface of the azure water. It, a giant mass of pale flesh, silently rises from the ocean. The residual water pours from its curving surface as it rises higher and higher. The top of the thing, rounded like the top of the tower, reaches their level and continues to rise.

Back at the surface of the water the pale fleshy thing grows in circumference. Whatever it's attached to, Darren knows he does not want to know. The long thing reaches a point in the sky twice as high as the tower and begins curling in on itself. Its tip touches a spot lower on the tendril, emitting a slick and slimy sound. The base of whatever the thing is begins to subside beneath the waves, though the large shadow of where it travels far beneath the surface stretches on forever deeper into the darkness. Its tip extends back into the air and flips to touch itself on the other side, spraying a bit of coagulated seawater on the tower that gets Darren and Kellen wet. It just barely misses the tower on its descent. Slowly, its tip reaches the top of the tower and continues to fall. It finally subsides beneath the surface, its giant flesh dimming as the water blurs its form, and the shadow grows smaller and smaller until it's disappeared, morphing with the unending darkness beneath the waves.

Darren feels himself breathing again, the tightness and coldness in his chest receding. "What… was that?"

"Something else I'm unsure of," Kellen says. "But its presence is going to force me to close the tower."

"You must!" Darren agrees, still staring at the water. "Your students can't be out here with that—thing! Great Dunlon, it was like a giant tentacle without suckers! Great— what *was* that!?"

"If it comes back it could destroy the tower just by flexing itself," Kellen muses. Somehow he still has his carefree, breezy tone. "Maybe it was a giant tentacle. Or, maybe it is a different species of invertebrate."

"We should get off this tower immediately!" Darren says, taking Kellen's arm.

"I suppose," Kellen says, and the next moment they're standing back at the spot on the beach Darren had first teleported to.

"There's no one in the tower currently, is there?" Darren asks.

"No, the students have all gone home for the day," Kellen says. He sighs sadly, the first emotion beyond his usual affect of mildly interested he's shown in a while. "I'll miss it." He raises his arms and the top of the tower crumbles down. Large cracks appear and the walls fall apart, returning to their original form of individual grains. In just a few moments the tower is destroyed and the ocean is left empty. "I hope the tree survives on its own," Kellen goes on, lowering his hands. "I'm going to miss watering it myself."

"It's going to get plenty of water without the tower," Darren assures him. "Hold on, wasn't your office still in the tower?"

"I moved everything out the first time I saw that thing come out of the ocean."

"You did? Okay, good. I remember you had a lot of good books in there." Darren pauses, taking a long moment to look back at the ocean. "You cleared your office out and didn't tell your students about that thing?"

"Well, that was the first time it came above the surface," Kellen says. "All I saw before were long shadows stretching across the ocean."

"*Dunlon*," Darren breathes out. "This is why I don't live near the ocean."

"This is rather unprecedented, even as far as the standards of various dangers of the ocean."

"I'd hate it if it were precedented," Darren says. He shivers, clutching the sides of his arms. "It was so smooth and large. Looking at it... I felt hopeless." They look in silence at the churning waters as the sun falls below the horizon. "Are you going to create a new tower?" he asks after a while.

"I'll have to, otherwise the students will get mad," Kellen says. "I only just got word about the Magic Tournament happening. The three Occult Towers were encouraged to participate."

Darren sighs. "We also have the Concilium to be concerned about on top of... *that* thing. I should've guessed they'd want the families of magicians to be gathered in one spot..." Darren trails off, getting lost in thought.

"You're thinking about it too, then?" Kellen questions. "Warfare?"

Darren nods. "Vespertine said other nations would be notified as well. Even if the event itself is straightforward, Lanmar would be at its most vulnerable to invasion. I still don't know what she is planning, though she seems to be the one at the center of it all. Oh, do you know who I'm talking about?"

Kellen nods thoughtfully. "Hmmm, yes, she very well might be planning something."

"I agree. I haven't told you yet, but I've applied to be a Concilium member to see if I can learn anything. So far she's been suspiciously honest about things like the kingdom's dark past with Giants, though of course she's lying about what the Concilium actually is."

"You should be careful," Kellen warns. "You're closer than anyone to being mind-controlled. Be vigilant of mind. By the way," Kellen adds, "who's Vespertine?"

Darren drops his head. "Why'd you act like you knew her in the first place?" he mutters, then says, "She's the tower master of Vale Tower. Only recently has she become more public, spearheading the reconfiguration of Lanmar's governance under the Concilium."

"The tower master?" Kellen questions. "Come to think of it, I never knew any of the Spatial magician tower masters. I don't remember how I even got in touch with Aveve."

"Aveve got in touch with you," Darren says, remembering the story with distaste. "You're the one who told me about it when you were appointed to the Tower of Bel. If you truly forgot, don't tell her that. She'll get mad."

"No matter," Kellen says, clapping his hands. "I'll go construct a new tower. I think... over there would be good." He walks off toward where the sand rises and becomes solid ground. "Oh yes," Kellen adds, turning briefly. "Good luck in the tournament."

"Thanks, Kellen," Darren says slowly. He watches the other magician tread off the beach until he is out of sight and then turns back to the ocean. His thoughts return to the fleshy thing that crept from underneath. He involuntarily shivers. *Both the state of affairs and the affairs of the state are deteriorating,* he thinks. Setting his sights back to the north, he teleports away, making sure to keep a good distance from the shoreline.

Chapter 15: Not

"I don't understand why you like the desert so much," Tang complains. "It's nothing but sand and nondescript rock formations."

I gaze on lovingly at the sand and nondescript rock formations spanning before us as we trot along. "It's the best," I say. "Most of the people you come across here are asocial or dead. Either way, you don't need to bother interacting with anyone."

"It's hard to travel," Tang goes on.

"It's easy if you center your aura in your feet," I reply. Sure enough, what I refer to as "trotting" is more so whizzing along the sands at the same speed as a horse's gallop. Both our feet touch down, barely disturbing the sand and making the lightest of footprints. Thinking of horses, I sadly recall that I had to untether Egol and let him go free since he would not fare well in Lynnor. "Anyway, why do you live so close to the desert if you dislike it?"

"I live in a garden," Tang says defensively. "Just about every species of flower lives there. It's like a dream."

"I didn't know you had such feminine tastes," I say. "Though for anyone with an allergy to nature it's probably a nightmare." A large, smooth surface of sun-dried rock sticks up two inches out of the sand that we step on that aids our already swift progress. Several large wood pillars rise up on the edge of the horizon, marking one of the several grand attractions of Lynnor: an amphitheater. The pillars stretch up into the sky four stories high, a grouping of wooden spikes encircling the pillars marking each floor at intervals. Each pillar narrows as they rise, honing and curving inward toward the center of the amphitheater to a single spiky point that claws the sky. Between the pillars are large swaths of tanned leather hide stitched together that are held up by the spikes on every floor of the amphitheater, skewering the hide in various places.

We race straight toward the amphitheater. "How's your arm?" I ask.

"How's your stomach?" Tang retorts.

I don't reply. The wound in my stomach has healed enough that what remains is a light scar. My running causes it to tingle, though it no longer hurts. Soon enough we reach the amphitheater. Scatterings of people mingle outside the leather walls while a line of people looking worse for wear progresses slowly up to a wooden hut stationed next to a part in a wall. "Remember when we used to compete here?" I ask once we stop running. The line of people, all competitors who are waiting to post their schedules for a bout, warily watch us, some surprised by the speed with which we arrive.

"I remember fighting for my life everyday," Tang says. "I hated it here."

"Right?" I state fondly. "Come on, let's look at the major fights this week." We move beyond the line and around the slit-opening in the leather that leads inside the amphitheater and find an electronic display. It hangs several feet above our heads from metal rods that stick through the leather wall. "These things always amazed me as a kid. Electricity in the desert!"

"They make enough money from tickets to afford it," Tang says.

The screen on the display fades to black before another image fades in, a list of competitor rankings from 1st all the way to 50th. I ignore all the others and quickly scan the top three names. "The Salamander, Wrath, Death, and Despair, and Kelsey," I mutter the names in ascending order to myself. "Wow. The names've gotten more extravagant. Who alone goes by Wrath, Death, and Despair?"

"It's probably a group," Tang says. "People can sign up to fight together."

"Ooh," I say. "Want to be a team?"

"No," Tang says. "I'm not here to fight."

"I wonder what Kelsey's got to be above Wrath, Death, and Despair. Maybe it's another fake name that is intended to deceive opponents and psych them out."

"Or it's probably just Kelsey," Tang replies. "You know, one of Instructor's other students."

"Nah. Wait, there was another student named Kelsey?" I ask seriously.

"She always watched us sparring," Tang says in a low growl. "If you've forgotten, you better not let her know—"

"Kelsey!" I proclaim, striking my fist and hand together. "I remember now! We never sparred, so that's why I didn't remember her. Good for her being number 1." An image of the shy girl with a brunette ponytail held up by a green ribbon squatted down in a sitting position comes to mind.

"She never wanted to spar with you because she liked you," Tang mutters.

"Everyone likes me," I say, waving aside Tang's subsequent objection. "Anyway, it may not be the same Kelsey. I wonder if the rules have changed so that we can challenge the top ranks."

"Unlikely," Tang says. "It'd be anticlimactic for the best to be challenged by anyone who hasn't proven themselves in the lower ranks. You're going to have to work your way up as we did before."

"But I want to fight Kelsey!" I say. "If it really is Kelsey, there's no other way I'll be able to ask her to come with us to Lanmar if I can't!"

"Are you doubting you'll be able to climb the ranks?" Tang asks, intrigued. "Finally starting to be humble?"

"No way, I can wipe the floor with anyone here," I say. "Not that I would with Kelsey, since she's a childhood friend." The display changes images to a list of fights scheduled for the week. The main event appears to be Wrath, Death, and Despair vs. Kelsey, though they're going to be fighting in one of the other amphitheaters of Lynnor. Another cool thing about the displays is that they show fights in real time when management enters them in computers in the respective amphitheaters all around Lynnor. "Dang it!" I say loudly. "They're not even at this amphitheater!"

"Since we're here, you might as well enter your name at the booth so that you can at least have a rank," Tang advises. "If you're really in a rush we can head over, but it looks like later in the week she's scheduled to fight here with someone named Frequency who's rank 6." Within the amphitheater applause erupts along with several loud jeers. The display changes again, back to the list of rankings. "Looks like the top 10 just changed," Tang comments.

"Balgan the Muscular just fought Mol," a hooded passerby stops to say. "Looks like Balgan lost and has dropped to rank 23."

"So lower ranks can fight the top 10?" I ask excitedly.

"You're looking to fight?" The guy brushes the stubble on his face with the back of a hand as he appraises me. "Can't say you're in for a good time the way you're built. But if you want to fight any of the top 10 you have to get to at least rank 30." He walks away to join a group of spectators who are watching the line beside the booth.

"I have no idea what he's talking about," I say to Tang. "I'm built *great*."

"As far as looks go, you're not physically intimidating," Tang says.

"I'm svelte," I say. "A compact powerhouse."

"Please don't make that your name when you enter," Tang mutters.

"I can't wait anymore," I say. "I'm going to enter my name and climb to number 1!" I rush off, leaving Tang who contentedly watches the display. The line is several meters long, just about the length between two of the large imposing wood pillars surrounding the amphitheater. I take my spot at the end of the line behind a generic muscular guy wearing a tight shirt that accentuates his biceps. His legs sticking out of brown shorts are equally large. The line moves forward unusually fast, and I watch five contenders leave the line before getting to the booth. "Why're they leaving?" I ask aloud to myself.

"They're not actual fighters," the muscular guy in front of me says, turning around. "They come every day and stand in line for show. My name's Striker."

I shake his offered hand with a nod. "Is that your fighter name, or your actual name?"

"Galley's my real name," Striker says. "I was born on a ship and worked the kitchen. My parents weren't very imaginative."

"It's a good name," I say honestly. "I'm Not."

"Not what?" Striker asks.

"My name is Not. It's like how you tie a rope, except you remove the 'k.' "

"Oh. Do you have a last name?"

"Not James," I say.

Striker murmurs vague interest. "Fresh blood, huh? I don't mean that in a bad way, that's what we call newcomers."

"No, I've been here before," I say. "Long ago when I was a kid." I think back on the reason for returning to Lanmar after leaving Lynnor in the first place due to a gambling debt. *I hope Margarine isn't around to collect.*

"You fought here when you were a kid?" Striker's eyes go wide and he stares at me.

"Yeah, when I was a little under 10. I stayed in the minor leagues, though I think I've improved since."

"Hm," Striker says in thought. "Your parents let you fight?"

"I lived alone," I say. "It was one of the ways I made money."

Striker shakes his head. "That's no life for a kid."

"Maybe. Though it was fun. By the way, it's your turn."

Striker shakes his head again, turning back to look ahead and step up to the booth we had crept up on as we talked. The fight coordinator slides a sheet on a flat countertop over to Striker who fills it out briefly before stepping away. "I guess I don't need to tell you good luck," he says when he passes me.

"Nah. Thanks for chatting with me." I step up to the booth and say, "Hey, I'm not yet registered."

"Please fill this form out," the coordinator says, a friendly woman wearing a neat tan-colored shirt and pants. She slides a registration form that had simple biographic information to be filled out. I oblige, sloppily swirling a pen the coordinator offers across the form. I get to the bottom of the paper and see there's an option to fill in a real name or pick a fake name. I write down "Not" in slanted letters and slide the paper back.

"Thanks very much," the woman says, placing the form on a pile of papers behind her that are stacked on a box. "Contenders don't need to pay to fight as a portion of money made from tickets will be taken by management. You will receive 50% for wins and 15% for losses so no matter—"

"I don't care about money," I say hurriedly, "I just want to be at the top. When can I fight?"

The coordinator smiles, maintaining her friendly demeanor, and says, "Please list your availability up to the end of the month and we'll arrange the fight. If you want to have more of a say in coordinating fights you may list an opponent's name next to yours in the column, though you both must have written an availability on the same date." She places a schedule form in front of me.

I pull the paper closer and mark myself with availability for every day of the month. "If possible, could I fight more than once a day?" I ask, putting the pen down and sliding the form back.

"Certainly," the coordinator says. She lifts the pen, taking the form, and marks a circle around my name. "Take this," she adds, handing me a smooth black knob-like piece of plastic smaller than my thumb. "That will beep to notify you of upcoming fights. Press the small button on the base to stop the beeping and put the large end in your ear. A coordinator will communicate with you the details of the fight."

"That's new," I say, taking the plastic device. "Fascinating."

"If you lose it you will be disqualified," the coordinator goes on. "Have a good day."

I nod, then turn and being pacing back over to where Tang is standing. In my haste I almost run over a woman cloaked head-to-toe whose height reached just below my shoulders. "Sorry about—"

"Not," the woman crooned.

Recognizing the voice, I pivot but am stopped by a hand she lashes out to catch my forearm.

"I heard you mention earlier that you didn't care about money. I sure hope that was just another one of your lies."

I grimace and glance at Tang still a ways off whose gaze is fixed to the electronic display. I know he is pretending not to notice. "Hi, Margarine. How fortuitous to see you… here."

"Like the lie you told me about returning here 'promptly' with the money I won from you," she pressed on, her hand forming an ironclad grip. "I don't suppose you happen to have that money on you?"

I wince, recalling the fiery gemstone I had plucked from the palace crown and left with Idrid. "I quite literally did, but I, ah, seem to have loaned it to my friend. You remember Idrid, don't you?"

Margarine's grip somehow tightened harder. "The orphaned half-Giant you took in, yes. I didn't take her for a gambler, but maybe your bad influence finally got to her. Is a deadbeat really who you are?"

"You can—oow*ww*—let go now. I've no reason to run now." She huffed out a breath and released me, the warmth of blood flooding back down my arm.

"Indeed. You know that I can go to the officials and notify them of your disrepute."

"Disre—That's just not true!" I shake my head emphatically. "You played a dirty trick, but that's not important because you still won the gamble," I change tacks hastily as her eyes flash angrily. "I have plenty of good-repute where I'm from, I'll have you know."

"Where you're from?" Margarine repeated.

"That's also not important," I say, wondering at myself for bringing up Lanmar after the events of the past week. "I know you can disqualify me at a moment's notice. But, because I joined the ranks, *you* know I won't take off. I'm sure you also know I have a plan. You'll be happy to know that I was not lying and that I do indeed care not for money, and that will happen to be a lovely byproduct of my plans."

Margarine's anger subsided quickly as she listened. She waits a beat before smiling, her tan skin crinkling around her almond-glossed lips. "Indeed, I am happy."

I match her smile. "Indeed, you get to exploit—*recoup* what I owe you."

"I'll hold you to that," she says, dropping the smile and whapping me with the back of her hand. "It seems you haven't cut the habit of mimicking things you hear." She shakes her head, muttering "Indeed," to herself before walking on. "I'll be watching," she calls over her shoulder. "And waiting."

I shudder, then quickly return to Tang's place by the electronic display. "I registered," I say excitedly. "I wonder who I'll get to fight." I glance up and see the rankings again. It shows ranks 1-50 again, though not much has changed. The screen flashes and it now shows rankings 51-100. I scan the names, not seeing mine. "By the way, how far do the rankings go?" I ask Tang.

"They've been rotating through them," Tang says. "The rankings go up to 234."

I grit my teeth and let out a slight groan of annoyance. "Well, I should've guessed." The screen changes several more times before it shows ranks 200-233. Right at number 233 is my name.

"Hey, someone dropped out," Tang says. "Looks like you've already made a step towards number 1."

"Hmph," I say. The plastic device in my hand emits a beep. I press the button at the thin end and slam the large end into my ear swiftly.

"Hello contender Not," another friendly female voice resounds in my ear. I wonder if it's the same coordinator double-tasking. "You have a fight today in 15 minutes at Midland Amphitheater with contender Declan. Please make your way to a designated contender area within the amphitheater."

"All right, I'm going in," I say, rushing off.

"I hope you die," I hear Tang mutter behind me.

Ignoring him, I enter the slit by the booth and see signs hanging along the tall backside of the stone stands that make up the actual amphitheater. There aren't installed floors within but well-walked upon sand paths. One sign directs fighters to follow the way to the left, which I do. Several ways into the amphitheater squeeze between the rounded stone stands encircling the inner arena, and I catch glimpses of crowds. I find the designated area which is labeled with the same name for fighters to wait before their fight. No one is there, a likely sign that the majority of fights had finished for the day. I walk over to a lone male coordinator in the same clean tan-colored clothes that must be a uniform for management. He has a black device in his ear as well.

"Please hand over your contactor," the man says. I take the device out of my ear and give it to the man. He places the device on a thin metal cylinder with a circumference of a mug that sticks out of the sand and reaches up to waist-level. The metal cylinder beeps. The coordinator hands me back my device which I place in one of my pouches on my hip. "Not," the coordinator says with a curious look though he refrains from asking anything, likely to retain a sense of professionalism. "You will be fighting with Declan, rank 230. Weapons are not permitted in the minor leagues."

I look over my shoulder at my sword sheathed on my back. "I won't use it," I say. "But I won't leave it anywhere."

The coordinator narrows his eyes. "If you wear it on your back that will be fine. If you do use it during the fight, you will be disqualified. Do you wish to know the details of your opponent?"

"Hmm…" I say, thinking. "No, I want it to be a surprise. It's more fun that way."

The coordinator nods. "Fights in the lower leagues are naturally lower-stakes. The rules are simple. If you knock your opponent outside the elevated area, if your opponent can no longer fight, if your opponent surrenders, or if you land ten hits on your opponent you win. Killing your opponent is not an immediate disqualification, but you would do well not to build up that kind of reputation if you want to survive."

I nod, feeling the excitement send tingles down my limbs. I wonder what kind of opponent I'll be facing, though don't have too high of an expectation since I'm at the lowest rank.

"Naturally, there will be a time limit so that fights don't go on too long," the coordinator says. "Since this is your first fight, your performance will be judged and you may be re-ranked into a higher position. Also, if you or your opponent is absent for a fight that match is a default win for the contender that shows up. If neither of you show up it'll be considered a draw. Everything make sense so far?"

"Yessir," I say.

"Right." The two of us wait in silence, the steady murmur of people resonating from within the amphitheater providing a constant background noise. The minutes pass until finally the coordinator holds a hand to his own "contactor" and signals for me to proceed into the arena.

I walk under a flap of cloth and onward between the amphitheater seats confidently, eyes locked ahead of me. There is no crowd blocking this entrance, and I stride into the open space. The seats descend into the floor which is also plain sand, and I'm met with a surprisingly full area that surrounds a square arena elevated two feet out of the sand in the center. Far above the wooden pillars encircling the outside of the amphitheater interrupt the view of the sky, their spiky points ending directly above the square arena in the center. I move to the arena and step onto the platform, turning in a full circle to get a good view of the crowd. There are quite a few spectators, only several rows either empty or with one-to-three people occupying them while the other rows are largely taken. Even so, the majority of the crowd looks uninterested. They're likely waiting for a more entertaining fight later on. I don't blame them, I doubt my opponent will last long.

A female announcer's voice rings around the amphitheater. "Ladies and gentlemen, for your entertainment today we have a newcomer that is making his debut at the Midland Amphitheater! Will he prove his worth? Or will he remain at the bottom of the barrel? Welcome, contender Not!"

Halfhearted applause comes from those in the rows closest to the arena while those higher up continue to chat among themselves and give minor glances my way. "That guy has a sword!" someone shouts.

"Thanks for letting me know!" I shout back, earning some chuckles from the crowd.

"Quite the comedian, this Not! As I'm sure you're all aware, weapons aren't allowed in minor league fights! So if Not pulls out his sword he will be disqualified! And now, his opponent, most of you know, has seen quite a few fights! He's battle-hardened and ready to put this newcomer in his place! Welcome, contender Declan!"

There's more half-hearted applause, though marginally more significant than the applause I received. At the other side of the inner amphitheater beyond the seats a tall man, though not as tall as me, enters under a flap and begins walking toward me. He's not particularly muscular, though he appears, at the least, toned. Oddly, he wears a single leather shoulder-pad on his left shoulder over a plain black shirt. He steps up onto the platform, taking up a position opposite me while watching me carefully.

"Let's see what you got!" the female announcer calls. "Let the match begin!"

I glance around once more, unsure of whether I should fight in a way that would make me popular or in a way that is most efficient. Not many seem to care, so I opt for efficiency. I turn my head to my opponent and begin to walk toward him.

"What's this?" the announcer shouts. "Not is approaching Declan! Will he make the first move?"

Are they going to narrate everything we do? I think. I put it out of my mind and continue forward toward Declan, the man's eyes widening in unease. Declan raises his left arm, fingers extending toward me. Something that smells like bottled lotion reaches my nose. *So he's a magician.* Pieces of the stone arena floor around me rise and clamp down around my feet. I stop walking, looking down in interest.

"There it is, folks! Declan's trapped Not using his signature earth magic! Not's in trouble now!"

I shake my head disapprovingly and continue to walk forward, the arena floor holding my feet in place crumbling away like it isn't there.

"Wha—What's this!? Not has broken free from Declan's entrapment! How did he do it? Is Not also an Elementalist?"

Declan takes a step back in alarm as I've closed the distance and no more than two feet are between us. My eyes drop to his stomach, then move to his neck, then his legs, searching for the best place to make a quick strike. Declan holds both of his arms down, pointing straight at the floor. I feel the ground underneath begin to shake.

"Declan's going for something drastic!"

Before anything can happen, I move behind Declan in less than a second and, making my hand flat like a knife, chop against the back of his neck just below the base of his skull. The motion is primarily for show, a façade to look like hand-to-hand combat—the real move is invisible and what Instructor had taught me about my body magic. *Through physical contact, I can drain the energy of magicians.* The ground ceases to shake, and Declan drops to his knees before falling to the floor, unconscious. I watch his body for a second to make sure he really is down, then raise my eyes to look around, waiting for a reaction.

"WHAT!?" the announcer shrieks, and the audience follows suit. A few who hadn't seen what happened simply shriek out of fright from the sudden uproar. "NOT TOOK DECLAN OUT WITH ONE STRIKE! INCREDIBLE!"

A coordinator, or perhaps an attendant or judge or nurse given he wears the same tan clothes as the other management staff, detaches from the sidelines and comes over to check on Declan. Whoever it is, finding a pulse above Declan's wrist, rises, nods, and signals the crowd by crossing his arms in an X.

"The judge has called it! Not has finished the fight with a single strike! Truly, this is a man to keep your eye on! What other feats can he perform? I look forward to seeing his next fight!"

The crowd picks up into larger applause, the spectators apparently respecting the skill it took to knock someone out with one blow. I nod slightly to the crowd, then take my leave back through the cloth flap the way I had come in. The coordinator, still standing alone in the waiting area, looks toward me and does a double-take. "The fight's over already?" he asks incredulously.

"Yeah," I say. "When can I fight next?"

.

Chapter 16: Maia

"What is going on now?" Maia asks.

"The tower's been surrounded by townsfolk," Mark says. "Again."

"Show yourselves, magicians!" come shouts from outside. Other students are gathered alongside Mark and Maia by the entrance. The crack between the door and the floor where sunlight filters in is interrupted by several shadows that shift restlessly. A fist pounds the other side of the door, the loud sound echoing around and up the inner walls.

"Do we have to confront them?" Maia asks.

"It'd be nice if Master Aveve did, though judging from last time…"

"I'm fed up with this!" one of the older students, the girl named Pina says. "I'm going to give them a piece of my mind!" She flings open the tower door and steps outside, confronting the large rowdy mob that recoils away from the tower. "Why don't you leave us alone!?" she shouts.

"I guess we should back her up," Mark says. He, Maia, and two other students go to stand beside the older student in solidarity.

"Why don't *you* leave *us* alone?" someone in the mob shouts back.

"Excuse me?" Pina says incredulously.

"We will not be oppressed by the privileged! You magicians think you can do whatever you want!"

"Privileged?" Maia questions softly. "We're kids... aren't we?"

"You people keep to yourselves in your little *magic* towers and suddenly come out and expect us to be ruled by you?" a mob member goes on.

Pina shakes her head fervently. "You people ostracized us in the first place! You're the reason we don't practice magic openly!"

"Hold on," Maia interjects again only loud enough for the students to hear, "Is that true?"

"Somewhat," Mark whispers in her ear, causing her heart to flutter nervously. "The Occult Towers are like schools, though they also were made to serve the purpose of keeping magician affairs outside non-magician affairs. It's why the towers are so far from towns, the exception being Vale Tower."

"You're too unmanageable to be allowed free reign!" another mob member shouts.

"You call us privileged and yet we're socially outcast and forbidden from being who we are!" Pina snaps back aggressively.

"Magic is unnatural!" the same mob member shouts.

"Two can play that game! What if magicians were to say non-magicians are unnatural?"

The mob erupts in angry roars. "You're threatening us!"

"Says the people who came here threatening us and telling us we can't live our lives!"

"You can't expect us to go along with being ruled by you people!"

"Why not?" Maia speaks up. "We were ruled by a non-magician up until a few weeks ago and we didn't care. Heck, most everyone I know who're non-magicians disliked James."

"That's because you're privileged with magic!"

"Now I'm just confused," Maia mutters.

Pina speaks next. "No, it's because it doesn't matter who we're ruled by as long as they leave us alone!"

"Easy for you to say!" a mob member shouts.

"Why?" Pina fires back. "Because we're magicians? Because we're privileged? Where I'm from a privilege is earned, awarded, and allowed! Who are you to say I'm not allowed to be me? That I'm granted the opportunity to be me... by you!? Isn't that the same thing you came here to prevent us from doing to you? To not simply be *allowed* to exist by a magician in power? Well, guess what, neither we nor anyone else has the authority to decide what you're allowed to be!"

"You don't know what it's like to not have it easy!" yet another mob member shouts.

"Who said magic is easy?" Mark asks. "We don't come out of the womb conjuring fruitcakes, you know."

"Yes," Pina says, reining in her emotions some. "It takes time and effort, the same as learning to sail a ship which is a privilege, by the way, since you need a license for that."

"Actually you don't," Maia says.

Pina turns to look at her. "What? Really?"

Maia replies, "Only if you're sailing a trade ship."

"Oh."

The mob, less certain, is silent for a moment. Finally someone in the mob speaks up. "That's a nice speech, though you have the ability to choose to sail ships or do magic. You can do both! We don't have that luxury!"

Pina, sighing, says, "It's not a luxury. You know how much time it would take someone to learn magic and sail a ship?"

"But you can still do both!" the member of the mob retorts.

"I can't stop being able to perform magic, same as you can't stop being able to not perform magic. If you have a problem with that, then I guess we're at an impasse."

"This is all very philosophical," Mark says. "That is to say, I like this conversation. But it's a bit distracting to others here practicing, so, if you could tell us, what is it you guys actually want from us?" he asks the mob.

"Uhmm…" the mob murmurs among themselves for several moments. "We want to be a part of the Concilium!" a member finally speaks. "It's unfair only magicians were accepted!"

"That's fair enough," Mark says, turning to Maia and the other students.

"But we have no say in who gets to be a part of the Concilium," Maia comments slowly. "Not that I'd want to be," she adds under her breath.

"None of us here have family members that are part of the Concilium," Pina tells the mob.

"You do!" a member of the mob shouts suddenly, and a hand flies up, pointing at Mark. "Your family is part of the government!"

"My parents are economists!" Mark says swiftly. "They have nothing to do with statutory affairs."

"Hello, everyone!" a familiar, deep woman's voice calls from somewhere behind the mob. One by one the people in the mob turn to look at Jasmine in a flashy sky-blue dress with a lengthy slit along her right leg reaching to her upper thigh. "There'll actually be a chance for anyone looking to be a part of the Concilium in the upcoming tournament."

"But that's a magic tournament!" members of the mob object.

"Everyone's allowed to compete!" Jasmine calls in her smooth voice. "It's not going to involve magician-only events, either. That way no one will be put at a disadvantage!"

"Really?" The mob begins to murmur among themselves, no longer angry but with slight interest. "But why is it being called the Magic Tournament?"

"That's referring to the magician towers," Jasmine says. "The three towers will be competing against each other. Think of it as a series of events for everyone, centered around the competition of student magicians. Like a decathlon between schools! Only, it'll be over three days."

"Doesn't sound too bad," someone murmurs in the crowd. The mob begins to break apart, walking away in different groups. Jasmine moves toward where Mark, Maia, and the three other students stand by the tower door through the departing crowd.

"That was quite a confrontation," Jasmine says to Mark and Maia.

"Where'd you come from?" Maia asks.

"I was in Chalman and noticed a mob forming and decided to join. Enough talk, come with me if you want to do that test we talked about."

Maia remembers the test Jasmine had mentioned that would tell her the types of magic she could perform and perks up.

"You two know this woman?" Pina asks.

"She's an Elementalist," Maia says. "She's been helping me."

"All right," Pina says, her face making a look of slight disdain causing the corners of her mouth to slant downward. She briskly nods to Jasmine before returning within the tower.

Maia begins to question Pina's sudden curtness in her head before she remembers that other magicians looked down on Elementalists. With the recently unstable relationship between non-magicians and magicians it is even more complicated to think about how magicians of different magics think of each other.

Jasmine, unfazed, flashes the other two students a smile before they follow Pina inside, and she paces around the tower toward the edge of the forest. Mark and Maia follow her over to a small stack of wood logs piled in a neat square behind the tower. Atop the logs is a thin, flat wooden board with a transparent cup half-filled with water resting on top. Jasmine moves to stand on the other side of the makeshift table and face Mark and Maia. "This'll be the test," Jasmine says, gesturing to the cup of water. "All you have to do is extend your will out around the cup. Think you can manage?"

Maia looks at Mark. He nods for her to go ahead. She reaches her hands out and holds them beside the cup, hovering in midair. She both sees and feels her will, now very much resembling an aura, roil from her skin and surround the cup. "What do I do now?"

"I told you that's all you had to do," Jasmine says, bending over to get a closer look at the cup. Inside, the water begins to stir by itself in a slow clockwise circle. Additionally, the water starts to bubble. Jasmine watches the cup, showing no emotions, while Mark and Maia watch with intrigue. "All right, that's enough," Jasmine says, standing up straight and putting her hands on her hips.

Maia recalls her will back to her body and the water in the cup becomes still again.

"The water in the cup reacts differently to different types of magicians, it being magically imbued," Jasmine says. "It's a rather simple test that anyone can try, as long as there's someone knowledgeable enough to create the water."

"You're not a Conjuror," Mark comments. Jasmine simply purses her lips in reply.

"Why couldn't I do this sooner?" Maia says, mildly annoyed.

"Because you lacked motivation to do your tower master's quiz," Jasmine replies. "Would you like to know what the results of this test show?"

"Yes," Maia says, a touch more annoyed that the woman even asked.

"The water moved in a circle, which indicates you're an Elementalist," Jasmine says. "But you already knew that. Also, as I'm sure you saw, the water began to bubble. What do you think that indicates?"

"Uh," Maia says while thinking to herself. "Well, Elementalists can also crystalize and evaporate water."

"That's true, but does the cup feel at all warm to you?" Jasmine asks.

Maia moves her right hand, feeling the outside of the cup below the waterline. "No, it's cool."

"What else could it be?" Jasmine asks.

"Parts of the water traded places," Mark says.

"Very observant, Mark," Jasmine says approvingly. "The water moving smoothly indicates Elementalist magic, though the bubbling wasn't smooth. Parts of the water traded places, or rather teleported, and not entirely in the same proportions. That caused some molecules to overlap, which caused significant force for the molecules to separate themselves, which in turn caused bubbles."

"Spatial magic?" Maia asks, slightly proud.

"Yes," Jasmine says. "There's still at least one thing left that changed in the cup."

"What?" Maia looks closer, her eyes observing the water. "What else happened? Did it have to do with Conjuring?"

"Yes," Jasmine says. "You can tell by the water level in the cup being a bit higher."

Maia sees the difference once Jasmine points it out and smiles. "Wow. I guess I can do a lot of different magic."

"Try tasting the water," Jasmine says.

Maia picks up the cup and raises it to her lips. She pauses right when she's about to take a sip and looks suspiciously at Jasmine. "You didn't do anything to the water, did you?"

"No," Jasmine says.

Maia hesitates, then takes the sip. "It tastes… sweet. There wasn't anything you added to the water?"

"No," Jasmine repeats a tad more slowly. She looks as if she is going to say something, but doesn't. "A different taste indicates Enchanting."

"Enchanting!" Maia says excitedly. "Do you know where I can learn more about it?"

"No," Jasmine says yet again. "You should focus on what you can do right now," she goes on briskly. "And focus on getting better. The Magic Tournament will be your next test to see how much you've improved."

"But Aveve said we could have the next few days off," Maia says.

"Practice," Jasmine insists. "You don't want to do poorly in the tournament, do you?"

"No," Maia says. "But it'd be nice to relax for a day or two."

"You'll get time to yourselves once you're done. The type of training I'll have you both be doing is simple and can be done by yourselves."

"Is it more thinking?" Maia asks sorrowfully.

"You'll be running," Jasmine says.

Maia and Mark share a look of surprise. "What?" they say together.

"Run from the tower to Chalman and then back," Jasmine says decidedly. "That should be good for now."

"Why?" Maia asks.

"Maia, magic isn't something you simply do with your mind. When you tested your magic just now with the cup, did you *just* use your mind?"

Maia stops, thinking. "No. I moved my hands."

193

"Indeed," Jasmine says. "Mind and body work together when performing magic, like a conductor and an orchestra. You can conduct your magic superbly, but if the orchestra is lousy there will be a disconnect and there will be discord and the magic will be diminished. For that, you must also train your body."

Maia thinks back to Master Kellen and how Greg said he enjoyed exercise. "Both Kellen and Aveve run up and down stairs," Maia says.

"Then they have the right idea," Jasmine says. "Go on, now. Run to Chalman then back here."

"Wait," Mark says. "I haven't gotten to see the type of magic I can do."

"Oh, right," Jasmine says, looking at the cup. "I'll go find some more water. When you get back, you can take the test. Now go!"

Maia and Mark flee quickly around to the front of the tower and start off down the road toward Chalman.

Chapter 17: Not

My next opponent is a muscular guy, which isn't anything new from the last ten or so people I've faced. His fighter name, as proclaimed by the announcer, is Thick, which I have to refrain from making a joke about. He faces me from the other side of the square arena, stretching his legs. I can almost hear the strain of his tight white shirt stretching around his muscles. I have no idea what workout routine most of the competitors here are using, though it's flawed in one key way. The flaw is that the majority of my opponents are training their muscles to be stronger without the thought of using them specifically for fighting. Without knowing how to attack or defend, muscles can be pretty pointless.

Thick, finally done with his stretching which I'm sure he'd done enough of behind the amphitheater stands and only now does for show, stands up and points a thick finger at me. "Don't go thinking you're hot stuff just by beating a couple losers!"

Almost every other opponent of mine had used a similar line. Intimidation seems to be the name of the game in the minor leagues. I notice Thick crouching low, getting ready to do something, and focus.

He breaks out into a run, sprinting straight at me with his arms held wide as if he is going to hug me.

The announcer's voice, ever the accompanying narrator, rings out around the amphitheater. "Thick makes the first move! He is going toward Not like he is going to clobber him!"

When Thick is five feet away and springs forward with his right foot I move. Ducking under his left arm in an instant, I make the same chopping motion against the back of my opponent's neck with a knife-hand as I've done for every other fight. The force along with his momentum sends Thick sprawling out of the arena, sliding several feet across the ground on his face and upturning the sand in the process.

I step down and turn him over so that he doesn't accidentally inhale the sand. His eyes are closed and he's out cold.

"Thick has been knocked out of the arena, and he is unconscious to boot! Not takes out yet another opponent twice his size with a single strike!" the announcer cries emphatically. "What is this man's secret? How far will he go!?"

The crowd's applause is even greater since my first match. I smile to myself, slightly giddy to be getting some fans. I wave once to the crowd before exiting the inner amphitheater. I meet with the coordinator in the designated waiting area for fighters. Today several other fighters are here as well. They each look at me with a semi-menacing stare, though there's also some respect. They must've heard the fight from the announcer.

"This was your thirteenth match and your thirteenth victory," the coordinator tells me, not bothering to conceal his admiration. "And…" he pauses, holding a hand to the contactor device he has in his ear. "Yes, this puts you at rank 149. Congratulations, contender Not. You are now in the intermediate league."

"Hey," one of the other fighters, another buff guy, says. "I heard you joined yesterday. You're the real deal." He gives me a thumbs up.

"Thanks," I say. "Is there a chance I can get any more fights in today?" I ask the coordinator.

"You can, though don't you think you've been progressing too swiftly?" the coordinator responds. "We won't stop you, but it would be better for business to let your name get out. Let rumors spread for a couple days, it'll create some intrigue, sell more seats, and get more money for you and the management here."

"I'm not interested in money," I find myself saying again. *But, I suppose it wouldn't hurt to have in case Margarine corners and rinses me. All the more reason to rise up the ranks quickly.* "I want to be number 1."

"You mean you want to face number 1," a low voice calls from behind me. I look over and see Tang standing outside the fighters' waiting area. "Remember why you're here."

"Ugh, fine."

The coordinator nods to me. "We will check for any intermediate fighters scheduled later today," he says. "We'll notify you for your next fight."

I nod and walk out of the waiting area to Tang. We both move to the slit in the tanned leather making up the outer amphitheater wall and walk back to the same electronic display hanging on the outside. "Have there been any more interesting changes in the ranks?"

"Kelsey and Wrath, Death, and Despair's ranks haven't changed which means Kelsey won her fight," Tang replies. "Frequency, who was rank 6, moved up to rank 5 which was previously Morose's rank. No other notable changes in rank regarding the top 10, and I haven't paid much attention to the other ranks."

"Except for me, of course," I say, rubbing the back of my head with a hand.

"Not really."

I feign pouting, looking at Tang from the corner of my eye. "Are you ignoring me on purpose?"

"No, I just don't have to pay attention to you when I don't need to," Tang says.

"I'm rank 149 now," I say, dropping the ridiculous face I made with puckered lips for a more serious one. "I've climbed a bit in just a day, though I still want to go quicker. Is there anything you've learned about the other fighters here?"

"Not much," Tang says. "Most don't want to talk to me, which is fine with me because I don't want to talk to them."

"It could be the hair," I say, looking his shoulder-length hair up and down. "Or the personality."

Tang ignores me. "Most of the minor league contenders are muscle-heads. The higher up you go there tends to be more magicians."

"I never got into the intermediate league before," I say excitedly.

"Yeah, whatever. Not that it should matter to you, but the type of magicians that rank among both the worst and the best are Elementalists. I overheard that the guy called Frequency is a special kind of Elementalist so he might be of interest to you, if you face him. Spatial magicians appear to consistently be the second-strongest contenders among magicians, and then Conjurors in third. The latter two shouldn't be trouble since they depend on their own will…"

"Elementalists aren't much trouble either," I say casually, bending down to pick up a smooth stone out of the sand. "Their magic augments the elements that they manipulate kind of like how we augment our own bodies, which greatly reduces their effect on me to the point of being inconsequential."

"Good for you," Tang drawls.

My contactor buzzes and makes a noise in my pants pocket and I quickly retrieve it. Sticking it in my ear, I immediately hear a fight coordinator's voice. "Hello contender Not," a female voice says. "You have a fight today in 30 minutes at Midland Amphitheater with contender Dulon. Please make your way to a designated contender area within the amphitheater."

"I've got another fight," I tell Tang. "Hopefully I'll get to continue jumping up ten or so ranks."

"Hopefully you'll choke and die," Tang responds, turning away and looking up at the display.

"Contender Dulon, rank 120, steps into the arena!" the female announcer shouts. "A wizened magician with many tricks up his sleeve, he overwhelms opponents with swift action! But will he be fast enough for his next opponent? Please welcome back, for the fifth time today, contender Not!"

The crowd cheers louder this time, and I can't help but notice it is louder than the applause my opponent received. Walking into the inner amphitheater, I see Dulon, a middle-aged man bordering on senior citizenry, standing atop the elevated arena in brown robes that sweep the floor. He eyes me warily.

"Nothing has stood in the way of this fresh contender, folks! However, this could be the end of his winning streak! Let's see what they've got!"

I step up into the arena far enough away from Dulon to set him at relative ease. So far I've been either letting opponents attack first or approaching them slowly before attacking. My opponent looks like the type who is cautious and actually thinks, which indicates I should be the one to end this fast. That is what I would do, though Dulon bows low, giving me pause.

"I hope to learn something from you," Dulon says. His voice is amiable, contrasting quite a bit from his serious, senescent face. He rises from the bow and takes up a fighting stance.

"Let the fight begin!" the announcer cries, and the thundering sound of a bass drum rumbles around the arena.

I wait and watch as Dulon points a finger at me. Bracing myself for an Elementalist wind-type magic, I get into a low stance. Instead, there's a *pop* and Dulon is suddenly holding a wide crossbow.

I look to the audience questioningly. My eyes find the closest audience member and I lock onto her. "Hey, aren't weapons not allowed?" I ask.

The woman, shocked that I'm addressing her, blushes and waves her arms frantically, signaling she doesn't know what to say.

"That's right, weapons aren't allowed!" the announcer shouts, apparently hearing me. "However, weapons of magic are within the rules! It looks like Dulon will make the first attack!"

"You should watch your opponent," Dulon tells me, pulling my attention back to him.

"Sorry," I say, turning in time to see a crossbow arrow flying dangerously fast at my chest. It's too fast for me to dodge. This is a first. I'm actually being forced to make a decision: stop the arrow, or let it hit me. The latter would be a gamble as it'd reveal the nature of my own power. There are more fights I have to think about beyond this one where I'd like to pull out all the stops. On the other hand, Dulon earnestly wants me to try my best given the concentrated look on his face. Still, it's too soon.

My hand reaches up and catches the arrow just as the arrowhead grazes my chest over my heart. It does not puncture the skin. I let go of the arrow, and it clatters dully on the floor.

"Not caught the arrow!" the announcer shrieks. "Is that even possible? How fast can he move!?"

The crossbow *pop*s out of Dulon's hand and is replaced by a different crossbow.

"Oh! Dulon has conjured a multi-firing crossbow! He is not playing around, folks!"

What to do? I think. I can stand in the same spot and let my opponent continue trying new weapons which will eventually force me to reveal my power, or I can go on the attack. It's still a bit too early to end the fight, though.

Dulon makes the decision for me by firing his triplex crossbow. Each arrow flies in a vertical line, the lowest approaching my abdomen, the highest approaching my head, and the middle one approaching my solar plexus. This time I dodge, taking a little jump to my right, then rush forward, narrowing the distance slightly but not all the way so as to allow Dulon time to counter. I hear members of the crowd shriek in fear behind me. I glance back quickly to see the three arrows disappear with pops. *Good man* I think, seeing Dulon's outstretched hand.

Dulon's crossbow then vanishes and he kneels down, placing a hand flat on the arena's stone floor. I slow my pace though continue toward him, curious. Dulon's fingers penetrate the floor like it's malleable, and he lifts up a large chunk of stone that he throws at me. I bat it away with the back of my hand. It's a bit more trouble than I anticipate and I feel its impact rattle my arm, enough to leave a bruise.

"Dulon's begun using Elemental magic! Truly, a jack of all trades!"

Dulon rips out another piece of the arena just as I'm about to reach him, though this chunk that he pulls up is like a wall. He uses it as a barrier to block me, then quickly jumps away. His hand digs into the arena again, pulling up another two-foot wide and seven-foot tall wall. I follow him while performing feints with my fists that Dulon reacts to, pulling up walls where my feints would hit if I followed through.

"What's this? Dulon is eluding Not by turning the arena floor into barriers!"

Dulon stops creating the walls out of the floor and ducks behind one out of my sight. All around are stone walls, like a small forest. The wall Dulon stands behind shudders and breaks, pieces of it flying in my direction.

"Dulon's back on the offensive, continuing to use the arena to his advantage!" the announcer calls.

I dodge out of the way of the debris behind a stone wall. In this spot I am surrounded by four individual stone walls, a fairly protected space. I notice all the walls around me shift, and realize what's happening the moment before it occurs. The walls shatter violently, sending up a large cloud of dust that covers the arena.

"Ooooh!" I hear the announcer's voice shriek between the sound of crumbling debris cracking against the floor. "Dulon caught Not with a shower of debris! He's surely been crushed!"

In actuality, the moment before the walls shattered I caught the smell of dry grass, a peculiar and unusual smell in the desert. It tipped me off that Dulon was fully using magic to manipulate the stone to crumble on top of me. This allowed me to shrug off the debris entirely, as the stone had residual will that allowed me to absorb the impact. It was pure luck that the dust obscured what happened, allowing my power to remain somewhat ambiguous.

The cloud disperses and the dust settles, and I can clearly see Dulon standing between the few remaining stone walls looking at me in surprise.

"What's this? Not is still standing! It appears he didn't take any damage from the violent shattering of rock! Is this man invincible!?"

I wipe a hand across my brow, flinging clots of dust and several pebbles out of my bangs. While I had taken no damage, Dulon won a point in my book. He got me to use my actual power.

I leap toward Dulon in a flash, the air rushing in my ears in a momentary burst of speed. Dulon doesn't have time to duck behind one of his stone walls or use further magic. I spin, the momentum sending my hand down toward his neck. Rather than knocking him out with my knife-hand, I delay the motion and let my palm fall lightly on Dulon's upper back.

Dulon flinches in place then turns his head to look at me.

I smile, closing my eyes for a brief moment, and nod at him.

"It looks like you've won," Dulon says, his voice still as friendly as before. "I forfeit the match!" he calls.

The crowd erupts into applause. The announcer's voice surfaces a few moments later, saying, "Never before have we had such an intense, fast-paced match in the intermediate league!"

"Your magic is impressive," I tell Dulon. "I haven't met a magician who could perform two types of magic."

"There aren't many who can," Dulon says. "I appreciate you sparing me. I'm relatively new, despite my age, though haven't had many losses."

"I bet," I say. "You seem like you should be much further up in the ranks. You're like Dunlon himself compared to the last guy I faced."

Dulon laughs lightly, his face crinkling even more. "I suppose we have similar names as well. I'd like to know how it is you took the full force of my magic... but this isn't the time or place to discuss it. Well, congratulations." Dulon walks away, leaving me alone in the arena to soak up the rest of the applause.

Chapter 18: Vespertine

"What do you call a bird without wings
Oh, the wind, it does blow
Or a bow having all but some strings
And the sea, winding, flows.

Is there ever a more sorry sight
Oh, the wind, it does blow
Than a lover lost in lonely night
And the sea, winding, flows.

If rulers stand upon others tall
Oh, the wind, it does blow
Who, then, do they turn unto to call
And the sea, winding, flows."

Low lighting accompanies the jester's pitchy tune in the royal chambers. The pale bare flooring made of quartz stretches long, carrying the blithe, tinny notes across the room to Vespertine's ears. She sits in a tall wooden chair facing the length of the room. Five more are similarly lined along the wall, while a larger, cushioned chair rests in the center of them, pushed several feet away from the wall to indicate higher authority for the sitter. All of them are unoccupied save for her own on the end. Her eyes lazily stare

on at the jester on the opposite end who is gesticulating out
of time with his song. Every now and then the individual
electric lightbulbs hanging midway up the long walls on either
side flicker. The walls themselves are painted with a light,
faded green with dull golden arches forming a simple pattern.
There are places where the paint has chipped away and
wallpaper is peeling. It all desperately needs redecorating.

A servant enters through the single door on the far
side of the room behind the jester and hurriedly paces the
room's length to Vespertine. His shoes clack along the quartz,
the sound adding a sort of offbeat tempo for the song. He
reaches the woman who casually acknowledges his presence
with a glance.

"Everyone's finished," the servant says in a hushed
voice. "All but current Concilium have moved on to the
second trial."

"Have them meet me here," Vespertine tells him.

The servant nods his assent, taking a short pause to
look disdainfully at the upholstery, then swiftly takes his
leave. He exits back out the single door at the other end of
the room, leaving Vespertine and the jester alone.

"The ruler's love locked underneath one

Oh, the wind, it does blow

Unceremoniously undone

And the sea, winding, flows."

"Don't make up stanzas, Lorenz," Vespertine calls.
"It's undignified."

"Embarrassment is a liberty only the dignified may suffer," the jester calls heartily.

Vespertine places an elbow on an armrest and leans against her hand, ignoring the jester's rambling.

"It's a tragedy to have desire

Oh, the wind, it does blow

But lack the means to ever acquire

And the sea, winding, flows."

The far door opens again and six Concilium magicians in their red cloaks sweep along the floor toward her. Lorenz sways out of their way, his bright red-and-orange-patterned tunic swaying with him. The magicians divide themselves between the remaining seats, leaving the larger imposing one empty.

"Did you enjoy yourselves?" Vespertine asks in welcome to the core Concilium members. She appraises each who are capable of Mind Control magic alongside a different kind of magic.

"It was a waste of time," Balnar, the man sitting to her immediate right with a stony face, says. Like his blunt features and way of speaking, he is blunt with his powers of Conjuring; when it rains, he conjures a coat; when in battle, he conjures a sword.

Vespertine lets out a light laugh. "It took some work to put together."

"It was better than doing nothing," Goldyck, another, younger, man three seats over, says. His power is also of Conjuring. "Playing with servants was kind of fun."

"Where are the toys?" Ponla, the woman sitting between Balnar and Goldyck, asks. Her power is of a peculiar Elementalism she favors using to manipulate manmade objects.

"You can bring them back," Vespertine says. "I wanted to be alone for a bit."

Ponla sighs, pulling the hood on her cloak up. Analise, sitting furthest from Vespertine, says, "You're too fond of them. They should be disposed of rather than kept around." The woman frowns in a parental manner at Ponla. Her power is of Teleportation.

"They're too much of a danger to be seen," Tethris, between Goldyck and Analise, agrees. His power is also of Teleportation.

"They retain their uses," Vespertine says. "We've already relieved problem servants from duty, so there's no risk if we let them roam the palace."

"More toys would be fun," Ponla says, tugging lightly at her hood to pull it even further over her face.

"What will you have us do in the tournament?" Balnar asks, ever the serious one.

"The country is slowly preparing for it, ignorant of our goal," Vespertine says. "The only confounding variables are the half-Giant, Darren, and the half-Giant's friend."

"Why are you having her participate in these trials?" Goldyck asks. "Surely she's aware that she's the odd one out."

"I've already told her she's the only non-magician," Vespertine says.

"What?" Balnar growls.

"She already drank the vesper," Vespertine assures him. "Her suggestibility should be at its highest. Once we also control Darren, we can use him to give her an order since they share a basic level of trust. Speaking of, we should begin giving him doses and preparing more. The Stirling Sea isn't quite saturated with enough vesper to circulate consistently into drinking water yet."

"Why do we have to go this roundabout way of controlling people?" Analise asks. "We can already control people more easily than your vesper."

Vespertine lowers her eyelids. The question isn't seeking clarification, as she's explained it multiple times already. It's challenging authority. *All the more reason to restate it plainly to put her in her place.* "I thought it was obvious. You can't control everyone at the same time. With vesper, everyone's highly suggestible. Coupled with Mind Control, we can fully dominate everyone as easily as the word of a trusted other can manipulate them."

Analise smirks and shrugs. "And you're certain your vesper can keep them controlled forever?"

"Not forever, no. Though that won't matter once the majority of our water supply contains vesper to keep everyone in a constant state of suggestibility."

"I don't like it," Balnar says. "How can we be certain we're immune?"

"The immunizations I gave you work. If you're that paranoid you can take antidotes daily."

"Darren and the half-Giant are largely within our control," Tethris says. "But the half-Giant's friend... Not? What do we do with him?"

"He disappeared after the lame speech he gave," Vespertine says. "Reports said he was traveling south somewhere. He's likely to come back for the tournament, which is where we'll dispose of him and the others."

"More wasted toys!" Ponla says with a sigh, rocking back in her chair.

"They know too much, or, at least, suspect too much to be reliably controlled," Vespertine says.

"A fam'ly of four unduly split

Oh, the wind, it does slow

Where four now just one, the rest remit

And the sea, unwound, goes."

"You can go now, Lorenz," Vespertine calls to the jester.

"Wheeze-a freeze-a, brango vango!" the jester calls back before exiting the room.

"Did he make up that song on the spot?" Ponla asks. "I liked it."

"He likes to insert James's family into his songs," Vespertine says. "Even though I told him to stop."

"Not killed James, didn't he?" Tethris muses. "Disposing of him along with the others is easier said than done. He and the half-Giant were reported to be the sole two responsible for the king's death."

"Yes, yes, though there's not much they'll be able to do once they're surrounded," Vespertine says while waving a hand dismissively.

"We shouldn't underestimate them, especially Not," Tethris goes on.

"What you take for underestimation is merely confidence," Vespertine says. "And, hardly unwarranted. Whether or not Not comes to the tournament is irrelevant. The northern and eastern nations are now involved."

"Both Thalidan and Vichaelis are?" Balnar questions seriously.

"They're moving forces as we speak," Vespertine says. "Since we don't control the entirety of the guard we can assure Lanmar that they're merely making arrangements for the Magic Tournament since it will be hosting all nations. Thalidan will send their forces from Endovir over the seas along the coast while Vichaelis will pass through and follow the Talwood's edge. From there, once the tournament is over, they will begin overtaking Lanmar."

"That takes care of both the Occult Towers, then?" Tethris asks.

"Yes," Vespertine says. "I'm certain Darren's warned the tower masters. Or, at least Kellen, since they're friends."

"The Concilium has roots in Thalidan, but I don't trust Vichaelis," Balnar says. "They're a precarious ally."

Tethris coughs into his arm. "We're dealing with entire nations. Thalidan was once the suzerain nation to Lanmar, so it's only natural Lanmar would coalesce with Thalidan. The rulers of Vichaelis must know this, and I doubt they'll stand idly by while two powers become a superpower."

"If they rebel, we'll deal with it," Vespertine says.

"There's too much at stake," Balnar says insistently. "Having both the nation of Vichaelis and this Not poses plenty of potential problems."

"Nice alliteration," Analise comments, and Ponla and Goldyck clap their hands together lightly in approval.

"We're more than prepared," Vespertine says, standing from her seat and pacing away slowly.

"Where are you going?" Balnar hisses, annoyed.

"The 'toys' are here," Vespertine replies as the door at the other end of the room opens. A man and a woman in plain, loose clothes enter and walk in step toward the seated magicians. "I don't care for them, and I tire of reiterating plans."

"Why do we still have them around, then?" Balnar asks.

"Insurance," Vespertine says, passing the man and woman at the halfway point of the room. She gives a cursory glance, noting their unnaturally porcelain-colored skin and rickety movement. She steps outside of the room then leans back in, taking the door handle. "They're Not's parents, after all," she calls before shutting the door behind her.

Chapter 19: Maia

This is not what I signed up for, Maia thinks while pushing herself up from a lying down position. Her hair is draping around her face. She keeps her body straight like a board, parallel to the ground, and eases herself down, bending her elbows for another pushup.

"Slow," Jasmine says for the millionth time.

"I *am* going slow," is Maia's exasperated reply. "If I go any slower my muscles will give out."

"That's the idea," Jasmine says.

Maia glances over at Mark who is doing pushups next to her. He has done a few more than she has which annoys her. She bends her elbows once more, her arms visibly quivering from the exertion. Somehow, she pushes herself back up.

"Keep going until you can't," Jasmine says.

Biting the inside of her mouth to distract herself, Maia goes down once more. This time when she tries to push her muscles refuse.

Jasmine squats down, balancing on her toes. "You feel that?" she asks amiably.

Maia relaxes her body, letting herself lie facedown on the grass. Some part of Jasmine must be sadistic.

"Rest for a minute," Jasmine instructs. Mark, still in a ready position, lets himself lie down too.

"My arms are burning," Mark comments, rolling onto his back. His chest rises and falls rapidly.

"That's good," Jasmine says. "Prepare for more."

"What kind of motivation is that?" Maia asks. "How much longer are we going to continue?"

"You've only just begun. The hardest part is next."

Maia thought sprinting to and back from Chalman would be the death of her. What could be worse?

"Get back into position," Jasmine orders. Maia and Mark slowly do as they're told. "All right… Go."

Maia does a single pushup and then feels her muscles immediately fire up with stress. She tries to do another but fails, her arms giving out.

"You're done," Jasmine tells Maia. Beside her Mark lies on his stomach, also having reached his limit. "All right, get up." They stand, both panting lightly. "How do your bodies feel now?"

"Hurt," Mark says. Maia murmurs an agreement.

"Imagine doing that every day," Jasmine tells them, sweeping a hand through the air dramatically before resting it on her hip.

"That's horrible," Maia says, shaking her arms out, which does little to relieve the burning sensation.

"Guess what? It's no longer going to be just your imagination. Tomorrow you'll be doing the same cardio and muscle training. And the day after that, and so on."

"All the way until the Magic Tournament?" Maia asks incredulously.

"You want to strengthen your magic, don't you?"

"I have a question," Mark says. "Why is it I can see some types of magic performed but not others?"

"You mean you can only sometimes see orenda," Jasmine says. "Give me an example of what magic you can't see."

"Like when I destroy an object I conjured," Mark says. "I go through the motions of conducting magic, you know, thinking, defining, focusing, and doing, and as I do the steps I can see my orenda more clearly. When I conjure an object, I can see my orenda sort of form an outline of it before it appears outside my body. But when I destroy I never see my orenda move from my body, and the object somehow still disappears. How is that?"

"You should already know this," Jasmine says. "The object you conjured already consists of your orenda, therefore you don't need to extend any of your energy again. You're simply manipulating your orenda that's already there."

"Isn't that bad?" Maia asks. "Doesn't that mean you're destroying a part of your own orenda?"

"Your energy rejuvenates," Jasmine drawls. "The same way your body recovers overnight while you're asleep. If you have any more questions, I hope they're better."

"What about your Elementalist magic?" Maia asks. "When you manipulate the air I don't notice your orenda."

"That's because you're still untrained and you're not paying attention. Look again." Jasmine lifts her hand from her hip and spreads her fingers wide. From the center of her palm the smoke-like substance representing her orenda spirals outward, getting thinner and less defined the further out it goes. The air reacts, rippling in the same pattern as her orenda.

"Oh, I get it. Because it's more spread out it's harder to see."

"That's a very important thing to know," Jasmine says, nodding. "Just because you can't see it, doesn't mean it isn't there. Some magicians trust their eyes too much only to be taken by surprise by a magic attack."

"Is there another way besides visually to sense magic being used?"

"Yes, though it is difficult to describe. It also works sensing another's orenda in general."

Maia considers the ways she has experienced magic. There was the time she fed the tree in one of the bottom levels of the Tower of Bel which Kellen described as a combination of several magics. The feeling she experienced she can only best describe as "touching" the unusual tree's will despite not physically touching it. It was like a wall, clearly defining that *this* was another living thing that could not be manipulated. It was unique, like how Maia now perceives Mark and Jasmine's individual orenda. Then there was the more recent quiz with Aveve in which students were asked to conjure two items at once. Aveve had asked her about the difference between a conjured object and a natural object and she had sensed that her staff which Tricia had conjured for her to use was not natural but consolidated will. Jasmine is right. It is hard to describe how she could sense orenda.

"Essentially, sensing others' orenda is like an involuntary function of our bodies, right?" Mark states, looking between Maia and Jasmine. "Like breathing. It often goes unnoticed, though we have some control over it."

"That's a good comparison," Jasmine says approvingly. "And like controlled breathing during exercise, by controlling your senses to perceive magic, particularly your own in relation to others', you can enhance your performance."

"How do you mean?" Maia asks.

"If you're performing magic cooperatively with someone else, it helps to control your magic to be compatible with your partner, or at the very least not get in the other's way," Jasmine says. "If circumstances call for a duel between magicians, it is also salient to use your sense of magic to your advantage. Elementalists can take advantage of Conjurors' short-range magic with distance. Conjurors can take advantage of Elementalists' limited manipulation magic with uncommon or unusual substances. In similar-magic combinations, Elementalists who specialize in manipulating air can counter Elementalists who specialize in manipulating water by oxidizing their water to limit their resources, or the other way around by liquifying the air. Any chink in a magician's magic can be exploited with trained sensing."

"It's too complex for me," Maia says tiredly.

"Practice and it won't be," Jasmine tells her. "I'll be leaving you now. Remember, tomorrow you'll do the same exercises."

"That's how you knew Aveve was watching over us when you stalked us to the tower," Mark says.

"Yeah. Well, until tomorrow." Jasmine walks away towards the Talwood, her long legs carrying her quickly across the grass.

"I seriously want to know where she goes every day," Mark comments. "She can't just be living in the forest."

Maia watches as Jasmine disappears amongst the trees. "Well, the sailors in my hometown also had stories about the Talwood."

"It's haunted like the Holt of Dunlon?" Mark teases.

"*No*," Maia says, annoyance stretching out the vowel. "Just that strange people live in the forest."

217

"Strange people?"

"Yeah. Forest-dwellers or something, who have weird-looking skin like oak and live inside the trees."

Mark tilts his head. "How'd you live inside a tree? They're way too small."

"I don't know. We should ask Jasmine about it, maybe she'd know. Or maybe she's a forest-dweller herself!"

"You think?" Mark says doubtfully, a playful smile on his face.

Rather than answer him, Maia turns toward Chalman and begins to walk.

"Hey!" Mark calls, following after her.

Chapter 20: Not

"You."

I turn at the deep, unsettling voice. A man wrapped in dust-colored, billowing robes stands before me. I narrow my eyes, wary. Somehow he had snuck up on me and I hadn't heard him approach. "Me?"

"Face me in the arena." The voice, again, comes out deep and quivers unnaturally. It's the way a voice would vibrate while on horseback, being forcibly shaken by the movement.

I appraise the man's stern face. A months-grown beard shadows the lower portion, accentuated sharply by the line of his chin. His eyes are a startling green that stand out from his dull brown attire. "Okay. When?"

"Now," the man says.

The crowd within the amphitheater erupts into cheers, breaking the otherwise stillness of the air. "Okay," I say. "I'll go tell a fight coordinator. What's your name?"

"Frequency. I'll go with you."

I make no reaction as I move to continue walking toward the amphitheater's exit. Recognizing the name to belong to the person currently in rank 5, I direct all my attention to him as he moves beside me. Still, I don't pick up a trace of sound coming from him. Even his breezy clothes don't make so much as a noise. "Why is it you want to face me?" I ask.

"You're now rank 88," Frequency states. "A day ago you were rank 233."

"You tracked my progress? I'm flattered." We pass the exit and move toward the booth just outside where a fight coordinator is stationed inside. There currently are no contenders waiting in line, the fights for the day largely finished or being finished at present.

"I moved up the ranks quickly as well," the man intones.

"Oh." It shouldn't, but it puts me off that someone else has done a similar feat.

"Someone like that is worth facing."

"I suppose they are," I reply, turning to the fight coordinator in the booth. "We'd like to schedule a fight together," I tell the woman.

"You've already laid out your schedule to be open literally every day this month, contender Not," she replies. "No further scheduling will be required."

"But we want to fight each other specifically," I say.

The woman turns her attention to Frequency and does a double-take. "My apologies. I did not see you, contender Frequency. You both wish to fight each other?"

"Yes," Frequency says.

"Very well." The woman pulls a paper out of the middle of a stack behind her, inexplicably locating my very own schedule. "What date do you wish to fight, so that I may write your name in?"

"Today," Frequency says.

The woman doesn't initially respond, though frowns slightly. For several seconds she looks to be restraining herself from saying anything. Then, "It looks like all the fights are wrapped up for today. The crowd will be at its thinnest. Are you sure you want to still fight today?"

"Yes," Frequency says.

Making a small nod, the woman quickly scribbles Frequency's name down in a column on the sheet and returns it to the stack. "I'll make the arrangements," she says.

"Great," I say, turning and walking back to the amphitheater's entrance. Frequency continues to follow beside me in all his uncanny silence. "Are you a magician?" I ask.

"Are you?"

I pause a beat to answer. "In a manner of speaking." More cheering erupts from the central amphitheater.

"Me too." Silence. My footsteps pad gently over the sandy floor. Even with my best efforts I can't fully conceal the sound of my own steps. Yet the other man is doing it without any perceivable effort. It's like I'm walking next to a ghost. "I suppose we'll see what manner of magician we both are," Frequency says finally when we reach the waiting area for contenders.

"It certainly makes it more exciting," I say. The male fight coordinator standing by the long entryway to the center of the amphitheater beckons us over.

"Not and Frequency," the coordinator says. "Please place your contactors on the metal podium."

We each do so before returning it to our persons.

"Your fight is up next," the coordinator says.

"Just like that?" I ask.

"This fight was unprecedented," the coordinator responds. "But, because both parties wanted it and were

221

available, and because one of them is among the top 10, it is sanctioned."

"Wow, I didn't know higher ranks got perks," I comment.

"Because this is an inter-league match between you, Not and Frequency, there are other differences in the ruleset that must be mentioned. As it is with the major-leagues, weapons will be allowed."

I shift in place, feeling the weight of my sword against my back. Will I finally get to use it?

"As death is more common, earnings are also increased for fighters. Since there was no time to charge anyone, whatever audience members remain within the amphitheater will simply be given free admission. Management will take percentages out of an average top 10 match's revenue and distribute it accordingly to you both. Another perk of the higher ranks," the coordinator says.

"How generous," I say. We three lapse into silence, awaiting the telltale excited chatter to diminish within the inner amphitheater to signal the final match's end. I turn to Frequency and ask, "You're really fine facing me? I mean, wouldn't losing put you all the way back in the intermediate league?"

"That's the way it goes," Frequency replies coolly.

I smile at that. "I suppose it is."

Within the amphitheater comes cheering causing the female announcer's booming voice to be incomprehensible amidst the noise. The fight coordinator holds a hand up to the contactor in his ear before gesturing for us to enter the inner area. "Good luck, both of you," he says.

Side by side Frequency and I walk down the long entrance toward the arena. We both swipe the cloth flap hanging in the way aside and step over to the elevated platform. Among the fifty or so remaining in the audience, all of them congregated in one area of seating, those sitting at the ground level closest to the arena look our way in interest. On the opposite side two contenders exit, one limping while being assisted by the other.

"Ladies and gentlemen," the announcer's voice resonates imperiously. "All of the scheduled fights for the day are now over. But. There is one final fight taking place today that you won't want to miss." The words hang in the air as the announcer pauses, letting the audience turn their attention to the arena where I now take up a position opposite Frequency on the stone platform. "Ladies and gentlemen," the announcer repeats, her voice rising fractionally in building intensity, "we have a top 10 contender in the arena tonight."

The audience makes a variety of "Oohs" and someone excitedly screams at the top of their lungs.

"Just yesterday he made his leap into the top 10. Not only that, he made it into the top 5. The match was hard fought, but he came out on top against Mol. Now, he has made a surprise appearance at the Midland Amphitheater. Please, welcome… Rank 5—FREQUENCY!"

The audience roars, the noise somehow louder than any of the fully seated matches I had attended. They all continue to clap and cheer while taking back their seats in their one section. After ten seconds the announcer speaks again, diminishing the applause.

"You may be asking yourselves why he is here tonight with us, ladies and gentlemen. There can only be one answer, and he is standing on the other side of the arena from Frequency. You've likely heard his name mentioned, I know I have. If you've attended recently, you likely have seen him fight multiple times. He made his debut at this amphitheater the same day Frequency took rank 5—at rank 233. Since then, he has climbed the ranks and sits at rank 88. Progress like that cannot go unnoticed, not even by members of the top 10. Ladies and gentlemen… Not!"

I raise my hand shortly before taking up a stance, keeping my legs spread so that I can quickly move in a direction. Locking eyes with Frequency, I wait for the announcer's call. The cheering continues for several more seconds, unwavering. Then…

"Begin!" the announcer shouts.

Crack.

The noise quells the cheers and the amphitheater is deathly silent. I immediately pinpoint the sound to have come from Frequency, though he hasn't moved. *Crack.* My eyes fall to his right hand. He flexes his middle finger. *Crack.* It's abnormally loud for his knuckles to resonate around the arena like the sound of a whip. *Crack. Crack.*

I'll give you a hint what kind of magician I am. I shudder, looking at Frequency hard. Did he… just plant a thought in my head?

I'm told this is disorienting. No, his lips are moving.

But you should be able to manage. I see. His lips form the same words that seemingly appear in my thoughts. His voice is so quiet it's entering my mind as if it's a thought. But what magic does this?

Here I come. Frequency raises his right arm to flatly point at me. Curling his hand back, he brings his thumb and middle finger together. *Snap.*

The sound begins moderately soft. Then, it amplifies exponentially. The entire amphitheater shakes as if the world itself buckles. It nearly throws me off my feet. I get low, bracing myself against the pressure that comes from Frequency's fingers like an explosion.

All of the audience is covering their ears. I glance overhead to see the tanned hides forming the amphitheater's outer walls billow as if blown by wind. But there is no wind. I finally realize what magic this is. It's Elementalism, and my opponent's name indicates exactly what is being manipulated.

Frequency smiles slightly. It's the first emotion that moves his face. *I've given you enough hints. Now, show me what you can do.* He brings his thumb and middle finger together and snaps again.

Everything—the ground, the amphitheater, the air, and I—shudder violently. I feel the vibrations rattle my bones and my brain and begin to feel nauseous. I clamp down on my body, forcing it into stillness.

As the arena finally stills, Frequency raises his other hand. Swiftly, he brings his hands together and claps once.

Again, the world shakes violently, much more than before. Except for me. When the impossible frequency of the initial noise reaches me, I absorb it. The remaining wavelengths that reverberate from all around me I absorb too. My nose pricks up, fully finding the scent of the magic. It smells like toffee.

Frequency, sensing his magic interrupted, lowers his arms to hang limply by his sides. All of the reverberating sound silences instantly. The contrast is deafening in its own way. *You know I'm an Elementalist* he states, crossing his arms over his chest. *Though I still don't know what you are.*

He's smart. He deduced that the only way his magic could have been interrupted was if I knew what it was, though he did not incorrectly deduce that my own magic was also Elementalism so that it cancelled out his magic. Perhaps he still thinks I could be an Elementalist, though I doubt it. The nature of what I did isn't the same as simply counteracting his soundwaves.

Frequency uncrosses his arms and holds them out before his body as if he's about to give a speech. Instead, he starts to sing.

"Oh… Down in the desert there's a place I go

In times of merry and times of woe

There many gather alike, whatever for?

Why, the finest ale of all Lynnor!"

His bass-y voice booms, creating a pleasant yet loud tune that also causes the amphitheater to shiver. Frequency's foot extends forward, and he begins to pace slowly toward me as he continues to sing.

"It's true, far and wide the land is desolate

But further liquid's tune resonate

Brings back all who know its taste and many more

Yes, the finest ale of all Lynnor!"

I press my hands over my ears, his song deafening to them. The ground and air around me seemingly becomes percussive in reaction. I glimpse that none of the audience are protecting their ears. So Frequency is not only amplifying his voice, he is changing the soundwaves' velocity to bombast only me again and again.

His words become unintelligible, morphing into a nonsensical cacophony around me. There's a minor drop in volume before I start to hear a dull ringing in both my ears. No, the noise around me is the same volume and only getting louder. The receptors in my ears are simply giving out. Even if I continue to manage absorbing the magic he's using, I can't afford to have my senses destroyed.

I yank my sword out of the sheath on my back and make a flurry of swipes through the air around me.

Frequency, about to step within swords-reach, steps back and freezes. My sword hums at several pitches as if someone is running their fingers around the rim of several champagne glasses. Whipping it through the air once more, my sword silences. I bring my elbow back in a ready stance, sword pointing toward Frequency.

Frequency remains unmoving, even no longer singing. Moments pass as the ringing in my ears diminishes and I realize Frequency was trying to talk to me in his unnervingly quiet voice. I tap my ear with my free hand, giving him a helpless shrug.

"Did you cut through my sound?" he asks finally at normal volume.

"More or less," I reply, my own voice sounding odd after that barrage of noise.

His eyes narrow. Kneeling down, he places a hand on the arena floor. Raising his arm an inch for a moment, he slams his palm back down. The stone beneath his palm shatters with a resounding *boom* and he picks up as many of the bits of rubble he can carry in one hand. He stands back up and, surprising even me, he tosses a pebble at me.

The pebble flies behind my guard and bounces ineffectually off my chest. Half a second later I'm thrown off balance, forced backward by the latent sound of the impact being amplified. Regaining balance, I check to see if my chest is bruised. No, I absorbed it all, though the initial impact felt physical, somewhat like the vibrations the body receives from a bass drum. I see. So not only can he use sound to deafen his opponents, he can virtually make physical impact with it if condensed to a small area.

"I see," Frequency says, echoing my thoughts. "You're like an anti-magician."

What a clever guy. He used the element of surprise not to take advantage, but to test the limits of my own power.

"Using my sound all-out on you would be interesting. Though, whether or not you can counteract it all would hardly matter if there's nothing left of the amphitheater."

I tilt my head and smile, catching his word choice to describe my magic. *He still doesn't know.*

"That makes physical attacks your weakness," he goes on. "So I have to land one on you."

I nod at him. "You can try."

Frequency pulls his arm back, readying to release his handful of rubble at me. Before he can, I release all the magic stored up inside me out through the tip of my sword. Frequency's hand releases the rubble, and it makes it several inches through the air toward me before it's obliterated.

The sound erupts from the end of my sword in a cone-like vortex that overwhelms Frequency. His eyes widen momentarily as he is sent flying back from the force off the ground, then screw shut in pain.

Quickly, he brings his hands together in the manner of a spear against the pressure. Immediately he drops out of the air like a stone outside of the arena as he continues to barely protect himself from the rush of noise. A portion of the amphitheater stands behind him are torn asunder, and beyond that the tanned hide of the outer wall shatters like glass. And then it's over.

I sheathe my sword and look for a moment at the gaping hole shrouded in a destructive haze of sand and debris in the otherwise intact amphitheater before shifting my gaze down to Frequency who is huddled in a ball on the sandy floor below the arena platform.

I nimbly run over to check on him. "You okay?"

He doesn't seem to hear me. Or maybe he does, though he makes no reaction other than to continue covering his head with his arms. After a moment, his body relaxes and I see that he's fallen unconscious.

For the first time I notice how neither the audience nor the announcer had made a sound for the duration of the match. Perhaps it had to do with their knowledge of Frequency and any sound they made could interfere with the match. I look over at the audience members, all their mouths agape and eyes wide and staring at me. I slowly wave at them to signal the end of the match.

A few moments later the announcer's voice quietly says, "Ladies and gentlemen… the victor of the match is Not." None of the audience applauds or cheers. In the same reserved voice the announcer continues, "Please make your way to the exits, as the amphitheater will be closing soon."

I can't tell if they're silent in awe or fear, or both, though the audience members rise and begin to leave. I stand and leave Frequency with several of the amphitheater's medical personnel who finally enter the inner arena through the usual entryways and eye the destroyed section of the amphitheater tiredly.

Before I make it halfway around the arena platform to the other end where I first entered, I hear a woman call my name.

"Not!"

I stop and turn around. Stepping out of the hole and waving her hand to clear the air around her I recognize a familiar freckled face.

"Not?" She has grown since the last time I saw her, obviously, and the way she moves is more mature. Still, she has her medium-length brunette hair in a ponytail and wears brown cargo shorts with leggings similar to her appearance in her youth. "Can you hear me, Not?"

"Yes." I move back across the sand to get within normal speaking distance. I see she also has a sword in a sheath on her own back over a plain blue shirt with an ocean pattern.

"Good, I thought Frequency might've made you deaf. Is he all right?" Kelsey turns her head to see him being carried out by the medics, her ponytail waving lightly in the air.

"Yes."

She nods then turns to me. "I first saw some contender named Not when I chanced a glance at the lower rankings, but thought it was only a coincidence. After my match yesterday I noticed the name had moved up tens of ranks and I had to see if it was an imposter or really you."

I'm taken aback by her friendliness in addition to her casual appearance here. I expected the current rank 1 to have bodyguards or be welcomed with fanfare or something.

"I guess I shouldn't have worried, though! I couldn't believe it when I heard that you had made it into the top 100 already and were being challenged by Frequency rank 5. Sad that I missed it," she adds, looking back at the hole in the arena.

"It's good to see you again," I say.

"You too!" she says, looking at me with a slight smile.

"I thought you would still hate me after what I did, like the others."

"No way!" Kelsey says emphatically. "Instructor had his reasons for everything. It's thanks to him I'm here at all."

"Rank 1," I comment. "That's pretty awesome."

"Thanks!"

There's a brief, awkward silence. I break it, saying, "I want to challenge you."   .

Kelsey's eyes widen marginally, though her same slight smile springs back to her face. "That's good. I mean, I was going to challenge you, but I was unsure how to bring it up."

"Huh?" I get distracted by several pairs of footsteps padding over the debris littering the floor by the hole in the amphitheater. Entering the same way Kelsey had are four people, three who look to be a trio of sisters and one who wears a long dark cloak with the hood obscuring the person's face. The person's build is bulkier than Margarine's, and I'm thankful it is not her. "Do you know them?" I ask Kelsey.

The four step into the inner arena and stand in a semicircle around me and Kelsey. "We've come to challenge Not!" one of the women announces.

"Where is he?" the second woman asks pointedly at Kelsey.

"I'd like to challenge him, too," a man's hushed voice emanates from the one with the hood.

"Okay," I say. "But why?"

"You're Not?" the two women say in unison, the third and seemingly youngest silently appraising me.

"And you are?"

"Wrath," the first woman says as if she herself is truly furious.

"Death," the second woman says somberly.

"And Despair," the third woman says meekly.

"What about you?" I ask, turning to look at the hooded man.

"What about me?" Kelsey asks, slightly annoyed. "I was here first, you know."

"I am The Salamander," the hooded man answers.

"Great. Okay, I accept all your challenges, but first I'm fighting her," I say, pointing at Kelsey.

"Why her first?" Death asks.

"She's rank 1!" Wrath says. "You should fight us first!"

"I'm rank 3, so me before them," The Salamander says.

"If I win and get rank 1, then you all will have a chance to beat me and get rank 1 yourselves," I say.

"That's assuming you'll beat me," Kelsey says, affronted.

"Come on," I say, taking her hand quickly and pulling her away. "I want to catch up with you since it's been a while."

Kelsey inhales sharply in surprise and blushes, though nods and allows me to pull her toward the nearest exit before the others can protest.

Chapter 21: Vespertine

It is a wonder to even Vespertine that such a city as Endovir exists in the same world that the antiquated architectural style of Lanmar does. Doubly so, knowing that it is the capital of the country that birthed Lanmar. She thinks this while gazing over the resplendent city, with its numerous onyx stone spires piercing the sky. Their bases faintly resembled Telnas's palace in a blocky fashion, though that is as far as the similarities go. The walls and spires have elegantly curving parapets reaching upward below every window much in the design of wings. Each spire has four windows facing different directions on every level making it seem like they could fly off at any minute. Each stony street weaving between the black buildings and spires all over the city is a gray like storm clouds. Despite their dull color each street is pristine and offsets the deluge of blackness from the buildings. No plant life grows within its limits, though decorative and jagged stone also of onyx reminiscent of trees jut from the pathways adorned with lights. The way the city in its entirety is arranged is elegantly chaotic.

"I've never been here before," Tethris comments uncharacteristically, his tendency being quiet and reserved.

"Why is it you've never traveled outside Lanmar before?" Vespertine asks. Her eyes spot the building she's looking for. In an area of the city where dozens of spires are clustered is the imposing residence of the capital and country at large's ruling body.

"Traveling is a means of escaping," he replies laconically.

Vespertine shifts her soft gaze to him, considering his words. "Even in times of adversity you always were one to find ways of entertaining yourself close to home. Much like me, which is why I asked you to take me here."

"I don't like people."

"Both good reasons," Vespertine says with a slight nod. She looks back at Endovir. Just beyond its northern side is a sandy shoreline that recedes beneath the northern Stirling Sea. The only thing that rivals the city's grandeur is the landscape surrounding it. The cliff they stand on with its gentle incline that rises behind them continues several feet ahead where it sharply drops at the edge. The jagged cliff face runs straight down to the low basin Endovir rests in, and on the other side a similar sheer cliff rises up the better height of Endovir's spires. The only normal means of entering and leaving the city is the southern mountain path between the cliffs and by ship across the northern sealine.

"The imperial palace is there." She guides Tethris with a finger pointing to the imposing building twice the height of the others with the dozens of spires rising from it.

Without a word he takes her arm and they teleport to its front doors. The walkway leading up to the doors is barren without a person in sight.

"This country is run by zealots," Vespertine reminds him. He glances at her with a blank look. A silent reminder to her that he can keep his mouth shut. She hesitates a moment, gathering her thoughts, then pushes against the tall and smooth stone door on the left.

They step inside and pace across the grand hall that runs directly to an array of seats similar to the inner chamber of Telnas palace where the former king and his council deliberated. The main difference is the imperial council of Thalidan had no king so all the seats are equal to each other, side by side facing the entrance. There also are roughly double the number of members making twelve.

Their steps clack lightly along the hard floor that mutedly reflects the light from spidery stone chandeliers overhead. Vespertine breathes in deeply as they approach the twelve members of the council. Finally, they stop and both give a respectful half-bow.

"Imperial Council," Vespertine says lightly. "I appreciate you seeing me."

"It is no bother," a council member, Nedici, says. He imperiously bows his head, his chin lightly brushing the collar of his pale white frock coat. The rest of the council members who wear the same religious garb dip their heads likewise. "But it isn't necessary. We already have contacts whom we can commune through, and we've already agreed with the matter you're here to discuss."

"I wish to finalize other details of our plan so that I may promptly get the tournament underway. We've agreed with what to do with Lanmar, but there is the matter of the eastern kingdom."

"You mean Emerus," another council member says. Several other members mutter under their breath something Vespertine infers to be derisive of the king.

"The Winnowing will make him and his country a non-issue," Nedici says. "All that needs to be done is taking Lanmar, then magician rule will be absolute."

"Yes," Vespertine says haltingly. "However, I must make a compelling arrangement with Emerus so that he'll follow along with our plan."

"Thalidan is a large country," Nedici says. "Promise him a portion of it as an incentive. He would hardly refuse then."

"Simply telling him that won't earn his trust."

"Too true. Your visit, then, has not been a total waste. Give him this." Nedici holds out his hand and a laminated sheet of paper appears in it. "A provision, should we be successful in retaking Lanmar, the eastern kingdom gets the eastern portion of Thalidan, signed by all members of the Imperial Council."

Vespertine steps forward and takes it, giving it a quick glance over before concealing it on her person. "This should do. Thank you very much." She pats it beneath her clothes once and adds, "You don't plan to abide by this provision."

"That is so. Your Concilium is a clever ploy," Nedici muses. "It is fortunate there are those still sympathetic to the teachings of the old gods that remain there. It would be a pity to destroy a second nation of non-magicians."

"A terrible waste," Vespertine agrees, lowering her eyes. "With that business done, I should get this to Emerus."

"So industrious," Nedici says approvingly. "You may stay long enough to at least dine."

"I'm afraid organizing an international magic tournament with only but five others is time-consuming," she says. "I hope, once all is over, we may dine together."

Nedici nods alongside the others. "Very well. May magic guide your way." The last phrase is echoed among the council and Vespertine and Tethris turn and take their leave.

Once outside with the door shut behind them, Vespertine points to the spot on the cliff they had come to before. Tethris teleports them up there and he lets go of her arm. Vespertine lets out a sigh, her body visibly relaxing. Her arms loosen and her shoulders sag a bit. Tethris watches her quietly.

"It's always like you're stepping on eggshells with those people," she says, straightening her back. The gentle sounds of faraway ocean waves waft up to them. "Say one wrong thing about magic and you're on their bad side. What do you think?"

Tethris is silent for a moment. "To the devout, dissent is blasphemy."

Vespertine lets out a short, light laugh. "Well said. You really were the right person to choose to come with me."

He shrugs. "Speaking is often unnecessary."

"But you enjoy it when others talk," she comments.

"When I speak, I'm repeating what I know. Listening tells me more about what I don't know."

"Right. We should get going to Emerus."

"What is The Winnowing?" Tethris asks.

Vespertine remembers she had not given him and the other members of the Concilium all the info about their partnership with Thalidan. "As part of our agreement, Thalidan and Lanmar will merge to be one nation, retaining the former suzerain's name. The Imperial Council also saw it fitting to put their own agenda into motion which they're calling The Winnowing." She pauses, tilting her head at Tethris. "Thalidan is a deeply religious nation that reveres magic."

"So I've read," he says.

"They value magicians above all others. That is why they are planning The Winnowing."

Tethris thinks it over. "Before they had said it would be a pity for a second nation to be destroyed. After the tournament they plan on destroying Emerus's kingdom?"

"It is known that the indigenous population of Vichaelis is made up largely of non-magicians. King Emerus isn't a magician as well. The recent death of James was likely seen as a divine signal for Thalidan's people to make a move."

Understanding dawns on Tethris and his eyes narrow. "The Winnowing is referring to the mass killing of non-magicians, not just the destruction of Vichaelis."

"I didn't want to mention it, but yes."

"You should disclose these details to the rest of the Concilium."

"Ironic coming from you," Vespertine says, then sighs again. "I don't want them to worry," Vespertine says, waving him off. "Telling them of a genocidal plot similar to that of the Giants years ago when we're so close to our own plan succeeding would only cause unnecessary concern."

"I can't help but be concerned. What happened with the Giants was what created the Concilium in the first place."

Vespertine nods. "I know. I—We, aren't going to go along with their plan. Look," she says, pointing to the Stirling Sea. "Already the water has changed. With the vesper, we'll be able to stop them from causing the death of thousands."

"I don't see any difference."

"It's there," Vespertine says confidently. "We've waited long enough. The time is coming close when everyone will have some level of vesper in their body."

Tethris puts the back of his hand on his hip and eases most of his weight to his left leg. "Whatever happens now, it's the only way to stop Thalidan."

"Yes," Vespertine says. "Now, let's go. To Emerus."

Chapter 22: Not

"Not many places to go around here, huh?"

"It is a desert," Kelsey says.

I walk around where she sits facing the expanding sands stretching far and away. The Midland Amphitheater, while dreadfully unfurnished, has a scarce wooden pavilion on the southwest side with four meager round tables each accompanied with a set of three chairs without backs. I take the seat beside Kelsey and gingerly set two large ale mugs down. The table is just large enough to fit a third mug, the management sparing all expenses to serve at most three per table.

"I don't drink," Kelsey says, eyeing the mug closest to her which contains the deep ochre of Midnight Delight.

"Me neither," I say, swapping the mugs so that the Midnight Delight is nearest me. In response to her questioning stare I say, "I'm only interested in alcohol."

"What does that mean?" she asks, cradling the mug of water I swapped over up to her lips and taking a tentative sip.

I procure a handful of crushed herbs from one of the brown pouches on my hip and, pinching some between my other hand's thumb and index finger, I sprinkle bits of the herbs into the Midnight Delight. "Its effects, such as inhibiting reasoning and causing drowsiness, interest me."

Kelsey's shoulders heave as she suppresses laughter, quickly swallowing so as not to choke on her water. "So you're not only a swordsman but you're also a chemist?"

"I'm neither," I reply, sprinkling a touch more into my drink before stuffing the remaining herbs back into my pouch. "I'm just a guy with a sword and some ingredients."

Kelsey's eyes shift, their corners no longer crinkled from laughter. "I talked with Tang. He said your sword is actually Instructor?"

"Yeah," I say.

She nods, taking another sip from her drink while her eyes nervously shift to mine then away repeatedly. "You know, I don't really know what that means."

"Well, it's pretty simple really," I say. "Instructor is my sword."

"Right," Kelsey says slowly, her eyes still shifting back and forth. "But how?"

"It just kind of happened. Is something wrong?"

"What?"

"You keep looking away."

"Oh. I was remembering how I never talked to you."

"That doesn't matter. I never talked to you either."

"But I wanted to talk to you."

I recall what Tang said about Kelsey liking me and I internally swear at myself. "Well, I hope you still do, because we're about to do a whole lot of talking." I see her cheeks redden marginally as she smiles. Then I regale her with the story of my journey from leaving with Instructor as my sword, to doing small-time looting, to meeting Idrid, and finally to what brought me here.

"It sounds like you're leaving out a lot," Kelsey comments once I'm done.

"You really do want to talk to me," I nod with a smile. "Most everyone wants me to shut up once I start talking."

"The others did get annoyed when you talked about yourself. It seemed like you were boasting."

"I never boasted! I just congratulated myself."

"To the others it was boasting."

"People should learn to appreciate their accomplishments."

"I think they do, they just do it more quietly."

I don't respond, gently shaking my mug around to swirl the liquid within to better mix the herbs in.

"I'm not saying you should stop," she says quickly. "I know you're not being egotistical."

It's my turn to stifle my laughter lest I fall out of my seat. "I didn't know you were so blunt."

"Er, well—"

"I like honesty," I say. "Anyway, you're right I left one or sixteen things out, but that's too long-winded even for me. What have you been up to?"

Kelsey blinks, thinking. "It's not that exciting. I stayed in Lynnor, practicing what Instructor taught each of us. Everyone else left shortly after the 7 days expired. Tang left first, pretty much immediately, followed by Lauren, both going north to Lanmar. Rodrigue and Saffrin went east to Vichaelis to work in the guard."

"I suppose it'll take too much time to find them," I mutter. Then I say, "It must've been lonely."

"Not really. Once I felt confident in myself I joined the ranks here and got acquainted with a lot of people."

"How long did it take to get to rank 1?"

"A couple years. It was kind of a shock when I got it, so I took a break for a while."

"That's impressive," I say. "You'd have been... what, a teenager?"

"Fourteen."

"That's a lot of years to be rank 1."

"I didn't stay rank 1 while I was gone. And when I came back to reclaim rank 1 I lost it several times."

"How'd you lose?" I ask.

"I either forfeited the match or didn't show up."

"So technically you're undefeated."

"I was defeated plenty of times while climbing the ranks, unlike you."

"I lost back in the day, too," I say, internally congratulating myself for my modesty.

Kelsey smiles and looks away again. "Are we being competitive about how many times we've lost?"

"Damn right we are. 27."

"30. I win."

"Crap in a bucket," I say. "Wait, if I lose to you and ranks 2 and 3 we'll be tied."

"Are you saying you'll lose to me?"

"No, I'm saying if I lose I can still win if I forfeit another match."

"You want to win at losing?"

"But if I win the match with you I'll lose," I continue, letting go of my mug to stroke my chin. I feel lengthy stubble pricking my fingers, signaling it is getting near the time for a shave.

"Either way, you'll win," Kelsey says, considering this just as deeply as I am.

"But I'll lose either way, too. It's a matter of what I'm wanting to win and lose."

"I didn't know you were so philosophical."

"I might be if I were talking about literally anything other than winning for the sake of winning."

Kelsey smiles, sitting back as far as she can without falling backward. "Even though you spout your achievements you just as easily tell your failures. That's what I remember best about you."

I feel a hint of guilt knowing that she must've paid a lot of attention to me while I paid her no mind. I'll have to make up for it now. "Would you like to try some?" I ask, sitting forward and offering my mug. She looks at me funnily then turns serious and starts to reach a hand over.

"I'm joking, you don't want to try this," I say quickly.

"Why? What'll it do?"

"Probably knock you out."

"Holy— What do you use it for?" Her eyebrows arc low over her eyes which reflect the dim overhead starlight.

"Thievery," I say.

"That's kind of wrong."

"You didn't seem to mind when I told you I killed the king of Lanmar."

"Yeah, well, that's more complicated. And also old news."

"Old n—!? What's new news then?"

"The Magic Tournament being held soon," Kelsey says. "It's coming up."

"Well," I say, stretching the "e" out for a good second. "How'd you like to join me in the tournament?"

Kelsey nods. "I was going to join anyway. Why, though?"

"Bad stuff is going down and it'll likely be at the epicenter of this tournament."

"You mean the Concilium? Tang told me about them as well. They seem like a group of wimps."

"Wimps that manipulate your mind are dangerous," I say.

Kelsey gives a meaningful look at the altered drink in my hands.

I raise a hand and shake it. "First of all, I'm not a wimp."

"That's not—" Kelsey begins.

"Secondly," I say authoritatively, "It's different since it's organic."

"Mmhmm," is all she responds with.

"All right, Miss Judge-y, I'm very particular with who I steal from."

"Is it a sense of righteousness driving your rationale? 'Cause I think the Concilium have a similar mindset."

"I've never thought anything of what I do as being right," I say. "That stuff is all arbitrary anyway."

"Is it?" Kelsey asks.

"Stick a hundred people in a room who all agree about something, there'll always be someone else somewhere else who doesn't. Heck, wait a couple years and stick the same hundred people in a room and they'll likely no longer agree."

"I'd think a hundred people would have an opinion that benefits more than any one person," Kelsey says.

"Do you really think that? I'm not saying people shouldn't attempt to create some sort of order based on morals. I'm just not convinced anyone else, no matter how many of them there are, know what's best for me."

Kelsey thinks for a bit. "We've slipped back into philosophical talk." She sips some more of her water, then says, "Perhaps you're right that it's not necessarily good for everyone if the majority makes the decisions. Or that a minority, like the Concilium, tries to do the same."

"Mmm," I say thoughtfully. "Behold the conundrum of politics."

"I still don't agree with drugging people."

I sigh. "It beats brute force."

"You got me there," Kelsey says, letting out a clear laugh. "But why?

I gaze at her. "Why what?

"Why are you wrapping yourself up in all this? It was originally because of your decision to leave politics behind that we met."

I consider this, tapping my fingers along the rim of my mug.

"Are you trying to do the right thing?"

Grinning, I shake my head. "You really did pay attention to what I said back in the day."

"Or you were really loud and made it impossible not to."

"Do you think that's what I'm doing?" My smile drops and my hands freeze, pressing into the side of my mug.

Her eyes flick to my hands, noticing my sudden tenseness. "I don't know. Tang said you were looking for the best fights."

"Well, knowing what I do now about Ja—my brother, I sort of feel like I have to."

"You mean him being mind-controlled?"

I don't answer. Somewhere in the darkness in the desert a lonely mewl echoes. "Will you help me? With the Concilium, I mean."

Kelsey's eyebrows lower, her eyes looking far off. "I will… if you can win. Are you really ready for tomorrow?" she then asks, her eyes steadily watching me for the first time.

"Fighting you?"

"Yeah. I mean, I heard you lost to Tang."

"Pfft," I say, though don't deny it. "He surprised me and got me to cut one of his arteries."

"It really is fifty-fifty with him," Kelsey acknowledges. "Sometimes he beats you, sometimes he passes out before he can."

"What about you? Are you ready for tomorrow?"

"You're a one-trick pony, Not," Kelsey teases. "While Instructor taught each of us unique abilities, I also took the time to study the other students' including yours. I think I've got this in the bag."

"Not fair," I say. "I don't even know what Instructor taught you."

"You'll have to wait and find out," she says.

Ten hours later I roll around the arena, keeping low as I dodge a flurry of punches from Kelsey who nimbly follows after me. "I think I've waited long enough," I say, panting slightly. I stop firmly in a crouch and bring the flat side of my sword out to deflect a punch.

"You're not giving your all either," Kelsey replies. She drops to the ground, using her arms to prop herself up, and kicks out at my chest.

I leap a couple feet off the ground and over her extending legs. On my descent I kick her legs away and she spins into an upright position. I land and also stand. We face each other and I take the moment to do some thinking. She doesn't carry a weapon, at least none that I've noticed. Yesterday she had been wearing a sword on her back which was odd. From the brief memories I have of the days with Instructor she never carried a weapon either. There's nowhere apparent she can conceal one as she wears pocketless shorts and a simple, breezy shirt that is a tainted off-color orange. While I specialize in swordplay, she seems to specialize in using her body as a weapon. This puts her at a noticeable disadvantage, hence why I haven't unfairly cut her. "If we keep this up, we'll be going for days," I tell her.

"Give me your best shot," she challenges me. She lifts her front leg to balance on the other, moving her fists close to her chest.

I try to infer what her magical ability is from what I know of her. My mind comes up with nothing, save from what I know of Tang's ability. I don't want to make the same blunder and deliver a serious injury that then makes her inordinately powerful. Or worse, simply cause a serious injury. On the other hand, I could use my ability and simply drain her energy with a tap of my sword or my skin. She's already trying to make this a close fight so it wouldn't be hard to touch her once. That, however, would also be rather unfair.

"If you don't use your ability, you won't win," Kelsey says, reading my thoughts.

She *is* rank 1, I think. She couldn't have made it this far without sustaining blows from the best of the best. Though she apparently wants me to get serious, which indicates a trap.

That leaves the safest option for the both of us, then. I lunge forward, pushing my sword out beside the leg she stands on. At this distance her only way to reach me is by kicking out with her other leg. Even then, I could take the hit while her back leg will inevitably be cut.

As anticipated, her front leg kicks out and hits my extended arm, but not fast enough. I see my blade sink just enough into her back leg before it is kicked away. I take a step back, shaking the aching away in my arm and appraise the minor damage I've done.

Kelsey remains standing on her back leg as if she felt nothing, her front leg curling in again ready to strike out the same as before. I see the spot where I nicked her leg and notice nothing is there except smooth skin.

"I didn't cut you?" I ask, wondering if I had actually missed.

"Nope," Kelsey says lightly. "Try again."

Tilting my head, I oblige. I feign a lunge just enough to get the responding kick from Kelsey. I twist my body out of the way of the kick and maneuver my sword to pierce the lower part of her shin. Yet again, when I draw my sword away I see my sword has no red on it, and her shin is uncut. "My sword is going through you," I say, confounded.

"There you go," Kelsey says. "You've figured it out."

"I don't think I have." What kind of magic does this? I'm only familiar with Elementalism, Conjuring, and brief encounters with Spatial teleporting like Darren's. *Well, regardless of what kind of magic it is, if I can't physically touch her, what can I do?*

Kelsey leaps with surprising speed, using hidden strength from her back leg, and speeds through the air at me.

I instinctively bring my sword up to deter her movement, though she follows through with her right hand. My sword passes cleanly through her torso, sticking upward out of her back. I only have a moment to look dumbly at the sight before her fist hits the side of my face and I am knocked down.

She jumps just out of range and gives me a small smile. I lift myself onto my knees and touch my cheek, wincing. "Ow." Kelsey gives me a "what-can-you-do?" shrug and begins to bounce side to side on her feet.

Shaking my head, I stab my sword into the arena floor. It slides into the rock smoothly, just a foot of the blade sticking out along with the handle at an angle. I let go of it and rise to my feet, dusting off the area of my pants over the knees.

"If that's how it is," I mutter, bringing my own fists up.

Kelsey continues to silently bounce on her feet, enjoying herself as I approach. She doesn't move to block my swing, instead giving a swing of her own fist. My fist passes through the side of her ribs while hers connects with my solar plexus.

The blow is enough to cause me to stagger again, though I'm able to stay on my feet and pirouette around her. She casually turns around, still bouncing.

Right, she has no need to block anything that won't hit her I think. I reevaluate what I can do, thinking quickly. Each time I've "hit" her she's hit me. That means her entire body isn't untouchable, at least when she's wanting to hit me.

I move in close again, swinging with my right fist. She doesn't move to block, again swinging her own fist. This time I don't focus my strength in my right fist and instead focus it on my left hand, which reaches up to knock her swing away. My right fist doesn't hit anything while my left does. She misses, and I take a moment to mentally congratulate myself when I'm once again hit by her other hand, this time in the stomach.

Kelsey, keeping close, sends out a flurry of punches. I block several of them, but soon enough the pattern is interrupted when one of her punches goes right through my arm and her next punch connects with my upper torso. If I stay close she'll simply batter me the same way, so I quickly leap backward, my heels teetering off the edge of the arena's platform. Regaining balance, I run around the arena's perimeter with her in hot pursuit. I'm only able to keep enough distance to not engage, though eventually I'll have to. Before then, I must do some more quick thinking.

She's landed five hits on me, meaning she can win with another five. No matter how I'm able to block her when she starts throwing punches, she can just as easily break the flow and get me off balance to land a hit. All the while, I'll be unable to land a hit myself since I have to be on the defensive. My best option is to get her to use her mysterious ability on one part of her body so that I can touch another part. I'll never have the advantage when she's on the offensive since I cannot react fast enough when a fist or leg passes through me. Which means I'll have to forget about defending myself and just attack.

I run past my sword sticking up out of the arena and get an idea. I turn around, sliding to a halt and face Kelsey suddenly. She skids to slow herself, though keeps her momentum, apparently prepared to continue throwing punches. I ignore whatever attack she is about to do and put all my strength into both of my fists, punching them both out at the same time at different heights. My left fist goes for her face while my right goes for her stomach.

I brace myself for whatever fate the rest of my body will endure, only hoping that one of my fists connects. It is my right fist that makes contact while my left passes through her face, and I feel the full weight of Kelsey's body collide with it. It's strong enough that she bounces back, all her momentum rebounding the other direction as she falls backward.

I look worriedly at Kelsey's face though see I didn't totally knock the wind out of her. She quickly turns her head, her eye catching that with her trajectory she'll land on the hilt of my sword sticking out of the arena.

She lands on her back, sword hilt passing harmlessly through her upper torso near her heart. The sight is deceitfully morbid. Before she can get to her feet, I rush over and plant a foot on her stomach to hold her down. I kneel, getting close to her face. She looks at me defiantly, eyes furious, though the corners of her mouth twitch up.

Smiling myself, I flick her forehead.

"Ow!" she says.

"That's for punching my face," I tell her. She glares at me, then her eyes soften and she nods. Standing, I lift my foot and remove my sword out of the arena and out of Kelsey.

She stands a moment later and the announcer screams, "LADIES AND GENTLEMEN WE HAVE A NEW CONTENDER FOR RANK 1: NOT!!!!!"

Kelsey stands up momentarily, brushing the back of her clothes free of dust. "How clever of you," she comments.

"I still don't understand what kind of magic it is you're using."

"It's Void magic," she says. "The rarer subfield of Spatial magic. You have no idea how difficult it was to master without hurting myself."

"I don't," I agree.

"NOT!" It's Wrath screaming from rank 2's Wrath, Death, and Despair. They each leave the stands and move to stand beside the arena. "You still have us to face!"

"I know!" I tell the three women. "Just… give me a break."

"THAT'S RIGHT, FOLKS!" the announcer shrieks. "NOT, NOW RANK 1, MUST NOW DEFEND HIS PLACE AGAINST RANKS 2 AND 3!"

"Is that today too?" I ask, still breathing heavily. "I forget."

"You're the one who accepted all our challenges," Kelsey replies. "When you're done, find me at the pavilion again and we can talk about what to do next about the Concilium. I'll get Tang there, too."

"Gah," I mutter as Kelsey jumps off the platform and exits the arena while Wrath, Death, and Despair replace her. "I'll make this quick."

Torion Oey

Chapter 23: Vespertine

The kingdom of Vichaelis is starkly different from the theocracy of Thalidan both in culture and geography. Navigating the mountainous northern country is an ever-precarious challenge whose only comfort is that regular temperatures are above freezing and snow is uncommon. The eastern kingdom, on the other hand, consists of flatlands and intermittent low hills that are easily traversed. Much like Lanmar, it is the home of many fine breeds of horses, a decent few indigenous and unique and subsequently much beloved by its people.

Tethris, a steady hand on Vespertine's shoulder, teleports the two across the warm gold-brown plains, following the road stretching onward toward the kingdom's capital. The woman eyes several large horses wandering in groups, most palominos whose colors match that of the plains. Some of the unique breeds Vespertine lacks a name for are nearly twice the size of Lanmar's horses. She turns her attention to the city ahead that rapidly enlarges itself in flashes as the two get closer. "We can walk to the throne room at the entrance," she tells Tethris.

Two more teleports and they arrive where the first buildings crop up. There are no walls to the city, the only indication of an entrance being the road leading into it. The buildings are far more traditional than the futuristic onyx buildings of Thalidan; plain, finely thatched roofs adorn plastered salmon-colored terracotta walls. The buildings are few and far between, leaving plenty of space for the trampled roads, though each's height and size can qualify as a tavern. The doorways are also large and doorless, providing enough space for even the larger horses wandering the surrounding plains to fit through which is likely the purpose of their design. Wooden shutters serve as window panes, allowing easier maneuverability than glass to open and close. Vichaelis, while slightly dry, has tropical weather thanks to the numerous rivers flowing from the northern mountains as well as several prominent oases, some of which are natural and some of which are human-cultivated. Its capital, through ingenuity in the science of valves, carries water from underground up to the surface. Along the streets Vespertine and Tethris walk are intricate sandstone waterways that allow the water to continuously flow, eventually returning underground only to be carried up again in the similar fashion of a fountain. Denizens stroll the streets, many of them leading horses who occasionally stop to drink from the flowing canals.

Tethris remains silent and Vespertine takes out the signed form by Thalidan's leaders detailing the arrangement between the three countries of Vichaelis, Lanmar, and Thalidan. She will write her name down beside the others' in Emerus's presence as a show of good faith and leave the document in his hands. Hopefully she can get this matter settled in good time.

They follow the street onward. Townspeople glance their way several times, noting the two's velvety red cloaks sweeping close to the packed earth. A building marginally grander than the others made entirely of sandstone rests atop several stone steps. Large archways provide multiple passages in and out. The central archway is bordered by a waterway on either side that flows down from within.

"Let's make this quick," Vespertine mutters only for Tethris to hear. They climb the few stairs and pass under the arch. She pauses to allow her eyes to adjust to the dimmer interior, the only source of light being provided from the sun outside. Shadows lining the parallel walls morph into the figures of guards, each outfitted with light chainmail and a tall spear in one hand. The guards remain unmoving, though she can feel their eyes watching her as she continues toward the sandstone throne set at the center of the room. The waterways converge somewhere behind the throne. Sitting on the throne, head propped up by an elbow on the armrest, is Emerus himself. She briefly met him once before alongside Lanmar's former king, James's father. Wearing a rugged brown tunic torn short at the shoulders and leather leggings, she recognizes his piercing hazel eyes set within the ragged features of a man who looks to have partaken in combat too many times in one life. Despite the wear and tear of his leathery face, it retains a sort of handsome smoothness gotten from good genetics. His fingers twist and tangle through his bushy golden-red beard that trails down about a foot in length from his cheeks. He says nothing, though his mouth quirks upward at their approach and his eyes bore into hers.

"King Emerus," Vespertine says in a hushed voice, stopping before the throne and bowing slightly. Tethris mimics the formality beside her.

"What have you got in your hand?" Emerus says. His voice is brighter than his appearance suggests, the tone similar to that of an aspiring youth joining the guard.

Quick to business Vespertine thinks in relief. "Provisions for your aid," Vespertine replies. "Shall I read them, or would you rather?"

"No matter," he says, rising suddenly and stepping down from the throne. His lengthy golden hair falls above his back and around his face, waving with his movement. He stops in front of her and holds out his hand. Vespertine, taken aback slightly, hands over the document. She looks up at his large and tall form reaching about a foot and a half over her. He takes the form gently without looking at it and returns to sit on the throne, placing it on an armrest.

"Finalization for the big event, then?" he asks.

"Yes," Vespertine says. "I'll need to sign it as well," she adds.

"No need. I recognize you as the interim ruler of Lanmar, however Thalidan does not."

Vespertine blinks. "I'm sorry?"

Emerus places his elbow on the armrest again, now atop the document, and strokes his beard. "This form is created by the Imperial Council, no? A signature from you, however honorable, would be ineffectual on such papers."

Vespertine breathes in slightly. "I assure you, the Imperial Council—"

"Treat nothing but their gods as sacrosanct," Emerus interrupts. "I don't know you well, Vespertine. But I can give you the benefit of the doubt. They, on the other hand, I cannot."

"Why agree to aid us in the first place?" she asks, managing to keep her facial muscles relaxed.

"If I refused, where would that put my country, between the conquests of Thalidan and the unchecked civil atmosphere of Lanmar?" Emerus poses. "You and I both know relations between magicians and non-magicians are tense."

"I'm working to create a rule of equality," Vespertine replies.

Emerus gazes at her for a long moment, his hand pausing in the strands of his beard. "You were among the few who opposed the eradication of Giants," he says suddenly. "I have reliable sources," he adds, answering the questioning look on her face. "It is why I'm worried for the future. You've been busy on the inner workings of Lanmar's governance, though while commendable you may have overlooked the stirring in its people's hearts. They are afraid, both magicians and non-magicians."

"I can only do so much," Vespertine says calmly. "Which is why I need you."

Emerus nods slowly. "The wise are aware of their limits while the fools believe they have none. I've agreed to help you and, by extension, Thalidan in stamping out unrest wherever it may be within Lanmar. If all goes well, relations will flourish like they never have before."

Vespertine nods her agreement, lowering her eyes momentarily, though her gaze flicks back up quickly.

He smiles broadly, catching her unease, and waves a hand outward. "Yes, that is a mighty big 'if.' But we, or at least I, am not one for dealing in prophetical hypotheticals." He blithely chuckles to himself. "All I'm sure of is I trust what you've said and I share your goal. Therefore, I will take you at your word. Not on Thalidan's word—yours. Let's leave it at that."

Vespertine smiles back and bows. "Thank you, Emerus. I will see to it that war does not befall any of our countries." Her eyes fall to the document under his elbow. "Shall I take that back, then?"

"No," Emerus says thoughtfully, picking it up and looking at it for the first time. "I think I'll hold onto it. Even if it's worthless to the Imperial Council, I doubt there are many papers out there with all of their signatures."

"Of course," Vespertine says. "I'm afraid, if there's nothing more you require, I must prepare for the tournament. Thank you," she adds genuinely, holding his gaze. She bows again then turns and exits, Tethris following alongside her.

Emerus returns the signed document to his armrest and rests his head on his hand. The two magicians retreat out of sight soon enough. He tilts his head in a nod and the guards lining the walls move in unison to the center of the room, stepping over the waterways, and face him in two single-file lines all the way from just before his throne to the door.

He looks at them each in turn, thinking things over. "Rodrigue," he says finally, the guard at the head of the line on his left stiffening in response.

"Yes?"

"You will lead a handful of the guard into Lanmar. Remain covert and make your way to the tournament grounds. You will get in touch with Vespertine and follow any orders she gives you."

"Understood," Rodrigue affirms, lifting his spear and letting it clang on the stone floor.

"Only bring magicians," Emerus adds.

Rodrigue, half-turned in the process of picking out guard members, faces front. "There are only seven of us in the kingdom," he states.

"Like I said, you're leading a handful. It would be a death sentence if I sent anyone else, since you will eventually face Thalidan's forces. Also, I can't emphasize this enough, remain covert. While you will be following Vespertine's orders, she does not need to know there are only seven of you."

Rodrigue nods, clanging his spear on the floor once, then moves between the lines of guards and tapping them on the shoulder to gather around him.

Emerus sits back and looks down at the document lying on his armrest. "The Imperial Council of Thalidan has written here that Vichaelis shall be granted land for aiding the conquering of Lanmar," he announces. "On Thalidan's end, they will move forces across the Stirling and along Lanmar's coast in preparation. On Vichaelis's end, we will move forces along the eastern border by the Talwood. That is what we've previously agreed to and what is written here. Instead, only a few will work to conquer Lanmar while our main forces will go north and press into Thalidan's territory."

The guards clang their spears in unison once.

"This is, plainly, an act of war," he continues. "However, the Imperial Council no doubt has other ideas. For all we know, they are moving forces to press into our territory. That would be the worst case, but we will nonetheless be prepared to meet them at our border."

"An even worse case is that Vespertine and Thalidan join forces," Saffrin, one of the magician guards who Rodrigue taps, says.

"True, that would be worse."

"You distrust her intent?" she asks.

"On the contrary, she is probably the only one among us acting for the benefit of everyone."

"To what end are we acting?"

"Survival," Emerus says.

Torion Oey

Chapter 24: Not

A dull metal twang vibrates along the flat edge of my sword as it taps the top of Death's head. The woman, last of the sisters making up rank 2, collapses unconscious on the arena floor.

"Remarkable, ladies and gentlemen!" the announcer shouts. "After a close match with Kelsey, the first we've seen of Not on the ropes, he in no time takes care of Wrath, Death, and Despair to defend his rank at the top! What is his secret? What sort of magic is he using?"

I sheathe my sword and sit at the edge of the platform, crossing my legs beneath me. I wipe at the residual sweat left over from my fight with Kelsey with the collar of my shirt. Wrath, Death, and Despair had been good opponents, each of them specializing in specific branches of Elementalism (air, earth, and water respectively), though once I tapped the first sister of all her magic their teamwork crumbled.

The announcer continues to talk while medics gather the unconscious bodies of Wrath, Death, and Despair. "Whatever kind of magician he is, he still has one challenge left today, folks! Now stepping into the arena, rank 3: The Salamander!"

I watch the robed man walk through the dim hallway and into the arena, passing the medics carrying Wrath, Death, and Despair on their way out. He steps onto the square platform and stands still, the obscured face beneath the hood turned toward me. *One more* I tell myself.

"Without further ado, let the match begin!"

A strange cracking sound rifles the arena, the surrounding audience shifting in reaction. It is reminiscent of Frequency cracking his bones, though the sound comes from The Salamander. All at once the shapes of spikes prod outward beneath his robes, ripping the fabric. They grow, the sound apparently coming from the spikes hitting and scraping each other, and the robes are torn as the shape of what was the man becomes another creature entirely. Each spike widens, taking on the mixed appearance of a snake's scales and a porcupine's needles. They protrude across the back of the creature as its body enlarges, growing to a size that occupies an entire corner of the arena platform. What were his arms are now legs that the creature uses to ease its upper half down to the floor, distributing its weight equally. The smoother, unlayered scales of the body mesh together under the spiky shell making up the creature's back. Where the shell covers the creature's head are two gaping holes where eyes should be, but they're empty. Under that is its mouth, toothless but its gaping jaws appear razor sharp and enough to snap a large boulder into pieces.

I raise myself warily, watching the creature. I have never seen a shapeshifter before, but the magic is unmistakable. Getting the privilege of fighting one who can take the form of an actual salamander entices me to draw my sword and prepare for a longer fight. That is, until I remember that I am on a time crunch and should get back to Tang and Kelsey quickly.

Within the holes in The Salamander's spiky shell a brilliant fire ignites, its flames emanating out and illuminating dark spots that are the creature's pupils. The flames lick between the various cracks of the shell's pointy scales. Within the gaping mouth even more fire emerges, spilling out and slowly dispersing over the arena floor. Beating a giant creature wreathed in flames like this normally would be incredibly difficult. But, since the form is magic-based…

I wait for the moment the flames from The Salamander's mouth cease when he has to inevitably intake air. In that moment I strike: I dart forward, body tilted forward to speed my progress, sword stretching out toward the mouth. In a flash, the metal of my sword *tings* against The Salamander's underjaw. In half the time it took for The Salamander to transform he returns to his human form, unconsciously lying on the floor and the remaining tatters of his robes not quite covering the indecent parts of his body.

The crowd erupts into cheers and boos alike. I ignore them, along with whatever inspiring narration the announcer shouts, and jog off the arena floor and out the inner amphitheater's exit. Returning my sword to my sheath on my back, I make my way out of the outer amphitheater and toward the pavilion where Tang and Kelsey are sitting at the same table I'd sat at the previous night.

"Not," Tang says when I arrive and take the remaining chair. "You're not dead. Shame."

"You'd miss him as a rival," Kelsey says, giving me a friendly smile. "How'd your other matches go?"

"You tapped them of their magic, you cheater." Tang swats the hilt of my sword poking over my back. "That's not what you said Instructor wanted you to use him for."

"It was clean," I say, defending myself. "No muss, no fuss, as they say."

"You absorbed all of their magic?" Kelsey asks curiously. "I was aware you could do that, though the amount I sense stored within your sword is enormous. How much did you take?"

"Enough to make them sleep," I tell her.

She gapes at me. "How much *can* you take?"

"I haven't found a limit quite yet," I say seriously. "Though, my sword is buzzing a lot, isn't it? I'll have to release some later."

"You're saying you could've done that to me at any time during our match?"

"That would've been disrespectful."

Kelsey, flustered, flicks her ponytail to fall over her left shoulder. "Ugh. And I thought I had the advantage."

"There's an easy way to counter my magic absorption Instructor taught us," I tell her.

"Yeah? How?"

"Make your magic inaccessible to me," I say simply. "In other words, don't use magic."

"Can we discuss battle tactics some other time?" Tang interrupts. "Are you done with the amphitheaters now?"

"We've got Kelsey," I say. "So, yeah."

"Great. We can go back to Lanmar now and leave this wretched desert." Tang stands, the back of his legs sliding his chair away. "Come on."

I look up at him slowly. "You know, I was just in three fights. I could use a break. Why are you so eager, anyway?"

"Isn't it obvious? The Concilium, of course."

"Well, yeah. You know, I never asked you why they mattered to you."

"They… one of them, anyway, tried to recruit me."

Leaning forward, I ask, "Who?"

"The woman you say leads them. Vespertine."

I slap my hands on the table. "You didn't think to mention that before? Never mind. When was this?"

"Just before you went and killed the king."

"Oh. So that's why Idrid found you in the capital."

"She's the Giant, right?" Kelsey asks.

"Half-Giant," I correct before turning back to Tang. "What did Vespertine say to you?"

"I forget."

I stare at him for a long moment. "Seriously?"

"Yeah."

"Then why do you care?"

"Because she tried to control me after I refused. I had to cut myself on my own sword and bolt before she did."

I tut, sitting back. "So she knows your power."

"All she can know is speculation."

"Why didn't you overpower her?"

"1: it was a public space. 2: she tried to recruit me before I used any magic, so she already knew something about me and *still* risked controlling me. She's either suicidal or more dangerous than me, and I didn't take her for a fool."

I pause and consider it. "She must know how to discern people's orenda like Instructor taught us."

A brief silence settles over us before Kelsey asks, "Why did you refuse her?"

Tang grimaces. "I remember her mentioning the royal family, which I want nothing to do with." He eyes me angrily.

"I have nothing to do with them, remember? I ran away."

"You're still one of them."

I narrow my eyes and raise a hand toward my blade. "I think I've got enough energy for another fight."

"Hold on," Kelsey quickly says, "that'll only end with one or both of you bleeding to death."

"Doesn't sound so bad," Tang mutters.

"Forget it! Let's wait for the sun to set. It'll be cold, but better than running across the desert midday."

"Fine." Tang returns to his seat, cupping his chin in his hands above the table.

"What were you two talking about while I was fighting, then?" I ask, letting my hand fall and relax. Tang remains silent, avoiding eye contact.

"Oh!" Kelsey says, lightly smiling. "Uh, catching up! And, uh, also the Concilium. We'll need to be prepared to counter Mind Control."

"From what I know," Tang speaks up, "you can't be forced to do something you truly don't want to do. The thing is, there are ways of tricking the mind to get around such barriers."

"So our best bet is subduing anyone who can use Mind Control before they have a chance to," I say. "But we won't know who they are until they use it. That is a dilemma."

Tang and Kelsey look at me. I look back at them. Blinking, I understand their silence. "Right! I'm immune, so I can be the decoy and identify who is a member of the Concilium if they use their magic on me. Good thinking."

"That leaves us kind of pointless, doesn't it?" Kelsey says.

"Not necessarily. They don't know who you are the same way we don't know who they are. They know me, which works in our favor since that makes me more of a target."

"I like that," Tang says, his lengthy hair blowing gently in a light breeze.

"We'll be participating in the tournament, too," Kelsey says sternly. "Even if it makes me a target."

"I won't sit it out, either," Tang agrees. "If nothing happens, at least I'll have a chance to beat you."

"You'd have a harder time beating Kelsey," I tell him.

"I want to beat you," he says stubbornly.

"Whatever. That's all settled, then."

"Not quite," Margarine chimes in, her cloaked form stepping up and overshadowing the table between us.

Crap. "Why, hello again, Margarine!" I say with a buttery affection that could cause an entire army to throw up. "Pull up a seat, kick back enough to fall off!"

"Who's this?" Kelsey asks calmly, though her wincing face betrays the disdain for my tone of voice.

"I've come to collect on that long-ago gamble," Margarine says.

I drop the friendliness and motion to a passing coordinator encircling the outside of the Midland Amphitheater. I'd noticed there being at least one hovering around monitoring me after my fight with Frequency. The coordinator sharply changes course and steps up expectantly. "About my earnings for today—"

"Staff are preparing it as we speak, contender Not," the coordinator says quickly. "We ask that you be patient, as the back-to-back bouts have—"

I wave my hand. "I'm in no hurry. But, I'd like to make a request regarding those earnings." I point a thumb at Margarine and say, "Could you allocate it all to this strapping specimen of sultry sourdough?"

The coordinator raises his eyebrows while Tang draws Kelsey's sword, Kelsey's winces becomes spasms, and Margarine moves as if to strangle me.

"How much is all of it?" I ask, ignoring the sword poised towards my chest and the rigid hands approaching my throat.

Without delay the coordinator says, "I don't know the exact number, but my estimate of a top-ranked fight multiplied by three is somewhere in the six digits."

Margarine's hands froze.

I smirk. "That should more than cover things, shouldn't it?"

"Indeed." She retracts her hands. "I'll oversee this myself. Take me to the accountants."

The coordinator gives me a quizzical look and I nod my approval. He spins on his heels and leads Margarine inside the amphitheater.

"Well, now that *that's* settled as well…" I stand and bat the sword Tang still has pointed at me away. "I'm going to take a nap over at the edge of the pavilion. Don't think of pushing me off, Tang."

Chapter 25: Maia

Each day leading up to the day all the students of the Tower of Vern would leave for the Magic Tournament is excruciating for both Maia and Mark. At least, as far as Maia could tell they both are exhausted from all the exercise Jasmine tells them to do. Mark could very well be faking his tiredness for her sake.

"I miss when thinking was the worst of my problems," Maia groans while lying in a bed on the second floor of the tower. She feels Mark shift on her right, sitting on the edge of the bed.

"Why are you both so tired all the time?" Lin asks, sitting on an adjacent bed beside Tricia and facing Maia and Mark's bed. Students stand scattered along the railing separating the floor from the empty plunge to the first floor, infrequently conjuring items with the accompanying *pop*.

"Running," Maia breathes out. "Lots of running. And then pushups."

"You're getting better at conjuring, though," Tricia says with a hint of jealousy lilting her voice a half-step up. "Both of you. So it must be good."

"We've all been busy with Aveve's own exercises also," Lin adds. "We've all improved considerably. To be honest, I don't think we'll be beaten by the other Occult Towers' students."

"Don't underestimate Kellen," Maia hears Aveve say over her own voice, both having said the same thing. She sits up in the bed and turns to the tower master.

"Hello everyone," Aveve says to the group of four. "Not bragging too much, I hope? We can't get complacent right before the tournament."

"No, ma'am," Lin says quickly.

"Every tower's students will have undergone similar training for the big event," Aveve says. "There's no telling who will win."

"Do we know what exactly we are winning?" Maia asks, patting down her clothes to free it of air pockets.

"No one knows except for those in charge, at least until the tournament starts," Aveve replies, giving Maia a conspiratorial wink. She looks at each of them in turn. "I advise you all to focus on yourselves rather than others. You will be up against students of many different fields and of many different skill levels. Don't let that intimidate you, since you can only do what you can."

"The other towers' students are Elemental and Spatial magicians, right?" Mark asks. "That's just two, isn't it?"

"Elementalism has many subfields," Maia says before Aveve can answer. "Technically one for each major element like fire and water."

"Very good, Maia," Aveve says approvingly. "That's at least four subfields, and another Elementalist subfield is Shapeshifting."

"I didn't know Ellies could do that!" Tricia says. "I mean… sorry, Maia, I meant Elementalists."

"Mmmhmm." Aveve continues, saying, "Spatial magic has two subfields: Teleportation and Void."

"I haven't heard of any subfields in Conjuring magic," Tricia says.

"That's because there are none," Aveve says.

"What? That's kind of lame."

"On the contrary, it speaks to the versatility of Conjuring. The only limit is your imagination."

"But you can't conjure living things," Maia says.

"Right, that goes without saying as a universal rule for all magic to never mess with life."

The four look at each other quietly for a while, awkwardly glancing up at Aveve who stands between the two beds with an absent half-smile on her face. Mark finally breaks the silence. "Was there a reason you came to speak with us, Master Aveve?"

"Hmm, no, not really. It's just good to talk with people sometimes, you know? Anyway, keep up the work. We'll be off to the tournament tomorrow."

Maia swings her feet off the bed away from Mark and sits up straighter. "Tomorrow?"

Aveve looks at her briefly then nods to herself. "Ah, that's right. There actually was a reason I came down here." Turning, she cups her hands around her mouth and shouts, "Tomorrow we'll be leaving for the Magic Tournament! Gather at the southern end of Chalman before noon and be prepared! We will be in charge of our own transportation!" Dropping her hands, she nods again to herself and mutters, "I think I'll go for a walk." She sweeps over to the stairway and rockets her way down to the first floor without adding anything further.

"What does she mean we'll be in charge of our own transportation?" Maia asks.

"Knowing her, she'll probably have us conjure a cart or wagon for horses to pull," Mark replies. "It's the most cost-effective and should be within everyone's ability."

"You should tell your boyfriend to stop using financial speak," Tricia tells Maia.

Maia blushes, glancing behind her at Mark who still sits facing away. They hadn't explicitly told them, yet they somehow knew that they are now a thing. Although, the thing is she doesn't really know what kind of thing "a thing" is. Not much has changed between them, but she does feel somewhat more comfortable with him.

"Geez, enough with the silence," Tricia says. "You could at least try to hide that you like each other."

"Why?" Mark asks seriously. "What's the point of being a couple if you can't show how you feel?"

Tricia and Lin look over Maia's shoulder at him. "Are you for real?" Tricia asks.

"What kind of boy says stuff like that?" Lin asks.

"A sane one?" Mark offers.

"At least that's settled," Tricia says. "Pretty much every boy is insane."

"I think we should go," Maia says quickly, overcome with embarrassment in response to the conversation.

"Sure," Mark says, standing up.

"Wait, you are still staying at his house?" Tricia asks.

"Uh—" is all Maia can get out before the two other girls gasp dramatically.

"You're still staying at his house!"

"Let's go," Mark says, running to the stairway and quickly descending at roughly the same speed as Aveve.

Maia laughs awkwardly and waves at the two girls who look on incredulously at her while she rushes after him.

Tomorrow comes soon enough, and students gather wearily by the edge of Chalman in a midmorning mist. The hanging vapor in the air seems to dampen everyone's mood as they wait for Aveve to arrive. They make minimal conversation with each other, scuffing their shoed feet along the dirt road. Maia and Mark stand together a ways off the road by a grassy incline, watching the bunches of magic students.

"Going somewhere?" Maia and Mark turn toward Jasmine with what little surprise they can manage while still being drowsy. She'd silently come upon them from behind. She is wearing the same grey robes from when they first met. Her hair falls long and straight around her head elegantly despite her dreary attire. "After all I've done for you it isn't very nice not to tell me about a field trip."

"It was mentioned only yesterday," Maia says while yawning. "I don't have a way to contact you, you just sneak up on us most of the time. What's with that, anyway?"

"Just a habit," Jasmine says, plopping herself down in the moist grass. "Is it time to be off to the Magic Tournament? I should've known I would've eventually found Not on my own if I'd just gone there myself."

"We weren't exactly keeping you here," Mark says.

"I'm well aware. But because I stayed, you benefitted from my magnanimity. Aren't you glad?"

Using her skills of inference from hours of listening to her former Elementalist mentor Greg use words she lacked a meaning for, Maia nods. "We're grateful," she says. "So are you going to travel with us?"

"I'm not sure," Jasmine says. "It might be entertaining to see how you all are going to get there."

"Horse-pulled carts," Mark answers. "Though, we're conjuring our own carts."

"Those are big," Jasmine says. "Will everyone be able to manage?"

"We've all been training so it shouldn't be a problem. If it is, others will likely share a ride."

Jasmine looks at Maia. "And what will you do?"

Maia looks back at the woman. "What do you mean?"

"Are you traveling by cart or by air?"

"By air?" Mark gives Maia a questioning look.

"I've been learning some Elementalist stuff on the side," Maia explains to him. "I didn't want to tell anyone until I really got it down."

"What exactly? You can fly now?"

"It's gliding, and I'm not at all sure if I can do it," Maia says.

"If you've been training properly these past weeks you can," Jasmine says. "Have you not tried it on your own?"

"Once, but that was before I met you," Maia says.

"Well then, how about a test? Travel to the Magic Tournament by gliding in the air."

"Go all the way to the Holt of Dunlon using air Elementalism?" Maia responds. "That's too far. Isn't it?"

"You've been running back and forth from the tower and Chalman every day. Your body should be far better prepared for extended time using magic."

"Maybe. But I don't want to travel alone."

"What'd be more fun?" Jasmine asks her.

Maia glances at Mark and sighs. "I can travel alongside you in a cart," Mark suggests. "I'll make it personal size, like a chariot."

"I, of course, will follow along to make sure you don't cheat," Jasmine says.

"This is kind of a lot of pressure," Maia says. Just then Aveve arrives, pacing down the road towards the gathered students. She is accompanied by a stablemaster and several men, each of them holding the reins of multiple horses. They disperse the students as they move forward, almost like a miniature parade. "And Aveve might not approve."

"Go ask her, then," Jasmine says. "I'll wait."

Reluctantly, Maia leaves Mark and Jasmine and walks slowly over to the overcrowded road and waits alongside the other students. The students continue parting to allow Aveve and company through. Aveve halts at the center of the crowd and begins giving out instructions.

"Students, one at a time, conjure a cart for yourselves or others depending on who you want to travel with. Horses will be distributed depending on the size and capacity of the cart, and you will be assigned a driver. Once situated, you will be on your way. Questions?"

There's brief silence in which Maia awkwardly waits for someone else to ask something. It goes on for a while and she decides to finally ask. "Would it be all right if I traveled another way?"

The students all turn their attention to her, making her feel even more embarrassed. Aveve sees Maia among the crowd and her face lights up. "Why, yes of course! I was hoping you'd have some other way of travel. Make sure to bring that spirit to the Tournament as well."

Standing still for a moment, unsure of what exactly she had heard, Maia nods. "Thanks." She quickly turns and walks out of and away from the gaping crowd back to where Mark and Jasmine are. "Frickety frick," she sighs when she reaches them. "She said I could."

"Good," Jasmine says. "We can be the last ones to leave, then. I know appearances are a big thing for teenagers and that Elementalism is thought of as the poor man's field of magic, so we don't have to worsen your reputation."

"Thanks," Maia says sarcastically, though is quite thankful for the woman's consideration no matter how backhanded it is.

"This might take a while," Mark says. Behind him a blanket pops into existence lying against the incline and he sits on it.

Maia chooses to continue standing. She is far too restless now to dare relax. It takes the better part of the hour before the last few students are situated with their carts, horses, and drivers. By that time the sun has well dispersed the haze and shines cleanly across the landscape.

"Tricia and Lin have gone ahead," Maia states. "Should we start?"

Mark stands up, his blanket disappearing. "Let's go." He follows Maia to Aveve who is just seeing off the final student whose cart is boxy and made of sanded oak.

"Are you both ready?" Aveve asks, looking fondly at them.

"Sure," Mark says. He lifts his hands, his eyes closing and mouth frowning in concentration. Maia senses the process of his will moving to his hands and sees his purple-y aura coalesce around him. A metal chariot pops into existence, Mark's hands gripping the top of its low rim. It is rather small—its shape is like a cup cut vertically through the middle. The walls come up above his waist, and it is just large enough for him to stand in. He steps onto the metal flooring, the chariot shifting forward slightly with its two large wheels under his weight.

"That's good, Mark, but there's no place for a driver," Aveve says.

"I wanted to drive myself," Mark says. "Shouldn't be too hard, right?"

"Harder than you think," the stablemaster comments, shaking his head. "You'll need to manage two horses for your chariot at least."

"You don't just attach the reins and follow the road?" Mark asks, stepping back out of the chariot.

"Follow the road, manage your horses' speeds, don't wear them out," the stablemaster replies. "And don't fall out."

"Sure," Mark says. He glances at Maia, then at Jasmine who remains sitting on the incline. "I guess she's waiting for us to get going."

Maia nods, shaking her hands to warm up. "I don't know if I can do it."

"If you're not sure you can, nothing beats trying," Aveve says supportively.

Maia nods again, psyching herself up. As the stablemaster outfits two thoroughbreds of pure auburn and attaches their reins to the chariot she quickly thinks over what she's going to do. The base thought: *travel.* The defining thoughts: *I will glide through the air.* In focusing her intent, Maia considers what she has to do to enact her will—manipulate the air to propel behind her, outward from her palms. *No,* she realizes, *that would only give her an initial boost.* Plus, she has it completely backwards. She wants the air to push against her, not the other way around with her pushing against the air.

Letting go of the incorrect method, she runs through the basics from the beginning up to focusing her thoughts. By the time she's got a solid image of what she'll do in her head (a habit she has picked up from practicing Conjuring which is largely about visualization) Mark's chariot is securely attached to the thoroughbreds and ready to go.

"Ready?" Mark asks, stepping into the chariot and peering closely at the reins to get a bearing of how he'll steer.

"Hey, kid," the stablemaster says. "These horses are trained so they'll follow the road even if you don't steer. There are several waterways between here and the Holt. Make sure to let the horses rest whenever you get the chance." He pauses, stroking his chin with mild irritation. "Any other situation I wouldn't let you go off with my horses, though since you're under master Aveve who assures me she'll look after everything, I'll allow it. Also, there is no need to rush. It'll be at least a week's travel. I've attached some saddlebags to both horses containing rations for them."

"Anything in there for us?" Mark asks.

The stablemaster shakes his head. "I figured you students could conjure your own food."

"True. Okay." Mark nods at Maia, giving her the go ahead. "Let's go."

Maia enacts her will, and suddenly she is throttling down the road with the wind whipping her face. Her mind catches up a second later and she realizes she is doing it. She is actually gliding in the air. The air behind rushes against her palms, winding between her fingers and elevating her off the ground. Her feet are suspended beneath her, hanging without feeling like they are hanging. The air pressing against her feet is like a solid object that perfectly cushions her body all the way along her backside and hands. It is like a pillow pressing against her—not too hard but not completely soft either. Where the air leaves her body she can sense it flying ahead of her some distance, her will sending it rushing on. She senses the air ahead decrease in speed, the absence of her will no longer pushing it forward, and it slows. She then whips by, the stilled air picking up once again to send her flying forward. It is a steady pattern of motion Maia uses her will to manipulate. Her hair streams behind her, the only part of her that does not feel like it is being snugly fit into an ever-pressing pillow. She doesn't dare turn her head to look back for fear she'll throw herself off balance. Her world is only what's in front of her. She takes a moment to smile as she watches the road flow beneath her and the grasslands pass by.

Jasmine's figure slides into her vision. "Enjoying yourself?" Out of the corner of Maia's eye she sees the woman is also gliding, her body suspended in the air. "Why don't you slow down a bit so Mark can catch up?"

Rather than easing up Maia stops her manipulation of air altogether. She lands hard on her feet, stumbling forward before catching herself. Without the wind buffeting her ears she can hear the metal wheels of Mark's chariot rattle a ways behind. Jasmine makes a sharp U-turn in the air, her body pivoting gracefully, and flies back to gently let herself down next to Maia.

"Strong start, but you can work more to ease in and out of it," Jasmine instructs her.

Maia takes several deep breaths, letting the invigorating feeling subside before she nods. "That was awesome," she says, her voice sounding lighter in her own ear.

"It never gets old," Jasmine agrees with a smile. Her rosy lips part for a second as if she is going to say something, though she drops her smile and says nothing and turns to watch Mark's progress. It's only a few seconds when Mark has his horses going at a steady speed. He soon reaches Maia and Jasmine and then passes them with an unsteady smile. "It looks like he'll need to get used to his way of traveling as well. Come on," Jasmine says to Maia. "Try it again, but match Mark's speed."

Chapter 26: Idrid

Weeks. She has no real measure for how long it's been that she's wandered helplessly around the forests surrounding the Holt, but that is how long it has felt like. Every now and then she sees a traveler who is also on their way to the tournament, and every time they point her in a new direction. No matter how long she travels in that direction she never finds it. Still, that hasn't stopped her from meeting person after person going the same way, so she has to be somewhere on the right track.

Idrid comes upon a small clearing, the area only slightly less narrow for her bulky form to fit through than the rest of the forest. She pauses, taking a moment to try and gather her bearings. Daylight passes through the canopy of leaves above, illuminating a good deal of the forest floor. It is her only comfort in allowing her to have some grasp of the time of day. Reaching her arms out fully, she stretches. A somewhat foul odiousness reaches her nose. The smell she recognizes as her own body odor, having become more prominent as the days pass without a change of clothes nor a bath. She sighs, taking a leather flask that she has strapped over her shoulder from her back, and gulps in refreshing water. The people she's passed on her way, while seemingly useless in giving directions, have been incredibly kind to offer her food and drink since she brought none. She finds it nice that they aren't put off by her size or, perhaps even more off-putting, her body odor.

Yet another traveler steps into the small clearing and almost bumps into her. The man, wearing tan traveling trousers and a tunic, takes a step back in surprise, his eyes widening. "Whoa. Sorry, I didn't see you."

"That's a first," Idrid says.

The man laughs heartily. "Not many can take a joke at their own expense, let alone make one themselves."

"Are you here for the tournament, too?"

"Yes," the man says. He unburdens himself of the large pack on his back that is causing him to slouch and stands up straight. Idrid notices his form, while not quite as large as hers being a half-Giant, is impressive for a human's. He lets his pack fall to the ground, reaching his hands up into the air to also stretch. His arms drop and he gives Idrid a curious look. "What's your name?"

"I'm Idrid," Idrid says.

"I'm Balnar. I've been traveling so long I've half a mind to burn this forest down to find my way."

"You're lost too?"

"Not lost, no. I've been going back and forth from the Holt of Dunlon and the closest town, transporting supplies. The ruddy tournament committee has a plethora of Teleporters at their disposal, yet they order me to do delivery services."

"You're part of those in charge of the tournament?"

"I wish I was," Balnar says gruffly. "Then I wouldn't be doing this job."

"Ah." Idrid appraises the man a moment more, noting his muscles. "Would you let me follow you to the tournament grounds?"

"I would," Balnar says, a smile flashing across his face. "Though what I'm transporting is actually going *off* the tournament grounds. Apparently not many have been there in a while, and since this is the first time an event's been held they're clearing the area of various… things."

Idrid gives him a questioning look at the vagueness of that last part, though doesn't bother asking. "So if I continue on this way I should reach the tournament grounds?"

"Yes," Balnar says with several nods. "Just go on ahead, that way." He points with his whole hand behind where he came from. It's not too far, though do you need any supplies?"

"No, I've got enough," Idrid says, shaking the flask in her hand. "Thanks for the info."

"Good luck in the tournament," Balnar says, shouldering his pack back over his shoulders. "That is, if you're participating. Otherwise, enjoy yourself."

"Thanks." Idrid watches the man trudge around her and out of the clearing. It is the first she's been told she's not far from the Holt, so she follows the direction Balnar told her. Her strides are large and would carry her almost twice the length of what a normal person's walking pace would if not for the trees in her way. A rich, oaky brown is one of her favorite colors, but this forest has quickly turned it into an eyesore.

Just then a flash of brilliant red sweeps in and out of view, passing between the trees ahead. Idrid, feeling like she recognizes the color, calls out. "Hey!"

The billowing red fabric returns into her line of sight from around a tree and she sees Darren looking at her quizzically. Recognition dawns on his own face and he calls back. "Hey! I didn't think I'd see you here!" In an instant he appears right in front of her, startling her.

"Has anyone said that that's disturbing?" she asks.

"Yes," Darren says matter-of-factly. "What's that smell, by the way?"

"Don't," Idrid warns him.

285

"Have you been traveling all this time?" he instead asks. "How've you not reached the Holt yet?"

"I guess I got lost," Idrid says.

"More than lost," Darren comments. "This isn't a very large forest."

"Yeah, well, let's just say I'm not good with directions," Idrid says defensively. She doesn't want to admit it, but Not had always been the one to guide her when they traveled.

"There has to be more to it than that," Darren says. "Didn't Vespertine say it would be a trial in itself to get to the Holt of Dunlon? Have you come across anything… trial-y?"

"No," Idrid replies. "Only other people also going to the tournament."

"Did they know the way?" Darren asks.

"Yeah, they all did," she says with a frown.

"And you followed their directions?" Darren waits, then takes her silence as answer enough. "Then they were misguiding you."

"They were nice enough to trust," Idrid says slowly. *Why did I trust them so easily?*

"Yeah, well, you shouldn't trust people who are too nice. Come with me, I was on my way there. Then we can get you a… Come on," he cuts himself off, opting not to say that she needs a bath. Idrid follows Darren through the forest for several minutes before they reach a break in the trees. Emerging from the forest, they both stop and gape at the sight before them which isn't much. Rather than an impressive hill previously inhabited by Dunlon himself is a slate wall that reaches twenty feet up and stretches on in both directions along the tree line.

"Is the Holt behind this wall, then?" Idrid asks.

"I... suppose?" Darren steps up to the wall and knocks on it, a hollow metal sound ringing in response. "It looks like the only way is around."

Idrid steps up to the slate wall and pounds it with her fist. She makes a large dent, though it's not enough to put a hole in the wall. "Maybe if I punch it some more."

The dent disappears, the wall unbending itself to return to a flat state, and then the sounds of more metal clangs ring out along the wall. The sounds get closer, until finally they cease, the final clang coming from the wall immediately in front of them. Then, the metal creaks outward, a door forming where none had been before. The pale face of a young woman leans out, her white-blonde hair falling in braids around her face. "Here for the tournament?" Her voice is light and childlike.

Idrid and Darren nod.

"You'll have to pass through this maze first," the woman says. "No going back once you're in."

"All right." The woman steps to the side as Idrid walks inside, Darren following shortly behind her. Idrid turns to see the woman move her hand, resealing the slate wall onto itself. *A magician* she thinks.

"Go on, then," the woman says, not moving.

Darren and Idrid look at each other, then around. Now they are sandwiched between two slate walls without a ceiling, the bare sky hanging overhead. "Which way do you want to go?" Idrid asks him.

"No idea," Darren replies, though starts walking right. Idrid doesn't question his decision and follows behind. She glances over her shoulder at the woman who remains where she is, watching the two go on. "Don't bother with her," he says to Idrid. "She wasn't among those who participated in the palace trial, which means she's likely one of the Concilium."

"You know her?" Idrid asks.

"Really only her name. Ponla. We've met on several occasions in and near Vale Tower."

"The Spatial tower," Idrid muses to herself. "What she just did to the maze wall wasn't that."

"No, she's an Elementalist. One of the Royal Guard."

"I thought Concilium were all Mind Controllers?"

"They don't have to be," Darren says. "They share the same goal, which Vespertine has yet to reveal. Still, she might not be, but... Most everything about her is circumspect. She doesn't associate with other Elementalists. Well, she doesn't associate much with anyone."

They reach their second choice of branching paths, one going deeper while the other continuing onward. Darren takes the one pressing deeper, Idrid monitoring her steps while following closely behind so as not to step on the backs of his feet.

"What have you been up to?" Idrid asks. She notices Darren glance over his shoulder at her shortly, his eyes narrowing.

"You wouldn't believe me if I told you, much less be interested," he says.

"Seeing as we're in a maze that's seemingly set up to just waste our time, how about you go ahead and tell me anyway."

Darren's shoulders rise and fall in a shrug of acquiescence. "I've been researching aquatic life forms in oceanic biomes."

Idrid perks up marginally. "Research?"

"Yeah. There's surprisingly little information about the ocean beyond how large it is. Did you know no one knows its depth?"

"Yes," Idrid says.

Darren looks back at her. "You do?"

"I like to read," she says.

"That's a good hobby. I didn't find anything worthwhile, though. Is there anything you might know?"

"Hm." Idrid thinks for a while as they walk. "Not about the ocean, no. At least, I can't remember anything important I've read about that would be worth mentioning. It's sort of like the Talwood in that regard... mysterious and big. I remember it was something my family was going to take me to see, before—you know." She sees Darren's back stiffen as he walks. She then asks, "What are you trying to find out?"

"It's just—um... creatures that are... uh... as large as, or larger than... um. The shoreline?" He glances at her again.

Idrid blinks at him. "The shoreline?" she repeats.

"Yeah. Give or take."

"What kind of shoreline are we talking about here?" Idrid asks. "Like, a patch of shore several meters long?"

Darren stops walking, turning to look back the way they've come. "Like from there," he says, pointing to the slate wall that makes up the perimeter of the maze they're walking away from, "to there." He points forward at another slate wall rising in the distance and marking what seems to be a dead end. "Or… probably longer. I just can't remember how large it was…"

Idrid judges the distance analytically. "Roughly 330 meters, then?" She pauses and looks worriedly at Darren's vaguely pale face. "And you're saying you saw something that large?"

"I mean, of what was visible above the water, yeah…"

Idrid's face reflects his. "What was it?"

"I don't know. It resembled a tentacle, but it was as smooth as bone. It was as pale as bone, too. But it was fleshy."

Idrid feels an involuntary shiver run down her body. "Just a tentacle, then? It wasn't attached to anything?"

Darren swipes a hand through his light brown hair and continues to move forward to the end of the path. "I don't know. It sank back into the ocean before anything else emerged. But it only seemed to be getting larger as far as I could tell."

"Where did you see it?" Idrid asks as they walk.

"By the Tower of Bel. Kellen—the tower master— called me over. He was the one who noticed it first."

"No one else has seen it?"

"Not that I'm aware." They reach the end and find that there are indeed no branching paths. "Let's go back," he says.

Idrid holds up a hand, signaling for him to wait. "Do you think I could just break through before Ponla or whoever comes?"

"Maybe," Darren says. "Do you think you can?"

She slides her hand along the hard wall. "If it's as thin as the outer one, yeah." She knocks on it, and a significantly less hollow sound resounds. "I don't think I can get through it."

"Do you still have that enchanted rock?" Darren asks.

"The gem? Yeah." Idrid stoops down and pulls it out of her malodorous left sock. She offers it to Darren who looks at her like she's offering him a turd. He composes himself quickly enough to calmly take the gem. "Can you use it?" she asks.

"Not to the effect of an Enchanter, but I should be able to do enough." His body physically relaxes. Idrid is unsure whether it is him concentrating or no longer talking about a horrid sea creature that causes him to become calm. He reaches his hand holding the gem out and presses it against the slate wall. Several seconds pass as Darren mutters things under his breath that sound to Idrid like a chant. The dim space between his palm and the wall where the stone rests lights up with a blinding light.

Idrid covers her eyes and turns away. The light pours around her and casts a dazzling white gleam that stretches all the way back to the outer maze wall. In an instant the light dies. Idrid looks back at the dead end and sees the wall around where Darren is holding the stone has become a sizzling hole twice her height. It continues clean through about four feet of solid wall before it ends at another pathway leading straight on and further into the maze.

Darren, blinking furiously, offers her back the stone. "That was a lot more powerful than I thought. Whoever enchanted it must've captured a ton of fire within."

Idrid warily taps it, anticipating it to burn her fingers off. Certain that it's cool, she takes the gem and stores it back in her sock. Behind her she hears the same metal clangs that emanated from the walls before Ponla appeared. "I think she's coming," Idrid says hastily. Darren quickly jumps through the hole, being careful not to touch the surrounding metal that is steaming.

Idrid makes it through just in time before the hole starts to close up and reform as a wall. She looks back and sees Ponla suddenly standing on the other side like she was there the whole time. The woman stares at Idrid, shaking her head while smiling oddly. The wall reseals itself, separating them a second later.

"We're at the end, I think," Darren says. Idrid, unnerved by Ponla's reaction, looks down the straight path deeper into the maze and sees there is no wall at the end. There figures in robes are walking back and forth, and beyond that a large grassy hill rises. The Holt of Dunlon. He looks at her, relief softening his eyes. "Let's get there so we can finally see what this tournament is really about."

Idrid adds, "And so I can take a bath."

Chapter 27: Maia

In the shroud of night Maia and Mark continue on their way toward the Holt of Dunlon; Mark is in an alert stance within his chariot that steadies himself from the bumpy road; and Maia is suspended midair in an inclined position as she's propelled forward by wind. Per the stablemaster's instructions Mark had taken every opportunity to stop his horses by fresh water and give them rest which had also given Maia some time to rest her will. Though she hates to admit it, even if only in thought, Maia is grateful to Jasmine for forcing them to exercise their bodies in the days leading up to their departure. Without any of it she would hardly have been able to cause a single rush of air, let alone create a perpetual stream that could carry her.

Jasmine, on the other hand, while she started the journey off with her usual carefree instructing, had gradually grown quiet as they traveled. She now has a stern look, brows half-lowered and eyes gazing forward in deep thought as she herself glides through the air. Maia had wanted and still wants to ask her about it but she does not want to risk talking while performing magic. A line of trees crops up into view, morphing out of the shadows. They come upon the trees rather quickly, Mark quickly reining in his horses to a slow trot. He brings them to a halt just before where the path cuts through the trees while Maia and Jasmine return to the ground. Maia lands hard again, feeling a slight pain go up her stiff legs when they touch down. She still has yet to master control of the air to let herself down more gently.

"Are we already there?" Mark asks.

"We made good progress," Jasmine says. "This should take us to the town of Woodside. From there we can make our way through the forest and finally to the Holt."

"Did we pass everyone on our way here?" Maia asks.

"Just about," Mark says. "Some students may still be ahead of us. Or they could've stayed in the previous towns and we missed them."

"None of them recognized me, right?" Maia asks.

"Unlikely," Mark says. "Only Tricia and Lin and me know you can do Elementalism."

"And I," Jasmine says. "It's 'and I know.' Saying 'me know' is bad grammar."

"Right," Maia says, shaking her head at Jasmine's particularity with getting language correct. "We can walk the rest of the way, then. Me don't want to fly into a tree if the road turns suddenly."

Mark stifles a laugh and shakes the reins on his chariot. The two horses start forward. Jasmine and Maia walk in pace with the horses, going nice and slow. "Just a few days left, then," Mark says. He glances at them both, Jasmine equal to his height while he's elevated by the chariot and Maia who matches his actual height a foot lower. "It's rather exciting."

"It kind of is," Maia agrees. "I'll be getting to compete against Elementalists I know. I wonder if they remember me."

"Does it feel weird?" Mark asks.

"Yeah. Though it'll be fun seeing Kellen. I want to show him and the others what I can do now."

"I wonder if the tower masters will be participating, too."

"Hush," Jasmine interrupts the two with a low voice. Mark and Maia look at her, though she doesn't look back. Her eyes are alert and scanning the road ahead. She seems to be listening for something while she continues to walk. It's dark and the only sounds Maia can hear are from the rattling metal of the chariot wheels and hoofbeats of Mark's horses.

Maia looks around while trying to sense if there is any magic close by. She feels nothing. "Wha—"

"Hush," Jasmine repeats immediately, stopping and crouching low. Mark pulls up on his reins to stop his horses again and waits, his head pivoting back and forth at the surrounding trees. Leaves shiver in the cold air, rustling against each other and the twigs they grow on. The only other sounds they can hear are those of woodland animals padding up and down the trees, their claws making light woody taps on the bark. The soft breathing of the horses calmly stirs the otherwise still air. Maia sees Jasmine slowly reach a hand beneath her dull robes and a *cling* of metal hitting metal resounds. Completely at a loss, Maia crouches slightly as well and moves beside the chariot as a sort of cover.

The faint moonlight overhead pattering through the leaves is all that illuminates the dim forest floor. The surrounding dark has a hue of blue Maia is well acquainted with, having strolled down the road from the Tower of Bel back to her hometown at night in the past. Something about the atmosphere here, at this time, is unsettling. Faint rustling of leaves stills as the breeze overhead dies down. Small animals continue to claw their way among the trees. For a second time Maia is about to ask Jasmine what is wrong, then a light mist rolls in from between the tree trunks. Like a transparent shroud, it casts the surrounding shadows in a fuzzy paleness. The mist touches upon her, and her clothes seem to grow a touch heavier. A drop in temperature falls upon them, each of their breaths coming out in small wisps. Maia shoves her hands into her pants pockets and peers up at Mark who is also crouching within the chariot.

No longer are they surrounded by the darkness of night that restricts their eyesight. The mist presses tighter and further obscures the path ahead and forest around them. Maia feels like her senses are tricking her. The horses' breathing becomes dampened along with the sound of the forest life. Maia puts her hand on the chariot wheel she crouches by and hears nothing. Looking at the metal wheel, she flicks it with a finger. The metal sound she is expecting to resound doesn't reach her ears. And then everything is silent.

Out of the corner of her eye she sees Jasmine rise slightly, a knife in her hand curving dangerously outward as the woman takes several steps forward. Maia can't see ten feet ahead of her, though she wonders if Jasmine sees something she can't.

The touch of a hand on her shoulder makes her jump and she whirls to see Mark standing behind her, his eyes glinting dully in the minimal light. "It's me," Mark says.

Maia lets out a breath of relief, knowing she isn't actually deaf. Looking back, she sees Jasmine continuing forward slowly. Mark drops his hand and walks forward as well, Maia close behind and peering over her shoulder with paranoia.

Jasmine stops suddenly by the left horse, causing Mark and Maia to stiffen and brace themselves. A figure shifts through the mist slightly ahead of Jasmine, his or her features too obscured for Maia to make out. Jasmine pulls her hand holding the knife back and in a flash throws it at the figure. The knife slices through the air and a damp thud emanates from where it embeds into the figure's head.

Maia looks away for a moment in cold shock. When she sees Mark staring at the sight wide-eyed, she turns back. The figure draws closer as if nothing is wrong, though Maia can make out the outline of the knife sticking out of the figure. Maia realizes while she can see the knife, she still can't see the figure's features when she knows she should. The cold of fear slides in her stomach and she unconsciously takes Mark's hand. Its body resembles the mist around it, only a slightly darker tinge of grey. When it was more obscured and further away it looked like a person, though now she doesn't know how she could've mistaken the thing for a person.

Whatever the thing is, it doesn't have a face. It is humanoid, but drifts through the mist like it has no legs. Glancing down, she sees the thing has the form of legs, though they are obscured by the mist. The faceless thing is within arm's distance of Jasmine, Jasmine preparing another knife to plunge into it. The figure swiftly falls back in an instant, becoming enshrouded in the mist beyond their sight. Maia looks all around as the mist withdraws just as swiftly, letting the darkness of night back in along with the faint moonlight. Ahead where the figure disappeared the path continues forward some meters before the warm lights of the town shine through the trees.

Not knowing how the town had suddenly appeared there, Maia notices the touch of Mark's fingers in her hand. She looks down and sees their hands intertwined. Blushing, she lets go and puts her hands back in her pockets.

Jasmine paces forward to where the blade of her knife glints on the ground, absent from the figure. She kneels, scooping it up, and looks at it closely. Sniffing, she stows the knife in her robes and walks back to where the two stand. "We should be safe now."

"What was that?" Maia asks finally.

"I don't know," Jasmine says.

"You stabbed the thing… didn't you?"

"Yes." She takes the same dagger out and shows them the blade. Maia recoils, expecting blood, though relaxes when she sees the blade is clean save for specks of dirt it picked up from lying on the road. "Do you believe in ghosts?" Jasmine asks.

"You're kidding, right?"

"Wait a minute, didn't you mention stories that sailors told you about the dead wandering the forests around the Holt of Dunlon?" Mark asks. "Do you think that was one of them?"

"Whatever it is is gone," Jasmine states, putting the dagger away. "Let's go to town."

Maia nods. Mark steps back into the chariot and urges the horses onward at a slightly faster pace than before, but still slow enough for Maia and Jasmine to walk comfortably beside. They reach the town with no further interruptions, thankful that the first building is a stable.

"Can you handle them?" Mark asks the stablemaster who comes around the wooden building to greet them. He leaves the chariot and horses for the stablemaster to handle, giving the woman a small payment, and moves to where Maia and Jasmine stand at the center of the road and gaze at the tall buildings around them. The trees hug each structure snugly like they grew that way naturally. It could be the town was built before the forest grew.

"Are we continuing on, or staying here?" Maia asks, her voice a tad lighter in hope when asking the last part.

"Let's stay here," Jasmine says decisively. "Better to be attacked by ghosts in the day than night."

"Sure," Maia says, trying to think how it would be better.

Chapter 28: Idrid

The tournament grounds are a stretch of grass that encircles the Holt of Dunlon. Roughly seventy meters span between the Holt and the slate wall making up the maze that separates the grounds from the surrounding forest. Large dark blue tents, most the size of royal houses, occupy the majority of the area all around the Holt. The remaining area is just enough for small crowds to wander around. At the top of the Holt a single massive blue tent melds with the wind, its sides rippling steadily. It is the late afternoon and getting toward the second eve Idrid and Darren arrived there.

"There's going to be an announcement at the top of the Holt, right?" Darren asks Idrid distractedly. He sits on a tree stump to the right of a shack-sized tent staring down at the map of the area, scanning it over and over again.

"According to the tournament staff," Idrid says. She paces in semi-circles around his stump, holding her own map she received from an overly friendly woman by the maze exit. She holds it out in front of her and infrequently glances down at it. The layout of the maze is far simpler than she would have guessed. There are roughly five rows encircling the Holt though only a few dead-ends that largely could only be found in 50/50 chances.

"Excited to see Not again?"

"Slightly," Idrid replies calmly though feels a small smile creep onto her face. She can't help wondering what he's managed to do since running off in Telnas. No matter if he succeeded in finding others that would help, she is certain he will show up.

A diminutive man in a white button-up shirt and silly salmon waistcoat steps through the nearby tent's flap and offers each of them their respective drinks.

"Thanks," Darren tells the barkeep, quickly folding up his map and putting it away in his cloak before taking the mug containing a fine wine. Idrid takes the other mug containing water, her hand wrapping all the way around.

"He'll probably be annoyed that the only bar in the whole place is this measly tent," she says before taking a sip. The barkeep enters back through the tent flap with a disgruntled huff.

"I didn't take him for an avid drinker," Darren says.

"He isn't one. He just—well. He likes to pay for others."

"All right," Darren says in disbelief. He stands up and Idrid walks in step with him, navigating their way closer to the Holt between the tents. Swaths of diverse people wearing even more diverse clothes walk every which way, all eager to get a sense for the grounds in preparation for the start of the tournament. They reach the beginning of the Holt where the ground begins to gently rise and progress steadily to the top. There the majority of the tournament-goers ascend and descend the hill while plenty more sit and overlook the tents scattered below.

As Idrid and Darren reach the same height as the top of the tents on ground level she looks back every now and then at the maze. She tries to picture where they are in relation to the image of the map in her mind. The pattern of the walls represents a portion she remembers from the eastern side of the Holt which matches with the current position of the sun hanging somewhere behind the top of the Holt on the other side. The Holt casts a short shadow. As they near the top Idrid and Darren are met with a face-full of sunlight that forces them to squint and protect their eyes with their hands. They make the rest of the way looking down at their feet. The earth flattens out and the tent at the top provides another shadow that blocks the sun from view. They take a look at their surroundings and see a steady stream of people moving around and to one side of the tent. A significant portion of them are young, somewhere in their adolescence. Idrid infers them to be students by the matching clothes they wear. Following the flow of people, they find themselves within the big tent. It houses a large barren area, though a length of rope sequesters the crowd around the outside of the tent from a 20x20 meter area in the middle. Tilting her head up, she sees various slits in the tent higher up that allow in sunlight that travels in small beams across the inside to shine at spots on the other side of the tent.

Idrid silently follows Darren, guided by the crowd squeezing themselves tighter to fit more and more people. As Idrid and Darren get uncomfortably snug within the crowd, both feel the breath of those behind them brush against their backs. Several individuals in the telltale red cloaks indicating Magic Guild magicians step inside the roped-in area. Idrid, her line of sight a solid foot taller than the majority of the crowd, recognizes the man she met in the forest. The studly man, Balnar, steps along the inside of the rope, sweeping his gaze over the crowd. She feels his eyes stick to her for a noticeable moment, though his serious face makes no reaction and his eyes move away. She feels like she should be surprised or annoyed to see him as one of the people supposedly in charge of this tournament after he lied to her but all she feels is disinterest. Following him up is the other magician she met in the maze, Ponla. She watches the diminutive magician's figure step along behind the rope, who in turn gazes back at the crowd with a hint of boredom that sets her eyelids marginally low over her pupils. Two other magicians circle the inside area along the rope, neither of whom Idrid recognizes.

"Any idea of who's Concilium and who isn't yet?" Idrid attempts to whisper so that only Darren can hear. She is unsuccessful as her words are drowned out by the chattering crowd around and he doesn't turn to acknowledge that she opened her mouth. Sighing, she folds her arms and waits in place, no longer being able to be bothered to move or be moved any further into the crowd. Several people bump into her and nudge her, though she doesn't pay them any attention. Soon enough the magicians in the center finish walking laps around the inner area and converge at the center. Balnar and Ponla take up positions facing away from each other while the other two do the same so that they're all facing a different direction like the major points of a compass. The sudden loud sound of someone clearing his throat echoes around the tent, causing the crowd to quiet.

"…ahem. Ah-*hem*. Well. Here we all are. At least, most of us." One of the two magicians Idrid doesn't know facing one section of the crowd talks, his casual voice somehow being amplified. "Ah. Well, that doesn't matter right now. Greetings, everyone, and welcome to the Magic Tournament. We are glad that so many are here to participate. That is, that's why you should be here now. If you will not be participating and for whatever reason you found your way up here, please make your way out of the tent and enjoy the amenities below as this meeting is only for those who will be participating. All right?" He pauses, looking over the crowd for a moment. "Ok. Well, then. Hello, everyone. My name is Goldyck. I'll be giving out information to everyone about what it is you'll be doing exactly, and my lovely assis*tants*—"

His voice becomes pained on the last syllable as Balnar elbows his side. Ponla, who faces Idrid and Darren's section of the crowd, makes an amused smile while Goldyck composes himself.

"Apologies. My associates will be handing out schedules of the next three days. Each day will largely be dedicated to a particular group. Those groups will be announced now. The first group are Occult Tower students. The second group are non-magicians. The third group are magicians. Group one will be partaking in events on the first day, group two will be partaking in events on the second day, and, yes, group three will be partaking in events on the third day." Chatter fills the tent and Goldyck looks the crowd up and down. "The reasons for separating people into these groups are self-evident, so I won't go over them." Some members of the crowd boo but Goldyck continues, unfazed. "Which group you belong to is also self-evident, so I won't tell you who among you are students, non-magicians, and magicians. As I mentioned earlier, certain groups will be participating on certain days, however some individuals may be required to participate on multiple days. These can be exceptions, but most importantly they will be determined by performances. Successful performances during events can lead to participation in further events. An example of this will be Occult Tower students who do well and may be scheduled to compete against another Tower's students who did similarly well on the second day. As many of you know, this tournament is not only a celebration of skills, it is a competition and, for some, a job application. Many people who are here and not participating aren't just here to simply enjoy the show—they're here to scout out special individuals.

"Those of us who are in charge of this tournament," he sweeps his hand at the other three standing by him, "are looking for members to join the Concilium who will be helping oversee the progress of Lanmar. Well. Popularity, acclaim, and professional development won't be all that you get during this tournament. There will be monetary and other rewards as well." Goldyck shifts his feet. The crowd has gotten politely quiet again, sated by the prospect of various rewards. "Okay. Then, we should get on to handing out schedules. Occult Tower students, please form a single-file line in front of Ponla," he gestures a hand to the childlike woman on his right who raises her hand halfheartedly. "Non-magicians, please form a single-file line in front of Balnar." He gestures to his left, and Balnar raises his hand. "Magicians, please form a single-file line in front of Analise."

Analise, the woman behind and facing the opposite direction of Goldyck, claps her hands once and stacks of papers materialize out of thin air beside her and the other two Goldyck referred to. The crowd begins to move, people eager to get to their respective lines. The sudden rush of people attempting to push their way against each other causes several fights to break out.

Idrid remains motionless, glancing at Darren. "I suppose we won't be participating together."

Darren, hearing her this time, nods. The people move around Idrid and Darren, allowing them some space. It is Darren's cloak that Idrid notices people looking at that is causing them to choose to move around them.

"Should you be wearing that?" Idrid asks.

"The Concilium already know who I am," he states. "And besides, I'm wearing this so Not can find us."

That's right Idrid thinks. Not is here somewhere. She tries searching the crowd moving in every direction though doesn't see him. She considers standing at the head of the lines and waiting there to see when he shows his face though decides against it. It'll take too long and he probably doesn't want to be spotted until... well, until he does.

"I'll go grab my schedule then." Idrid makes a path to the small line forming in front of Balnar, the crowd parting hurriedly so as not to be barreled through. She steps behind the thirteenth person in the non-magician line. Everyone in the line and everyone in the other two lines are appraising each other, likely analyzing the competition. Those in front of and behind her give wary glances at Idrid. "What," she says when the guy in front of her looks at her for the fifth time. He doesn't turn around again.

The line progresses fast, and she comes face to face with Balnar again. "I'm glad you made it," he says. "No hard feelings, I hope."

"Nope," Idrid says, taking the sheet Balnar offers. She scans it, seeing the various events of the second day listed by times.

"Enjoy the tournament," Balnar says.

Idrid moves out of the line and sees Darren stepping through the crowd and ignoring the line in front of Analise. He comes up to Analise and, stooping down shortly, snatches up a schedule from the magician stack of papers and turns to leave. Analise simply nods at him with a polite smile while those in line make noises of disapproval. Idrid goes to follow Darren's red-cloaked form back through the crowd and out of the tent. He detaches from the majority of people trickling down the Holt and moves around the corner of the tent to the side where the sun is setting. The light casts a pink glow that sets upon the upper portion of the tent.

Darren stops and turns to Idrid, looking down at his schedule. "I suppose I'll have to enjoy myself for the first two days," he murmurs. "What does your schedule look like?"

Idrid looks over at Darren's sheet. "Similar to yours, though events on the second day are highlighted in red. They look to be scheduled so that everyone can participate in just about every event for their day. The last event is one that the entire group must participate in… it looks to be a brawl."

"A brawl?"

"Everyone versus everyone," Idrid says.

"Oh. The same thing appears on my day too," Darren says. "That sounds like utter chaos."

"The students won't have a brawl as the last event of the first day… right?"

"We can find out," Darren says, folding his schedule into fourths and sliding it within his cloak. He looks up and smiles. "There's a student I know."

Idrid follows his gaze and sees a familiar girl standing next to a boy, both wearing matching violet shirts. The girl looks Idrid up and down with a curious expression that widens her eyes.

"I've seen you before," the girl says plainly. "You were with that guy. Not. But why are you with Darren now?" Her eyes move over to Darren. "Hi, by the way." The girl's eyes bug out and she does a double take, looking at Idrid. "Wait, were you with Not when he—uh, the king was murdered?"

Idrid flashes a grimace. "This isn't the time or place," she says, looking at the tent and hoping that everyone on the other side of the thin fabric did not hear them.

"Somewhere more private would be better," Darren agrees, then freezes. His smile drops away slowly and a tall woman in dull grey robes rounds the corner of the tent and stands behind the boy and girl. The woman's lips part in surprise before twisting upward.

"Well, well," her deep voice drawls. "Fancy seeing you here."

Chapter 29: Maia

"They know each other," Maia whispers to Mark.

"You know each other?" Darren asks Jasmine and Maia.

"What does it really mean to know someone?" Jasmine pontificates while checking her fingernails.

"We don't really know each other," Maia says. "She just taught us stuff."

"Taught you stuff?" Darren's eyebrows rise skeptically.

"Magic stuff. Oh, she knows Not and is looking for him."

"You know Not?" Idrid asks.

"You're still looking for him?" Darren asks.

"I wouldn't be if you hadn't punched me in the face," Jasmine remarks. "He took something that's mine that I'd like back."

"Oh?" Idrid crosses her arms.

"It was a cloak, much like yours, Mr. Teleporter."

"Darren," Darren says.

"Yes, this precocious girl already mentioned you to me."

"Precocious?" Maia murmurs to Mark, slightly affronted.

"Talented," Mark supplies.

Jasmine lowers her hand and sighs. "Neither of you are with him, which must mean you don't know where he is either."

"Since you're still after the cloak, I could punch you in the face this time," Idrid volunteers and takes a step forward.

"Careful, Idrid," Darren warns.

Jasmine's eyes narrow at Idrid, a small smile playing on her lips. "Is that jealousy or loyalty?"

"What's there to be jealous of?" Idrid asks, frowning.

"What indeed," Jasmine muses suggestively.

Idrid blinks, then barks out a single laugh. "He drugged you and took your cloak. That's all."

It's Jasmine's turn to frown. "It was a *very* nice cloak."

Maia watches the large woman called Idrid and Jasmine shortly, then turns to Darren who watches on with a look of helplessness. "I don't think this is about a cloak," Maia comments. Everyone turns to look at her. She looks back, confused. "What?"

"He drugged you?" It's Mark who asks, turning to Jasmine.

"He had good reason," Idrid says.

Jasmine's eyes narrow further. "To steal from me," she says in a lower voice than usual.

"You were going to steal from him," Idrid retorts.

"Neither you or him sound completely good," Mark states to Jasmine. "No offense."

"What's done is done," Darren says. "Can we—"

In an instant Jasmine's hand points out at Darren, a blast of air rushing forward. It hits him in the face, forcing him to cover his eyes. Before they can react the air around Maia and Mark erupts and Jasmine flies between them, moving straight for Idrid.

Idrid raises her hands defensively, though Jasmine ducks under them and hovers a foot off the ground immediately behind her. Jasmine brings her hands up to either side of Idrid's head just over the large woman's ears. Fingers' curling and uncurling, Maia senses the air around Idrid's head deplete. In response, Idrid's eyes droop and she staggers, now having trouble standing.

"Hey!" Maia says, horrified.

"If you're precious to Not, I can use you to find him," Jasmine says calmly, her gaze fixated on the back of Idrid's head.

Darren recovers, eyes blinking furiously, and quickly assesses the situation. It takes him too long. Jasmine's hand flicks out for a brief second, sending another blast of air at his face now from just a couple of feet away from him. He is once again forced to protect his face.

"Stop!" Maia cries at Jasmine. Jasmine makes no show of stopping. Idrid stumbles to her knees, her eyes shifting unsteadily. Then, her hand reaches over her shoulder and curls around Jasmine's throat.

Jasmine's eyes widen and Idrid lets out a grunt of exertion as she swings Jasmine's entire body in an arc over her head. With her grip still around Jasmine's neck, she forcefully brings the magician down at the ground in front of her.

Jasmine catches herself before she is slammed by creating a pocket of air that cushions her fall. She grabs the wrist of Idrid's hand constricting her throat and begins

309

applying pressure. Maia is about to shut her eyes for fear of the worst, but then Jasmine disappears.

Idrid falls forward, catching herself with her hands on the ground. She looks up and around in confusion. The sound of a body thumping on the ground behind them causes Maia and Mark to turn and see Jasmine lying there breathing heavily with her hands over her throat.

Maia turns back to see Darren standing up straight, one of his eyes peaking out between a crack in his fingers. He lowers his hands, revealing an angry frown. "That's enough, okay?"

Jasmine boosts herself into a standing position using the air to push her, and gets into a low stance. Idrid is back on her feet and gets into a similar stance.

"HEY!" Darren shouts, causing the two women to look at him. "How's this?" he starts in a calmer voice, glancing down the Holt at a majority of people's faces turned toward them and several climbing up and approaching them. "If you're going to fight, do it during the tournament. For now, let's go back to our housing."

Jasmine and Idrid appraise each other while glancing down the hill, evaluating their options. "We're scheduled on different days," Idrid says.

"Remember what Goldyck said? Those who perform well can participate in more events. Did you read the bottom of your schedule?"

Idrid shakes her head but doesn't move to take her schedule out.

"I did say that!" Darren and Idrid turn toward the voice and see Goldyck approaching them from behind. "I'm glad you were paying attention, Darren. And, may I say, I'm glad to see your friends are so eager to get to it."

Maia senses Jasmine starting to use magic while Idrid and Darren's backs are to them and she quickly grabs Jasmine's hand to stop her. Jasmine exhales a breath, then relaxes.

"That was smart, whoever you are. You too," Goldyck comments, looking Jasmine and Maia in the eye in turn. "We'll be making sure no fights break out outside tournament events, so please save your energy for the events themselves." Maia lets go of Jasmine's hand slowly as Goldyck turns. "Well. That's all." He briskly walks away back to the far corner of the tent and disappears around it.

"Dinner?" Darren asks finally to everyone.

Maia blinks and looks around. "All of us?"

"Yeah. We can all get acquainted, and that way know better why we'll later be at each others' throats."

Maia and Mark share a look.

"I'm joking," Darren says, though his lack of a smile is unconvincing.

"Doesn't sound like a bad idea," Jasmine relents. "Lead the way."

Darren gives Idrid a meaningful look and she, too, relents and starts walking down the Holt. Darren walks beside the large woman and they begin to discuss something.

"That wasn't half-bad, by the way," Jasmine murmurs for Maia to hear. "You sensing what I was going to do. It's nice to see hard effort pay off."

"Hmph," Maia says and begins following the other two. She knows she should be upset with Jasmine for attacking them, though she can't help the small bit of pride sneaking its way into her chest.

Somehow the group manages to find a table in the dining hall of a general housing building at the southern end of the Holt without further antagonism between Idrid and Jasmine. Maia knows she and Mark have rooms there along with the rest of the Conjuring students, though she is unsure about the other three. The dining hall is situated around the entryway, a large open space with 6-people tables organized in rows. With how well it is all lit, electric chandeliers hanging from the ceiling, and how upkept the furnishings are, Maia doubts the stories she's heard about the Holt of Dunlon being abandoned being totally accurate. And, with the number of people bustling between tables and climbing the stairs in the entryway to their rooms, it's about as busy as the port of her hometown.

Darren and Idrid sit opposite Maia and Mark while Jasmine sits at the head of the table furthest from Idrid. They share looks while picking through their food, plates full of mashed potatoes and chicken breast. Darren is the first to interrupt the silence. "Let's start with why we're all here."

"We're competing against the other tower students," Mark says.

"We're here to join the Concilium," Darren says.

"What?" Maia glances between Darren and Idrid. "But they're bad."

"We know," Idrid says. "All we're doing is keeping tabs on them."

"So you're spies," Jasmine says.

"In a manner of speaking," Darren says. He waits for Jasmine to give her answer.

She rolls her eyes and says, "I'm here for Not. And the tournament."

"What do you want from him?" Idrid asks.

"Payback," Jasmine replies.

"Okay," Darren intercedes before Idrid can talk back. "How's this, then? We find Not and you two can settle your differences. Yes?"

"Sounds fair," Jasmine says coolly, scooping up her fork to begin eating.

Darren looks at Idrid who only nods after some seconds. "Good. In the meantime, I'd like to know what you know about the Concilium."

Jasmine looks up from her plate with her fork carrying a bit of the potatoes half-raised to her mouth. "I don't know much," she says, then bites down over her fork. "Only that they use forbidden magic."

Darren looks around the table to make sure no one is eavesdropping before saying, "Mind Control."

"Yeah. That guy I saw you and James with was one of them, right?"

"Right, Filento."

"I knew that some who were in contact with James were Concilium. That's all, I don't know who specifically."

"You knew. As in before the Concilium announced themselves to the world?"

"Some acquaintances told me."

"Who?"

Jasmine eats another scoop of her potatoes and chews slowly before swallowing and letting out a breath. "Woodlanders. The people who live in the Talwood."

Idrid sits forward slightly. "You know them?"

Jasmine sits back, surprised. "You do?"

"Not and I ran into them. Just before you two met, I think."

"Hold on," Maia chimes in, "You mean Woodlanders are real, too?"

"We can't confirm the dead walking around being real yet," Mark says.

Darren looks at both Maia and Mark. "I'm confused, but I'm going to ignore that last part. Who are the Woodlanders?"

Jasmine gestures her fork at Maia. "Like I said, they're people who live in the Talwood. They pointed me in the direction of Maia who they said would guide me to Not."

"You're talking about predicting the future?" Idrid asks.

"That among other things. They're knowledgeable in magic, and use it as a means of monitoring what's happening around the spanses at any given time."

"They sound powerful," Darren says modestly. "How come I haven't heard about them?"

"They stay hidden," Jasmine says.

"When we found them it was like we were led there," Idrid says. "It was weird. I think they used magic to lead us to them and away."

"What part of the Talwood do they live in, then?" Darren asks.

"I don't know. They live in massive trees, so somewhere in the center."

"That narrows it down to a couple hundred miles," Darren states.

"I don't know either," Jasmine says. "Like the big woman says, they only let you find them."

"What did you call me?"

Darren holds up a hand to calm Idrid. "So… Your friends who are Woodlanders led you to Maia who they said would eventually lead you to Not, and they knew about the Concilium. Since they didn't tell you who they are specifically, that doesn't narrow down much either."

"How many people were in contact with James?" Maia asks with a mouthful of food. "Like, who were his buddies who were also magicians?"

"A rough estimate would be hundreds," Darren says. "That would be those who lived in and around the palace. Give or take twenty guests every suppertime, only several returning every now and then."

"It's useless trying to narrow it down this way," Idrid says. "We already know the Concilium are members of the Magic Guild as we've seen during our trials to become a member."

"We don't necessarily know if there are others not joining this new Concilium," Darren says. "But I agree it's unhelpful guessing who out of hundreds uses Mind Control."

Some commotion in the entryway drags their attention from the conversation. Three men stagger to one of the tables closest to the door and shakily collapse into its seats. A fourth man, just as shakily, walks to the table and slams his fist down onto it, the noise quieting the majority of those feasting in the dining hall. "IT WAS HIM!" he bellows.

The other three men whose arms are clasped in front of them on the table to prevent serious shivering both shake and nod their heads.

"You can't convince me otherwise!" The fourth man jerks toward an adjacent table completely full and looks intensely at everyone. "James is alive!"

"What did he say?" a person from a table nearby Maia's murmurs.

"THE KING IS ALIVE!" the man shouts. "I SAW HIM!"

Darren stands up, his seat scuffing the wood floor, and disappears. He then appears standing beside the disturbed man grasping the back of his shirt.

The man flinches and whirls before relaxing slightly as Darren says something to him. "Yes! He was by the exit to the maze! You'll see!" He points out the door of the building. "Go! Look, and you'll believe me!"

Darren turns to Maia's table and beckons them to him. Unquestioningly, they all rise and move to Darren and follow him through the door, Idrid and Jasmine moving swiftest. No one else follows them out, though several begin trying to calm the man. Darren leads the group from the housing building between the tents, his cloak whipping quickly in the chilly air of the night. There are poles fitted with lanterns scattered at intervals that provide the few people still wandering about the tournament grounds with abundant light. Maia keeps her eyes on the back of Darren's cloak, making sure not to lose sight of the spot of red moving between people. Fortunately the little crowds of people part for them, seeming to know something is up with the purposeful way they move.

The further they move into the eastern portion of the tournament grounds the air gets chillier and a light mist hangs low over the tents just above their heads.

"That's not how mist works," Maia says between breaths to Mark who is walking fast beside her.

"I figured," Mark replies.

There's a break in the tents and they find an open patch of grass stretching all the way to the exit of the maze. Darren is less than halfway to the maze's exit, though the mist hangs lower and thicker, touching the ground some feet in front of the exit and obscures everything behind it.

"Is this?" Mark asks, not needing to complete the question to refer back to the first night they arrived at Woodside.

"It's like it," Maia says. They both stop walking, watching as Jasmine and Idrid move behind Darren who is about to reach the maze's exit. "Should we follow?"

"They're adults," Mark says. "They should be able to handle it."

"But if it *is* the dead, or ghosts..."

Mark doesn't say anything. Maia feels guilty, but is content staying where they are and waiting for the others to return. Darren stops at the exit and turns to Idrid and Jasmine, his mouth moving. They talk for a moment, Maia and Mark unable to hear a word of it, and then they meld with the mist and enter the maze's exit.

A calm quiet settles over them. The only noise comes from tournament-goers conversing back from the way they came.

Maia's breaths come out like bits of smoke. "Why would Not be inside the maze?"

"My best guess is he doesn't want to be seen," Mark responds.

Something like a tree branch cracking resounds from their left. They both turn and see him—Not—in dirty and fraying travelers clothes approaching them. His grey hair over his eyes waves with his movement, stepping carefully over the grass.

"Not?" He stops several feet away, his posture stiff and straight. Maia can't tell if his complexion is pale or if it's the mist muting his skin tone. His arms sway limply.

"My brother," Not says, his voice sarcastic. "You know him?"

"James?" Maia asks. "I… uh, everyone does. Though not personally."

His head turns upward slightly, allowing the moonlight and lights from the electric poles to reflect off his grey eyes which glare back at Maia. "Not personally." He laughs sharply, a grin that doesn't reach his unblinking eyes flashing across his face. "Such a name has the potential for too much wordplay."

"Yes?" Maia agrees tentatively. "Are you okay?"

"I'm dead," Not says.

Maia shakes her head, confused. "What're you talking about?"

His head falls suddenly with a loud *snap*, his hair falling over his face. Maia lets out a cry and jumps back as a tear in his clothes forms, and with it a cut that follows diagonally down from his right shoulder blade. No blood trickles out, just a dry and empty scar opening and revealing dry skin underneath.

"That's not Not," Mark says, backing away with her.

"Am I Not?" he asks, his head hanging limply with his face obscured and staring at the ground. Maia can see the top of his cheeks protruding from the way his head hangs, indicating he is smiling. "Not James." His body contorts in on itself, more bones cracking as his left shoulder unnaturally touches his chest while his right shoulder bends sharply to touch his back. His arms stick outward at odd angles, twisting his body gruesomely while his head and neck remain straight. "Not." His body shivers from a quiet laughter that emanates from his lips. In an instant his body flies backward through the mist, disappearing out of sight.

Maia and Mark stop backing away and stare at the empty space before them. Slowly Mark looks at her.

"We didn't find anyone," Darren says, suddenly standing behind them.

Maia and Mark jump and spin around. "Dunlon," Mark breathes.

"Frickety frick!" Maia says, her body involuntarily shaking once. "Don't just appear like that!"

"Sorry," Darren says. Loud thumps against the ground alert them to Idrid pacing toward them, followed by Jasmine a short ways behind. "Not must already be on the tournament grounds."

Maia looks for a moment at Mark and asks, "Why do you want to see him so badly?"

"He's helping us stop the Concilium," Darren says.

"He's my friend," Idrid adds, stopping beside Darren.

319

Mark looks like he is about to tell them about what just happened though Maia waves a hand to silence him. "What?" Mark asks her, though she shakes her head.

"Nothing. We should go back to the dining hall."

Darren nods, looking up at the sky. "The mist is clearing. It's strange that it is here at all."

"Magic," Jasmine huffs with annoyance, stopping beside Maia. "I can't tell what kind, but it's unnatural."

"You're probably right," Darren says. "Let's go back."

Darren, Idrid, and Jasmine go on ahead while Maia and Mark hang back a bit before starting to walk.

"Why didn't you tell them?" Mark asks.

"Because what if Not's dead?" Maia replies. "Do you really want to tell them that?"

"Do you really not?" Mark asks.

Shaking her head, she says, "We don't know who or what that was."

"So then why?"

"Because," Maia says, knowing she's being difficult but unable to stop herself. "If we tell them and it is him and he's not dead, Jasmine might actually kill him, and if we tell them and it is him and he is dead, it'll upset Idrid."

"Okay, but what if it isn't him, dead or not?"

"I don't know!" Maia says exasperatedly.

"Okay, fine. I won't tell them for now."

Maia nods. "Thanks. We can tell them, but I want to find out more first."

Chapter 30: Vespertine

A trio of horn players stand side-by-side outside student housing, facing the two-story building. They each wear rose-colored uniforms befitting one of the royal band. In unison, they twirl their polished silver trumpets and let loose a single, triumphant note as clear as the cyan sky above. The students who are all lined up in groups according to their respective Occult Tower face the trumpeters. A gathering of onlookers wanders over from their own housing. Each tower's students wear a monochromatic shirt designating what tower they belong to: blue marks students of the Elementalist tower, pale yellow marks students of the Spatial tower, and violet marks students of the Conjuring tower. Vespertine paces to the left of the trumpeters, following the first row of students to its end before doubling back to the trumpeters. Standing behind the horn players are Balnar, Analise, Tethris, and Goldyck, all wearing their velvet Magic Guild cloaks. The moment she steps in line beside the trumpeters they cut the note they play and swing their trumpets to their side in a parade rest position.

"The first day of the tournament has begun," Vespertine calls. She does not have to shout loudly as there are roughly forty students in every group. "And the first event of the day is about to begin. Students of Elementalism, Conjuring, and Spatial magic—you all will show your ability today. I look forward to seeing each of you perform. I'm sure you will do your tower masters proud. I will now announce what you all will be doing in the first event. Please turn your attention to the forest beyond the maze." Vespertine looks over her shoulder past the Concilium members and at the grey slate wall running in either direction around the Holt. The wall begins to move, and a space opens up as the wall splits. Across the stretch of grass beside the wall stands

Ponla, rhythmically tapping her knuckles against the wall to manipulate it. Once a fairly wide part in the wall is open, Ponla drops her hands and skips over to stand next to Tethris.

"Thank you, Ponla," Vespertine says, turning back to the students. "The first event is waiting for you all in the forest surrounding the Holt of Dunlon. You will find several species of trees there. A most uncommon tree in Lanmar grows only in this forest. They are known as Blood Elms because of the color of their sap. The sap is considered a commodity for its tanginess and sweetness in syrup-making. A male Blood Elm cone is smaller and lighter in color than female cones, which are larger. They contain pollen sacks that are released via air to attach to female cones. Your task is to find these trees and collect their cones—that is, one of each. Bring a male and female cone back here, and you will have completed the first event."

She signals with two fingers for the trumpeters to raise their horns and blow another loud, triumphant note. Dropping her hand to silence them, she nods at the students. "The first event has begun. Good luck."

"This isn't what I had in mind when the first event on my schedule said 'Search and Collect,' " Mark says to Maia as they jog with the other students between the part in the maze wall. Many of the Spatial magic students teleport and reach the forest before the others. "Are we each expected to bring two types of cones back?"

"I think we can work together, but we each likely have to bring our own," Maia says. Thanks to the running Jasmine made them endure they aren't nearly as breathless as most of the other students already are. They quickly become immersed in the forest and cut to the left to follow the maze wall east, deciding to get far away from the main body of students without much competition. "Can you tell the difference between these trees?"

Continuing to jog, careful not to trip over an upturned root, Mark appraises the trees they pass. "Pines typically have branches along the lower trunk while others' branches are higher from the ground, right?"

Maia looks up at the trees as she jogs. "Most of the forest's trees have tall trunks so their branches all look high up." It is true, the nearest branches are roughly four times their height stretching above their heads.

"The branches also aren't very long, right?" Mark continues to look around. "Forget it, it's better if I don't pretend to know the differences between trees. Let's start with what Vespertine told us with the sap."

Maia hears a *pop* and sees a thick knife appear in Mark's right hand. "Maybe you shouldn't run with that," Maia suggests, watching its edge swing back and forth pointing at Mark's face.

Mark looks back, checking to see how far they've run from the other students, then slows into a walk. "Let's try this tree." He steps over to a light-toned tree and digs his knife in between a crack in the bark. He leans in close to the knife and waits for a moment. Maia waits behind him. "No," he says finally, pulling his knife out. "The sap is clear-colored."

Maia compares what the light tree looks like to the others in their vicinity. "How about that one?" She points at a tree growing close to the maze wall. Its bark is slightly darker and its branches are different in height. They move over to it and Mark sticks his knife into the bark. A few seconds pass as Mark checks for the sap to come out.

"Not this one," Mark tells her.

A little exasperated, Maia turns on the spot. No matter what other tree she compares the two they've tried to, they all look the same. "I can't tell the difference," she says finally.

"Maybe we should try another area. They're supposed to be uncommon."

"SALUTATIONS, MAIA!"

Maia's head shoots up to see her old Elementalist mentor Greg falling from the highest branches overhead. He wears the same plain and loose clothes she always saw him in with the same loop of rope serving as a belt for his pants. A blast of air shoots up from the point Greg is going to land that catches his fall for a second and he touches down a second later on his feet.

"Forgive my incursion, but I had to see for myself that you were participating in the tournament. And, it seems, you are."

"Who's this?" Mark asks, pulling the knife out of the tree and approaching him.

"Whoa." Greg takes a step back and raises his hands defensively. In them are differently sized pine cones.

Mark looks down at the knife with a bit of sap and resin hanging on its edge and he lowers it. "Sorry. Hey, did you find the cones?"

"It's my mentor, Greg!" Maia says with a wide smile. She still considers him her mentor even though they've been apart so long. "How are you?"

Greg lowers his hands to fold them across his chest. "Good, now that I've seen you're doing well."

"No hard feelings about being a Conjuring student?" Maia asks.

"It's just a setback. You and the Spatialists will capitulate in the end."

"Sure," Maia says, glancing down at the cones he holds. "Where'd you get those, by the way?"

"These aren't the right ones, I'm sorry to say," Greg says. "I don't have a knife, so I was comparing the cones to each other up there."

"You can tell what the cones of a Blood Elm look like?" Maia asks.

"Yes. And, being the magnanimous guy I am, I'll join you two to help find them."

Jasmine would like him, Maia thinks.

Mark wipes the residual sap from his knife on his pants and nods. "That's good. I don't really want to stab every tree in this forest."

"Leave it to me. But, know that I am only doing this because I want to face you in the upcoming events." Greg flies back up the trunks of the tree, manipulating the air to send him up and up and land back on the tallest branches.

Mark gives Maia a serious look. "Was he your boyfriend?"

"What? No! Why would you think that?"

Mark shrugs, a smile breaking through his seriousness. "Just a question. He seems a bit old for you, anyway."

Maia makes a tutting noise, feeling the sudden redness in her face subside. "Go stab that tree over there."

"A report," Tethris says to Vespertine and the other Concilium members as they wait for the students to return. He looks around at the tournament-goers who have followed after the students and now wait by the opening in the maze. "From the palace. The servants confirmed James's body missing."

"Since when?" Vespertine asks, tapping her fingers on her arms.

"Last night."

"The same time it was reported that James was here at the tournament," Goldyck says.

"A new toy lost," Ponla says with a hint of sadness.

"He's dead, Ponla," Balnar says disgustedly.

"Not everything is a toy," Analise agrees. "The king and queen are exceptions."

"Hm," is all Ponla says.

Vespertine looks between the five of them. "It could be a coincidence and his body was moved sometime earlier. Either way, it's clear that the person that was actually seen last night was Not. Has there been another sighting since I arrived?"

They all shake their heads. "Those five who I saw picking a fight with each other didn't find him either," Goldyck says. "I don't know about the two students and the woman they were with, but Darren and Idrid still are the only ones I can confirm who are onto us."

"That's no matter," Vespertine says. "Once they know about what will happen, it will have already happened. All that will be left is to move the pieces accordingly."

"Thalidan's Council has confirmed they have armed ships sailing down the western coast toward Fairbreeze," Tethris says. "Their arrival will coincide with the final day of the tournament. Emerus has sent soldiers and stationed them in Chalman and Ferry."

Vespertine frowns. "They're already stationed there? What are they doing?"

"They have been instructed to follow your orders," Tethris explains. "At the moment they are fitting in as farmhands and loggers."

She thinks for a moment. "Very well. You can teleport there and tell them to continue 'fitting in' until the final day. In the meantime, let's try and find Not."

Nods all around. "Toy," Ponla murmurs, twirling a lock of her hair around her finger.

"Blood!" Mark exclaims, pulling his knife back with a trickle of red staining it. "I mean, sap. This is a Blood Elm!"

Maia moves to stand beside the tree and gaze up. Far above Greg is straddling one of its branches and peeking around in search of some cones.

"Found one!" Greg calls. "Catch!"

Maia watches a streak of yellow fall and she covers her head. The cone bounces off the forest floor, soft pine needles cushioning the fall. "Geez," Maia says, kneeling and scooping it up. "I don't want to crack my head open!"

"Sorry!" Greg calls back. Another cone falls a few feet away with a heavier thump, its color brown and a couple sizes larger.

"So this is the male one, and this—" she goes to pick up the other cone, "—is the female one."

"Looks like it," Mark says. Two more of each kind fall to the ground nearby. Mark winces, stepping away from where they fell. "Is he trying to kill us?"

"Eliminate the competition, win," Maia jokes.

"Ha. Hee. Hoo." Mark stoops and picks up the other cones.

A rush of wind casts the pine needles blanketing the ground to the side and Greg lands gently. "Task complete," he says. "Let's make our way back and you can tell me what's happened since you left." They begin following the maze wall back to where the woman Ponla made the opening.

Maia nods, almost comfortably slipping back into the role of his personal student. "You go first."

"Where to begin?" Greg starts. "I got a new mentee to train under me. He's got some promise, though he has yet to photosynthesize a tree. He's progressed past where you left off, anyway."

"I've progressed too, you know," Maia interjects.

"I don't doubt it. Anyway, Kellen rallied everyone up in preparation for the tournament and had everyone practicing day in, day out. Can't tell you what specifically, as we're planning on winning, but I can say that I've become quite good with manipulating the earth."

Maia becomes excited. "Is that what you're going to specialize in?"

"I think so," Greg affirms. "Other than that, Master Kellen deconstructed the old Elementalist tower and created a new one a few weeks before the tournament."

"He what!?"

"Oh, I forgot I wasn't supposed to tell you that. Well, don't tell anyone and keep it clandestine. Master Kellen told the students it was for their safety, though I suspected there was something more and asked him about it. He confided in me that there was a behemoth lurking in the ocean and not to tell the other students. Oh, wait."

"A behe-what?"

"Okay, keep that clandestine too. He described it as a long tentacle-y thing spanning the entire ocean, though I'm not sure I believe it to be that big. Whatever it was, no one else has seen it. To be honest, part of me thinks it's another weird myth Master Kellen has been researching like the Solar Flare."

"The Solar what?" It's Mark who asks.

"That's right," Greg says to himself derisively. "That was supposed to be clandestine too."

"Why do you keep saying 'clandestine'?" Mark asks with a little frustration.

"He likes to use big words," Maia explains.

"Keep it clandestine," Greg says. "It's a magical stone that houses the power of a star. Allegedly."

"All right, whatever," Mark says.

"I've never heard anything about a behe-whatever while in Fairbreeze," Maia says. "It sounds like something sailors would know."

They reach the new opening in the maze wall and make their way through a crowd of onlookers who begin to give them a light round of applause. Some other students are already back. Several of them are Elementalists while the majority are Spatialists. *This sort of task does seem to not be in a Conjuror's favor,* Maia thinks. Beside Vespertine and the other Concilium members are two wide buckets that hold the different types of cones.

"Let's converse more at the end of the day," Greg says. He moves ahead to place his cones into the respective buckets. Mark and Maia do the same shortly after and return to stand alone as the first of the Conjuring students to finish.

"We should probably let him in on the Concilium stuff," Mark says quietly to Maia who eyes Vespertine. The woman looks back at them thoughtfully, far too long for either of their comfort. "Maybe he could also help us with uncovering what we saw last night."

Maia winces at the memory. "If anyone would be helpful to tell, it'd be him," Maia relents. "Ok, we should tell him. For now let's worry about what our next challenge is."

Chapter 31: Idrid

"This is a strange tournament," Idrid comments, watching as the Concilium members divide and lead the students off in mixed groups after the first event ends. "What're the cones for?"

"Probably to breed more Blood Elms," Darren states. "Vespertine is known to experiment. It's really the only thing known about her other than being the Spatial Tower master."

Idrid sees Maia get selected by Balnar to join a group of three Spatialist students and two Elementalist students and they begin to walk away and off toward one of the larger blue tents. The girl glances back at Mark who is then selected for a different group. "Let's follow her," Idrid says, starting after Maia's group.

"You don't want to keep an eye on Vespertine?" Darren asks behind her.

"Jasmine said a prophecy or whatever from the Woodlanders predicted Maia and Not would meet," Idrid says.

"Do you believe in prophecies?"

"The Woodlanders weren't wrong about James and the Concilium," she replies, stepping through a crowd of onlookers who are slowly walking in the way of their pursuit of Maia's group. The crowd, seeing Darren's red cloak, parts for him to walk through. He follows Idrid around the tent and inside where Maia and the other students are instructed to move to the center of the area. He and Idrid find empty space by the outer edge of the tent to observe the second event. Maia looks around at the few clusters of people who already were there waiting or are just getting there now and spots Idrid and Darren. She waves slightly before turning her attention to Balnar who stands like a guard before the students in the center of the tent.

"She's the only Conjuring student in the group," Darren says. "Let's hope the event is in her favor."

Balnar begins to announce the second event as more people trickle into the tent. "Congratulations and good job on the first event. As you've no doubt noticed, we've separated you into groups and split off from the others. The group you are now in you will stay in for the following events. The event here with me now is simple. Objects will appear that you will be required to collect. Other objects will appear that you will not be required to collect. The objects you are looking for are green, and everything else does not matter. Each green object you collect will count as one point. They will appear and fall to the ground. If they touch the ground, they will no longer count for points and disappear. Any questions?"

The students all shake their heads.

"Kind of juvenile, isn't it?" Darren comments.

"They *are* kids," Idrid replies. "And weren't our trials to become part of the Concilium similar?"

Balnar gestures with his arms, signaling for the students to spread out. They de-cluster, moving into a loose circle around Balnar. He walks out of the center and joins the crowd at the outskirts. He turns, lifting a hand with his fingers extended upward. Five objects appear at once with five simultaneous *pops* at the ceiling of the tent and plummet down. The students scatter out from under a ten-foot flag pole, a wool coat, a claymore, a hooked metal object, and a green-painted wooden chair. None of the students manage to react quick enough to attempt catching the chair midair. The flag pole impales the hard earth along with the claymore while the chair cracks and splinters upon impact. The metal object thunks on the ground and the coat flutters down shortly after.

"Is that a door handle?" a spectator murmurs, pointing to the metal object. The objects disappear a second later before anyone in the crowd can respond, and five new objects appear in the air forty feet up. Students move again to dodge their trajectory and protect themselves.

"It looks like he's trying to kill them," Idrid comments as a glass plate and a vase shatter into sharp fragments on the ground. Maia stands still directly beneath a green-painted wooden beam spiraling downward. She extends both her hands with her palms upward and the beam stops sharply in the air. Maia flinches as the beam bounces slightly against the wall of air she created, coming close to her hands, though holds firm with her magic.

"Point, Maia," Balnar calls, and all of the objects disappear. He raises his other hand and seven objects appear in the air. The green object flashes in the morning light provided by the slits in the tent, a tinted wine bottle turning clockwise as it falls. The students frantically get out of the way of the other objects and converge under the glimmering green wine bottle. The bottle disappears out of the air and reappears in a spatial student's outstretched hand. The bottle hits his hand with a loud *smack* and eludes his grasp, bouncing off the floor.

"I see," Darren says. "This task is specifically difficult for Teleporters."

"Hm?" Idrid murmurs as a question.

"Teleporters have to make a series of exact calculations in order to teleport objects. One important factor is the momentum of the object. Even if the Teleporter successfully teleports the object, it will continue with its initial momentum. It's impressive that Balnar can conjure these various objects at once, and at a distance."

Idrid watches as another series of objects smash on the ground, among them a green-painted plant pot unsuccessfully caught by any of the students. "So what you're saying is if the object is too heavy or dangerous to catch, all a Teleporter can really do is move it from one spot to another."

A green jacket appears amongst a variety of furniture in the air and flutters downward. None of the Spatial students try and magic the jacket to them. Maia and several other students whip up an air current that pushes and pulls the jacket multiple directions in the air. A strong wind blows the jacket closer to one of the Elementalist students. Maia, seeing that it wouldn't go her way, extends her hand out and pushes at the air to create a large gust. The jacket is blown past the Elementalist student and into the surrounding audience whose hair and clothes ruffle in the harsh breeze. The Elementalist looks at Maia with annoyance.

"Smart of her to take away a point from another," Idrid says. "But why didn't the Teleporters do anything?"

"An object that's not static is difficult to teleport," Darren explains. "A jacket being worn is more easy to account for, but one fluttering, furling and unfurling like that, is something else."

"Wow," Idrid comments. "It's good Maia has an advantage, but is this really fair for those students?"

"Who cares if it's fair?" comes a sarcastic voice from behind her. She turns and recognizes familiar long, unruly dark hair falling around the man's face and over his shoulders. He wears a tan traveler's garb and a sword belt with his curving scimitar sheathed at his waist. Standing next to him and behind Darren is a woman Idrid doesn't recognize who is similarly dressed with a straight sword protruding over her left shoulder, though her face is lit up with a friendly smile.

"Tang!" Idrid states, surprised. "Where's Not? You didn't—"

"No, I didn't kill him," Tang says with an air of regret. "And don't ask me questions I don't have an answer for."

"Fine. Who's this?" Idrid asks, gesturing to the woman next to him.

"Who are any of you?" Darren asks, his interest piqued at the mention of Not, causing him to turn away from the spectacle happening at the center of the tent.

"I'm Kelsey," Kelsey says with a short wave. Idrid sees that her hands are rough, noting the woman must be similarly experienced with fighting like Tang. "We're what you can call Not's old buddies."

"Not me," Tang says. "I'm more of a rival-slash-enemy."

Kelsey continues, saying, "Not went off on his own when we reached Woodside several days ago. He didn't want to wait around for us."

"You don't know where he is now," Idrid states, anger sinking into her words.

"We're not his handlers," Tang says sharply. "When he gets an idea, he jumps on it."

"Excuse me." Kelsey raises her hand up to her shoulder-level as if she's in a classroom. "If you don't mind me asking, but are you... a real Giant?"

The woman's innocent sincerity in asking conflicts with the anger Idrid has when hearing her race brought up.

"Half-Giant," Darren corrects for her.

"I thought so!" Kelsey says. "I've never seen a Giant, though I figured they just looked like tall people."

"If you thought so, why didn't you specifically ask if I were a half-Giant?" Idrid says.

"Well, because a relationship between a Giant and a human is unheard of. Where I'm from Giants are a myth."

"Would you stop saying 'Giant'?"

"Sorry," Kelsey apologizes. She slowly looks Idrid up and down. "You're Idrid, right?"

"Yeah."

"Not and Tang mentioned you," Kelsey says.

"They didn't mention how I was a half-Giant?"

"Well, yes. Not also mentioned that Tang should—"

"NO!" Tang's sudden shout causes the majority of the audience to look their way. Even Balnar momentarily pauses from conjuring objects to glance at them. Tang looks at the center of the tent and quickly points at Maia. "You're losing points! Conjure something for yourself!"

"No audience participation, please!" Balnar calls.

Maia's face reddens, though she nods. The next moment she's conjured a small wooden rowboat on the floor. A green cup falls onto it and shatters in pieces within the boat.

"Point, Maia," Balnar announces.

"Conjuring something to catch the objects for her," Darren muses, clapping along with some of the crowd. "Smart."

"Why'd you shout?" Idrid asks.

"She was about to say something she would regret," Tang says. "And by regret, I mean she'd be dead. Because I'd kill her."

"You want to fight?" Kelsey challenges him.

"Yes," Tang says without hesitation. "But first I'm going to fight Not, which won't happen until the final day."

"You're participating as magicians?" Darren asks. "Are you magicians?"

"Technically we are," Kelsey says.

"Physical magicians, as Not likes to say," Tang adds.

"He's never said that," Idrid says.

"He never had a reason to around you."

"Really?"

"He doesn't discuss his early life, yeah?" Tang says. "Not around others unless they're from his early life."

"Whatever. Not has his reasons."

"Excuse me, I couldn't help but overhear, but I thought I heard someone using a lot of negatives over here." Jasmine scooches up close behind Tang and Kelsey, causing them to inch away with irritation. "Could it be that Not is around?"

"Now who the hell are you?" Tang spits.

"Warm," Jasmine comments sarcastically, then puts her slim smile back on. "I'm Jasmine. Don't tell me you're also friends of Not's?"

"I'm here to kill him," Tang says.

"Fight," Kelsey euphemizes.

"So not Not's friends," Jasmine says. "I could use your help."

"She actually wants to kill Not," Idrid comments.

"Not kill!" Jasmine says with feigned alarm. "Though maybe maim or torment."

"A sadist?" Tang turns on her and puts a hand on the hilt of his sword. "It doesn't matter. If you get between my blade and him, I'll kill you."

"He really means kill this time," Kelsey says, putting a hand on her own sword and facing Jasmine. "I will too."

"Aw," Jasmine pouts. "And I was going to ask what you meant by 'physical magicians' to learn more about him." She gets on her tiptoes and looks over Tang and around Idrid at the students moving around the center of the tent. "Maia's doing well, isn't she?"

"Where've you been skulking?" Idrid asks.

"Around," she replies vaguely. "I'm looking forward to the last day. It seems we're each eager to have a go at Not." She glances down at Tang and Kelsey's hands still on their swords' hilts. "Calm down, I was only joking before. I've reevaluated my purpose, and I don't want to kill or hurt Not."

Idrid raises her eyebrows skeptically. "Really? Why is that?"

Jasmine shrugs. "Because he's already dead."

Chapter 32: Maia

"That's the end!" Balnar calls, putting a stop to the students' frantic movement. "The final scores: Emir with one point; Uon and Flannery tied with two points; and Maia with four points." The audience claps lightly for the students. The two who scored no points are Spatial students and Emir who scored lowest is also a Spatial student. They each hold a grim look that exudes resentment toward the two Elementalists and Maia. Maia is too breathless and elated to care. "Good job, everyone. Please take out your schedules and look at the map of the tournament grounds. You will notice numbers corresponding to certain events. Those numbers are written over tents where the event will take place. Your next event is number 7."

Maia quickly pulls out her crinkled schedule she'd folded and stuffed into her pants' pocket and sees the tent with the number 7 on the western side of the Holt. The event is titled "Tag." She looks up to see Balnar conjure a clean white paper that he tacks onto the interior tent wall.

"Performances will be displayed for every event like so inside each tent," he tells the students. "The next event starts at noon. Do as you like before then."

The surrounding audience begins to funnel out of the tent while some choose to stay and observe the next group of students who would be participating there. Maia glances at the Spatial students who quickly leave as well. She turns her attention to where she last saw Darren and picks out his vibrant red cloak among the bustling crowd. The large woman Idrid is with him, though their backs are turned to her. Curious, she moves to stand with them. As she approaches and gets closer she sees they are with Jasmine who stands alongside a man and woman she doesn't

339

recognize. Each casually rests a hand on the swords they wear, the man's at his hip and the woman's behind her back. Maia slows, searching their faces for a hint to what they're doing. Jasmine is smiling in the patronizing way she usually does while the others' faces are serious and pale. Stopping behind Darren and Idrid she asks, "What's up?"

Darren momentarily acknowledges her presence while Idrid doesn't turn, continuing to stare Jasmine down.

"Maia," Jasmine says thoughtfully. "You didn't happen to see Not, did you?"

The question catches her off guard. She fails to stifle her reaction, though she hopes it comes off similarly to genuine confusion. "Uh, no. Why?"

"Interesting," Jasmine says. Her eyes dart to the crowd moving around them, making sure none are paying attention to them. "Then you wouldn't know that he is dead."

Maia's face takes on a similar color as the others. Her thoughts return to the previous night when Not or something else approached her, broken and cut.

"This is a dilemma, though," Jasmine goes on, putting a finger to her chin. "The Woodlanders couldn't be wrong in telling me you would meet him. Does that mean you've already met him? Did you meet him but fail to recognize him? Or, did you meet him and recognize him but fail to tell anyone?" Jasmine carefully watches Maia for a reaction to each of her questions. Idrid finally turns to look at Maia, though her eyes are distant. "Or, maybe you have yet to meet him? The question would then be why would you meet a dead body?"

"Enough," Idrid says. "How are you certain that he's dead?"

Jasmine blinks. "I saw him."

"Where?"

"There's a tent," Jasmine says vaguely.

Idrid steps directly in front of Jasmine, the man and woman with swords stepping out of her way. She puts a hand gently on Jasmine's shoulder who for her part doesn't flinch. "Show me."

"Not now," Jasmine says. "Tonight."

"What?" Idrid puts her other hand on Jasmine's bare shoulder.

"Not having another fight?" Balnar steps up beside the swordsman and gazes steadily at Idrid whose hostility is broiling. Each of her arms are visibly shivering. "If so, I'll be forced to disqualify you from the tournament and, subsequently, the Concilium."

Idrid lets her arms drop to her sides, though leans in close to Jasmine's blank face. "Tonight, then. Until I see, I won't believe it." She turns and walks between Balnar and the swordsman, her legs swiftly taking her out of the tent.

"This is a tournament," Balnar says slowly, appraising each of them. "At the very least, look like you're enjoying yourselves." He paces away, leaving them to look at each other.

Maia shifts her feet. If Jasmine knows and has confirmed it, then that means there's no point keeping it a secret what she saw the other night. "Um…"

"You did good, Maia," Darren says brightly, patting her on the back. "Don't worry about any of this. Just focus on the next event."

"…Oh. Thanks," she says, looking at the swordsman. "You were the one who told me to conjure something, right?"

341

"Yes," the swordsman says in an equally hostile tone to Idrid's. He continues to glare at Jasmine who is absently rubbing her shoulders where Idrid touched her.

Awkwardly, Maia nods and says nothing.

The swordsman nods back, then looks at the swordswoman. "Let's go."

"Where?" she asks.

"To find him, obviously," he replies. "That bint said she saw him in a tent. If she won't say, let's search them all." They both walk away, leaving Jasmine, Maia, and Darren alone.

Darren and Maia appraise Jasmine for a reaction, though she appears not to have been listening. "Do you believe he's really dead?" Maia asks.

Darren shakes his head. "No matter what I believe, I know he's not someone who'd die easily."

Maia nods uncertainly. "Okay." She looks at Jasmine, noting the blank stare she is giving the ground. "I'm going to prepare for the next event, then." Jasmine stops rubbing her shoulders and slides her gaze onto Maia.

"Good," she says shortly, then paces out of the tent.

"She seems different," Darren comments. "First she was almost gleeful about telling us Not is dead, now she's not emoting at all."

Maia shrugs. "My mom acts the same regarding my dad."

The sunlight seems to set the tournament grounds in a pale light rather than livening up the healthy green grass and deep blue tents. Jasmine lets her feet carry her toward the one tent on the grounds that serves alcohol, glancing every now and then at the faces of the tournament-goers. Most are preoccupied with their schedules they hold in their hands, boasting to one another and non-participants about how they'll win. Uninterested, Jasmine pushes past them all. She is lightheaded, her thoughts jumbled yet focused enough on getting a drink to ground herself. She reaches the shack-sized tent serving as a bar that has a solitary stool placed at the entrance and moves inside. There's an immediate wooden countertop within, and behind it is a slender barkeeper who is entertaining himself by stacking wooden mugs on top of each other. He places the mug he holds down and stands up straight when Jasmine enters.

"Need a drink?"

Jasmine moves her head ambiguously up and down and side to side, her dark hair bouncing slightly along with the movement.. The barkeeper interprets it correctly and begins filling a mug with the warm orange liquid of Summer's Fire. She puts a coin on the countertop before taking the mug and stepping back outside into the pale light. A lone cloud floats over the sun and momentarily darkens the area. She sits down on the stool by the tent and takes a sip, grimacing at the bittersweet taste. People pass her and the bar tent by, all enjoying themselves too much to stoop to drinking before noon. One tall yet hunched man wearing a brown hood low over his face shambles closer and stops outside the tent, turning to Jasmine. She gives him a cursory once-over before looking down at her drink and taking another sip. He has a ridiculously scraggly grey beard wildly falling from his cheeks and chin. His appearance and the way he shivered and shambled even while standing still reminds her of an aged rat.

He groans slightly, gesturing a quivering hand to the drink in her hand. His voice is almost comically wizened. "Ahh—Shummer's Fiyer." Slowly, he retracts his hand into his baggy brown robes. "It'sh not quite my faaay-vorite drink." The way he nods to affirm his statement is jerky like he's having a seizure.

"No?" Jasmine asks, deciding to engage with the old man. "What is your favorite?"

"Ahh—it ish that Midnight Delight. I think I'll have shome now." He puts a hand on his back just above his hip and stretches, puffing his chest out. She hears several bones crack in response. "Ahh. Body'sh not what it used to be." The man slumps back into his hunch and shambles within the tent, leaving Jasmine alone for the moment.

Looking down at her drink she decides she also prefers Midnight Delight. The plain bitterness sustains its taste longer than Summer's Fire. She enjoys the few moments of solitude before the man shambles back out of the tent with a mug of Midnight Delight cupped in both his hands.

"Don't mind if I shtand by, do-ya?" Without waiting for a response he slowly moves to her other side so that he doesn't stand in the way of anyone else looking for a drink. "Besht not to drink at thish time."

"You are."

"Ohh—sho I am." The breath of his subsequent chuckles flutters the fringe hairs on his beard. He brings his mug to his lips then pauses, the mug shivering. "What'sh thish? You sheem to already be intoxshicated."

She looks up at one of the man's unobscured pale eyes looking back at her. "What?"

"I shee it in your eyesh," the man huffs, lowering his mug and unsteadily stooping to balance it on the uneven

344

ground. "You're not quite yourshelf." He slowly turns himself while stooped down, causing Jasmine to worry he'll topple himself over. He somehow manages to face her and he shakily scratches his beard. "Yesh… How much have you had to drink?"

"This is the only one," she says, turning the mug she holds around in her hands. "Have you had too much to drink?"

"No," the man responds, stressing the "o" slowly. "Thish is no mere intoxshication, then. Hmm. Guessh I'll have to."

Jasmine says, "What?" as the man raises his hand to her face. She leans back on her stool, though his hand follows her.

"Don't you worry," he reassures her. She watches, perplexed, as his hand draws closer above and between her eyes toward her forehead. His fingers brush her skin softly, and she feels a warm sensation beneath his touch. Then, she passes out.

Noon comes around fast and Maia, who arrived early to the third event, watches as the other students in her group enter the tent. The Spatial students still have subtle contempt pulling their mouths downward when they see her along with the two Elementalist students. She shyly shifts her feet as they position themselves around the center of the tent. The same relative size of the audience occupies the edge of the tent. The woman, Ponla, who Maia met when she first got to the tournament and entered the maze sits casually atop a wooden crate that's four feet high, dangling her legs over the edge as she watches the students.

"Are you all here?" she calls to them. They all nod, none of them speaking. "Good. I already know, but it's good you all know. The game you'll be playing here is tag."

"Game?" Emir questions under his breath, Maia remembering the name of the Spatial student that Balnar called to have received the only point among his tower's students.

"There are three rules. A tag is when you touch another's hand. Tag other students, and don't get tagged by other students. Ready?"

Maia barely has time to process what it is she's supposed to do before Ponla shouts for them to begin. The other students warily back away from each other, each quickly assessing the others' abilities in relation to the event. Realizing she's at a clear disadvantage against the Teleporters, she tries to think of what she can do to prevent herself from getting tagged.

Too soon, Emir teleports in front of her and swipes his hand across hers, grazing her skin.

"Point, Emir!" Ponla calls happily as Emir disappears and reappears where he was previously standing several feet apart from the others.

Thinking better of staying still, Maia breaks into a full-out run, moving straight for one of the other Spatial students she lacks a name for. The first student, who is a boy, easily teleports away. Knowing he would, she turns her course toward the last Spatial student. She also teleports away. Now that she's gotten enough speed, Maia pushes her arms behind her back and feels a rush of air fill her palms and lift her off the ground. The space within the center of the tent is large enough for her to maneuver, and she quickly whizzes toward Emir. His eyes widen at how fast she's moving, though he still has time to teleport away. The two Elementalist students

Uon and Flannery warily bring their hands up and Maia senses that they're manipulating the air in front of them to be solid. She doesn't care, as she's not aiming for them. With the continuous gust of air sending her flying around the tent, if the Teleporters wanted to score another point from her they would have to immerse themselves in the wind and then they'd just be sent flying. She knows she can hardly catch a Teleporter, so she settles for the next best thing which is to continue moving. Now it's an endurance battle.

She chases the Teleporters down who always teleport away when she's just about to reach them, though she always angles herself to continue chasing them relentlessly. For what feels like the fifth time she's flying toward Emir he suddenly falls over.

Maia looks down to see the ground entangling itself over his feet, pulling him a foot into it. She flies clear over him and angles herself away from the outer edge of the tent, careful not to run into the crowd. When she looks back she sees Uon racing over to where Emir lies, slapping his splayed hand before sprinting away.

"Point, Uon!" Maia hears Ponla call. A tremendous rumbling sound overtakes the rushing air Maia manipulates and a giant wall of dirt rips up out of the ground in the center of the tent, dividing the students on either side. Before she flies face-first into it, Maia ceases the air current and skids to a halt. Looking at Ponla, she sees the woman standing atop her four-foot crate and smiling. Ponla points a finger between Maia and both Emir and Uon and another wall of dirt erupts out of the ground and puts them out of her line of sight. Maia is now cut off from everyone except for the small section of the crowd on her side of the tent. More rumbling shakes the earth and Maia looks up to see Ponla now walking along the top of the walls. The woman stops at the center where the walls converge and she begins turning slowly in place, looking down at each corner she has separated. The walls begin to turn with her as if she is their focal point, shifting along the ground with even more rumbling.

Maia moves so that the wall doesn't collide with her. This is obviously part of the event, Maia thinks, though she wonders how she is going to get to the other students now. She hasn't reliably manipulated the earth outside of entering and exiting the Elementalist tower, and she doubts Ponla will allow her to make a hole in the rotating walls. Glancing up, she also knows it would be too dangerous to lift herself up that high and get over the walls.

"Point, Flannery," Ponla calls.

Continuing to move out of the way of the wall, she considers making a hole to go underneath. The thought of the rotating walls falling on top of her scares her too much to try.

"Point, Uon."

The Elementalist students seem to be taking advantage of the new terrain and getting the upper hand. She has to do something or she'll not have any points. Spinning on her heel, she focuses her resolve to blast a hole in the oncoming wall. Pulling both her hands back and positioning her legs shoulder-length apart, she shoves her hands forward and palms the wall. Rather than coming apart, the wall recedes on itself and a square hole large enough to fit through appears. Maia quickly steps through it and sees Flannery and one of the Spatial students dodging each other. They notice Maia and move apart. Flannery looks between her and the Spatial student, then gives Maia a nod.

Agreeing to the implied temporary coalition, Maia nods back. She conjures a black blanket large enough to envelope her and tosses it into the air. Manipulating the air, she sends it whirling toward the Spatial student who is half-paying attention while moving out of the way of the rotating wall. The blanket spreads out, covering the remaining area from the Spatial student's sight. Maia and Flannery follow the blanket's progression. The student, unable to teleport, swipes his arm at the blanket to tear it out of the air. When he does, both Maia and Flannery quickly tap his hand that grips the blanket.

"Point, Maia and Flannery."

Satisfied, Maia races away. The Spatial student is frustrated, his red face a clear sign of it. Before anything more can happen the walls stop rotating and Ponla looks down at each of them individually.

"That's the end." Ponla's walls of dirt recede back into the ground, revealing the rest of the tent. Ponla stops descending when her feet reach ground-level and she paces back to the crate in the crowd and lifts herself onto it to sit. "The final scores are: Maia with one point; Emir with one point; and Uon and Flannery with two points. Good job." Maia looks at the same two Spatial students who, again, scored no points. Both their faces are flushed with frustration, the girl cracking her knuckles. "Look at your schedules. Your next event will be in the tent with the number 5 on it. It will begin in an hour." Ponla waves them away dismissively before turning to pick up a pen and write the scores down on a paper resting atop the crate beside her.

Sighing, Maia looks around at the crowd who lightly applaud and doesn't see anyone familiar. It's been a while since she's seen Mark, so she resolves to find him before their next event. She wants to tell him about the events thus far, as well as tell him about what Jasmine said. *I hope Aveve doesn't make losing any of the events at this tournament conditional for expulsion...*

Torion Oey

Chapter 33: Idrid

"What in the spanses is she doing?" Idrid and Darren stand under the warm glow of a lamp while tournament-goers breeze by, their shadows melding together in the dark cover of night.

Darren looks up from the schedule for the first day. "Hmm?" he asks distractedly.

"Don't tell me she got drunk and passed out," Idrid mutters then strides toward the beer tent. Jasmine rests upon the lone stool outside, her form slumped backward with her head lolling with each of her deep breaths. Some old man stands beside her with a hand on her back that keeps her propped up. The man's ratty beard is flecked with drops of liquid. He takes a deep swig from a brown mug and emits an emphatic "ahhh" after he swallows.

"That'sh shome powerful shtuff," he says in a rickety voice that cracks more than once.

Idrid reaches the man with Darren shortly after and crosses her arms. "Who are you?"

He pauses, the mug in his hand shivering in his grip for a second, then he takes another long drink. "Ahhh. Shorry, misshus, I didn't shee you there. I'm jusht a traveler. There I wash, enjoying the tournament, and then I came upon thish woman who couldn't sheem to keep her liquor. Hah."

"What're you drinking?" she asks.

"Thish ish water," the man says, sloshing it towards Idrid, some droplets falling out of the mug and to the ground.

"We'll take her," Darren says, moving to Jasmine's other side and lifting her arm.

"Ah, friendsh of hersh, eh?" The man raises his head to allow some light to fall on the lower part of his face that is unobscured by his hood. "Good thing you came along. Yesh." Jasmine begins to stir when the man lets go of her back. Idrid reaches out and catches her other arm to steady her. "She'sh probably going to be very weary," the man advises.

"Are you going to make it all right?" Idrid looks up only to see that the old man is no longer there. "Where'd he go?"

"Wait," Jasmine murmurs softly.

"Come on, we're getting you to housing," Darren tells her.

"What?" Jasmine's eyes open and they flit between Idrid and Darren. "Where'd you come from? Why is it nighttime?"

"Apparently you got drunk," Idrid says with a hint of satisfaction.

"Crap in a bucket," Jasmine says, detaching her arm from Darren to pry her other arm away from Idrid's hold. "Wait, no I didn't. I just had a sip."

"That's what they all say," Idrid says.

"*Several* sips," Jasmine hisses. "Then some old guy talked to me. Where is he?"

"Disappeared in the crowd," Darren says. "Did… did you get drunk because of Not?"

"What?" Jasmine looks up at him for the first time and whatever color in her face drains away. "I said Not was dead."

Darren gives her a long look before uttering a single word in the most sincere condescension rivaling that of a parent speaking to his toddler: "Yeah."

She blinks. Her face screws up, tightening. Then she relaxes and opens her mouth. "The Concilium tricked me." She jumps to her feet suddenly, her legs wobbling slightly. Despite her desire to see the woman fall, Idrid reaches out to steady Jasmine. "Come with me," Jasmine says and paces away purposefully without Idrid's help.

"Where are we going?" Idrid asks with Darren in pursuit.

"I'm not sure yet," Jasmine replies. She impatiently pushes through streams of people who're either oblivious of their surroundings or don't have a chance to move out of the way of the woman cutting a path across the tournament grounds. She makes it outside the area where the tents are clustered around the holt and begins walking fast along its edge. In the space between the tents and the surrounding maze there are fewer people, though still groups who are huddled together here and there, most nearer the line of tents where tournament lights provide illumination. "Come on," Jasmine huffs out in annoyance. She scans the area between the tents and walls, stopping intermittently to check more closely between the tents.

"Who're you looking for?" Idrid asks.

"I'm not sure exactly." Jasmine freezes suddenly with her eyes locked straight ahead. There a thin mist wafts in the air, seemingly coating the grounds in a dull white hue. "We're getting closer," Jasmine says, trudging forward with yet more speed. Idrid actually has to walk mildly fast to keep up for once while Darren pants behind her in a light jog. The mist damply touches upon their skin and causes them all to shiver. Jasmine continues along the line of tents then cuts between them, moving back onto the main tournament grounds. Idrid makes sure to keep a line of sight of her with the moist air hanging ever tighter with the thickening mist. Overhead the lamplights are muted, obscured orbs of light. The blue tents rise up and out of sight in the pale darkness. People are more carefully maneuvering around each other while Jasmine blazes through. Jasmine stops suddenly yet again beside a large tent, looking it up and down.

Idrid halts behind her, and Darren beside Idrid, and it is then that Idrid notices the mist seems to emanate from between and beneath the walls of the tent. What's more, the mist clings to the walls of the tent like a veil before drifting away.

"What'd I tell you guys?" Jasmine breathes. "The mist is magic." She walks beside the tent, slapping a hand along the wall of the tent that causes the fabric to ripple along with the veil of mist. They reach the opening and move inside, undisturbed by any of the nearby tournament-goers.

The entirety of the interior is illuminated with obscured orbs of electrical light hanging along a low fence encircling the center of the tent. Above them and hanging below the square ceiling are more electrical lights that, while not cutting through the mist well enough to shine upon the ceiling, are visible to Idrid from the ground. The audience space is deserted save for themselves. The event space in the middle of the tent, however, is occupied by two people at the very center. A man stands taller than the other and wears ragged clothes that are torn in places. The one on the right, roughly a foot shorter than the tall man, wears a familiar red cloak with the hood down. It is from that one's outstretched hand that a trail of mist pours forward and blossoms out in all directions.

Idrid and the others step silently over the low fence designating the event area within the tent and move closer. It's the tall one on the left she recognizes first who has telltale frazzled silver-grey hair hanging above his grey eyes. "James." She turns to Jasmine and whacks her arm.

"Ow!" Jasmine bats Idrid's arm in retaliation though her hand bounces off the bigger woman's beefy arm ineffectually.

"You said Not was dead," Idrid grunts. A mixed feeling of satisfaction and relief tilts her lips up.

"Your friend was manipulated," says the woman standing next to James. Ponla takes a step forward, ceasing her Elementalist magic creating the mist, and waves at them all like a child would to a friend. "By me. I did the same to Not when I was out playing in the fields of Telnas one night. Come to think of it, it was actually the night before he killed James."

"Now that's obvious," Jasmine says. "But what was the point?"

Ponla puts her hands in the inner pockets of her cloak and shrugs. "Toys are fun." James's body shudders beside her, and there's the sound of a bone cracking.

"Toys?" Jasmine responds, confused.

"Is that really James?" Darren asks.

"Yeah," Ponla says.

"But he's dead," Darren says.

"Yeah," Ponla says. "It's his carcass."

Darren shudders in revulsion. "I've got too many questions."

"Why were you standing here like you were expecting us?" Jasmine asks.

Ponla shrugs again. "Maybe I was."

"Has anyone else walked in here and seen… him?"

"No, just you," Ponla replies. "This is boring now. Don't you want to find Not?"

Idrid takes a step forward, now a measly ten feet between them. "Where is he?"

"I don't know," Ponla says. "You should've found him by now."

"What do you mean?"

"Your friend isn't being manipulated now, is she?"

Jasmine doesn't move, though responds. "You didn't stop mind-controlling me?"

"I never was," Ponla says.

"Then why do I remember being told to tell them," Jasmine says, referring to Idrid and Darren, "that Not was dead when I saw James and then doing it?"

"You've had vesper," Ponla says.

"What?"

"You all have," she goes on. "It makes you easy to manipulate."

"What are you talking about?" Idrid asks.

Ponla sighs with boredom though begins explaining. "Vespertine created a substance she named vesper to control everyone without the use of magic."

Idrid asks, "Is that even possible?"

"You'll see," Ponla says. James's body cracks again, his left shoulder collapsing so that his arm hangs unnaturally out of its socket.

Idrid takes a step back, unnerved by the body whose eyes continuously move to each of them on repeat. "What are you doing to him?" Darren asks haltingly.

"Just playing. You'll see there is much more magic can do beyond what you know."

"Why are you telling us this?" he asks.

"I thought it would be more fun than not telling you," she says.

"Are you not part of the Concilium?"

"I am, for however long it lasts."

Idrid considers this to be a bleak thing to say about one's own organization. "What are Vespertine's plans?"

"I'm not going to tell you that," Ponla says. She turns to Idrid and asks, "Aren't you going to find Not already?"

"We haven't seen him."

"You have," Ponla insists. Her gaze slides off Idrid and sticks to Jasmine. "At least one of you has." She suddenly swipes her hand through the air. The surrounding mist begins to ebb away. James's body falls forward and sinks into the ground, the earth reforming a flat surface over it.

"What are you all doing here?" Vespertine walks into the tent, followed by Balnar. "Why are you practicing Elementalism, Ponla?"

"Playing with toys," Ponla says, her mouth forming a sweet smile.

"They're guests," Balnar growls.

Idrid, Darren, and Jasmine look at each other uncertainly. The surrounding lights finally cut through the dispersing mist and warmly light the inner tent.

"Did she rope you into one of her antics?" Vespertine asks, directing the question at Idrid.

Idrid thinks over what Ponla just disclosed to them about the mind-controlling substance vesper and wonders how to answer.

"They came to me," Ponla says. "They heard about the rumors of James and thought the magic mist had something to do with it."

Vespertine looks at each of them in turn. "They're not rumors," she says finally.

Ponla walks casually around and past them to stand by Vespertine, her smile broadening slightly. "No, they're *not.*"

Vespertine shoots Ponla a glare, then says, "You all should return to the festivities outside. And you, Idrid, should get some rest before it's your turn to partake in the events."

Idrid nods slowly, taking the opportunity to make her way out with the others.

"Be sure to find Not," Ponla says to them before they leave.

Vespertine, Balnar, and Ponla watch the wide slit in the tent where the three exit. Several seconds later Vespertine turns to Ponla. "That was surprisingly good work."

Ponla's same sweet smile is stuck on her face. "Thanks."

"Using one of them to confirm Not being here was a brilliant idea."

"You could stop calling them toys," Balnar puts in.

"Toys are better than anything else," Ponla says.

"We'll have to make sure to get Jasmine to intake more vesper," Vespertine continues. "And make sure we don't wholly activate its effects again until after the tournament."

"Ugh," Ponla groans, dropping the smile.

"Was it necessary to tell them about vesper?" Balnar asks.

"Patience," Vespertine says. "Only two days left."

Torion Oey

Chapter 34: Darren

Day two of the tournament arrives with little fanfare. Darren is unsurprised given the current sociopolitical climate that, when the Concilium arrives to direct the participants outside their housing, there are fewer non-magicians than the first day's students. People are grouped together and sent off to separate tents where the day's events will be held. Darren, along with Jasmine, follows Idrid's group into a tent and observe as the participants are tasked with a show of strength that has them duke it out between themselves.

"What do you remember from yesterday?" he questions Jasmine as Idrid is paired off to wrestle with a burly man roughly her same height.

"I told you all I remember," Jasmine snaps. Her hair is uneven and splayed while her slim-fit black dress is wrinkled, leaving the most obvious guess for Darren as to why she has a short temper this morning.

Darren runs through the events again out loud. "You found James being controlled by Ponla in a tent, though you didn't know it was Ponla who was doing it, and she controlled you with something called vesper which made you think it was Not. Under that control, you went and told us Not was dead, then went to the bar tent where you passed out for most of the day. We found you and with you we found Ponla who told us about Vespertine's vesper but not her plans." He pauses and claps politely with the rest of the crowd as Idrid and the burly man at the center of the tent begin to grapple with each other. "Vespertine and Balnar came in and didn't know that we were all there and what Ponla was doing. Though, Vespertine then told us the rumors about James being at the tournament were true, which indicates she had known to some extent what Ponla was doing with James. But why would Ponla bother burying James's body?"

"She probably thought some common folk would come in and see," Jasmine says, huffing out a breath that blows strands of her hair away from her face. "Or maybe Vespertine doesn't know what Ponla's doing."

"Ponla told us about vesper, which Vespertine definitely wouldn't want us to know about," Darren continues to think aloud. "And Ponla was talking like she didn't care about the Concilium. I don't know where that puts her in the grand scheme of things."

"She said we've all had it," Jasmine points out. "Whether we believe her or not, I was controlled without knowing it which isn't normal Mind Control. When you're mind-controlled, you know you're being mind-controlled."

Darren gives her a short look before turning back to Idrid who sticks out a foot and sweeps the burly man's leg out from under him. "You sound like you've been mind-controlled before."

" 'Cause I have," she replies. "While escaping the palace I found myself in Vale Tower. Magicians paralyzed me and forced me to collapse on the stairway. It's an experience like you're arguing with yourself, though reason goes out the window and the only way to win is to drown out the part of you that is being controlled."

Idrid pins the man to the ground on his stomach, holding one of his arms while his other ineffectually tries to reach back to push her off. Analise, the Concilium judge for the event, gives Idrid the point and a second pair take the center of the tent to begin grappling. Idrid moves to the other side of the tent where the other pairs wait their turn. Her eyes find Darren and she gives him a nod, signaling she's fine.

"Let's take the worst case scenario then," Darren suggests. "Ponla is right and we're all susceptible to some new form of Mind Control. For all we know we're being controlled now. How do we know, and how do we stop it?"

Jasmine shrugs. "I wouldn't know if it were happening to me again. When I was told Not was dead and controlled to tell you, I believed it myself. Only after I was somehow un-controlled did I realize it was a dumb thing to believe." She glances over at him. "So I suppose the only way of knowing would be someone who isn't being controlled who can tell something is off."

Darren nods slowly. "Though that won't help if we're all being controlled."

"I still don't know how I got un-controlled," Jasmine says. "Ponla didn't seem to be lying when she said she wasn't mind-controlling me. But that could be the new form of Mind Control making me believe her."

"We'll get nowhere if we doubt every thought we have," Darren says. The second pair of participants both fall to the floor in a tangle and Analise calls it a draw. "You passed out, and when we found you and you woke up you seemed back to normal. That is, mildly unpleasant and visibly annoyed."

Jasmine mutters something incomprehensible.

"Yeah, like that. I think Ponla was telling the truth that you met Not."

"When?" Jasmine asks slowly.

"Either before or while you were passed out," Darren says. "The old man who was looking after you might've seen him. Though, he didn't seem totally of sound mind either."

"So?" Jasmine prompts Darren impatiently.

"I think Not must've been the one to undo whatever was mind-controlling you."

"How?"

"He's immune to magic." Jasmine's eyes widen at that. "It's the only thing I can think of that would counter whatever Mind Control was happening with you. Either that, or you really drank yourself into a state incapable of being mind-controlled."

"Didn't happen," Jasmine says. "So that's what Not's magic is. It makes sense. It also makes sense why Ponla was insistent on us finding him."

The third pair of participants finish their grappling with the victor being yet another burly man, and Idrid is called back to the center of the tent to grapple with him.

"Well, that means we have to find that old man and get him to tell us what happened while you were passed out." Darren watches as Idrid, seemingly tired of the process of getting into the battle of strength, throws herself forward, leading with her right shoulder, and knocks the burly man over. The crowd loves it and erupts into applause. The man hits the ground hard and seems to have the breath knocked out of him for he doesn't try to get up and instead takes a moment to regain his breath while lying on his back.

"This concludes the test of strength!" Analise calls. "All the other events should be finishing up shortly as well! Everyone, please gather at the tent marked 8 on your schedules. There we'll be having a joint event with some students who performed well yesterday!"

"Joint event?" Jasmine repeats.

"They mentioned before the first day that participants would get the chance to do more," Darren says. "I wonder how they'll do the event with magicians and non-magicians."

"The non-magicians aren't gonna like it," Jasmine says.

"You don't need to tell me that," Darren replies. "Come on, let's follow Idrid there."

"Welcome, ladies and gentlemen, to the first *brawl!*" Vespertine announces loudly, her voice carrying clear and sharp across the tent. The tent is one of the larger ones and holds roughly a neighborhood's block in length and width for the non-magician and student participants for the event. Along the outer edge where the audience encircles the center of the tent Darren and Jasmine stand. Darren watches Idrid shift uneasily at the center of the tent alongside the other non-magicians and students. Glancing over to the audience on his left he sees Tang and Kelsey giving them surreptitious glances, though they both refuse to come closer.

"I think you put them off the other day," Darren tells Jasmine in a hushed voice. "You should tell them what you said wasn't true."

"Not yet," Jasmine says. "I want to find Not first."

Vespertine continues to announce the event. "Non-magicians will be paired off with a student and, together, will fight each other. This is truly, in the traditional sense, a brawl, though victors will not be decided by who remains conscious. If you or your teammate has had enough, you will step out of the brawl. Judges will step in if we see any foul play or someone is being beaten into unconsciousness. The goal is to get your opponents to surrender, not cause brain damage or the like. You will be judged on the effectiveness of overpowering your opponents. Seriously hurting others will result in removal from the tournament and receiving no prize." Her red cloak flaps with her swept hand as she gestures to a podium at the front of a section of the audience where the other Concilium members sit slightly behind and atop a small platform. On the podium is a crystal clear gourd filled to the brim with gold coins that refract every beam of light brilliantly. "That will be your prize. 1,000 gold pieces."

"What about the cup?" a man in the audience calls, earning a round of laughter.

"The cup goes to the victor as well," Vespertine says with a thin smile. "We will begin pairing non-magicians and students." She walks from the center of the tent where the participants continue to shift uneasily and over to the platform with the Concilium members.

Balnar stands and announces the first pair. "Earl and Greg." Greg, an Elementalist student Darren is somewhat familiar with from having talked occasionally when visiting Kellen in his tower, steps forward. The participants shift as his partner moves to stand beside him. To Darren's surprise it is the rickety old man he saw with Jasmine. His arms can be seen to visibly quiver folded beneath his baggy robes that cover him completely aside from the lower part of his face where his scraggly beard falls over his chin.

The two make quite a pair Darren thinks as they move to stand toward the outer edge away from the other participants huddled together and waiting to be called.

Analise stands up on the platform and then calls, "Idrid and Maia."

"What's an old non-magic guy doing in a tournament?" Jasmine asks more to herself than to Darren. "And in a brawl no less?"

"No idea," Darren says while watching Idrid and Maia move away from the unpaired participants and to a spot near but comfortably distant from Greg and the old man. Darren ignores the rest of the pairings since they're all overly large burly men save for a few normally-proportioned individuals who seem like they've had their share of honest farm work. He is focused on how Maia will fare, especially against her former mentor.

"The pairs are decided," Vespertine announces from the center seat of the platform behind the podium with the glamorous prize. "Let the brawl commence!"

Greg moves quickly, skirting the outer edge of the area they're allowed by the audience and away from Maia. The old man, Earl, turns and paces effortfully after him, though Greg is already twenty paces ahead and beginning to engage with another pair.

"He shouldn't leave the old guy behind," Darren comments. "If one of them goes down it'll be over."

As if responding to the comment, three pairs of participants move in on Earl walking slowly toward where Greg is tripping up a burly man by shifting the ground under his feet. The old man notices them approaching him and turns slowly. "Oh my—" is his response as Idrid sprints across the tent and knocks over the largest man among the six participants. He backs away as the others turn their attention to Idrid who puts a foot on the largest man's back to pin him down.

Maia comes to her aid, flying through the air and landing next to Idrid. She conjures a polygonal metal object with a *pop* and slides open its lid. The largest man's student partner, Flannery, one of the Elementalist students who Maia had in her group on the first day, points a finger out at her. A stream of flames flick through the air toward her.

Angling the polygonal object she conjured, Maia catches the flames and closes the lid.

"Well look at her," Jasmine says with a hint of pride while a familiar woman's voice in the audience shouts gleefully. "She found a use for it."

"Fantastic, Maia!" Aveve's voice coos nearby Tang and Kelsey.

Maia tosses the object into the`air and it *pops* out of existence. She then pushes her arms forward at all of the nearby participants, sending a strong gale to blow over them as well as the audience nearby. It's not enough to knock them over, though it is enough to intimidate them into retreating.

Idrid pushes Flannery's partner away with her foot who quickly gets up and retreats with Flannery. While they all begin engaging each other and the rest of the participants she turns on Earl sidling away toward Greg. Greg, for his part, has overpowered a pair by trapping their bodies beneath the ground and is looking over to check on Earl. His eyes move over Earl's shoulders and meet Maia's.

"Are we fighting them?" Maia asks Idrid.

"We may have to," Idrid says. "But don't touch the old guy. I want to ask him some questions."

Overhearing them, Earl turns and points at them with a finger. "Get them, Greg!" he cries, shuffling away. "They're after me!"

Greg shakes his head and moves ahead of Earl to block Idrid and Maia's way. He stands there, hands on his hips, and says, "Are we in for a duel, then, Maia?"

She doesn't respond, preparing for what Greg may do. The ground beneath her feet begins to tremble, and she senses that he is going to try and trap her also. When she tries to manipulate the earth she finds that it is unresponsive and continues to slide beneath her feet. A lone student teleports beside Greg and rears back, readying a punch. Maia recognizes him to be Emir.

"I have a score to settle with you," he says to Maia.

Without turning, Greg waves his left hand in a circle and the earth beneath the Teleporter's feet cleanly turns 180 degrees. Emir's punch flies forward, hitting nothing but air, and his momentum sends him stumbling away. Greg then snaps his same hand and the ground where he stumbles shoots up a foot off the ground in an instant. Emir's unsteady legs buckle and he is hurled off the ground, carrying him even further away.

Maia, realizing she won't be able to out-magic Greg with the earth, pushes herself off the ground and into the air, hovering in a continuous upward gale.

Greg smirks, his hands curling, and the ground then begins to curl in tendrils that snake upward. One tendril of earth loops around her ankle and begins to tug her down. Idrid kicks her leg out at the tendril of earth and breaks it up, causing it to crumble away.

Maia glides around Greg to his backside while Idrid advances on him. While he's busy manipulating the ground beneath Idrid to sink and enclose around the bottom of her feet, Maia blasts air at him.

He raises his other hand and Maia senses the wind change its path and move harmlessly around him. She doesn't know how he is able to simultaneously manipulate the ground and earth, but she knows his abilities are still beyond her own.

She ceases the gust of air carrying her and lands back on the ground. There's only one option she can think of. In a flash she conjures a blanket and darts forward. She hurls the blanket over Greg's head. Greg, completely caught off guard, puts all his magic to manipulating the air and sending the blanket flying away. Idrid catches the other edge of the blanket before it can blow away and, together with Maia, pulls it down over him.

"Hey!" Maia hears Greg's annoyed voice. She and Idrid pull it hard and touch it down to the ground, the fabric forcing Greg to the ground as well. The blanket begins to shake and Maia suspects Greg is going to do something with the earth. After a moment not sensing any magic, she instead hears his muffled laughter. "Okay, I give up! A blanket is too much for me."

Maia smiles and lets go of the blanket. Idrid does the same, and Maia makes the blanket pop out of existence. Greg is lying down on his stomach in a comfortable sleeping position as if he is in bed. His eyes, too, are closed, though his mouth is turned upward in a grin. His eyes open and he sits up.

"You could've escaped," Maia says.

"Yes, but good effort should be rewarded," Greg replies. "Besides, I am several years ahead of you."

Idrid humphs and casts her gaze around the combating participants. Already most of the pairs have surrendered and moved out of the center of the tent. She spots Earl at the other end of the tent shuffling away from a student and his burly non-magician partner. Somehow he had ended up over there. She watches as he stumbles, serendipitously moving out of the way of a punch the burly non-magician throws at him.

"Reminisce later," Idrid tells Maia. She paces forward to where a three-way battle between pairs is happening at the center of the tent.

Maia moves to follow, though Greg says, "Why don't you move the ground?" She turns back and raises her eyebrows. "You know, trip them up and let Idrid finish the job."

"Okay. Thanks." Maia goes on to follow Idrid who is already punching and blocking another non-magician. She sprints over and does as Greg told her. The ground beneath the first non-magician shifts, throwing him off balance. Idrid bats her arm at him, sending him toppling.

She puts her foot on him and growls, "Surrender." The non-magician puts his hands up and nods fervently. Idrid turns on the second non-magician who Maia quickly unbalances. Idrid again knocks him clean over and orders him to surrender. The man also agrees, and both pairs are no longer in the brawl. The last pair, aside from the one following Earl at the edge of the tent who still haven't managed to land a hit on him, prepare for Maia and Idrid's pattern of attack.

Maia sees that the student is Uon, another Elementalist, so she decides rather than engaging him to instead separate him from his non-magician partner who isn't a totally buff guy. She puts her hands out and creates a wall with the air between Uon and his partner. Sensing the magic, he turns and begins to counter it. Before he can, Maia moves the wall of air with her will and forces Uon to be pushed away.

Idrid, knowing it is her turn, steps up and raises her hands.

"I surrender!" the non-magician says quickly before Idrid can do anything. She lowers her arms and nods at him.

"Good."

Uon, forcing the wall of air to finally disperse, looks at his partner incredulously.

"And that's all folks!" Vespertine shouts.

The other pair following after Earl and still swinging punches that don't land turn, confused. They object, saying, "But we haven't surrendered yet!"

Vespertine looks over at them with a disdainful frown. "You've been throwing punches at an elderly man for the past five minutes that, if any had landed, could have seriously injured him. His partner had also already surrendered, making all your efforts pointless. None of the judges intervened because you were deemed incapable of touching him."

"We're disqualified?" the non-magician says gravely. "But if we weren't actually hurting him, why?"

"Even just attempting to cause serious harm to an old man of all people is worth disqualification," Vespertine says.

"Thanksh," Earl huffs out. "I wash getting tired. Oh, Greg shurrendered? Oh well."

"Idrid and Maia," Vespertine continues to announce. "You both have won the brawl, and this prize. Congratulations!"

She extends her arms wide and the surrounding audience cheers loudly. Idrid and Maia awkwardly look at each other, then together pace over to the podium in front of the Concilium.

"This concludes the day's events!" Vespertine says. "Please, enjoy yourselves, but don't think the tournament is nearing its end! The magicians will have plenty to do on the final day. Additionally, an exhibition match will be held to close off the tournament."

"An exhibition match?" Darren restates. The crowd begins to buzz with excited chatter.

"That's right. The tower masters will be dueling each other in a three-way battle using each of their unique magic.

It will be a sight to behold, so don't leave, for you'll be missing out on something never before seen!"

"That actually sounds amazing," Jasmine says.

"It does," Darren muses, though turns to Earl who is making his way back into the crowd with his shuffle. "But we still have to find Not. Come on, before we lose the old man again."

Torion Oey

Chapter 35

"Idrid!" Maia catches up to the large woman and matches her pace. "Where are you going? We still need to collect the prize!"

"You can take it," Idrid replies, the crowd parting before her so she can follow the retreating back of Earl. Maia stops for a moment and watches Idrid pursue the old man. Glancing back, she sees Vespertine and the other Concilium members watching her. Maia turns away and follows Idrid out of the tent.

"Idrid!" Maia calls to her again. She again catches up to Idrid and asks, "Are you actually a non-magician?"

"Huh?" Idrid questions back.

"I've sensed magic coming from you for a while," Maia says. "Though it's only coming from a part of your body."

"Magic…" Idrid muses, continuing to follow Earl who is wandering toward the holt. "Can all magicians sense it?"

"Well, probably," Maia says, unsure.

Idrid stops abruptly and takes something out of her shoe. "Here. Take this."

Maia retrieves the ruby stone out of Idrid's offered hand. "A gem? This looks valuable… but—it's warm!"

"It's been in my sock for days," Idrid says, starting to walk briskly again.

"No, I mean—ew—uh, I mean it's radiating warmth. What is it?"

"Apparently it contains fire," Idrid says.

"Oh, cool! Why are you giving it to me?"

"If magicians can sense magic, it'll be concealed by another magician's magic," Idrid says. "Theoretically."

"Thank you! But, uh, that wasn't where I sensed it…" She mumbles the last part as the large woman pushes on away from the tent and after Earl. They make their way off the main grounds and up the holt itself toward the top. Despite the old man's shambling pace, Earl is speedily walking ahead.

"Idrid!" Darren calls from somewhere behind them before appearing suddenly in a brisk walk next to them. "You're after him too, then?"

Jasmine, carried up the holt on a gust of wind, lands next to them at a jog. "Where is he going?"

"Why are we all following him?" Maia asks, confused. She only just notices that the entire holt is barren save for themselves and Earl. Looking backward, she sees all the tournament-goers wandering between the tents.

"Because he's Not," Idrid says.

"What?" Darren and Jasmine exclaim. All their paces increase to catch up to the man who reaches the crest of the holt and slips inside the large tent at the holt's center.

Maia jogs a little farther but stops at the opening of the tent while the three adults go in after him. Questioning her own need to be there, she turns around and looks over the tournament grounds. The high sun sends brilliant rays that glisten along the tops of the sea of tents. They are the only things that seem to move, rippling in a light breeze. Looking more closely, she notices something is off. None of the people, all the size of toy figures, are actually moving. Maia glances to a different area of the grounds. No one is moving there. She glances to the left. No movement. Everyone is standing stationary, as far as she can see. But wait, people at the tent that had just held the final event for the day are moving. She can't see who they are, though they're moving toward the base of the holt. A shrill, loud ring like a bird's call shatters the air. It echoes over the holt and dissipates over the maze and surrounding forest. Maia's eyes dart around, trying to make sense of what she is seeing. Everyone begins to move and walk in unison toward and up the holt from all sides.

"What...?" she breathes, taking a step back. Not one person goes against the crowd—everyone below is making their way up toward her.

Whirling and running inside the tent, Maia finds Darren, Idrid, and Jasmine in the midst of a confrontation with the old man.

"Sho... you've come to shee me, eh?" Earl says slowly. He flourishes his right hand, the sleeve of his dreary robe flapping out, and raises it to stroke his beard.

"Drop the act, Not," Idrid says.

"You shay I shouldn't drop the act?" He swaps his hands to continue stroking his beard.

"You just admitted it's an act," Idrid says.

"Well, shoot me through with arrows and call me holy." He throws his hood back, pulls off his beard, and a head of stark medium-length grey hair poofs out, falling over and around his face. Not's eyelids flutter as he blows lightly at strands of his hair, and his pale gaze moves across the opposing group of four. "How've you all been?" His eyes meet Maia's. "Hey, kid. Don't know you that well, but you did good in the last event."

"What in the spanses have you been doing?" Darren asks.

"Enjoying myself," Not says. He pulls his ratty beard up and over his face, a nearly invisible string holding it together. "Have you seen Tang and Kelsey around?"

"Briefly," Darren replies.

"What was that noise before?" Jasmine asks Maia.

"I don't know," she says. "But something is happening outside."

"Not, the Concilium have something that controls people," Darren says. "According to one of them, we're all affected by it."

"You seem fine now," Not says. "Though she wasn't," he adds, pointing at Jasmine. "What're you doing here, by the way?"

"Looking for you," Jasmine says shortly.

"Guys, there's something weird going on out there," Maia says.

"What?" Darren asks.

"I—" The entire tent tears away from the top of the holt, spiraling upward in a cacophonous torrential wind. Somehow they all stay on their feet while the wind whips up their clothes into a frenzy.

Not's fake beard is ripped from his hand. He shrugs off his robes which fly up and after the tent which is now a speck moving away across the sky. People surround them on all sides, all unmoving, blank-faced, and staring at them. The Concilium members stand at intervals among the crowd, though Ponla and Vespertine are together and pacing toward them. Ponla lowers a hand and the wind subsides. Slowly everyone's clothes come to a rest and there is relative silence save for the combined breathing of the crowd. Ponla and Vespertine stop twenty feet from the group.

Jasmine looks up and then back at Ponla. "Impressive."

"We're all here, then," Vespertine says. "Finally."

Not straightens the sword on his back that must've been concealed by the robes then pats down his hair.

"Will you come with us?" Vespertine asks him pointedly.

Not looks around at Maia, Jasmine, Darren, and Idrid, expecting one of them to say something. "Where?" he asks when no one does.

"Your previous home," Vespertine says.

Maia shifts her feet uneasily, her mind frozen under the hundreds of blank stares watching them.

"Never had one," Not replies.

A strange look overcomes Vespertine as if she is as fragile as porcelain. It disappears a second later, and she then calls, "Kellen!"

The Elementalist tower master steps out of the crowd from behind her and raises his hands to the sky. Everyone except the blank-faced crowd looks up. A point in the sky darkens and a storm-colored mist stretches out. It rapidly becomes a cloud that continues to expand, darkening the top of the holt below. A light flashes with the cloud and the sound of sparks resounds down.

Maia feels a strange tingling sensation on the top of her head like someone is playing with her hair. She takes a step back in surprise when she sees Not running toward her with incredible speed.

The air above her fills with a streak of light that crashes down on top of her. Not's outstretched hand catches the lightning and it splashes back in a shower of blue sparks. Embers peter out in the air before touching the ground.

Maia, cowering, uncovers her head and looks up at Not standing over her. Her thoughts finally catch up to the present. "Did Kellen just…?"

"He's being controlled," Darren says in a low voice. Maia glances at him, noting the dark expression on his face. It's the first time she's seen him angry. Then again, it's the first time she's seen him *anything*.

"What do we do?" Jasmine asks, her hands curling and uncurling to create a current in the air.

"They're all controlled," Not says. He shakes his hand, remnant sparks flashing between his fingers. He withdraws his sword and looks on at Vespertine with a stony face. Three more figures step out of the crowd behind her, causing his face to pale. Tang, Kelsey, and Lauren of all people stand side-by-side, each sharing the same blank expression.

"Darren," Not says quietly. "Take everyone out of here."

"I can't take you," Darren responds.

"That's fine. Leave me here."

Maia feels Darren's hand on her arm. Jasmine glances down at Darren's other hand that touches her shoulder, her face looking as if she wants to swat it away.

"Idrid," Darren says. "Hold onto me."

"I won't—" The earth beneath Idrid's feet juts out, sending her flying through the air towards Vespertine and Ponla, the latter of whom holds out her hand in a fist.

"Wait—!" Maia shouts, then she's surrounded by trees beside only Darren and Jasmine and no longer on the hill.

I watch Idrid tumble through the air helplessly. Thankfully, she is caught by an invisible force, likely air manipulated by Ponla, and lands relatively gently on her knees before Vespertine. Vespertine leans forward to whisper something in Idrid's ear.

Sucking in a breath, I see my friend stand and turn around, her face a similar blank slate as everyone around me.

"You're alone," Vespertine says. "It's hard, isn't it? Being the one person with total control of yourself, but lacking the control to affect anyone."

I run my hand along my blade, transferring the lightning I absorbed into it. I feel the skin under my pinky and thumb opening from the edges of my sword by accident. *I'm trembling.* The cacophony of smells from all directions, the scents of magic and magicians underlying the foremost smell of chlorine, is overwhelming. "What else is new," I mutter to myself, clenching my cut hand into a fist. Then, loud for her and the others to hear, "Give me back my Giant." Idrid's eyes remain clouded. *Damn.*

"Will you come with me?" she asks again.

I look between everyone, weighing my options which are annoyingly scarce. I turn in a circle, stopping to face away from Vespertine and eye Balnar. A *pop* emanates and a two-handed battle axe appears in the grip of his right hand. He twirls it casually, almost effortlessly, and only using the same single hand.

"You don't have to," Vespertine's voice calls. "Yet."

Balnar looks over my shoulder then nods. He steps to the side, murmuring something to the crowd who then part and open up a path down the hill. He looks at me and gestures with his head in an offer to run.

I spin around and release the lightning from the tip of my sword straight at Vespertine. Kellen waves his hands and the lightning bends straight up as if being reflected. It flashes across the sky with a resounding *crack* and disappears the next moment.

Gritting my teeth, I turn back to Balnar and walk to the part in the crowd. *There's really nothing I can do.* I freeze when two people step into my path. Both my parents stand before me. They are thinner than I remember; paler, too. Wispy strands of their matching silver-grey hair fall over their shoulders which are covered in ragged outfits.

They look at me—Gallain, the previous king, my father, with grey eyes, and Maria, my mother, with pale blue eyes. Both are unclouded unlike everyone else around.

"Ashu," Gallain whispers.

I recoil at the name. I look back at Vespertine who holds out her open palm and moves it forward, offering me to go on.

"Why?"

She retracts her hand and tilts her head, her straight-cut brunette bangs hovering just over her eyes. "They'll tell you."

I look finally at Idrid, searching for a hint of autonomy that I know I won't find in her expression. *I can't do anything.* Facing my parents, I stiffly walk between them and down the hill, away from everyone I should be with, followed by the two people I never wanted to be with.

"You let him go," Ponla comments with a hint of disappointment. "Along with the toys."

"What's next?" Balnar asks, crossing the center of the holt to where Vespertine and Ponla stand on either side of Idrid.

"We wait for news from the Imperial Council," Vespertine says. "They'll have arrived at Fairbreeze and begun coordinating with our magicians there by now." She gazes at the sea of blank faces along the top of the hill. A short breath tumbles out of her, followed by her heartrate picking up. She cups a hand over her mouth as another surprised laugh escapes. "Look at them... It's actually working... We're so close to preventing a war."

Balnar and Ponla share a proud smile, Balnar patting Vespertine on the shoulder.

"Darren and the others are less important, but why'd you let Not go?" Tethris says after teleporting over to them.

"He wasn't ready," Vespertine replies. "This was the best option with our circumstances. He'll be back." She looks sideways at Idrid who gazes blankly at the spot where Not descended the holt. "And he has a sword."

Acknowledgements

This book would not exist without paper (or digital technology as the case may be).

Some people I want to thank: Rosemary Sease, for concept art for the cover; Pat Oey, for unpaid editing; Nolan Bushnell, for certain things; Tim Oey, for other things; and Pat Oey again, for being the haha.

Some dogs I want to thank: Truly, the incorrigible barker; Padfoot, the rambunctious leash-chewer; and Tessa, the curious licker, may she rest well and continue licking Piper and Merlin in the afterlife.

I'd be remiss to not extend further thanks to readers for also existing. Without you, this book would not have been read.

About the Author

Torion holds a B.A. in Creative Writing and Psychology and an M.S. in Psychology. He has had short stories featured in *Galaxy's Edge Magazine*, *Cohesion Press*, and *NonBinary Review*. He dedicates his free time toward writing and critiquing speculative fiction both personally and in separate writing groups; he also likes to play volleyball. Torion has published several novels, including the first in this book's series *Not James*. You can find latest news about him at his website torion.us, and you can contact him at torionoey@gmail.com.